I0660087

JEANNETTE AND JEANNOT;

OR,

THE CONSCRIPT'S VOW.

𝔄 𝔯𝔬𝔪𝔞𝔫𝔠𝔢.

LONDON:

PUBLISHED BY E. LLOYD, 12, SALISBURY-SQUARE, FLEET-STREET.

JEANNETTE AND JEANNOT:
OR, THE CONSCRIPT'S VOW.

CHAPTER I.

THE CONSCRIPT AND HIS BETROTHED.—JEANNETTE'S MISGIVINGS.—THE NOTARY. HE LOVER'S VOW.—DEPARTURE FOR TOULON.

"DEAR Jeannot, how can you bid me be reconciled to this parting, when in losing you, I lose all that most fondly attatches me to this earth? You speak too of the glory that is to be gained under our renowned Emperor Napoleon, but there is death as well glory to be found in the field of battle; and, alas! my heart sinks with dread, when I think of the danger you will be exposed to, when engaged in the bloody strife that every year carries off so many of the bravest sons of France."

These words were addressed by the young and loving Jeannette, to the object of her heart's dearest affection, at their last interview, just previous to his departure for Toulon, where he was to join other conscripts, whose turn for military duty, had now arrived. Jeannot's grief at the compulsory separation was scarcely less than her own, but the laws of conscription were severe against those who attempted to evade them, and there was, besides, the shame of being regarded as a coward by those who obeyed with alacrity the call made upon them by their country. As no alternative remained, therefore, he put the best face he could upon the matter, assuring her that the danger was not so great as she imagined, and painting in the most vivid colours the honours and promotion that was certain to reward those who fought bravely in their country's cause. Jeannette listened to him with tearful eyes, and with a voice almost choked with emotion, she continued—

"You are going far away from me, Jeannot; and when you leave, there will be none to love and console me—I fear, too, that time and absence will make you forget me, though my own heart will follow, wherever you may go, even though the ambition of the emperor should lead you to the world's utmost extremity."

"Nay," replied her lover, "this is unkind of you, dear Jeannette, for I have ever proved the constancy of my affection, and no circumstance can change the feelings of a heart that is yours, and yours only."

"So others have said before," she replied, sorrowfully, "and yet how many instances have I known of broken vows, when those who over fondly loved have been separated."

"But I hope you will not judge me by the inconstancy of others?"

"If I do so," she replied, "it is because my affections are so entirely yours that I feel as if the loss of your regard would send me broken-hearted to the grave. Surely Napoleon dreams not of the countless miseries he inflicts upon his people, or he would not tear so many of his faithful subjects from their homes and families, for no other purpose than to gratify his own boundless ambition for empire!"

"Ah, Jeannette," exclaimed her lover, "but ought not every Frenchman feel grateful to the man who has raised his country to be the terror and admiration of the whole world? He found France in a state of the wildest anarchy and confusion, and in a few years, by his own wonderful abilities, has made her what she is. Do we not, then, owe him our gratitude? and would it not be an eternal disgrace if those who own his sway were to refuse their assistance when he is still aiming to raise their native land to the highest pinnacle of fame?"

"But he does so by the yearly sacrifice of the blood of thousands of his faithful subjects."

"And it must ever be so with other countries as well as this, whilst war is the plaything of monarchs," answered Jeannot. "Our great Napoleon knows that he is at the head of a brave nation, and, relying on the people's regard for him, he seeks to strike terror into the hearts of his enemies, by showing how completely the confidence of his subjects is with him. But you women understand nothing of this, and can see nothing in war but blood, rapine, and cruelty!"

"Have we not bitter reason to repine when we are constantly losing those whom we most tenderly regard?" asked our heroine. "Alas! there are few women in France who have not to mourn the loss of a husband, or a father, a lover, or a brother. These are the heavy curses that war brings with it, and scatters over the whole of our empire!"

"So say all your sex," answered Jeannot; "but we who have to bear the brunt of the affray, are still willing to hazard our lives in the service of the man that we almost idolize. Half Europe already acknowledges the power of France, and before long, the army that is assembling at Boulogne will invade England, where mines of wealth will be divided amongst the conquerors!"

"Ah!" sighed Jeannette, "such are the stories that Napoleon deludes the people with, but the elders of our village shake their heads doubtingly whenever the subject is mentioned, and all declare that the English are too brave to suffer an invading army ever to land upon their shores."

"I don't know anything about their bravery," answered the young conscript, "but our emperor has taken down the pride of other nations, and I don't see why England should fare better than they have. And when we have made ourselves masters of the country, Jeannette, all its wealth, as well as its broad acres of land, flowing with milk and honey, will be divided among those who have taken part in the conquest. Only think, love, how happy you and I shall be if it should be our good fortune to settle in one of the snug cottages of England!"

"The prospect is anything but a cheering one to me," exclaimed the maiden— "for I love France too well to wish for a home in any other country. But you men care not where you pitch your tents, and perhaps, Jeannot, perhaps you may fall in love with one of the fair daughters of England, and forget your poor, ever-constant Jeannette."

"Nay, you surely don't think I can ever forget you?"

"I don't know what to think of it," she replied, "for such things have happened, and no doubt will again, though I would fain hope that, in this instance, I may have been too severe."

"You are indeed," he exclaimed, "for as well might I believe it possible that you would bestow your affections, in my absence, upon some one else."

"Who else?" she asked, eagerly.

"Ah!" exclaimed Jeannot, "have you forgotten that I have a rival in Henri Dupont, whose earnings as a mechanic are more than double mine as a poor, plodding farmer?"

"For shame, Jeannot! Did I not dismiss him for you, with a request that he would never speak to me on the subject of love?"

"You did, but women are sometimes fickle, as well as men."

"But Henri Dupont is also a conscript, and goes with you to Toulon, so that there can be no cause for jealousy."

"I am not jealous," he exclaimed, "and perhaps it was wrong of me to taunt you with what I know is impossible, though I have good reason to believe Henri is as warmly attached to you as ever he was."

"How know you that?" she asked with alarm.

"Because I have been told so by those that he confides all his secrets to."

"Then believe me, they have only said so to annoy you, and then enjoy a laugh at your easy credulity. Henri himself would never dare say so much, for my answer was so decisive, that he can never dare make another proposal for my hand."

"Ah, Jeanette," he exclaimed, "you know not to what desperation love will sometimes drive a man. Vanity makes him believe it impossible that he can be utterly rejected by her who is the object of his affections, and not unfrequently he will again urge his suit, though to all but himself it must appear to be a hopeless one."

"And if he was to do so," answered Jeannette, "the reply still would be that my heart is already engaged. But we have said enough upon this subject, for, surely after my denial, you will no longer believe that I am false to the solemn promise made to yourself."

"Do not mistake me, dearest," exclaimed her lover, "for I know your heart too well to believe that it can harbour duplicity or falsehood. But you were rather hard upon me just now, in hinting that I should forget you during our separation, and I thought it only a fair retaliation to jest with you upon the possibility of your also forgetting the vows that have been exchanged between us.

But this is no time to talk of such matters, for we are about to be separated, and it may be our sad fate never to meet again in this world."

"For Heaven's sake, don't talk so, Jeannot!"

"Well, I'll not alarm you, love," he replied, "for to speak the truth, I leave this place in the fullest confidence, that, after having fulfilled the duty I owe to my emperor and my country, I shall return to claim the hand that has been so often promised me."

"Then you have already forgot that foolish notion of yours about Henri Dupont?"

"Believe me, Jeannette, I never seriously thought of it, for I have the fullest confidence in your constancy, and all the reports that mischievous people may raise, will never convince me that you are false."

"And your affection for me will never fail, even though hundreds of miles may separate us?"

"How can I cease to think of you with love," he asked, "when I have received so many proofs of your affection? On the contrary, I shall ever look forward to the time when we shall be united by the holy rites of religion, and that thought alone will be sufficient to urge me to the honourable discharge of the duty that I owe to my country."

"But if you should be wounded, who is there to watch over your sick bed as I should?"

"True," replied Jeannot, "but amidst the turmoil and chances of war, we must resign ourselves to our destiny, however hard it may be. And as for that matter, our emperor sets a noble example to his troops, for he willingly shares with them in all the difficulties and privations that are the constant attendants of an active military life."

"And so he ought," exclaimed Jeannette, "for those who are so anxious to make war, should be the last to shrink from any of its consequences, however severe they may be. Besides, he has been brought up to such scenes of strife and bloodshed, so that he feels less than those, who, like yourself, are forced to devote themselves to his service, whether they like it or not."

"Ah, Jeannette," exclaimed her lover, "how differently you and I think upon that matter. The emperor, it is true, is fond of war, because he has always been successful against whatever enemy has opposed him, but you forget how much gratitude we owe the man that first came forward when our country was in a fearful state of anarchy and confusion, and has since raised it to be one of the most powerful in the world. Other monarchs now tremble at his name, and France stands amongst the proudest of the dominions of the earth."

"Don't you think, Jeannot, his subjects would be much happier, and far more contented, if he would live in peace with his neighbours?"

"It's not for me to give an opinion as to what Napoleon ought or ought not to do," answered the young conscript. "All I know about it is, that war abroad makes peace at home; and I have heard older folks than myself say, that if our army should ever return to France, and live a life of idleness, there would be such commotion and disorder, that not even the authority of our emperor could check it."

"In that case, what chance is there of peace?"

"There's not the slightest, Jeannette, so pray don't deceive yourself with a hope that you'll never see fulfilled."

"Then it must be years before you return home," exclaimed our heroine

"Nay, that will very much depend upon myself," answered her lover, "for good conduct as a soldier is rewarded with every indulgence, and who knows but, if I do my duty faithfully, I may be raised from one rank to another till you hear of my being made a general."

"A general!"

"Yes; why should not such good luck fall to my share as to anybody else? The emperor looks not to birth or fortune when he has promotion to bestow, but gives it to even the humblest of his followers if they earn it by their bravery."

"I hope, then, his favour will not fall upon you, Jeannot."

"And why do you wish that?" asked her lover, reproachfully.

"Because, should you rise to greatness, you might forget the poor humble girl you once loved."

"Surely that is not your real opinion of me? You don't think, Jeannette, that I could ever be base enough to forget her whose love I have always looked upon as the dearest prized treasure that could have been bestowed upon me. If that is what you think, I would rather be looked upon as a coward, that is undeserving of reward or promotion."

"Believe me, Jeannot, you are wrong there," exclaimed our heroine, "for though I may have expressed a wish that high promotion should not be your lot, I so thoroughly detest a coward, that my love would not long survive the news of your dishonour."

"Good! I'm glad to hear you say that, because I know you will never have reason to be ashamed of me on that account. Indeed cowardice is unknown in the French army, or it would not have gone on conquering and gaining fresh glory as it has done, ever since the illustrious Napoleon placed himself at the head of it. So make yourself easy upon that point, Jeannette, and whenever an account of a great battle reaches you, look carefully through the gazette, and perhaps you may see my name honourably mentioned by the emperor."

"I will," she replied; "and more than that, I'll try to think that, in spite of rising in the world, you still remember with affection the humble village maiden you have left behind."

"Nay, if it will increase your confidence, I will make a solemn vow never to bestow my love upon another."

"Do so, Jeannot," exclaimed a voice behind them, "for the girl loves you, and it may soothe her during your absence to know that you are bound to her by a solemn pledge, as well as by every principle of manly honour."

These words were spoken by Monsieur Narbonne, a venerable notary, who having been for some time a listener to their conversation, now came forward to tender them his fatherly assistance and advice. The lovers looked somewhat abashed on discovering that they had been overheard, but Jeannot quickly recovering himself, said—

"It seems, monsieur, that you have heard our conversation, and, as a friend of both parties, I would ask your opinion, if love like ours can be turned to indifference by separation?"

"Genuine love will survive all things," replied the old man, "but, for the satisfaction of both parties, I see no reason why you should not both make a vow of fidelity to each other. It puts an end to doubt, and frequently softens the pangs that are occasioned by a lengthened separation. So kneel down, my children, upon the green turf, and yonder moon shall be the witness of the solemn vow you are about to make."

The two lovers knelt as they had been directed, and the old man taking off his hat with one hand, raised the other towards heaven, and in a deep, earnest tone, demanded—

"Are both of you willing to swear eternal love to each other?"

"We are," they replied.

"Do you also swear that neither time nor circumstances shall ever make you forget that vow?"

"We do," again ejaculated the lovers.

"Will you be indifferent to the calumnies of others, supposing evil-minded persons should raise reports calculated to mislead you?"

"We will."

"And when the time arrives for your meeting again, will you pronounce to each other those holy vows that are to last till death?"

"Again the lovers answered in the affirmative, and the notary having assisted them to rise, said—

"You will now remember, my dear children, that the vows you have uttered registered in heaven, and will be brought against you should you ever break them. Be faithful to each other, and, though your happiness may be deferred for a time, your reward will be great and permanent when you meet to part no more."

"Alas! monsieur," cried Jeannette, "how dare I venture to look for his return, when every hour of his absence is fraught with danger?"

"Trust in Heaven," answered the old man, "and your confidence will meet with its reward. That there are dangers to be encountered in the scenes he has to go through, is not to be denied, but the chances of his safe return are many, and even if he should fall in battle, you will have the melancholy satisfaction of knowing that his life has been sacrificed in the defence of his country."

"Ah!" sighed Jeannette, "but our country would not need defending if the emperor was less fond of quarrelling with neighbouring kingdoms."

"True," answered the notary; "but Napoleon acknowledges no will but his own, and certain as we are that he has at heart the good of France and the people he has been called upon to govern, it is our duty to yield our obedience when he calls upon us to follow him to the field."

"You seem to forget, monsieur," exclaimed our herione, "that thousands are every year sacrificed to the ambition of one man."

"So it may appear to those who give not the subject its due weight," answered the old man; "but much blood would be spilt amongst our own countrymen even if there were no foreign war, and for my own part I would prefer its being shed for the extending of our country, than that the brave citizens of France should draw their swords against each other."

"Then you see no crime in war?" exclaimed our heroine.

"That depends upon the cause that leads to it," he replied. "Many wars that I could name have been absolutely necessary, and I am not prepared to say that the one we are now engaged in could have been avoided."

"And yet it seems most cruel and unjust," exclaimed Jeannette, "that the blood of the young men of France should be sacrificed in a quarrel that they have nothing to do with."

"All are concerned in that which involves the honour of the land that gave them birth," answered the notary. "It may appear hard to Jeannot and others who have been drawn as conscripts, but let them recollect the consequences of their remaining at home at a time like this, and I believe few of them would regret the call that has been made upon them."

"Don't suppose that I have made any complaint, Monsieur Narbonne," exclaimed the young man, "for I admire the gallantry of our emperor, and would follow him to the world's end to fight in his cause."

"Then you care more for the emperor than you do for me!" cried Jeannette, half reproachfully.

"Indeed you do me a great wrong, then," he replied; "but two duties call upon me at the same time, and Monsieur Narbonne here knows that I must join the army, or run the risk of being hunted out and punished as a deserter. Besides, only think how the disgrace would cling to me all the rest of my life, if I was to hang back like a coward, when everybody else show their willingness to assist in a good cause."

"But war is a bad cause, Jeannot, and the people would soon put an end to it, if they had the spirit to refuse to engage in it."

"And what, in that case, would become of a country that was menaced by a foreign foe?" said Monsieur Narbonne.

"It's not for woman to argue upon a subject like that," answered our heroine, "but I believe all this strife between nations might soon be brought to an end, if all people were of my way of thinking. However, be that as it may, I see my own chance of happiness nearly destroyed by the forced absence of Jeannot, and I may therefore be pardoned for having said more upon the matter, than I should otherwise have done."

"You forget that your lover, if he meets the approbation of his superiors, may return home with honourable proofs that he has faithfully discharged his duty to his country."

" Oh, monsieur," exclaimed Jeannette, "that's just what he has been trying to make me believe, but I have heard quite enough to convince me that those only get exalted in rank who have interest, either in themselves or their families, with those who have the power to bestow honours."

" Such used to be the case under the former rulers of France," answered the old man, " but Napoleon acts upon wiser and better principles, and those only can look for promotion who have deserved it by acts of bravery or good judgment in making an attack. And if proof is wanted, it may be found in the commencement of his brilliant career before Toulon, when he distinguished the two common soldiers for their bravery, and afterwards raised them to the highest military rank. One of these was Duroe, the other Junot, both of them since created Peers of France, and their subsequent career of glory shows that our emperor at once formed a just estimate of the men."

" That may be all very true, monsieur," exclaimed Jeannette, " but such will never be the lot of poor Jeannot ; for though I know him to be brave, I fear he'll never survive long enough to obtain reward, however he may merit it."

" Have you made up your mind, then, that he will be killed in battle ?"

" What else can I think," she asked, " when I know the fearful peril that all men who take part in such scenes as he is about to enter upon. Besides, even supposing that he should be taken prisoner, how could I ever expect to see him again, since all who speak upon the subject say there is no prospect of peace for many years to come ?"

" Hush !" exclaimed the old man, " if you speak thus before him, his courage will begin to droop."

" Then here let the subject end," cried Jeannette, " for I would rather endure years of suffering than say anything that would make him deserve the foul name of coward. Jeannot," she added, turning towards her lover, " I have said more than I intended, and more perhaps than you should have heard from the lips of her, who is as jealous of your honour as she is of her own. It is our destiny to part just when our prospects in life were beginning to brighten, and for a moment I have given way to all a woman's weakness, but Monsieur Narbonne has brought me to a sense of duty, and I can now bid you depart on the errand to which you have been called by destiny. This night, you and your comrades leave the village for Toulon,—go, and may the God of battles aid and direct you !'

" That was spoken like a heroine of old," exclaimed the notary, " and no doubt Jeannot will remember your words, even at the moment when he is about to engage with the enemies of his country. If he does, they will nerve his arm to redoubled exertion, and we may hope before long to hear that he has deserved well from the gratitude of the emperor."

" Does the emperor reward all who deserve it ?" asked Jeannot.

" I have never heard of his omitting to do so," answered the notary, " and there is no reason why he should overlook your lover any more than others who have merited his patronage. Jeannot is young, of robust constitution, and from what I have seen of him, is warmly attached to the country which gave him birth. He will not, therefore, be wanting in courage when the moment for action comes, and you may afterwards call me but an indifferent prophet if my prognostication does not come true, that he is destined to fill many a page in the glorious annals of France."

" Why, surely you don't think it's my destiny to be a great man !" exclaimed Jeannot.

" It would be presumption for me to make such an assertion as that," answered the notary, " but at all events it will be your own fault if you are not esteemed a brave one."

" I'm glad to hear you say that, monsieur," exclaimed the young conscript, " for your words will never escape my memory, and they will go very far towards making me what you have said. I shall think, too, of Jeannette ; and what can serve to fill my heart with more courage than the thought that she will hear of my actions, and love me all the better for having done my duty?"

"Well said, my good fellow," cried Monsieur Narbonne;—"I am rejoiced to hear you speak so, and Jeannette looks her approval of your words, though her heart is too full to give expression to what she would otherwise have uttered. That you will deserve well of your country, I have no doubt, and let us hope that before long the return of peace will bring you back to her whom you so fondly love. But it is now time that you take farewell of each other, for within an hour Jeannot, with his fellow conscripts, must be on his march for Toulon. If you have anything to say to each other, I will retire for a short time, and then return to conduct Jeannette back to her mother's cottage."

"We have nothing to say that may not be spoken in your presence, Monsieur Narbonne," exclaimed our heroine, collecting all her fortitude for this trying moment. "Jeannot and I have held our last interview together for some time to come, and as the betrothed of a soldier of the empire, I will not show that weakness and want of self-command that we felt when we first strolled forth from home to renew our vows of constancy and affection. Jeannot," she added with forced firmness, "you see I do not weep;—my voice falters not, though it has now—and perhaps for the last time—to pronounce that dreadful word—farewell!"

As she uttered those words, she threw herself into the arms of her lover, offered up a few short words to Heaven as a prayer for his preservation from danger, and then, disengaging herself from his embrace, eagerly took the arm of Monsieur Narbonne for support, and then hurried away with him, without venturing to take another last fond look at him whom she had parted from. Jeannot stood watching her as long as she remained in sight, and then, heaving a deep sigh, he was about to hurry off in another direction, when his footsteps were suddenly arrested by the well known voice of Henri Dupont, who was standing within a few paces of him.

"Hilloa! friend Jeannot," exclaimed the new comer, "surely this parting hasn't made a coward of you?"

"Coward! why should you think so?"

"Only because you look so pale and agitated, that one would almost fancy the thought of fighting had made you sick already of the new life you are just going to commence."

"You seem to have been listening," answered the young man, coldly, "and if so, you might have known what it was that has agitated me."

"Humph! you have just seen Jeannette for the last time, and are suffering from love-sickness."

"I have seen her for the last time," he replied, "and it may be that I feel deeply at a separation that may be eternal. That, however, does not prove me to be a coward, as you may afterwards have to acknowledge when the hour of strife and danger comes. But you, Henri, have none to part from that you care much about, so that you can hardly judge of those who have."

"Well, never mind about that," answered the other; "I expected to meet you in your favourite lovers' walk, and came to give you notice that all is now ready for our march to Toulon, and all those who are not assembled when the trumpet sounds will be reported as deserters, and dealt with accordingly. So make haste, my lad, for you and I don't want to be the last in the field."

They now moved on in the direction of the village, and after proceeding some little distance in silence, Jeannot asked of his companion if he had heard much of the conversation that had just taken place.

"Why," answered Henri, "to tell you the truth, I heard too much to be exactly agreeable to my own vanity."

"I understand you; you were there some little time before the arrival of Monsieur Narbonne?"

"I was, and of course heard Jeannette express herself anything but favourably towards me."

"Which ought not to have occasioned any surprise, since you knew her to have been previously engaged."

"Well," answered Henri Dupont, laughing, "I can't say I was at all surprised at her confessing her indifference towards me, but I thought there was something like absolute dislike expressed, and that, you know, puts quite a different face upon the matter."

"It is not in Jeannette's nature to dislike anybody," answered the lover, "but she has a notion that her refusal to see you has not been accepted in a right spirit. In fact, I have heard her say before now, that she wished you would not throw yourself in her way on every occasion that offers itself."

"And yet, after all," replied Henri, "I only did so out of pure friendship, for I have known her longer than you, and perhaps presumed too much on that account. However, I am not likely to offend her again in that way, for this war is likely to last a long while, and I shall not return to my native village for many a year to come. Besides, Jeannot, I am aware that she is betrothed to you, and after the solemn pledge that has passed between you just now, I should be a treacherous scoundred, indeed, if I tried to draw away her affections from the man I esteem as my best friend."

"Well, I'm glad to hear you say that, at any rate," replied Jeannot, "for though I could never dream of treachery on your part, I must needs confess that what Jeannette said just now did give me a little uneasiness. And yet it ought not to have done so either, for we have always been such firm friends together, that it was not likely you would be base enough to deceive me."

"That's right, my boy," exclaimed Henri, "always do me the justice to think that, and the good feeling that at present exists between us will never be broken. As for Jeannette, I must confess that I have felt for her a regard that may be said to amount to affection, but no sooner did I learn that you had entire possession of her heart, than I retired from the field, determined not to contest with you for a love that I felt convinced was entirely hopeless."

"Then Jeannette was quite mistaken in supposing that you still sought her hand?"

"Oh, she is entirely mistaken there, I can assure you," answered his companion, "but that's not so much to be wondered at, for women, you know, are by nature rather weak when their vanity is concerned, and it may be that she has mistaken some little attention on my part for a determination to continue my suit."

"And I was rather afraid it was so myself," exclaimed Jeannot, "for lovers are proverbially given to jealousy, and I thought it a pity that our long friendship should be disturbed by an act of yours that must have been dishonourable. So as we now understand each other better, there's my hand, and from this time forward let us never have an unkind word between us."

"Ay, and there's my heart with it," cried Henri, grasping the offered hand of his friend with seeming sincerity, though at the very moment he was cursing him at the very bottom of his heart. "Now then," he added, "we perfectly understand each other, and whatever you may hear to the contrary from others, always believe that I would not forget your regard for any gratification of my own."

"I will listen to nothing against you," answered his too confiding friend, "for I well know that there are too many people in the world that are never so well pleased as when they are trying to set others by the ears. And yet why should you give me this caution, Henri, when you must be well aware that I am one of the last to pay attention to the ill-natured rumours of evil-disposed persons?"

"That is very true, but I thought to prevent the chance of misunderstanding between us."

"There can be no chance of it after the satisfactory explanation that has taken place just now," answered Jeannot, "besides are we not going out together to fight the battles of our country? and as both will be absent from home exactly the same time, you will not have the chance, even supposing you had the inclination, of trying to supplant me in the affection of Jeannette.'

"Exactly so," returned Henri, "and therefore it's a pity you should have harboured this notion even for a moment; however, you have acted throughout the affair with your usual candour, and I therefore hope this is the last time we shall have to speak upon a disagreeable subject."

"Hark," exclaimed Jeannot, "I hear the trumpet sound that you just now spoke of."

Soon as these words were uttered they separated, each taking a different road. Jeannot was thinking as he walked along, how pleasantly the disagreement between himself and Henri had been overcome, and how they should enjoy each other's friendship and confidence; little suspecting that any treachery was at work against him. On the other hand, Dupont was brooding over revenge, and thinking in what way he could get Jeannot into disgrace with his superiors, and by those means lessen him in the estimation of Jeannette. He had not been in this train of thought long when he saw one of his own company, a dissipated young man, coming towards him. Knowing this man to have an antipathy to Jeannot for his sobriety, and general good conduct, he accosted him with,—

"You know Jeannot Lamont, I believe?"

"To be sure I do, and have no great respect for him, my boy, for he's a great deal too steady and sedate in his habits, which is very bad for others who do not live quite so much within rule, because the contrast is rather apt to show off their defects."

"You don't like him, then?" exclaimed Henri.

"Not a bit of it."

"And you may suppose I don't," returned the other. "So suppose you and I put our heads together, to see if we can do him a mischief?"

"What sort of mischief do you mean?" asked Jacques Denon. "In a word, do you want to get rid of him, in order that the road may be open for you to marry the girl?"

"No," exclaimed Henri, in alarm. "I would not shed his blood, nor engage others to do it; but it has been his pride to deserve the praise of the officers that are over him, and I would give my next month's pay if we could only contrive some plan to get him into disgrace."

"Oh, if that's all," answered his comrade, "there's no very great difficulty in your way. Does this Jeannot like the taste of a good drop of wine?"

"No; he is particularly sober in his habits. But what made you ask that question, Denon?"

"Why, I was thinking if we could only contrive to make him drunk, or even a little tipsy, it might do great things towards getting him a very severe punishment. There would be the black hole to a certainty, for the first offence, and, to an equal certainty, he would be imprisoned for a longer period if the fault was repeated."

"I don't think that notion of yours would be of any use," exclaimed Henri, after a pause, "for the fellow happens to be so confoundedly steady in his habits, that he never takes anything stronger than *vin ordinaire*, and a man could never take enough of that to get into his head."

"Did you ever try to tempt him with anything better?"

"Oh, yes, I have asked him to join me with a bottle of real good stuff many a time, but I might as well have asked him to take poison, for he's always resolute in his refusal, and at length I've given up pressing him upon that point any further."

"Psha!" ejaculated Jacques Denon; "you are not half a fellow to carry on a plan of operations. You should stick to him hard and fast, till he will drink; and when he has taken a glass or two, I'll be bound he won't refuse to take as much as would answer your purpose."

"Why do you think so?"

"Because very little serves to get into the weak heads of those milk-and-water fellows that are not fond of their cups. Now this Jeannot, according to your account, is one of those sober chaps that will never be social with their comrades, and he's just the one that we may easily get into our leading-strings, if we choose to try."

"Don't be too sure of that till you know more about him," exclaimed Henri, "for, though a good natured fool in many respects, he can be as obstinate as anybody when he likes. Now, anything approaching to drunkenness has always been his abomination, and if he was ever asked to join us in a social glass he would be sure to think that it was only done as a snare to get him into mischief."

"Is he aware, then, of your dislike to him?"

"I believe he has not the least suspicion of it," answered young Dupont; "but then he has so often asked me not to press him to drink, that he would be sure to suspect there was some treachery intended if I were to urge him any more."

At this juncture Jeannot was seen to be slowly approaching the spot where they were standing.

"Psha! you only think so," exclaimed Denon. "However, by good luck, here he comes, and, if you have no objection, I'll try what sort of influence I have over the young fellow."

"Oh, do as you like about it," whispered Henri, as Jeannot approached; "but remember, caution must be the word, or he'll be awake to the trick we want to play him." Then turning towards his intended victim, who by this time stood by his side, he added, with a laugh of apparent good humour, "Why, how is this, Jeannot, can it be possible that you have ventured into so wicked a place as this canteen?"

"I should not have done so," replied the young soldier, "but, having just received a kind letter from Jeannette, in which she also desires to be remembered to you, I could not help coming to tell you, though, to do so, I was obliged to enter a place that I have foresworn, as the very root of all vices."

"Nonsense," exclaimed Jacques Denon. "Why should there be more vice in a place of this kind than in any other?"

"It's not for me to explain why it is so," answered the young man; "and, perhaps, you may think me foolishly prejudiced for the notion I have taken of the matter. Be that as it may, however, I quarrel with no man on account of his opinion, and I hope no one will attempt to interfere with mine."

"Bravo!" exclaimed Jacques, rapping the table with mock applause.

"And so," rejoined Henri Dupont, "you have had the exquisite pleasure of receiving a letter from Jeannette?"

"I have," he replied.

"And she has really condescended to mention my name?"

"Yes."

"Well then," exclaimed Jacques, "as the news seems to be so very agreeable to you both, I don't see how we can be so ungallant as to omit drinking the young lady's health. Here's to the pretty Jeannette, and her speedy marriage with the man of her heart!"

"Here's Jeannette, and her speedy marriage with the man of her heart!" repeated Henri; and raising the wine cup to his lips, he drained off the contents to the very last drop.

Jeannot stood by quite unmoved.

"Halloa! how is this?" exclaimed Jacques. "Here's the young lady's lover refuses to drink a toast that has been given in honour of the fair object of his affection. That's prettily said on my part, I believe, Monsieur Dupont?"

"It was kindly meant, I have no doubt," returned Jeannot; "but I have a strong objection to drinking, and all I can do in return for the compliment, is to thank you for it from the very bottom of my heart."

"Come, come, old fellow," exclaimed Jacques Denon, "that's but a milksop way of returning thanks, that we are not used to here. So off with your cup of wine, and prove by the sacrifice you make in doing so, that you deserve to have the love of such a girl as Jeannette Corville appears to be."

Thus urged, and unwilling to subject himself to any further ridicule, Jeannot raised the cup to his lips, and returned it empty to the table.

"Aye, there's something like spirit in that," cried Denon; "and now, I begin to see something like hope that, by and by, you'll be a fit companion for the soldiers of the grand army. And now, having done honour to our first toast, there's another that we can hardly pass over without disrespect to a most worthy female. Here's health, long life, and happiness to Madame Corville, the excellent mother of the no less excellent Jeannette!"

"Excuse me, my good friends," said the young man, "but I have already departed from my natural habit, and will take no more wine to-day."

"What! refuse to drink the old lady's health. For shame, Jeannot; I thought every Frenchman respected age too much to treat it with such marked disrespect."

"I have already told you my objections," answered Jeannot, "and having given way in one instance, I little thought you would press me to drink a second time."

"Well then, oblige us this once, and you can do as you like about drinking any more afterwards."

The young soldier stood irresolute for a moment or two, and then seeing that he would only be laughed at, if he hesitated any longer, he again raised the wine cup to his lips, and a second time it was drained to the very bottom. Unused, as he was, to taking intoxicating liquors, the effect was immediately felt, and from that moment he cared not what excess he might fall into. At the request of Henri Dupont he took a seat beside him at the table, and in the excitement of the conversation that was purposely introduced, he drank off three or four more cups of wine in quick succession, so that he soon became what is usually termed "half-seas over." He was not so far gone, however, as to be incapable of taking care of himself, nor was all the persuasion of his companions able to make him drink a drop more of the liquor that had taken such an effect on him.

"Very well, my good fellow," exclaimed Jacques Denon, as he thrust back the offered cup, "we'll not ask you to take any more with us to-day, because you are not used to it, and if the fumes of the wine should happen to mount to your head, there's no saying what would happen if our commanding officer should happen to hear of it."

"I thought the commanding officer was gone out to dinner with the governor of the citadel," exclaimed Jeannot, in the thick, husky tones that denote inebriation.

"So it was expected," replied Henri; "but he was obliged to give up a good dinner, because news arrived suddenly, that the Emperor Napoleon may be expected here from Paris every moment."

"The emperor expected!" cried Jeannot, with alarm.

"Yes, we have been looking for him some time, and now, at last, we are to have the honour of being inspected by him."

"And he will find me drunk," groaned the young conscript.

"Nonsense, man," exclaimed Jacques; what have you got to be afraid of, I should like to know? The emperor wont order us out till to-morrow, and by that time you'll be sober enough."

"But I shall be reported."

"Who by?—Do you think Dupont and I can't keep a secret, and who else need know anything about you having taken an extra drop of wine, if you are sensible enough to keep your own counsel?"

"There's always some good-natured friend ready enough to make mischief," answered Jeannot, "and if I'm seen intoxicated, it will soon reach the ears of the commanding officer, and then, instead of standing, as I ought to do, with my fellow soldiers, in the presence of the illustrious Napoleon, I shall be imprisoned in the black hole for having forgotten my duty! Fool that I was, to be led away against my own reason, when I had so long forsworn all intoxicating liquors!"

"Humph!" muttered Jacques, " you are a much greater fool for quarrelling with yourself without rhyme or reason. Are men to be always so much upon their guard, that they are never to be overtaken by drinking a little drop too much? In truth, Jeannot, I see you are a cup too low, so just take off this other drop, and that will set you all to rights again, so that you will be able to return to your room without anybody knowing that you have been enjoying yourself in the society of your friends."

Rendered desperate by what he had taken, and scarcely conscious of what he was doing, Jeannot swallowed the contents of the cup that was offered to him, and then rising from his seat, proceeded with staggering steps towards the door, till Henri Dupont caught him by the arm to prevent his falling to the ground.

"Halloa, old fellow," exclaimed the latter;—"this will never do, or the affair will soon be blown all over the place. Come, come, keep your body up, there's a good chap; or, if you like it better, sit down a little while, till you recover yourself."

"I'm drunk, I tell you!" hiccupped the conscript.

"Well, we both of us know that," replied Henri, unable to suppress a smile of exultation at the success of his stratagem. "There's no occasion for you to tell us that you have had a little too much, but the fault is not so much yours as that of your confounded head that can take so little to set your brains whirling."

"There's no denying that I'm drunk," again muttered Jeannot, in the same tone of stupid helplessness. "I've been fooled into taking what I ought to have thrown into the kennel, and I shall feel disgraced for the rest of my days.—Oh, Jeanette! Jeannette! could you see me at this moment, how utterly would you despise me!"

"Psha!" exclaimed Henri, with apparent friendship, "how is Jeannette to know what has taken place here?"

"Oh," he replied, "the story will no doubt find its way to her, and then my disgrace will be complete."

"Jeannot," exclaimed Denon, "are you a man, or do you want to become a child again, that you give way to all this weakness. Suppose your betrothed should happen to hear of your having taken too much for once in your life, is that any reason why she should think any the worse of you? No, no, women don't like those milk and water husbands that never enjoy themselves over a social glass."

"But the emperor!"

"Well," exclaimed Jacques Denon, "what are you to the emperor, or what is the emperor to you?"

"I have broken one of his strictest regulations."

"And so have a good many others done before you," answered Henri, "and yet I never heard of any worse punishment for drunkenness, than a few days' confinement."

"Confinement!" exclaimed Jeannot, stung by these words, "and do you think I could ever look again upon the broad face of day, if I was once subjected to the disgrace of imprisonment?—No! if it should ever come to that, I'll die rather than afterwards become a laughing-stock for my comrades in arms!"

"Well, you are a strange fellow, certainly," cried Denon, "but at any rate I'm glad to see that you are getting a little more sober than you were."

"I feel rather better," answered Jeannot, "but my legs still seem too weak to support me to my room. Besides, I've to cross the barrack yard, and the air will make me worse when I get in it."

"Nonsense," returned Denon, "it will make you better. Shake yourself a bit, man, and you'll soon get rid of your queer sensation."

Jeannot, without making any reply, started upon his feet, and after steadying himself a bit, made his way towards the door, from whence he emerged into the yard of which he had spoken. As he did so, the fresh air took an immediate effect, and to save himself from falling he made a bold rush across the quadrangle, which was formed by the buildings which constituted the barracks.

"We've done for him at last," chuckled Henri Dupont, as he and his comrade watched him partly on his way, and then closing the door, they returned to the canteen to drink more wine to the success of their stratagem, and exult over the anticipated fall of the man whom they had plotted to ruin.

Little suspecting the malice of his enemies, Jeannot continued to run staggering on, till he came near the door of the principal officer in command. Here a sudden thought flashed upon his brain, that he was in danger of being seen, and turning suddenly round he ran with no little violence against a stranger who happened to be passing at the time; Jeannot reeled back, and as he endeavoured to recover his equilibrium, his eyes encountered those of the person who he had so rudely, yet so unwillingly assaulted. The stranger was habited in a grey great coat, and his military hat and boots showed that he followed the profession of arms—a fact that was no sooner comprehended by the young soldier, than he became sobered by the reflection, that certain punishment awaited him for the breach of discipline which he had been guilty of. Conscience-stricken, and deprived of the power of speech, he stood irresolute whether to turn away or remain where he was, whilst the stranger, placing his arms behind him, stood gazing sternly upon the culprit. At that moment a fresh source of alarm burst upon the youthful conscript, for the peculiar dress, and, above all, the well-known attitude of the person before him, proved that he was in no less a presence than the Emperor Napoleon. Overcome by the astounding discovery, and believing that all was lost, he threw himself upon his knees and earnestly besought pardon for the offence of which he had been guilty. The countenance of the Emperor,—for it was indeed he,—somewhat relaxed its severity at this demonstration of sorrow for past offences, and Jeannot, auguring well from that circumstance, began to recover slightly from the alarm into which he had been thrown by this unlucky rencontre.

"How is this, young man?" exclaimed Napoleon, in a tone less severe than might have been expected. "Are the orders from head-quarters so little regarded that the first thing on my arrival here, is to find a soldier rendered incapable of service, if called upon suddenly, by an act of intemperance which is strictly forbidden."

"Pardon, sire!" cried the penitent, "pardon me a fault that I shall never cease to be ashamed of."

"How know you that I am your Emperor?"

"Ah, your majesty," exclaimed Jeannot, "how could I be mistaken in the person of our illustrious sovereign?"

"Humph! one would imagine that you had been brought up a courtier."

"And yet," answered the young conscript, "there is no other man in the world that I could bow my knee to."

"Your name?"

"Jeannot Lamont."

"Well, you are educated for a soldier. Are you a willing one, or, like too many others, have you only entered our army because compelled to do so by the act of conscription."

"Must I tell the truth, sire?"

"Certainly."

"Then it must be confessed," he replied, "that, if left to my own choice, I should have preferred the peaceful pursuit that I was brought up to. But when I was told that the Emperor required the services of all who are able to handle sword or gun, I willingly gave up my own inclination to follow the fortunes of the man, whose sole object seems to be the raising of France to the head of all nations."

"You love your country, then?"

"So well, your majesty, that I am willing to shed the last drop of my blood in her service."

"Rise from your knees, young man," exclaimed Napoleon, "for your candour and noble feelings have already obtained my forgiveness for the foolish excesses you have been guilty of. But tell me, are you in the habit of committing these acts of intemperance?"

"I am not, sire; our general here will inform your majesty that no complaint has ever been made against me."

"I shall inquire particularly into that circumstance," answered the emperor, "and if your assertion is borne out, the indiscretion of to-day will not interfere with your future advancement. But remember, there must be no repetition of it, or you will not escape scathless, and you will lose the confidence of your sovereign."

"Sire, you may rely upon my promise," replied Jeannot, "for this is the first time in my life that I have drank to excess, and I solemnly promise that it shall be the last."

"Perhaps the over indulgence was occasioned by this being the birthday of some loved friend."

"No, sire, I have not even that poor excuse to make."

"Humph! there is honesty in your words, and something tells me you will make a good soldier. But tell me, how was it that you were betrayed into this act of folly?"

"Pardon me, your majesty, if I am silent upon that point."

"Why should you be silent?"

"Because I cannot enter into an explanation without getting two of my comrades into trouble."

"Oh, I see how it is; you suffered yourself to be persuaded against your own inclination?"

"I did."

"And did they get as much intoxicated as yourself?"

"No, sire, I left them perfectly sober."

"That answer saves them!" exclaimed the emperor, "for had they also disregarded my orders, I should have held it my duty to insist upon the disclosure of their names, that they might be punished by way of example to the whole army. In times like these young man, our country requires its defenders to be brave and vigilant, which can hardly be expected from men who give way to evil habits that produce inervation and a carelessness, which are amongst the chief things that disorganize and ruin an army. For the present, however, I shall not inquire more particularly as to who were your companions in this drinking bout, but you may tell them from their emperor that he will keep a vigilant eye upon all the conscripts in these barracks, and the first that may offend against the rules of military discipline will receive the punishment they deserve. And let these words of mine be spread among all your companions, for this warning may not be without the best results. And now, tell me, young man," he added, changing the conversation in his usual rapid manner, "does satisfaction generally prevail among the conscripts, or is there a feeling against what may be termed the cruelty and hardship of forcing men to leave their homes and occupations to follow a profession for which they entertained no liking."

"Sire——"

"Nay, I know what you are about to say," interrupted Napoleon. "You fancy that I want you to act the part of a spy upon your comrades, and have too much honourable feeling to be one, even though urged by your sovereign. But do not misunderstand me, for all I want is to know the feelings of my people, in order that I may apply the proper means to remedy them. Tell me, then, if there is any dissatisfaction against the system of recruiting the army by conscription?"

"Since your majesty has asked me the question," replied Jeannot, "I must confess that many people do complain of the hardship that compels them to leave their homes and families to engage in wars that they consider unnecessary."

"Humph!—they grumble, but I suppose that is all?"

"They go no further, sire," answered Jeannot, "and I believe the most errant grumbler among them would fight for your majesty whilst a drop of blood remained in his veins."

"Then I have lost none of my popularity?"

"It is impossible your majesty can do that," answered the young soldier, "whilst you lead them on from one great victory to another, till the whole world seems stricken with fear at the bare mention of your name."

"All but haughty England," muttered the emperor half aside, "and she also must submit before long, unless I am very much mistaken." Then speaking aloud, he added,—" You, Jeannot Lamont, know the feelings of the people better than I can possibly do, and it is your opinion that my name is still respected among them ?"

"I can answer for it, your majesty, that it was never more so than at the present moment. All regard you as the saviour of our country, and are willing to follow your footsteps, even should you lead them into the most inhospitable countries of the world."

"No one is anxious for peace ?"

"I will not say that," answered Jeannot, "for the trade of our country has suffered so severely from this long war, that thousands are expecting immediate ruin if the rights of free commerce are not soon restored to them. I am, however, speaking too boldly, though I trust your majesty will pardon me, since I have been led on to do so by the questions I have been required to answer."

"You have spoken exactly as I could have wished—honestly and fearlessly— and without caring or remembering that you were speaking to another than your own equal in rank. In fact, I believe, if I had more such men to confer with upon matters that I cannot otherwise make myself acquainted with, I should better understand the wants of those I have been called upon to govern. This meeting, therefore, of ours, so unfortunate in its commencement, has not been without useful instruction, to him who was vain enough to believe that his own sovereign will was sufficient to rule the nation."

"Your majesty, then, has forgiven the disgraceful state of intoxication in which you found me ?"

"You have my full pardon, Jeannot," replied the emperor, "and especially as the suddenness of the recontre appears to have completely sobered you. Go, then ; return to your own room, and make a firm resolution never again to be guilty of excess either in drink or otherwise. Act with prudence, snd should your bravery in the field merit my favourable notice, depend upon it I shall not forget to reward it."

With this the emperor turned away, and entered the house of the general in command, leaving Jeannot standing where he was, and scarcely believing but that he was in a dream."

In the meantime Jacques Denon, who happened to be passing by a window, perceived Jeannot talking to a stranger, who, to his utter astonishment he soon discovered was no less a personage than the Emperor Napoleon himself. Having satisfied himself of this fact, he called to Henri Duport, and directing his attention to that which had so greatly excited his wonder, he exclaimed—

"What are we to think of this, my boy ? The emperor cannot but see that he has been drinking too much, and when the discovery is made, Jeannot may look out for squalls."

"But he seems to have become sober all on a sudden."

"It's enough to make him so, if he is not," returned Jacques ; "for the emperor is very strict against drunkards, and the young fellow must have heard by this time that he is to be shut up in the black hole for his misconduct."

"I don't know what to say about that," exclaimed Henri with a tone of evident chagrin, "for Napoleon seems to be in a tolerable good humour, considering the state he found Jeannot in."

"But Jeannot himself don't seem as if he felt very comfortable in his present situation."

"How can he ?" demanded Henri Duport, "when it's impossible for him to know how this affair will turn out? By Jove! it would be a glorious thing to hear that he had been ordered into confinement, for the disgrace would be so great that Jeannette would never have a good opinion of him again."

"Which is exactly what you want ; and you would therefore have something to thank me for, since it was my suggestion to make him drunk, and not only that, but it was through me that he was persuaded to empty the wine cup three or four times."

"Look!" exclaimed Henri, "the emperor has left him without any seeming anger, and Jeannot remains standing where he was in complete astonishment."

"And he appears to be as sober as a judge too."

"Ah!' exclaimed Henri, "fright has done that, no doubt, and'so our intended victim escapes, because there are no longer any traces of his former intoxication. But never mind ; we have been disappointed this time it's true, but nevertheless we'll make another trial of our skill in mischief-making, and perhaps the next time we may be more fortunate."

"So," exclaimed his companion, "you are determined not to let him escape, then?"

"How can I, when I know my only chance with Jeannette is to make him commit some act of folly that will set her against him ? Besides, I never had any great liking for him, and nothing would gratify me more than to get him into disgrace."

"Well, my boy," exclaimed Jacques, "you may depend upon my assistance at any time that you may require it."

"And what will be the use of it, if we are always to fail as we have now?" asked the other. "Everything seemed to be going on as favourably as possible, and his falling in with the emperor ought to have crowned the affair with success, when lo and behold ! he gets off, as if nothing at all had been the matter with him."

"But you surely don't expect that he will always have the same good fortune."

"Why the truth is, I thought the affair might have been brought to an end without even trouble or difficulty, but the very first attempt we make fails, and we are now as far off from gaining our object as ever we were. He may begin to guess to that some scheme is in progress against him, and if once that notion should get into his head, there'll be an end for ever of all the fine prospects that I was foolish enough to picture to myself."

"Do you always give up at the first failure of a scheme?" asked Jacques Denon."

"I never plotted anything before," he replied, "and that perhaps is the reason why I feel so disappointed now. Egad ! what could possibly be more provoking than to see him slip through our fingers so easily, when it was supposed we had so nicely caught him?"

"Well," exclaimed Jacques, "we have made a dead failure, that is certain ; but never mind, take things easily as I do, and believe that if things go contrary once there'll be better luck next time. We can't always be unsuccessful you know, and I should think you'll never be tired of trying, so long as there's a chance of setting Jeannette against her lover."

"Not so long as there's a chance of it," he replied, "but if things go contrary-wise, as they have done in the present instance, we may plot and arrange plans to very little purpose. So I fancy all chance of my marrying Jeannette may be supposed to be at an end, unless indeed her lover should happen to be shot or run through the body in the first engagement."

"Which is likely enough, if that's any consolation to you, for he's no coward, and will not be looking out for his own safety as long as there is a blow to be struck. However, even putting all that aside, we may yet find means to prevent his marriage with Jeannette, if you have only heart enough to follow up some of the many plans that I shall be able to propose."

"As for that," answered Henri Duport, "I don't mind what I do to prevent a marriage that I've always set my face against. Besides, though he believes me to be his friend, I bear him the greatest hatred, and have only been prevented doing him a mischief, by the certainty I felt that some one would be busy enough to find me out."

"Then you had better leave the management of the whole affair to me, for no one will imagine that I can have any ill-feeling against a person that I never saw or heard of, till chance brought us together in these barracks."

" Will you then undertake to lead Jeannot into some scrape that shall forfeit the love of Jeannette ?" asked Henri.

" At any rate I'll try my best," answered Jacques Denon, " and the next time he shall not escape quite so easily, as he has just done with the Emperor Napoleon. In short, I feel vexed that he has managed to defeat what I thought an excellent plan, and shall not feel satisfied till I have turned the tables upon him."

" Then there's still hope that Jeannette will be mine ?"

" I don't know how that may be," answered the other, " for everything will depend upon whether she finds out the share you've had in getting her sweetheart into trouble, for if that should come to her knowledge, I rather think you would have very little chance of finding favour in her eyes."

" How is she to know that I have anything to do with it ?"

" Aye, there's the rub," exclaimed his friend, " for I have often wondered myself how people have managed to get at secrets that seemed to have been kept all snug and close. But in this case, there's not much trouble, for Jeannot will no doubt guess that you have had a finger in the pie, and of course he'll take care that the girl shall know the mischief you have done him."

" And if she should hear of it," returned Henri, " all chance of making her my wife will be at an end."

" Why to be sure it would," answered the other, " and for that very reason I should advise you to forget Jeannette, and look out for some other girl that has not already given her heart away to a rival. There's plenty enough disengaged, and that will be glad to wed with a young fellow like you, that has devoted himself to the honourable profession of arms."

" That may be all very true," exclaimed Henri, " but when a chap is over head and ears in love, it's not very easy to give up the object of his affection. Besides, I've made up my mind to prevent the match between Jeannette and Jeannot, and I'll not be disappointed whilst there remains a single chance or hope of success."

" Well," returned his friend, " you know I'm ready enough to assist you, and there shall be nothing to complain of as far as I am concerned ; but, remember, I've cautioned you against the danger of a discovery, and if anything unpleasant should happen afterwards, I'll not take any of the blame of it upon myself."

" I only want your advice," replied Henri, " and when that seems to be good the active part of the business shall be under my own management. As for Jeannot, he has not the least suspicion that I envy him the love of the girl, and I think with a little care we may keep him ignorant of that part, till we have carried matters so far, that Jeannette will forbid him to continue his addresses to her."

" Well, we shall see how that may be, by and by," exclaimed Jacques, " but at all events we must keep quiet just at present, and make a fresh beginning when this drunken bout has been forgotten. Then, perhaps, we may write an anonymous note or two to the girl, describing her lover as growing more and more wild in his way of life, and as having almost forgotten her, amidst the more exciting scenes of a military career. That will soon give rise to anger on her part, and anger will before long grow into a downright dislike towards him."

Several comrades soon joined them, and as the conversation which had occupied their attention could no longer be carried on, they accepted an invitation to join in a drinking carouse, and returned to the canteen, where they kept up the scene of boisterous mirth till the regulation of the place obliged them to retire to rest."

CHAPTER III.

JEANNETTE BEGINS TO HAVE HER MISGIVINGS—THE EFFECTS OF AN ANONYMOUS CORRESPONDENCE.—AN ARRIVAL.—CONFIRMATION OF THE EVIL REPORTS, AND THE DESPAIR OF OUR HEROINE.

SIX months passed away since their separation, and though Jeannette received several letters from her lover, all of them breathing the same warmth of affection, she fancied his love was less ardent, and that, though professing the same sentiments of love he had ever felt, he was, in fact, transferring his admiration towards some more favourite object. It may appear singular how such a notion could have entered her mind, but the wonder will immediately cease when the reader learns that, in the interval we have named, she had received several anonymous communications, warning her that Jeannot was acting the part of a hypocrite, and repeatedly asserting that he was no longer worthy of the tender regard with which she had been used to favour him. These, at first, were looked upon with doubt and suspicion, but when the assertions were frequently repeated, and proof offered if required, she began to feel convinced that there must be some truth in the unwelcome reports that reached her. Then it was that, in her answers to the young conscript, she hinted at the unpleasant rumours that had reached her, and implored him, if he valued her peace of mind, to send back an immediate reply to remove the doubts which so greatly harassed and perplexed her. As may be imagined, Jeannot lost no time in obeying the request, and for a period our heroine felt convinced that his character had been cruelly maligned; at length, however, other anonymous communications were received, which once more awakened her suspicions, and then, scarcely knowing what construction to put upon the affair, she spoke to her mother upon the subject, and earnestly requested the old lady's opinion as to the truth or falsehood of the evil communications that had been so darkly conveyed to her. Madame Corville was busily engaged with her spinning wheel at the time, and suspending her operations suddenly, she directed a searching glance towards her daughter, and eagerly inquired if she had any idea who her anonymous correspondent was.

"I have not the slightest," she replied, "except that he appears to be one of Jeannot's comrades, and as such he has opportunities of frequently observing him."

"Perhaps it's some one that owes him a grudge, and takes this paltry way to revenge himself."

"That is exactly what I fancied myself," replied Jeannette; "but the writer, whoever he is, professes the greatest friendship for the man he is acting the spy upon, and, as an excuse for his conduct, assures me that he is urged only by a feeling of indignation against the treachery from which I am likely to suffer so severely."

"Depend upon it, my dear," exclaimed Madame Corville, "there is something at the bottom of all this that neither you nor I can fathom. If your unknown correspondent was urged by an honourable motive, he would not conceal his name, and in my opinion you ought to send back a reply, stating that you can place no reliance in the reports of one who is coward enough to stab another man in the dark."

"I should have done so before now," replied our heroine, "but I have no means of directing a letter to him."

"Then it will be better to pay no heed to such communications, and by and by the slanders will entirely cease."

"Am I to understand that you believe I may still rely upon the constancy of Jeannot?"

"I really see no reason to doubt him at present," answered Madame Corville, "for we have always seen him to be a strict lover of truth, and surely a man of that kind should be the very last to be suspected of anything like deception towards the girl he professes to love."

" True !" exclaimed Jeannette; "I have argued that way myself, and should have forgotten the evil reports that have reached me, but that they are so often repeated, that at length I scarce know what to think. I will not, however, entirely give him up without further inquiry, though it must needs be confessed I know not what source to look to, for a confirmation or denial of the charges that have been brought against him."

" But you know what his previous character has been, and surely he cannot have changed so suddenly as to become all at once the heartless deceiver of the girl he has always professed to love. For my own part, I cannot believe it possible, and, having some little experience of my own, I could almost take it upon myself to declare that Jeannot is still as warmly attached to you as ever he was."

" Then he has been most cruelly injured by some villain who has a motive of his own to serve."

" That's exactly my opinion upon the subject," exclaimed the old lady, "and depend upon it, my dear, you will, before long, see reason enough to rejoice in having listened to the suggestions of one who is able to judge better than yourself. Besides, he tells you that he has found some little favour with the emperor, and it's hardly likely that he would be guilty of an act that, if known, would bring upon him the scorn, if not the anger, of one who would not countenance a dishonourable act."

" But," answered our heroine, "some people tell us that Napoleon chiefly regards those that distinguish themselves by bravery in the field, without caring anything for their character in other respects."

" Ah ! my dear child," cried the old lady, "it may be all very well for folks to repeat these things of the emperor, but a great mind like his cannot approve of dishonour even amongst the meanest of his subjects. That Jeannot has deserved some kindly notice from him is a great thing in his favour, and I should not be at all surprised if this lover of yours rises to be a person of consequence by and by."

" I hope not !" sighed Jeannette.

" And why do you hope not, you simple girl ?"

" Because he might then indeed think me beneath his notice; and if I should live to be despised by him, what greater misery could possibly be inflicted upon me ?"

" How is this ?" exclaimed Madame Corville; "a few minutes ago you were inclined to give credit to the reports raised against him, and now your words seem to prove that he will be faithful only so long as he remains in his present humble condition. However, there's no accounting for the whims and notions of young folks when they are in love."

" If I am anxious in this instance," replied Jeannette, "it is as much on his account as my own—for who afterwards could regard him with favour if he were to prove faithless after the vow he made never to give his affection to another ?"

" Which vow ought to be quite sufficient to convince you that he will never forget his promise."

" I have tried to believe it of him, mother, and should never have listened to the scandalous reports of others, but for their having been repeated so often, that there appears to be something like truth in them."

" You forget, then, that there are few people lucky enough to be without enemies ?"

" Unfortunately, I know it to be the case," answered the girl, "but I never heard that Jeannot had an enemy, and it appears to be almost impossible that he can have made any in the short time he has been away."

" It's as likely as not," exclaimed the old lady, "that this secret correspondent of yours is some paltry fellow that is jealous of the notice that has been taken of him by the emperor."

" If that should be the case, Jeannot would soon be able to guess the person to whom he owes all this ill feeling."

"Then write to him immediately, and candidly relate all that has been stated against him."

"Nay," replied Jeannette, "I would have done that sooner, but for the dread I felt lest Jeannot should suffer his anger to overcome his prudence. He is hot and impetuous at all times when his honour is brought into question and, were he to learn what has been said of him, I know not where the mischief would end."

"Of course he would lose no time in seeking out the author of all these calumnies—and who could blame him if he visited the slanderer with all the punishment he deserves?"

"But in doing so he would risk his own life."

"And ought a brave man to think of danger when his honour is to be cleared up?" asked Madame Corville.

"Perhaps not," answered her daughter; "but I cannot help a feeling of dread creeping through me whenever I think of the consequences that would very likely follow if he was to know the mischief that is constantly working against him. Luckily, so far he is quite unconscious of what is going on, and I have taken every care to conceal that fact from him, lest he should fall into some serious dilemma."

"But, my dear, you will not be able always to keep him in this state of ignorance."

"I know it, but the fact shall be kept from him as long as possible."

"And soon, with all your care, it must come to his knowledge, so that I think the sooner he knows what his enemies are about the better it will be. In fact, it is hardly just that he, who is most deeply interested in the affair, should be the last to hear that a secret foe is endeavouring to do him a serious injury. Nay, I could almost find it in my heart to write and inform him of the mischievous reports that are continually reaching you through an anonymous correspondent."

"For Heaven's sake, reflect before you take so dangerous a step!" cried Jeannette, with alarm.

"I don't mean to say that I shall positively do so," returned her mother, "but in yielding to your fears, I must needs confess that poor Jeannot is hardly dealt fairly with. A man ought to know when he has a secret enemy to deal with, or he runs a chance of being utterly crushed without an opportunity being afforded him to defend himself. However, for the present, I shall content myself with watching how this affair goes on, and if the scandal is carried on much further, I may think it high time to put your lover on his guard."

"Will it not be better to leave that to me, who has his interest so deeply at heart?"

"Perhaps it may, but you must not withhold the information from him too long, or I may be tempted to send him a letter, explaining the whole affair, and calling upon him to prove to my satisfaction the utter groundlessness of these base charges."

"If you do so," cried Jeannette, "you will give him reason to believe that we have given credit to the reports."

"And have you not said that you almost believe them?"

"Sometimes," answered the maiden, "I scarcely know what to think, though I must confess that my inclination is to believe that he is faithful and stedfast to the vow he made on the evening of his departure for Toulon. His letters, too, are still full of kindness as ever they were, and I should hardly suffer a doubt to cross my mind, but that I have heard before now, of men who have been faithless when far removed from those whom they have professed to love."

"So you think Jeannot must needs be added to the number?"

"Indeed, mother," she replied, "if I had seriously thought so, I should have written to release him from his engagement long before now. In spite of these painful rumours, however, I have still no slight reliance on the honour of Jeannot, and am content to wait till something arises, either to clear his character, or prove beyond a doubt that he is guilty of the charge that has been brought against him."

"That may be all very well in some cases," observed Madame Corville, "but in this I think it scarcely just that your lover should lie any longer under an imputation, that so seriously affects his character. At all events, he should be put upon an equal footing with his secret foe, and there is no other way of doing so, except by informing him of the means that have been taken to destroy him in your estimation."

"Jeannot has not been injured in my estimation."

"Luckily for him it may not be so," exclaimed her mother, "but for all that, there's no thanks to the secret assassin, whoever he may be, that has set all this mischief afloat."

"Be assured Jeannot shall suffer no injustice as far as I am concerned."

"But he must suffer injustice so long as you entertain a thought that he has broken faith with you."

"Indeed, mother, I neither can nor will believe it of him."

"That's good hearing, at any rate," answered Madame Corville, "and yet I'm sure I understood just now, that you were inclined to believe his affections to have been transferred to some other female."

"Oh, I know not what I say when these cruel rumours get the uppermost, as they sometimes will, in spite of myself," answered Jeannette, scarcely knowing what reply to make. "I have endeavoured to believe that nothing will ever make him inconstant to his vow, and yet there are times when my brain feels almost maddened at the bare thought of being neglected by one in whom all my love—all my hopes of future happiness, are fixed. But henceforth, your counsel shall be my only guide, and when next I receive one of those anonymous letters that have given me so much uneasiness, I'll ask your advice as to what course I ought to adopt."

"Throw it on the fire, my love, and try to forget that an aspersion has been cast upon the character of your lover."

"Nay, the innocence of Jeannot must be proved, before I can forget the accusation that has been brought against him."

"Why should you pay the slightest regard to an accusation brought by a slanderer that has not the courage to come forward and make his charge in a straightforward, manly way? Treat him with the silent contempt that he deserves, and in a short time, you will be troubled with no more of his diabolical communications."

"Had I known where to find him," answered Jeannette, "I should have sent back all his letters unopened."

"You know his hand-writing, then?"

"So well, that I could pick it out from amongst a thousand letters."

"And have you never seen anything similar to it, before you received his first communication?"

"Never;—and therefore, I suppose, my correspondent must be an entire stranger to me."

"That don't follow, Jeannette," replied her mother, "for a person with the cunning that he appears to possess, would find means to prevent a discovery taking place through any carelessness of that kind. For instance, he would either so disguise his hand that you should not be able to recognise it, or get some other person to write the letter, in order to prevent the discovery of his secret. However, be that as it may, I would advise you to write without delay to Jeannot, informing him of all the particulars relating to this mysterious affair, and inviting him to prove that he has been assailed by the most groundless calumnies."

This Jeannette promised to do, though it was not exactly in accordance with her own views; and she was about to commence a letter, when a knock was heard at the door, and directly afterwards a soldier, apparently worn out with travel and fatigue, entered the apartment in which she and her mother were seated. They both rose with some alarm, but the stranger motioned them to be seated again, and then, throwing himself into a chair, he endeavoured to make an excuse for his intrusion, and inquired if he might ask for hospitality till the next morning.

"You are a stranger," answered Madame Corville, "but having the appearance of a soldier, I will not close my door against you."

And with that she spread before him such refreshments as her cottage afforded, desiring him to make free with the humble fare that it was in her power to bestow.

"Thank you, dame," replied the stranger, as he helped himself without further ceremony; "this is exactly the sort of kindness I expected to meet with from Madame Corville; for I was told, even as far off as Toulon, that beneath her roof, I had only to ask and receive the very best that her means would afford."

"You are from Toulon, then?" inquired Jeannette, eagerly.

"Yes, mademoiselle," he replied, "I have travelled direct from there on foot, and have not lost much time on the road, I can tell you."

"Are the conscripts still there?" again asked our herione.

"Oh, yes," he replied, "they were in their barracks up to the time of my leaving the town, but, if all the reports are true, they are not likely to remain in idleness much longer."

"What do you mean by that?" demanded Madame Corville, as she perceived that her daughter exhibited symptoms of alarm at the intimation that had been thus conveyed to her; "are there rumours abroad of any fresh invasion that our brave general is about to make?"

"There are something more than rumours," answered the stranger, "for the Emperor Napoleon has picked a quarrel with the King of Prussia, and he has sworn to deprive him of his dominions if once he leads his army over the frontiers."

"And, I suppose," exclaimed Madame Corville, "the conscripts in Toulon are to be draughted into the invading army?"

"Exactly so," he replied, "the young fellows acquitted themselves so well at at an inspection a short time ago, that the emperor, delighted at the precision of their movements, declared that they should immediately form part of the grand army that has the honour to be headed by himself. Aye, and the lads were s flattered by the distinction, that their cries of 'Vive Empereur!' might almost hav been heard at this distance."

"Foolish fellows!" cried Jeannette, "how little do they think of the perils they are about to encounter."

"As for that, mademoiselle," exclaimed the stranger, "what would military life be, unless there was danger attached to it? For my own part, I have been a soldier from the age of eighteen, and no part of the time has ever been so dull as when there was no enemy to fight against. No, no, peace is all very well for a parcel of women and children, but not for such as Pierre Langrais, who enlisted for the purpose of serving his country, and not to receive pay for doing nothing at all."

"Pray, Monsieur Langrais," interposed the dame, "do you happen to have heard of a young man named Jeannot Lamont, one of the conscripts you have just been speaking of, at Toulon?"

"Oh, yes," he replied, "and people say he's likely to turn out a smart fellow when he begins to smell gunpowder. By the bye, now you remind me of him, he is a native of this place, if I am not mistaken?"

"He is."

"And there is a girl here, to whom he was to have been married if he had not been carried off with his brother conscripts?"

"My daughter, Jeannette, here, is the person you allude to."

"Well," exclaimed Pierre Langrais, "it's singular that I should find myself in the presence of the very girl I was speaking of."

"You say," exclaimed Madame Corville, "that he is likely to be an honour to the profession he belongs to?"

"There can be no doubt of that," answered the man, "after the very flattering notice that has been taken of him by the emperor. To be sure, Jeannot is said to be a bit of a gallant amongst the fair sex; but that's nothing, for soildiers, you know, are privileged to break as many hearts as they can, and no one ever thinks any the worse of them for it."

"Is Jeannot paying his attentions to any female in Toulon?" asked our heroine, eagerly.

"Bless your heart, my dear," replied Pierre Langrais, laughing. "there's at least a dozen girls that he's after, and if he had been allowed to stay there much longer the number would have been doubled."

"You are jesting with me, because you see how much your words are likely to annoy me," exclaimed Jeannette, endeavouring, though in vain, to recover her usual calmness.

"Nay, why should I be so ungrateful as to say anything to annoy the daughter of my hospitable entertainer?"

"Because, if I mistake not, you are the person who has written a number of anonymous letters, or have sent them here to complete the mischief that has been attempted."

"Nay, you wrong me there, mademoiselle," exclaimed Pierre, "for we are strangers to each other; and even if I was inclined to act so perfidious a part, there must be some motive, which I am sure cannot exist in the present instance. In short, I would rather speak words of comfort to the betrothed bride of my friend Jeannot, than utter a word that might be likely to make her think badly of him."

"You tell me he is unfaithful."

"Then I cannot have made myself very clearly understood," replied the visitor, "for though I said he had made himself agreeable to some few of the pretty girls of Toulon, it don't follow that he has forgotten the pledge he has made to you. Besides, soldiers are privileged to make love, and many say civil things without being supposed to have turned their backs upon those they have left behind them."

"In other words," exclaimed Madame Corville, "you have only been teazing my daughter all this time."

"Indeed I have not," he replied, "for I have spoken nothing more than the truth, and mademoiselle Jeannette is at liberty to put her own construction upon what I've said."

"But he has some secret enemy, or these anonymous letters would not have been sent to my daughter."

"There's no denying that," he replied, "but I hope you don't suspect that I have had anything to do with so base a transaction."

"I should be sorry to think so badly of a man that has asked my hospitality," returned Madame Corvil'e. "It seems, in fact, to be impossible, and I therefore request that nothing more may be said upon so disagreeable a subject."

"May I ask," said Jeannette, "if you are about to return to Toulon?"

"That will depend upon circumstances," replied Pierre Langrais, "for having received rather a severe wound towards the close of the last campaign, I have permission to visit my home in order that I may return to head quarters with health and strength enough to do still further service to my country. And I hope a few weeks will restore me; for I am no coward, and would not shrink from my duty whenever I may be required."

"Have you been much in battle?" asked Jeannette.

"Aye, maiden, in several."

"And have never been wounded till the last one?"

"I have never been seriously hurt till then," he replied, "and that is something to say, for it has generally been my fate to be in the thick of the fight; however, the emperor has a pretty good notion of my courage, and such are the men that he always chooses whenever there is warmer work than usual to do. But I see how it is, mademoiselle; you are thinking of the chances that your lover may have of escaping from the perils of the career he is about to run."

" You have indeed guessed my thoughts," sighed our heroine ; " and yet it is foolish of me too, for, since he owes the duty to his country, my own feelings should be forgotten in the one reflection, that he may be spared to reap the reward of his bravery."

" Ah !" exclaimed Pierre, " it's all very well to talk of reward, and all that sort of thing, but unfortunately we common soldiers seldom mount higher than the first or second step of the ladder."

" And they say Napoleon rewards all that may deserve it."

" So he does, mademoiselle," answered Pierre Langrais, " but only consider the hundreds of thousands of brave fellows that he has under his command, and then say if he can bestow his favours upon all that may deserve his notice. As far as thanks go, I have received them publicly, but the honour, gratifying as it is, puts no money into one's pocket. However I am no grumbler, and will wait patiently to see if any piece of good fortune should by and by turn up."

" It seems hard, too," observed Madame Corville, " that men, who are forced to go as conscripts, should derive no better reward from it than the paltry pay they receive."

" There's no doubt about its being very hard," replied Pierre Langrais, " but if the emperor waited for people to volunteer into his service, he would never have been able to boast of being at the head of such an army as he can now lead against the enemies of his country. In fact, we Frenchmen never think ourselves so well employed, as when employed in the service of our native land ; and 'tis well that it should be so, for, to all appearances, we have work enough cut out to last us for some time to come."

" Is there no chance of peace, then ?" asked Jeannette, anxiously.

" As far as present appearances go, we have hard fighting to go through for a long while," he replied. " This quarrel with the King of Prussia will cost many thousands of lives, and before the affair can be brought to a conclusion other countries will join in the fray, so that there's no saying how long a time it may last."

" Can anybody be found to justify such scenes of bloodshed ?"

" I don't know much about justifying such things," answered the soldier, " but wars have been carried on from a very early period of the world, and, judging by affairs as we find them, I don't see any chance of their being brought to an end in a hurry. Indeed, so long as nations fancy there are reasons for falling out, their rulers will expect the people to risk their lives in defence of their country."

" Without caring for the misery and desolation they bring into the houses of their subjects," exclaimed Madame Corville.

" Whether they care for it or not, I don't know," returned Pierre Langrais, " but it is quite certain that war is a game they are too fond of, to give up so long as people are ready to hazard their lives in a cause that they can feel little or no interest in. So you see monarchs are not so much to blame as those who are willing to sell their services for the sake of the trifling pay they are to receive for them."

" But Jeannot was obliged to follow the profession of a soldier, because the emperor fancies he wants more men to carry on his wars against foreign nations," exclaimed Madam Corville.

" And no doubt the emperor is right."

" How can it be right to sacrifice the lives of thousands of men that feel no interest in the quarrel ?"

" That's a question," answered Pierre Langrais, " that you and I had better not argue. We neither of us understand it, and ' the least said the soonest mended,' is a saying that ought to be more attended to than what it is."

" Indeed," said Madame Corville, " then, according to that doctrine, we little folks have nothing to do but yield with submission to the will of the great ones."

" And in many instances we ought to do so," returned the soldier, " for as no nation can do without a head of some kind, the people must obey the laws as long as they are not absolutely bad. Not that I am going to excuse tyranny, for when once people begin to feel that they are living oppressed, it's high time for them to relieve themselves by all fair and honourable means."

"But, not by such scenes of bloodshed as were witnessed in our late revolution," exclaimed Jeannette.

"Aye, mademoiselle," returned the soldier, "now you are speaking upon a subject that I know something about, for it so happens that I was at the taking of the bastile, and have fought ever since in the sacred cause of liberty. I therefore know the heavy debt of gratitude which we owe to Napoleon, who, finding our country in the midst of misery, has raised it to be among the first in the w orld."

"That may be all very true," answered Madame Corville, "but great as our emperor is, he owes the greater part of his success to the bravery of the troops that he has had to command."

"Then you don't give him so much credit as most people do?"

"We women understand little of such matters," replied Madame Corville, "but there are few among us, I believe, that don't thank him for all the benefits he has conferred upon our country. War, however, is a game that none of us like, and we believe France would be much more happy and contented if she were at peace with all her neighbours."

"And so we shall be, if success continue to follow us as it has done ever since Napoleon has had the command of our armies," exclaimed Monsieur Narbonne, who, as an old friend, had entered the house without the usual ceremony of knocking.

Madame Corville shook her head doubtingly, but Jeannette, glancing eagerly towards the notary, inquired if he thought there was a prospect of speedy peace.

"That we shall all live to see more quiet times, I have no doubt," he replied, "and the steps the emperor is now taking are exactly calculated to bring about that peace which we all are so anxious for. He will not, however, do anything against the interest of France, nor shall we see an end of the war till he has taught foreign nations to respect as well as fear him."

"In that case," exclaimed our heroine, "there is not much chance of Jeannot's return for some time?"

"Perhaps not, but you may expect to see him long before the period of his service expires."

"By the bye," interposed Madame Corville, glancing towards her guest, "this stranger, who I must introduce to you as Pierre Langrais, has just come from Toulon, and brings us news of Jeannot."

"Indeed! then of course he is able to contradict the rumours that have reached us?"

"Not quite so far as we might have wished," she replied; "but, whatever my daughter may feel inclined to think upon the subject, I am thoroughly convinced the young man has been basely libelled for purposes that are yet to be discovered."

"I hope you don t suspect me of having libelled him?" exclaimed Pierre Langrais sharply.

"At present I suspect no one in particular." she replied, "though I believe, in spite of the secresy, it will not be a very difficult matter to discover all that have been in any way concerned in the plot to ruin the young man. At any rate, it shall not be any fault of mine if the whole affair be not brought to light in a very short time."

"What does this visitor of your's report concerning him?" demanded Monsieur Narbonne.

"He is cautious in what he says," she replied, "but we can discover sufficient to convince us he has been attracted by some of the pretty faces he has seen in Toulon."

"And have these weak inventions of the enemy made Jeannette jealous of her lover?"

"I am not jealous, monsieur," exclaimed our heroine, "but the reports, I confess, have made me somewhat uneasy, because I know long absence will bring about great changes in the opinion one person may have had of another."

"And you believe it possible your lover may prove false to the vow he pronounced in my presence?"

"I am rather afraid of it, monsieur."

"Then learn to do him more justice in future," exclaimed the notatary, "for I have known Jeannot from infancy, and have always found him honourable and true to his promises. Like other people, he may have his enemies; but you, at least, should have more faith in his word than to believe that he would be guilty of so cruel an act as that of deserting the woman whose affections he has gained."

"Thanks, monsieur," cried Jeanne te "a thousand thanks for the hope with which you have once more filled my heart. It was wrong, I know, to harbour a thought that my love could be unfaithful, and yet, assailed as I have been by anonymous accusations, it was not easy to rid my mind of a suspicion that he might have forgotten me."

"And yet," observed Monsieur Narbonne, "the very fact of the accusation being anonymous, ought to have convinced you that the person who made the charge was ashamed to do so openly."

"I hope, monsieur, you don't think that I have had anything to do with it," exclaimed Pierre Langrais, on observing that the notary glanced towards him as he spoke.

"My suspicions are fixed upon no one in particular, just at present," answered the old gentleman, "but it shall be no fault of mine, if the cowardly calumniator be not discovered before long.—Jeannette tells me that the letters bear the post mark of Toulon, so that we may fairly conclude the mischief-maker is to be sought for there."

"Perhaps so," returned Pierre, "but, in my opinion, the man that could form such a project, would take good care to prevent his plot being discovered by so simple a thing as a post-mark."

"Time will show whether I be right or wrong;" answered Monsieur Narbonne, "but, at all events, I will spare no trouble to discover the truth or falsehood of the charge that has been made. Nay, if no other means can be found, I will make a journey to Toulon and satisfy myself by a full and careful inquiry into the subject."

"Then you must be quick about it," exclaimed Pierre, "for the emperor is about to commence another campaign, and Jeannot is among the conscripts that are to be draughted into the grand army."

"In that case, I will set off to-morrow," replied the notary, "for no time should be lost in refuting or proving an accusation upon which so much depends. On arriving there, I shall immediately commence my inquiries, and then, Madame Corville, you may depend upon hearing from me, without any unnecessary delay."

The good old man waited not to hear the fervent expressions of gratitude that were poured from the lips of Jeannette and her mother, but immediately took his departure homewards. The remainder of that night was passed in making the necessary preparations for his journey, and at an early hour on the following morning he took his seat in the diligence that was to convey him to the town where his inquiries were to be made.

A few days' travel brought the old man within sight of the lofty towers of Toulon. When the diligence was drawn up in front of the hotel in the town, he was the first to alight; of such importance did he consider his mission, that he had determined not to lose any time in the prosecution of his researches after the truth or falsehood of the allegations against his young friend. He made his way directly for the quarters of the conscript, and enquired for Jeannot. The person to whom he first addressed himself was a young soldier whom Jeannot knew perfectly well, and described himself as a friend of the young conscript in question. Monsieur Narbonne hearing this, thought it would not be imprudent to state the case to him, which he accordingly did at length, commenting on the most important parts with great force. After the old notary had finished his narrative, the young soldier said—

"Then it appears to me that some kind friend of Jeannott's has been writing to the girl about his flaunting with others of the fair sex, ever since he has been quartered in the good town of Toulon."

"Such has been the tenour of the anonymous letters I have been speaking of," answered the notary, "and, unfortunately, Jeannette hardly knows whether to believe or discredit the assertion."

"Ha! ha! ha!" laughed the young man; "perhaps the damsel has been equally forgetful of her vow?"

"Indeed, you never made a greater mistake in your life," answered Monsieur Narbonne, sharply, "for the girl is still constant to her first love, and any offer that might be made by a rival suitor would be rejected with the scorn it merited."

"Humph!" exclaimed his companion, "so you think, then, that no other person would have a chance?"

"I am certain of it."

"She is a favourite, I find, and therefore you believe her to be the paragon of her sex?"

"I speak of her from long experience," replied Monsieur Narbonne, "and no sneers will ever make me think differently of her."

"Pardon me," returned the young soldier, with mock gravity, "for I would not, on any account be supposed to doubt the constancy of the damsel towards her lover. And yet it appears to me rather odd, that, with all her love for Jeannot, she should believe the first idle rumours that she happens to hear against him."

"But the rumours have been so often repeated, that it was almost impossible to discredit them. On the other hand, however, both her mother and myself have exerted ourselves to the utmost, in order to convince her that the report proceeded from some villain who had bad motives of his own to carry out."

"Which seems to me rather a bold assertion, when it's considered that you know neither the person nor his motives."

"But I can make a tolerable guess at them, though," exclaimed the old man, "for, if I be not mistaken, Henri Dupont is the person who either sent the letters or caused them to be sent, and if so, his reasons may be very easily seen through."

"He is a rejected lover, I suppose?"

"Exactly so," replied the notary, "and not a very honourable one either, for he has continued to annoy Jeannette with his visits, though she long since told him that her hand had been promised to Jeannot."

"But lovers—like all other persons—ought not to despond after one or two failures. If their passion be sincere, they will continue to plead till long after all hope has forsaken them."

"That is a point that I shall not attempt to argue," exclaimed Monsieur Narbonne, "but they have no right to feel aggrieved, if, after all, they find themselves still rejected. At any rate, Jeannette, like most other girls, thinks she has a right to make her own selection, and as her choice has fallen upon Jeannot, it is cowardly as well as base on the part of a rival to attempt to destroy his character by means of anonymous communications."

"So far your argument may be all very well," returned the other, "but I don't yet see clearly why you should charge Henri Dupont with being the author of these letters."

"I have not exactly charged him with it," replied Monsieur Narbonne, "but I think, if a strict inquiry be made, we shall find that he has been at the bottom of all the mischief."

"Of course you intend to see him, before you leave the town?"

"Certainly, but I wish to see Jeannot first, however; he may be able to give me information that will render all the rest of my task easy."

"And in the meantime," observed the young soldier, laughing, "I may perhaps tell him of the plot you suspect he has been engaged in."

"You are perfectly welcome to do that," answered Monsieur Narbonne, "for, unlike himself, I have no wish to do anything in a sly or underhanded manner. Let him therefore know all, and if in any way I have wronged him by a thought, I shall not be above offering him an apology, or any other amends that he may require."

"That's handsomely said, at any rate," exclaimed the other, "and I think I can answer for it that Henri Dupont will not feel in the least offended at a suspicion that he will easily be able to put an end to."

"You seem to understand him very well."

"Quite as well as I do myself," he replied, significantly.

"Then, if my words have wronged him, I will trust to your good offices as a mediator," exclaimed the notary. "And now, having thus far explained myself, and the motives that have brought me here, you will perhaps inform me where I am likely to meet with Jeannot?"

"That's more than I can tell," replied the conscript, "but he went with a comrade to the Café Bordeaux, where he may still be, for aught I know to the contrary, for there's generally a little gambling going on, and the place is a good deal frequented by our people."

"Where is it?" demanded Monsieur Narbonne.

"Exactly opposite the entrance that you came in by."

"You say gaming is carried on there; do you happen to know whether Jeannot has ever indulged in that fatal passion?"

"I have not yet heard of his having done so," answered the other, "for the Emperor Napoleon has given strict orders against any soldier playing for money, and those that disobey run the risk of being severely punished for their folly."

"Under those circumstances," exclaimed Monsieur Narbonne, "he has acted with great imprudence in entering a place where he might be tempted to break the orders of his commander-in-chief."

"You give him no great credit, then, for firmness of mind, if you suppose him to be so easily led away from his duty."

"I know well what he used to be when in his own quiet native village," answered the notary. "He was then a good example to all the young men in the neighbourhood; but in this place he finds himself altogether differently circumstanced, and I am almost afraid he might not be entirely proof against the persuasions of evil advisers."

"Then he would scarcely be deserving of pity, if he got into a dilemma through his own folly."

"How easy it is to blame another for doing that which under similar circumstances we might be induced to commit ourselves," exclaimed Monsieur Narbonne. "For my own part I should severely censure the conduct of Jeannot if he were to listen to the suggestions of evil counsellors; but how much more should I abhor the conduct of the man who would induce him to commit an act against discipline, knowing at the same time how serious the consequence of a discovery must be. However, I will now leave you to go in search of my young friend, and whether I find him or not, I will return here to let you know how I have proceeded. But before I go, you will perhaps tell me who I am to ask for."

"Inquire for Henri Dupont, and he will be readily found."

Saying this, he hurried through the nearest open door that led to the interior of the barracks, and left Monsieur Narbonne to ponder in amazement whether to follow or to go in search of Jeannot, for whom he now began to feel the greatest uneasiness. The latter course was adopted, and again crossing the court-yard, he made his way towards the street which had been pointed out, and soon found himself opposite a building, the large, flaring inscription of which informed him that he was in the immediate vicinity of the Café Bordeaux. For a momen the notary paused irresolute what to do, but while he was thus considering, the sound of a tumult within attracted his attention, and then, impelled by a feeling of dread that he could not account for, he rushed across the street, entered the door which was now surrounded by a crowd of idle spectators, and, guided by the sounds of discord, entered the room in which the strife was going on. The place was full of people, but forcing his way through, the throng he discovered two men, one of whom was Jeannot, and the other a conscript, both of whom had thrown off their military coats and were just at the moment engaged in deadly strife with their drawn swords. Monsieur Narbonne waited not an instant to consider what should be done in such an emergency, bounding forward with a cry of mingled horror and despair, he, at the imminent danger of his own life, threw himself between the infuriated combatants, and with a vigorous blow, applied on each side, sent them both reeling back as if they had been struck by the arm of a giant. Murmurs from all parts of the room immediately followed, and the notary would have been severely handled but for the arrival of a piquet guard, who at the moment entered the scene of strife, and arrested the two combatants on a charge of having disobeyed the military regulations. The room was then cleared of all intruders except Monsieur Narbonne, who, at his own earnest request, was permitted to remain a few minutes with the person of whom he had come in search, and who was discovered under circumstances so disgraceful to himself.

"Jeannot," exclaimed the worthy notary, breaking through the silence that was embarrassing to all parties, "I am not here to reproach you for an act that must have been committed under the sudden excitement of anger, but was brought here by a chance, and little suspecting that my labour would terminate thus dismally."

"Monsieur," answered Jeannot, "it would be useless to make any excuse, because no sufficient one could be found for the madness I have been guilty of. Punishment I richly deserve, and could bear it without uttering a murmur, if it were not for the thought of the anguish it will occasion poor Jeannette, when she hears that I have brought it all upon myself."

"How did the quarrel occur?" demanded the notary.

"Aye, that is perhaps the worst part of it," exclaimed the culprit, "for it will be no excuse to our emperor, when he learns that the dispute began over a game at hazard."

"Then you have doubly offended against the military regulations!"

"I have," he replied, "and therefore, little is to be expected on the side of mercy. when the offence is so greatly aggravated. I will, however, take all the blame upon myself, so that Corville, my late antagonist, beg pardon for the part he has acted in this unfortunate affair."

"Jeannot," exclaimed the other prisoner, taking him by the hand, "you are a noble-hearted fellow, and if I had known as much of you before as I do now, we should neither of us have stood in this disgraceful position. But why should you care more for me than you do for yourself, when both are equally culpable?"

"Not equally so," answered Jeannot, "for it was I who commenced the quarrel, and I therefore ought to be the only one punished. Besides, I have heard you say that you have an old and heavily afflicted mother, and the blow would break her heart, if she should hear that you have been disgraced by punishment."

"The truth is, both are to blame," interposed Monsieur Narbonne, "and it now only remains to try whether the emperor may not be induced to extend his mercy towards two men who have offended against his laws in a moment of unbridled passion."

"It will be but a poor excuse to him," exclaimed Jeannot, "when he learns that we first committed ourselves by gaming, and then added to the offence by drawing our swords against each other. The first act of military insubordination might have been punished by a few months' imprisonment, but the second is considered to be of so dangerous a character, that the offender is always sentenced to death, and that doom is seldom or never mitigated."

"And into this cruel situation you have brought yourself by your own want of self-control !" said the notary, in a tone of reproach that he could not possibly curb.

"There's no denying that I deserve your rebuke," answered the culprit, "but as the offence is committed, nothing is left but to meet my fate, whatever it may be, with fortitude. Had it been my lot to havefought in the battles of my country, a more glorious death might have been mine, but as I have broken through laws laid down by our emperor for the government of the army, I will submit cheerfully to his decree, and thus make all the recompense in my power, by offering myself as an example that may prove of service to all others, who too soon lose all control over themselves."

"But, my good fellow," exclaimed the notary, "neither you nor Corville shall lose your lives ignobly, unless Napoleon is deaf to the prayers and earnest supplications of his people."

"Which in this instance he will be."

"Then you and I fortunately differ, for I believe your chance is not quite so desperate as you imagine."

"What possible hope can there be for either of us ?"

"Not altogether in the emperor's clemency, perhaps," answered Monsieur Narbonne, "but as he is preparing to plunge into a desperate war against Prussia, he will need the services of every soldier he has, and will therefore rather pardon two men who are still willing to do their duty both to him and to their country, than send them to end their earthly career in ignominy. So you see I have not uttered a hope, without having some foundation for it, and you may rely upon my word, when I say that no exertion shall be spared to save you and your comrade from the dreadful consequences you have brought upon yourselves."

"I know how generously you will devote yourself to the task," answered Jeannot, "but even supposing you were successful, how can I hope that my poor heart-broken Jeannette, will ever bestow another kindly thought upon me ? She gave me all her love, and, villain as I am, I have forfeited it by one moment's indiscretion."

"You know not the heart of Jeannette, if you believe that it can be changed by that which all will consider a misfortune."

"Will you try to make my peace with her, by making my offence appear as light as possible ?"

"I will, if it be necessary," answered Monsieur Narbonne, "but I already feel quite convinced that she will be more lenient in her opinion than you imagine. Nay, even when evil rumours against you reached her ear, she boldly denied their truth, though it was but too evident that they sorely afflicted her."

"Who is the enemy that has tried to poison her mind against me ?" he exclaimed.

"That is a mystery I have not yet been able to discover," answered Monsieur Narbonne ; "it was, however, for the purpose of ascertaining the truth or the falsehood of the reports that I came here, and now, alas ! I find you in a situation I little expected."

"Come, prisoners," exclaimed the officer of the piquet, "the indulgence you asked for must end now, for we have our duty to perform, and if any neglect should be found against us, we may find ourselves in as bad a dilemna as the one you are in."

"Another minute or two and we will go with you," said Jeannot, and then once more addressing himself to the notary, he said—

"I have now, monsieur, only to thank you for the offers of assistance you have made, and to request that you will do your utmost to console poor Jeannette and her mother, under the severe affliction they will feel on my account. Tell them both that I am entirely resigned to whatever may be my fate, and that nothing will give me so much grief as to know that they feel acutely for the sufferings and punishment I have brought upon myself."

"And yet," asked the notary, "how can you imagine that they will not feel for one whom they both love ?"

"But their grief will not serve me in the least, although it cannot fail to add to my uneasiness, if I am assured that my madness has plunged them into misery."

"That I can easily believe," answered Monsieur Narbonne, "and you may therefore rest satisfied that I will do my utmost to put the fairest complexion upon this unfortunate business. They will not be indifferent to the consolation I afford them, and I hope it will soon be in my power to convince them that I have not falsely represented the probability of your getting through this difficulty. So now, Jeannot, farewell for the present; this night I return home with the sad news of your having fallen into disgrace, and when Madame Corville and her daughter have assured me that they rely upon the exertion I am about to make, I will set about my task with a heart lightened of half its present troubles, by the hope which inspires me, that my efforts will not be altogether in vain."

They then embraced, and when the two prisoners were led away, Monsieur Narbonne left the cafe, and, hardly conscious of which way he was going, directed his steps once more towards the barracks, which were then occupied by the conscripts. Contrary to his expectation, he found Henri Dupont seated precisely on the same spot where he had first of all met with him, when he was unacquainted with his name. The young conscript addressed him with as much freedom as if nothing particular had occurred, and after a few common-place observations, abruptly changed the subject of conversation by inquiring how Jeannot liked the awkard situation in which he had so suddenly and unwisely placed himself.

"You have heard of his unfortunate predicament, then?" exclaimed the notary, with some surprise.

"Oh, yes," he replied, "the news soon reached us here, and as Jeannot was not a favourite with a great many of our people, you may suppose the intelligence created no great deal of regret."

"Then I can pity as well as despise the inhuman wretches that could exult even in the downfall of an enemy."

"Ah, it may be all very well to say that," exclaimed Henri, "but it's the way of the world for all that; so Jeannot has no more reason to complain of want of sympathy than anybody else. Besides, pity wouldn't save life, now that he has done something that will send him to the guillotine."

"Those that expect him to be condemned to an ignominious death will be disappointed," answered the notary, "for he has got friends, who will not omit anything that may serve to obtain his pardon from the emperor. In short, no great crime has been committed, for the quarrel was an unpremeditated one, and, as no life was sacrificed, Napoleon will scarcely want to destroy two men who may prove brave soldiers, just when he happens to be most in need of them."

"Ay," exclaimed Henri Dupont, "but you forget what a stickler he is for military discipline."

"Indeed I have not forgotten it," answered the notary, "but at the same time I cannot help remembering that he has many of the good qualities that belong to humanity. Besides, experience has taught him long before now that the lives of brave men are well worth preserving. and it is not likely that, merely to intimidate others, he will give over to death a couple of men whose faults, when weighed justly, are of no very great weight."

"So you may think," exclaimed the conscript, "but Napoleon's notions of most things don't agree with those of other men, who know nothing about what is required to render an army of real service, when it is absolutely required."

"But the emperor has been known before now, to forgive those who have offended against the laws."

"I dare say he may," answered Henri Dupont, "but there must have been some very extraordinary reasons for his doing so, that neither you nor I, or anybody else can comprehend. Besides, he sometimes does strange things upon the impulse of the moment, that he would not do at other times, so that it would be but a sorry dependence, if you have no other foundation to rest your hopes upon."

"I see how it is," exclaimed the notary, half angrily, "you are no friend of Jeannot's, and are unwilling to see any chance by which his life may be spared."

"At any rate," returned the other, "it would take you some little trouble to prove that I have ever been his enemy."

"You have been his rival in love, and we all know there can be little friendship when that is the case."

[JEANNETTE DISGUISES HERSELF.]

"That must not always be set down as a rule," exclaimed Henri, "for I myself have long since forgiven him, and if it had not been for this unfortunate scrape into which he has got, I should have been one of the first to have congratulated him upon his marriage with Jeannette. However, I suppose all chance of that is over now, and the poor girl must either look out for another love, or make up her mind to pass her life in a state of single blessedness."

"But if Jeannot is pardoned—which I think extremely probable—she will be the first to show that her kindly feelings are not in the slightest degree diminished by receiving him again upon precisely the same footing as before."

"How very easy it is to reckon without our host," exclaimed Henri Duport, in a tone that was meant to be extremely jocular, "Jeannette may be gracious enough to overlook the affliction he has thrown her into, but, supposing he should receive the emperor's pardon—which, by the bye, I don't think is quite so likely as you do—he would be immediately sent away with the army into Prussia, and the chances are that he would never come back alive, for the war will be a warm one, and it is understood that no quarter will be given on either side."

"At all events, he'll have as good a chance of returning safe and sound as any of his comrades," answered the notary, "and even if he should not, it will be far better to die in the field of battle than to perish disgracefully by the hand of the executioner. Things may, however, turn out brighter than present appearances seem to justify, for I believe him to have a gallant spirit of his own, and, as brave acts always attract the favourable notice of the emperor, he may rise from the rank of a common soldier to be the general of a legion."

"By the same rule, monsieur," exclaimed Henri Duport, "I also may become a great man. Indeed, my chances are much better than his, for Jeannot has two or three times committed himself since we have been here, whilst I have not once received the rebuke of a superior officer."

"Perhaps that may be because you have managed to keep your offences from becoming public."

"Even if that should be the case," laughed Henri, "I deserve some little credit for eluding the vigilance of those who believe that nothing can occur here without their knowledge. However, this is no boasting matter either, tor when once we soldiers are found out doing anything wrong, there's no saying what may be the end of it. And that I suppose, is what Jeannot thinks, so that he will not have a very easy mind all this while that he's kept in suspense."

"Does that afford you any satisfaction ?"

"Oh, dear, no ; but one can't help wondering what must be the feelings of our friends when they are in trouble."

"Well then," exclaimed the notary, "in order to relieve your mind upon that point, I must tell you that Jeannot will make himself tolerably comfortable in the absolute certainty that his friends—and they are many—will never relax their exertions, whilst there is the slightest hope of saving him from the consequences of his indiscretion."

"Indiscretion, monsieur," ejaculated the young conscript; "upon my word, you have a mighty fine way of speaking about what military law calls a very serious offence."

"It might have been," answered Monsieur Narbonne, "but, fortunately for all parties, neither of the combatants were slain or even injured. So far, then, no great harm has been done, and the imprisonment they will have to undergo previous to the court martial, will be a sufficient punishment for the offence they have committed."

"So you may fancy," returned Henri, "but the emperor, though kind to the soldiers that are obedient to his regulations, is fearfully severe against those that neglect them. In short, though many instances could be named, in which the extreme punishment has been inflicted, I know not of a single one where a free pardon has been given."

"I have heard of Napoleon's magnanimity, though," exclaimed the notary, "and so may you too before long, if you wait till a proper application for mercy has been made in favour of Jeannot. But enough of this, as I find you have no generous feeling towards my young friend, and I will not therefore, as I intended to do, ask you to visit and console him in his heavy affliction."

"It matters to me very little whether you ask me or not," replied Henri, "for I shall go and see him in his confinement, as often as the commandant here will allow me. Indeed, we have always been friends, though, for a time, rivals in love, and it's not very likely that I shall forsake him just when he most wants comfort and consolation."

"Perform your promise faithfully," exclaimed Monsieur Narbonne, "and I will not forget to acknowledge hereafter that I have wronged you by my suspicions. And when next you see Jeannot, tell him to keep up his courage, for that, however dark his destiny may appear at present, there are those labouring in his behalf, who will never relax their exertions till they have obtained his pardon."

"I'll tell him what you say," answered Henri Duport, "but if his opinion and mine agree at all, he will at once see the folly of depending upon promises that can never be carried out. Gaming and duelling are always punished more severely than anything else, and as he has been guilty of both offences almost at the same time, I can afford him very little hope of getting off."

"You will at least tell him what I have said," exclaimed the notary, "and he will do as he pleases about the possibility of succeeding in what I have undertaken to attempt. I will now leave you to your task, and, remember, I take my departure in the fullest reliance that you will perform your duty faithfully."

He then left, for the purpose of securing a place in the diligence which was then about to start for his native village, and no sooner was he out of hearing than Henri Duport burst into a low, derisive laugh, and muttered to himself—

"Aye, monsieur, trust to me as much as you please, but Jeannot has, luckily for me, got himself into trouble, and it is not very likely that I shall lend a hand to get him out of it."

———

CHAPTER V.

JEANNETTE'S DETERMINATION ON HEARING OF HER LOVER'S DISGRACE.—SHE CONSULTS HER COUSIN.—A NEW PROPOSITION.—THE DISGUISE, AND COMMENCEMENT OF OUR HEROINE'S MISSION.

IT will be more easy to imagine than describe the excessive grief of our heroine, on learning from the lips of Monsieur Narbonne the hapless situation in which the rashness of her lover had involved him. At the entreaties of her mother, however, she eventually so far subdued all outward manifestations of her sorrow as to join occasionally in the conversation that ensued, relative to the means that were to be taken to rescue Jeannot from the dangerous position in which he had placed himself. She heard the suggestions of the notary, but, excellent as his intentions were, she could not but perceive that little hope was to be gathered from them; and when, at length, a sudden thought struck her, she declared that, be the difficulties or perils of the task what they might, she would proceed without delay to Toulon, and, by her own prayers and entreaties to the emperor, endeavour to procure a merciful consideration of her lover's case. Madame Corville heard her with surprise, and could scarcely believe the evidence of her own senses.

"What!" she exclaimed, "can it be possible, Jeannette, that you are serious in making so rash a proposition?"

"Indeed, dear mother, I was never more serious in my life," she replied. "This is not a case that admits either of delay or hesitation, for the liberty, if not the life, of Jeannot is at stake, and is it for me to stand coldly by, when, perhaps, by a little exertion, properly directed, I may be able to restore him to his former position? Nay, I will even be guided by the opinion of Monsieur Narbonne, who, I am sure, would not counsel me to forsake my betrothed lover in the hour of his utmost need."

"Is your appeal to me seriously made?" he asked.

"It is, monsieur."

"Then, to confess the truth, I would rather it had not been made," exclaimed the old man; "for I see perils and difficulties in your way, which one so young and inexperienced as yourself cannot be supposed to foresee. In fact, I scarcely deem it prudent for a female to visit alone a place that is notorious for its profligacy and gaiety."

"That may be true in some cases," she replied; "but my errand is one of so sacred a nature, that surely insult cannot be expected. Besides, shall I not be near Jeannot, and will any one dare to offer me an insult when it is known that I have journeyed far to implore pardon for one who is as dear to me as my own existence?"

"But, my dear Jeannette," exclaimed the old gentleman, "you are pretty, and where there are youth and beauty to attract, little safety can be expected for their possessor."

"In some instances it may be so," answered our heroine, "but, generally speaking, I think everything depends upon the conduct of the woman herself. You smile, monsieur, as if you thought me vain, but indeed my confidence in this instance has been produced only by the deep anxiety I feel for the hapless object of our care."

"My dear child," exclaimed Madame Corville, "this determination of yours is too rash and sudden to be decided on at once. Reflection will show you the imprudence of the proposed step, and the fatherly advice of Monsieur Narbonne, if properly considered, will deter you from a step that I tremble to think of."

"In that case, mother, you must admit that I have more courage than yourself," cried our heroine.

"My child," answered the old lady, "rashness is too often mistaken for courage, and in this instance I see that my remark is well applied, for you have not yet given sufficient thought to the project you have taken into your head."

"Can there be any rashness," she asked, "in volunteering to attempt the rescue of Jeannot, when I know him to be in danger?"

"It would be well, and even praiseworthy, if you could aid him without prejudice to your own character," answered Madame Corville. The world, however, is too censorious, and people—instead of praising your heroism—would condemn the act as being wanting in that modesty and decorum, which should be the chief characteristics of the sex you belong to. I am no less grieved than yourself for the cruel misfortunes that have befallen your lover, but Monsieur Narbonne has generously offered his services, and I am sure he will leave no effort untried that may effect his object."

"Ah!" sighed Jeannette, "but Monsieur Narbonne, kind and generous as I know him to be, cannot feel the intense anxiety that I do, and which is so essential to the success of the task he would undertake."

"You think I should want zeal?" observed the notary.

"Indeed, monsieur, you mistake me," answered our heroine, "for I know how ardently you would work in the cause, and that no trouble would be thought too much, so long as there appeared to be a prospect of success. But your hope would sink sooner than mine, and the moment that failed, there would be an end of all further energy."

"And you think *your* energy would rise with the difficulties you had to encounter?"

"I am, indeed, vain enough to believe so," she replied, " though you and my mother, perhaps, imagine that I should sink under the first disappointment I might happen to meet with. But time proves all things, and you may both, by and by, have to acknowlege that my spirits are not to be bowed down by a few reverses."

"May I inquire," exclaimed the notary, "if it is any part of your design to see the emperor?"

"It is,—that is to say," she added, checking herself, "if I am not positively prohibited seeing him."

"I am glad that suggestion struck you," exclaimed Monsieur Narbonne, "for the emperor is always very averse to have his leisure broken upon; and even where interviews are granted, it is generally remarked that he grows more and more impatient till it comes to an end. So you see, Jeannette, there is a chance of putting him into an ill-humour, and I need not tell you what would be the consequence were he to become angry in the instance we are speaking of."

"Ah!" cried Jeannette, "I see how it is, Monsieur Narbonne, you are trying to put me off this project."

"I confess my anxiety to do so," he replied, "and it is my opinion, that, after giving this affair a few hours' thought, you will begin to think of it somewhat as I do myself."

"What!" she exclaimed, "do you think it likely that I will forsake my poor Jeannot when most he needs a friend?—No, no, monsieur, I feel that in his misfortunes I love him more than ever; and were it possible to save his life by the sacrifice of my own, I would yield it up with pleasure for the sake of obtaining his pardon."

"You are a noble, generous-hearted girl!" cried Monsieur Narbonne, gently pressing her hand, "and I wish from my very soul that it was in my power to prevail upon you to trust me with the task you have resolved to take upon yourself. Believe me, I will set out on my return to Toulon without delay, and if exertions will save your lover from disgrace, I promise that mine shall be made to the utmost."

"It is quite in vain to urge me any further, monsieur," she replied, "because I know no one will labour so hard as I will in his behalf; and if my efforts should fail, it will at least be some consolation for me to know, that I trusted not to another that task which it was my duty to take upon myself. I have spoken to you plainly, Monsieur Narbonne; but believe me, I am no less grateful for the generous offer of assistance that you have been pleased to make."

"Then why not accept the kindness, when you know that everything will be done to save Jeannot?" asked Madame Corville.

"Don't urge me any further upon the subject, dear mother," she replied, "for though I may be deemed obstinate, it is only because I fancy no one can feel so deeply interested in this affair as myself. Besides, Jeannot will expect at least thus much from me; and I could not bear that he should have to reproach me even in his thoughts."

"Reproach you!" exclaimed the notary. "Has he not much greater reason to reproach himself, not only for the folly he has been guilty of, but also for the misery he has brought upon all those who have ever felt any regard for him. But I see, Jeannette, you are not best pleased at my plain way of speaking, and I will therefore say nothing more that may add to your affliction at a moment like this."

"You have not yet told us, monsieur," whispered Madame Corville, "what degree of punishment is generally awarded to those who break the army regulations."

"It depends entirely upon the previous character of the offending party," answered the notary, "for our emperor is careful to make a distinction between the really vicious and those who commit an error without premeditation. In Jeannot's case all is favourable so far; and for that reason I am inclined to hope he may escape with an admonition to be more guarded in his conduct for the future."

"Still I'm afraid," said the dame, "it will stand in the way of his promotion."

"That will depend entirely upon himself," replied Monsieur Narbonne; "for no doubt his conduct, whether good or bad, will be frequently reported, and, should it prove to be satisfactory, his previous misconduct will be forgotten. In short, the forthcoming Austrian invasion will afford ample opportunities to all those soldiers who are inclined to distinguish themselves, and if Jeannot only has the chance given him, I have little doubt we shall soon hear of his having wiped out the stain that at present tarnishes his honour."

"And then," exclaimed Madame Corville, "there will be nothing to prevent his rising in the army, as many a brave Frenchman has done before him."

"Certainly not, my dear madame," answered the old gentleman; "for Napoleon knows, better than any other man living, how to gain the hearty devotion of his soldiers; and hundreds of gallant fellows can testify that promotion in our army depends, not upon pride of birth, but the valour which is displayed in the field of battle. And the result has proved the wisdom of his conduct; since no army in the world can produce so many successful generals, who have been raised to eminence through their own acts of heroism. Every Frenchman, however low his origin may be, who fights in the defence of his country, knows that certain reward and promotion are bestowed upon those who deserve it, and the consequences are seen in those extraordinary acts of gallantry that electrify and astonish the world. And take my word for it, if your young friend Jeannot has only the chance given him, he will yet make ample amends for the act of indiscretion that has marked his first outset in life."

"Ah! monsieur," cried Jeannette, "you know not how proudly you have made my heart beat by those few words of yours. Yes, yes, Jeannot's pardon must be obtained, in order that he may have an opportunity of proving his attachment to the emperor and the cause of his country."

"You forget, my dear child," exclaimed her mother, "that we must first petition the emperor to pardon this one fault, and even when that is done, it is not by any means certain that the entreaties of Jeannot's friends will be attended to."

"But no life was lost, nor was even a drop of blood spilt, in the foolish quarrel that led to all this mischief."

"So far it was fortunate," answered the notary, "but the emperor, in forming his judgment, will not look so much at that circumstance, as at the breach of discipline, that, if not checked in time, would lead to the entire disorganization of the army. For that reason he is generally rigidly severe whenever cases of this kind are brought before him, and I therefore cannot help fearing that he will consider some sort of punishment necessary, as a warning to those who might afterwards be guilty of the same folly."

"Will he not incline to the side of mercy, if I plead for it upon my knees?" cried Jeannette.

"I am afraid he will not give you the opportunity."

"By refusing to grant me an interview?"

"Exactly so," replied the old gentleman. "The emperor has a great aversion to what he calls *scenes*, and has given orders to exclude from his presence all persons whose object is to plead to him in behalf of those who have offended against the laws."

"Is he, then, sternly resolved never to pardon those who may have been guilty of an error?"

"I must not go quite so far as to say that," answered Monsieur Narbonne; "but as he always strictly investigates every case of delinquency that occurs in the army, he thinks, probably, that his own judgment is formed upon the best and safest foundation. At any rate, it is quite certain that he seldom changes his determination for any argument that may be brought forward."

"And yet," sighed our heroine, "I understood just now that you were in hopes Jeannot's pardon might be obtained."

"I think so still," he replied, "but everything will depend entirely upon the manner in which it is carried out. We must soothe rather than irritate him, and if we can only convince him that mercy in this instance will not be misapplied, I believe our chance of success may not be very remote. At all events, the experiment will be well worth trying, and I am ready to give my services in a cause, that I feel so deeply interested in."

"There, my dear," exclaimed Madame Corville, "you hear what our kind friend says, and surely you can no longer persevere in your own wild scheme, of seeking an interview with the emperor?"

"I'll not deceive you by making a promise that I should be almost sure to break," answered Jeannette. "Torn, as my heart is, with a thousand fears, I cannot remain here whilst the fate of my lover is involved in uncertainty. Besides, I would visit him in his confinement, for surely this is no time to let him believe that he is slighted by those upon whom he has most reason to rely."

"At least, then, you will allow Monsieur Narbonne to accompany you?"

"Monsieur Narbonne's kindness, in making the offer, will never be forgotten," answered Jeannette, "but in this instance I would go to Toulon alone and un- aided. The duty is one that I have taken upon myself, and I am not afraid of encountering danger when the object aimed at is of so much importance."

"You forget," exclaimed her mother, "that a female should not venture upon so long a journey unprotected."

"No one will attempt to interfere with me," she replied, "and even if I should be mistaken, have I not ever shown courage enough to protect myself whenever I have met with either insolence or disrespect? So, fear nothing for me, for this will end better than you expect, or I am mistaken in the character of the emperor."

"But you will be a stranger in Toulon."

"True."

"And will not know how to find your way about the place."

"I shall be able to discover the head quarters of Napoleon, though," she re- plied, "and greatly shall I be deceived if his imperial majesty does not yield to the entreaties of one of the humblest of his subjects."

"May I ask," exclaimed Monsieur Narbonne, "what talisman you possess, that you make so certain of carrying your point with a sovereign who never acts but upon his own impulses?"

"To tell you the truth, monsieur," she replied, "I have not yet formed any plan, for in a case of this kind I think it better to be guided by circumstances. When I reach Toulon, I shall then see more clearly how the ground lies before me, and will act accordingly. One thing, however, is certain; I will at least attempt to obtain an interview with the emperor, and, if I should unfortunately fail in that, my next effort will be to communicate with him in writing."

"My dear child," exclaimed the old man, "Napoleon never receives letters till after they have been read by his secretary, and I need hardly tell you that not one in fifty ever reach the person they are intended for. So, in that respect—as I fear will be the case in every other—you will be doomed to meet with nothing but disappointment."

"Aye, monsieur, it may be all very well to tell me so, but I shall not put my project aside for all that. In spite of all you and my mother have said to alter my determination upon this subject, I am now as sanguine as ever I was, and there is still a something that whispers me to go over, for that my cause cannot fail to prosper."

"Foolish girl!" cried Madame Corville, "you little think of the cruel disap- pointment you will have to endure!"

"Indeed, mother, you are wrong there," she replied, "for I know too well that even the best directed efforts often end in the most bitter disappointment. Such may—as you have said—be the case with me, but even that, I can anticipate with- out flinching from the blow, because I feel that when all hope has been extinguished, I shall soon find forgetfulness of my sorrows in the grave."

"My poor Jeannette!" cried her mother, "why do you thus afflict me, when my sufferings on your account are already so great? Monsieur Narbonne has generously offered to attempt all he can on behalf of Jeannot, and yet you are still determined to encounter dangers that fill my heart with the most sor- rowful forebodings."

"Dearest mother, urge me no further upon this subject," exclaimed our heroine, "for I have vowed to Heaven that I will not forsake Jeannot in his afflictions, and no persuasion shall ever induce me to forget the solemn promise I have made."

"Whither are you going now?" demanded Madame Corville, with alarm, as she saw her daughter was about to leave the house.

"To my cousin Suzette's."

"For what purpose?"

"To tell her of my design, and ask her if she has any objection to accompany me on my journey."

"Good Heaven! then you are about to set out immediately?"

"I am," replied Jeannette; "why should I delay, when every instant may be fraught with danger to Jeannot?"

"Nay, go not—I command you, go not!"

"Till now, mother, you have always found me obedient to your slightest wish," answered our heroine, "but so urgent is the business which calls me hence, that I must hazard even your anger by refusing to obey your command. Heaven knows I love you no less than I have ever done, and yet, for the first time in my life, I shall leave my home with the sad consciousness that I have deeply offended you."

"Stay, Jeannette!" exclaimed the notary, taking her hand and leading her towards Madame Corville. "Look upon these tears, that have gushed forth through your own wilfulness, and then say whether you will not bid them cease by returning to that duty which every child owes to its parent. Embrace her, Jeannette, and leave not your aged mother to weep for the waywardness of her daughter."

"Forgive me, mother!" exclaimed our heroine, throwing herself upon the bosom of Madame Corville—"forgive me this one act of disobedience, and in all things else I will be to you the warm-hearted, dutiful child that, till this time, you have ever found me."

"Will you, then, abandon this journey to Toulon, of which I have so great a dread?"

"I cannot — nay, I will not do that, let the consequences be what they may," cried Jeannette. "Ask of me anything but that, dear mother, and no sacrifice that I can make shall be too great, so that it turns aside your wrath."

"I have but one desire, and that you are resolved not to comply with," answered Madame Corville. "Go, then, self-willed as you are, and wonder not on your return home if you find that your disobedience has broken the heart of your mother."

The old lady then tore herself away from her daughter's embrace, and half in anger, half in hopes that Monsieur Narbonne would yet succeed in changing the resolution of her child, she retired to her own room, there to give way to the grief which had so heavily, yet unexpectedly, befallen her. The good notary did indeed try all his powers of persuasion to induce Jeannette to forego her purpose; but all was in vain, for the warm-hearted girl believed that no one else would take the trouble to labour with so much zeal in behalf of her lover as she herself would, and, relying upon the forgiveness of Madame Corville as soon as the first gush of her anger was over, she left the cottage and proceeded to that of her cousin Suzette, who she generally consulted upon such matters as were not easily to be decided by herself. Her arrival was cordially welcomed, but she was still weeping, and that naturally gave rise to a few anxious questions as to the cause of her grief. As briefly as possible Jeannette narrated the troubles that had overtaken her lover—the consequences that his rashness might lead to—the design she had formed to obtain his pardon, and the opposition she had met with both from her mother and Monsieur Narbonne. Her cousin listened with attention to her narrative, and at its conclusion inquired if she still determined to proceed on her journey to Toulon.

"Alas!" sighed our heroine, "what course can I adopt when I find myself surrounded on all sides with difficulties? I left home with the firm determination to proceed there directly, but as I came along, the thought of my mother's affliction has almost made me change my purpose in order that I may return home to release the suffering of her to whom I owe all duty and submission."

"Then, of course," exclaimed Suzette, "you mean to abandon Jeannot to his sad fate?"

"Nay," she replied, "instead of abandoning him, I would willingly lay down my own life for the preservation of his."

"Perhaps you are afraid of the dangers and difficulties you may have to encounter on the way?"

"Neither dangers nor difficulties will deter me, if I have but my mother's consent," answered our heroine.

"And that I can see clearly enough you will never have."

[JEANNETTE MEETS WITH THE EMPEROR.]

"Why do you think so?"

"Because," replied her cousin, "though Madame Corville is one of the worthiest of women, she has her full share of obstinacy whenever she takes anything into her head. Now, it seems, she has a notion that something very terrible will happen if you attempt this journey, and it is therefore hardly to be supposed that she will consent to your going, after she finds that you begin to waver in your resolution."

"But if I should go without her leave she may never forgive me."

"Leave that to me, and I'll answer for it that Madame Corville shall not be angry with me after I have explained to her the absolute necessity for your interfering in behalf of poor Jeannot, who I believe she loves almost as much as she does you."

"She does."

"Well, then, how can she wonder at your anxiety to save your lover from punishment?" asked Suzette. "Besides, in my opinion, it is nothing more than your duty to make every effort in your power to lend him a helping hand, and, as far as I am myself concerned, you may rely upon my giving you all the assistance in my power."

"Will you accompany me if I go?" asked Jeannette, eagerly.

"I would if it had been possible, and should have been much pleased to have engaged myself in so romantic an adventure," answered her cousin. "I am sorry to say, however, that it is impossible, though I may perhaps be able to assist you in other things that will be equally serviceable. For instance, I'll see your mother, and after showing the necessity for what you have done, will obtain her pardon for a step that you were bound to take."

"And do you think, Suzette, she will ever forgive me for acting against her positive injunction?"

"Why to be sure she will," answered the other, "for when once the step is taken there will be no help for it, and she may as well say nothing more about it. I can, however, do something more for you, Jeannette, that will prevent you from meeting with insult, if you think proper to undertake this journey."

"What talisman do you speak of?" asked our heroine.

"Oh, it is a very simple one, I assure you, my dear cousin," answered Suzette. "You have merely to disguise yourself in the garb of a man, and you will pass on your way without danger."

"Disguise myself as a man?"

"Aye," answered her cousin; "or, to explain myself better, I think you would make a very tolerable looking conscript, and as a great many of them are now making their way towards Toulon, your appearance on the road would not attract any particular attention."

"But even supposing I was inclined to follow your wild plan, where should I be able to find such a dress as I should require?"

"In this very house," answered Suzette. "In short, I have carefully preserved the military garb of my poor brother, who died six years ago, and I think they will fit you to a nicety. So now tell me, Jeannette, what think you of my notable plan?"

"That it is as wild a one as you could have thought of," she replied, "and if anything could add to the anger of my mother, it would be the learning that I had so far forgotten the modesty of my own sex as to assume the garb of another."

"You are wrong there, depend on it," exclaimed her cousin; "for it would reconcile her to the task you have undertaken, since it would afford her a tolerable certainty that you might pass on your way free from insult. At any rate," she added, opening a drawer, and looking out the garb she was speaking of, "you shall judge for yourself, and then tell me whether there is any reason to be ashamed of making your appearance before the public in this costume."

"There is no reason whatever," answered Jeannette, "but I am afraid the world would deem my conduct too flippant."

"Never mind what the world says, as long as you are not conscious of deserving its censure," answered the other. "So now, at all events, try how you look in military costume, and if you don't like yourself in it, why you can only go on your journey as you first of all intended. By the bye, Jeannette," she proceeded, whilst assisting her cousin to put on the disguise, "you have not yet told me how long you are likely to be absent on this extraordinary mission of yours."

"That, of course, must depend entirely on circumstances," she replied. "My chief business at Toulon will be to see the emperor, and of course it will be useless for me to return until I have obtained an answer from him one way or the other."

"And so you really expect to have an interview with him?"

"Why should I not?"

"There you have fairly caught me," answered Suzette, "for I can give no other reason, than that great people have generally an objection to being interfered with by little ones."

"But Napoleon was not always the great man he is now."

"Very true, my dear cousin—he has indeed risen from a small beginning; but then it has been all owing to his own extraordinary ability as a soldier, and people that get up in the world by their own exertions are apt to think a good deal of themselves."

"Ah!" exclaimed our heroine, "but the emperor is said to be kind and generous to all that have a favour to ask of him. We have instances of that every day, or I should not have been bold enough to think of asking him to forgive poor Jeannot the fault he has been guilty of."

"Well, never mind that just now, but do me the favour to look at yourself in the glass," said Suzette, who having finished her cousin's toilette, was anxious that she should judge for herself of the complete transformation that had taken place in the course of a few minutes. Jeannette, sad as her heart was just before, could scarcely forbear bursting into a laugh as she gazed upon the reflected image of herself, but when her cousin added to this the smart military cap, she could no longer restrain her mirth, at the martial air she had been so quickly made to assume. At length, having fairly had her laugh out, she discovered one omission, and inquired if she ought not to be armed, according to the most approved military fashion."

"No, my dear coz," answered Suzette, "you will not appear at all singular in that respect, for the conscripts are never trusted with their swords and muskets till they are established in barracks. Indeed, I don't see that arms will be necessary, for they would only be an incumbrance, without being of any service, for you really wear so fierce an aspect, that few persons would be bold enough to offer you an affront, so long as you support your new character well."

"Ah! my dear Suzette, you are only laughing at me, I see."

"And who can help laughing at such a change as this?" she asked. "However, we must now begin the more serious part of this business, and, in the first place, I would ask when you think of commencing your journey?"

"Indeed, Suzette," she replied, "I am already half inclined to give it up altogether."

"What! have you become a coward as soon as you have assumed this gay martial costume?"

"No," exclaimed Jeannette, after a few moments' consideration, "I will not abandon my purpose, though it must be confessed my heart misgives me at the very outset of the business. But I shall become bolder as I proceed, and if I am but fortunate enough to obtain an interview with the emperor, I have confidence sufficient to believe that my task will not have been attempted in vain."

"By the bye, Jeannette," said her cousin, "I forgot to ask you before, but there is one thing that will be absolutely necessary towards the success of the project you have in view. You require money, both for your journey there and back, and to defray the expenses you will be at, whilst remaining at Toulon. Let me know, then, how your purse is furnished, for, if you have not sufficient, I have a little store of my own laid by, which cannot be devoted to a better purpose than that of assisting the generous task you are engaged in."

"Thanks, a thousand thanks, dear Suzette, for this kind forethought of yours," answered our heroine, "but I have with me more than will be sufficient to satisfy the moderate wants of one, whose sole purpose is to preserve her lover from the punishment he is threatened with. I have somewhat more than fifty francs, which, economically applied, will defray all my expenses, even if I should be about a fortnight."

"You will hardly be so long as that, if you travel by the diligence."

"But I shall not be able to afford the expense of riding all the way, and must therefore be content to walk about half the distance, which I shall be able to do without feeling much fatigued."

"Instead of doing that, my dear," exclaimed Suzette, "you had better accept from me of the loan of another fifty francs. You will then be able to reach Toulon without fatigue, and, what's still better, will save a very great deal of time."

"Nay," she replied, "the difference in the time will not, I am convinced, be of the slightest consequence, and as to the fatigue, I should indeed be unfit for the task I have undertaken, if any notion of that sort was to make me unwilling to encounter all difficulties that might happen to come in my way. For Jeannot's sake, I will suffer even death itself, though it should be accompanied with the most dreadful tortures."

"I know your noble spirit, dear Jeannette," replied her cousin, "and feel the fullest assurance that you will not flinch in the slightest degree from the difficult task you have imposed upon yourself. It is uncertain, however, whether you will have an opportunity of seeing the emperor, and if you should be denied an interview, there will, of course, be an end of all hope."

"Unless I could find any friend, who, having access to him, would plead for my poor Jeannot."

"There are none that you would trust like yourself," answered her cousin, "nor, indeed, should I advise you to place confidence in any one, for the promises of most people are forgotten as soon as they are made. Rely, therefore, entirely upon yourself, and if you cannot see the emperor immediately, wait patiently till an opportunity occurs, and you will do more good in a few minutes, than you would otherwise be able to accomplish in a month."

"But it is not always that Napoleon is to be seen."

"That may be true," exclaimed Suzette, "but just now they say he is so much occupied in making his military preparations, that I dare say he may be seen every hour of the day in the streets of Toulon. You will, therefore, do well to have with you a paper ready prepared, and containing a brief narrative of the facts respecting Jeannot. That you will, I have no doubt, soon have an opportunity of presenting it to the emperor, and when you have effected your object so far, I dare say a successful termination of your labours will be the result."

"You think, then, Jeannot will be pardoned ?"

"I think it very possible ; and were I in your place, I should look forward to it with some certainty. But we are now wasting time, Jeannette, that might be more profitably employed, for you ought to be on your journey by this time, in order that you may reach the end of it with as little delay as possible. I will accompany you a league on your way, and on my return home afterwards will call on your mother to inform her that she is not likely to see you again till you can bring her good news of your lover."

They soon afterwards set out on their way. Jeannette, still disguised as we have seen, proceeded cautiously along, as if still afraid of being recognised by some one who knew her. As she went on, however, her confidence gradually returned, and, inspired by the cheerful conversation of her cousin, she began to think more hopefully of the mission she had undertaken. At length, the sound of wheels struck upon their ears, and looking back they saw the Toulon diligence toiling up the hill which they had just ascended, and at the suggestion of Suzette, her cousin agreed to ride the next half-dozen leagues, which happened to be the most dreary part of the road she had to travel. In a few minutes afterwards the vehicle halted, and Jeannette having mounted it, was soon on her way towards the place where the most important results were ere long to be made known.

CHAPTER VI.

OUR HEROINE ARRIVES AT THE END OF HER JOURNEY.—MEETS AN OLD FEMALE ACQUAINTANCE.—RESUMES HER FEMALE ATTIRE, AND COMMENCES HER MARCH.— MEETS THE EMPEROR.—THE PETITION.—THE INTERVIEW, AND ITS RESULT.

PARTLY by riding, but chiefly by walking, to save an expense which her poorly supplied purse could not afford, Jeannette reached the busy town of Toulon towards the close of the third day since she left home. A perfect stranger in the place, she wandered up and down numerous streets, not knowing where to stop, and fancying that everybody must be aware of the disguise she had assumed. At length, as dusk was coming on, she heard her name pronounced in an accent of surprise, and looking round towards the spot from whence the sound seemed to have proceeded, she perceived an elderly female, whom she at once recognised as an old neighbour of her mother's, who had left about half-a-dozen years previously to reside in some far off town. She approached the woman, called her by name, and, after having expressed her satisfaction at having met with some one she knew, requested to be recommended to some place where she might lodge for the short time she was going to remain in the town.

"Before I do that," said Madame Germaine, glancing suspiciously at the dress of the applicant, "I must know whether you are the daughter of Madame Corville, and if such is the case, why I now meet you in the unseemly garb of a man?"

"Permit me to rest myself," answered Jeannette, "and if I do not give you a satisfactory explanation, I will at least tell you nothing but the truth."

The old lady instantly complied with this request; and leading the way through a passage, conducted our heroine into a neatly furnished apartment, in a recess of which stood a bedstead, concealed by means of a long curtain, which reached from the ceiling to the ground. Having desired her young guest to be seated, Madame Germaine once more requested to be informed why she had disguised herself, as if fearful of being discovered."

"Alas!" replied Jeannette, "I can scarcely give a satisfactory explanation for an act that I am heartily ashamed of. The disguise, however, was assumed at a moment when I feared discovery; though I now see the folly of placing myself in a situation that must expose me to the suspicion of having some improper object in view."

"Is your mother aware of this?"

"She is not?"

"Does she know of your visit to Toulon?"

"No, Madame."

"Then you have left her house secretly?"

"That is too true," answered Jeannette with downcast look.

"You have not been imprudent enough, I hope, to run away with a lover," exclaimed Madame Germaine.

"There, at least, I can excuse myself," said our heroine; "for he to whom I am betrothed with my mother's consent, is at this moment in the conscript barrack in this town."

"And you have taken this long journey in disguise for the express purpose of seeing him before he leaves with the rest of the army?"

"On the contrary," she replied, "he has fallen into disgrace, and I am afraid will be condemned to receive a severe punishment."

"What is the name of this lover of yours?"

"Jeannot Lamont."

"Ah," exclaimed the old lady, "I have heard his case spoken of, and it must be confessed the people hereabouts feel a great deal of sympathy, for his offence was duelling with a fellow soldier, and it is the general opinion that he was not in fault."

"But does Napoleon himself think so?"

"That is more than I can tell you," answered Madame Germaine, "for the emperor keeps his thoughts to himself, and none are ever permitted to know them till the last moment. However, I will not lead you away with false hopes, for if an unfavourable view should be taken of your lover's case, he will, as most people imagine, receive a very severe punishment as a warning to others."

"I am here to see the emperor," exclaimed Jeannette, "and to try if any prayers and entreaties can move his heart to pity for one who has offended only through momentary thoughtlessness."

"And you expected to obtain an interview in this disguise that you have so foolishly assumed?"

"Indeed, madame, I scarcely knew what I did," replied Jeannette, "but my chief motive for disguising myself in the garb of a man, was to escape the chances of insult which women are subject to when they are alone and unprotected."

"Ah," exclaimed the old lady in a greatly subdued tone, "if that was your only motive, I both honour and respect it, for prudence is an excellent virtue in young persons, and even your mother would not be angry if she was aware of all the facts of this extraordinary case. So you shall be my guest during the time you remain in Toulon; and as disguise will no longer be necessary, I will supply you with proper clothing from the wardrobe of a niece of mine, who is now on a visit at some distance from this town."

Jeannette was truly pleased at this offer, and having partaken of some refreshments which Madame Germaine had placed before her, she asked if it was known how soon the army was to be put in motion for the purpose of passing the Prussian frontier.

"No, no, my child," she replied, "that's all kept secret enough, I can tell you, for the emperor never lets an enemy know too much, but keeps everything dark till he is ready to pounce upon him when he is least prepared for an attack. However, it is said that everything is ready, so that when the orders are given, the whole army may be set in motion at an hour's notice."

"Do you think," asked our heroine, "that there is any chance of my obtaining an interview with him?"

"A very poor one, I am afraid."

"Why do you think so?"

"Because his mind is too much occupied just now with this new war against the King of Prussia, to think of anybody else. He sees no one but his field-marshals and his generals, and some of them are constantly with him, so that there's but a poor chance for those that want to trouble him with their prayers and petitions."

"But mine," sighed Jeannette, "is one upon which so much depends."

"Aye, my child," answered the old lady, "all people think their own affairs of the most importance, and, of course, it's only natural that you should fancy the same. By the bye, my dear, as you are likely to remain with me three or four days at the very least, it would be well for you to write to Madame Corville, your mother, to inform her of your arrival in Toulon, and of your being under my protection during your stay here. You will find writing materials on the table, and whilst you are engaged, I'll step to the door for a moment to watch for a neighbour who I was looking for when you happened to pass."

Being left to herself, Jeannette wrote a brief note to her mother, describing the few incidents that occurred on her journey, her unexpected meeting with an old acquaintance in the person of Madame Germaine, the hospitality with which she had been received, and expressing her still ardent hopes that the chief object of her journey would yet be successfully achieved. Just as she had folded and sealed her letter, the old lady returned with the hall porter, to whom the epistle was delivered, it being part of his duty to convey such communications to the post-office at the proper hour. This being done, Madame Germaine, again returned to the subject of Jeannette's visit to Toulon, assuring her that she would do all in her power to further the object she had in view, but at the same time expressing it as her opinion that no good would result from the long journey she had undertaken.

"I should also have been afraid of it," answered Jeannette, with a sigh, "but that Monsieur Narbonne, the notary, says he thinks the emperor is more likely to pardon a fault now that he is in so much need of every man that is able to carry arms in defence of his country."

"I hope it may be so, my dear," returned the old lady, "but he is determined to enforce the strictest discipline in the army, and there is no way of doing so but by proving by example that punishment is certain to follow every disobedience of his orders. It is true, Jeannot has not been guilty of any great offence, but I'm afraid it will not be passed over quite so lightly as you and his other friends could have wished."

"Alas! you almost dishearten me, after all the trouble I have taken to reach the end of my long journey."

"Nay, that is the last thing I would do," exclaimed Madame Germaine, "for I admire the heroism of your conduct, and would do all in my power to assist in bringing your task to a successful termination. Name, therefore, any way in which you think I may be useful, and you shall have no reason to complain of my want of sympathy in your cause."

"At present," answered our heroine, "I know not what course will be best for me to adopt, for I am a stranger in this place, and my heart sinks within me when I reflect upon the difficulties I may have to encounter before I can see him who alone has the power to grant pardon to those who have offended against the law. Indeed, even if the opportunity is afforded me, I almost fear my lips would refuse me utterance, when most my courage will be required."

"Then why undertake the task at all?"

"Because, when the difficulty is not very near, we all of us fancy we shall be able to overcome it," answered Jeannette. "I thought it was nothing to seek an interview with the emperor, and to supplicate him for pardon, but now that I find myself upon the very point of bringing the affair to a termination, my spirits fail me, and I feel that I shall play the part of a coward, at the very moment when all my courage—all my fortitude, would be most required."

"In that case, your labour will indeed have been taken in vain," exclaimed Madame Germaine, "for the emperor is said to be of a hot, impatient temper, and he may be in no humour to listen, whilst you are endeavouring to stammer out the favour you would ask."

"But my foolish dread must and *shall* be conquered."

"Aye," returned the old lady, "that's speaking somewhat more to the purpose, and if you only hold to the resolution, there's no saying but it may serve to assist you through the task you have taken upon yourself. Your looks, Jeannette, tell me, that you think I am already contradicting myself, but the truth is, I find you are easily discouraged, and therefore the best thing I can do is to fill you with confidence, in order that you may proceed as fearlessly in your design as when you set out from home."

"You would have me see the emperor?"

"There would be no harm in the attempt," she replied, "but the question is, how are you to obtain an interview?"

"I know of no other way," returned our heroine, "but by presenting myself at the place where he is quartered, and sending a message to say that I request permission to see him upon an affair of the most pressing importance."

"That, my poor child, will not do," replied Madame Germaine, "for he is in the habit of receiving many such messages as that every day of his life. He is completely harassed with applications of the kind, and I have heard it said that he has given orders for all persons to be dismissed, whose business is not previously known."

"Would it give offence if I was to address myself to him, if by chance I should meet him in the streets?"

"That," exclaimed the old lady, "would depend entirely upon the circum-

stances under which the meeting might take place. If his mind was occupied at
the time with any very important matters, he might be seriously displeased at the
interruption, but if, on the other hand, he should be in one of his good humours,
it is quite likely that he would not only listen to your request, but also give it a
favourable consideration."

"Ah! then I'll watch my opportunity, and think my labour not ill-bestowed,
even though I may have to wait for weeks ere I succeed in accomplishing the
purpose that has brought me here."

"You will not have to wait long, depend upon it," answered Madame Germaine,
" for though no one yet knows exactly when the troops are to leave Toulon, it is
pretty generally believed that the event will take place in the course of a very
few days."

" And before that time," exclaimed our heroine, "I suppose Jeannot and his
fellow prisoner will be tried by a court martial."

"No doubt of it."

" Then there is not a moment to lose," she cried, " for if they should be con-
victed of the offence, all hope of pardon will be at an end."

" That, I think, is pretty certain," answered the old lady ; " so if anything is
to be done, I should advise you by all means not to lose any time about it.
Tomorrow morning you will rise refreshed from the fatigue you have gone through,
and I will then show you about the town, in order that you may afterwards know
the most likely place where the emperor is to be met with in his rambles through
the town."

" Does he ever walk out alone ?"

"Sometimes he does, but more frequently he is accompanied in his walks by
some of his generals. Not, however, that they would be any hindrance to you, for
when he stops to speak to any one, they always retire some little distance, and
are not expected to interfere, unless he happens to ask them a question. So, if you
should meet him with any of them, don't let that hinder you from presenting
yourself."

" And in the meanwhile," asked our heroine, " is there any way by which I may
see poor Jeannot ?"

"There is no other means but through an order from Napoleon."

" For which I may have to wait some days."

"Perhaps less time than that," answered Madame Germaine, " for you may
chance to meet the emperor in the course of the morning, and, if you should be
lucky enough to do so, no doubt he will give the permission you ask for. So,
with that hope, you had better retire to rest, and to-morrow you will commence
your task free from the fatigue that has been occasioned by your long journey
from home."

Jeannette was really glad to accede to this well-timed suggestion, and following
Madame Germaine to the next room, she found every accommodation as nicely
made as if her arrival had been looked for. This was easily to be accounted for,
as the old lady's niece happened to be absent on a visit at the time, and her
leeping apartment being thus vacant, was given up to Jeannette for the period
during which it might be necessary for her to remain in Toulon. But it was long
ere our poor wanderer could close her eyes in slumber, for her thoughts were
occupied by the unfortunate situation of her lover, and the too self-evident chance
that all the pains she had taken would prove in the end to have been thrown away.
At length, however, she fell into an uneasy sleep, disturbed by dreams of evil omen,
in which she fancied all her worst fears were realized, and that Jeannot had been
condemned to a severe punishment, in spite of the efforts she had made to obtain
his pardon. From this state of trouble and affliction she awoke in the morning,
and having dressed herself in the female attire that had been provided for her in
the meantime, proceeded to the next room, where she found Madame Germaine
was waiting breakfast for her.

" Ah! my dear," exclaimed the old lady, in a tone of approval, "now, indeed,
you look something more like yourself, and I can talk to you a little more at my

ease than when you were disguised in that military garb, that made you look as fierce as if you were going to be one of the body guards of our great Napoleon. So now, my lass, take your toast and chocolate, for you have a long walk before you, and we may not return till a late hour for dinner."

"And to tell you the truth," answered our heroine, "I don't feel half the confidence of success that I did last night."

THE CONSCRIPT JEANNOT.

"Indeed! What reason have you to despair in so short a time?"

"I can scarcely tell," replied Jeannette, with a sigh, "except that I have been troubled with ill-boding dreams during the short time that I was able to sleep. Everything seemed to go against me, and when I awoke it was with a feeling of hopelessness that I never experienced before."

"Oh, if that is to be the case," exclaimed the old lady, "you may as well give up the attempt at once, for there is little chance of your succeeding unless you enter heart and soul into the business."

"I know it," replied our heroine, "and it has been my endeavour to keep up my spirits, and perhaps I might have succeeded better in doing so if it had not been for what you said last night."

"Ah! you thought I threw cold water upon the affair?"

"It might have been a mistake," answered Jeannette, "but I fancied you were not so full of hope as myself."

"Foolish girl!" exclaimed Madame Germaine, "you must have a poor heart indeed, if you always give up as easily as that. It's true, I did say there were difficulties in the way, but that was not done so much to put you off the affair altogether, as to prepare you against disappointment, in case the emperor should refuse to grant the pardon you ask for. However, think no more of what I have said, for your purpose is a good one, and is well worth pursuing, since the emperor—whatever may be the determination he comes to—cannot but feel admiration for the noble effort you have made to procure your lover's pardon."

"Do you think he will refuse my humble request?"

"Ah!" exclaimed the old lady, "that is a question that can only be answered after you have seen him. He is sometimes taken with very extraordinary feelings of generosity, and if it should be your good fortune to find him in one of those humours, the efforts you have made will not be thrown away. So keep up your courage, and look forward to a prosperous termination to the long journey you have taken."

"I will follow your friendly counsel," she replied, "for already do I feel a stronger assurance that Jeannot may escape the punishment that must have disgraced all the remainder of his life. Untiringly I will watch till I see the emperor, and then plead, with all the eloquence of a loving heart, for that grace which he alone can bestow."

"Remember one thing though," exclaimed Madame Germaine, "you must not attempt to palliate the conduct of Jeannot, or the favour you ask for will not be granted. Admit that he was carried away by the ardour of a young spirit, and promise, in his behalf, that he will repay the kindness of his emperor by fighting bravely in his defence whenever the time for action arrives. That's the kind of argument that will be most likely to succeed, and if well-applied, the chances will be in favour of your returning here with good news."

"I'll try my best, at any rate," exclaimed Jeannette, "though, to confess the truth, I tremble already at the thought of presenting myself before so great a personage as Napoleon."

"Aye," answered Madame Germaine, "and you are not the only one, by many thousands, that tremble even at the bare mention of his name. You, however, have little reason to be afraid of him, for, even though he may not grant your request, he will at least respect the purpose which led you to seek the interview with him."

"But suppose he refuses to hear what I have to say?"

"I don't think there is much fear of his acting in that way," returned the old lady; "for though he certainly is a good deal worried by the sort of applications that you are about to make, he knows that it is one of the penalties that great people are obliged to bear, and the best thing he can do is to put up with the inconvenience with the best grace he can. Indeed we never hear of his making any complaints upon the subject, though, as a matter of course, not one case in fifty that go before him receive such an answer as the applicants wish for. However, it is now time that we should start on our errand, for the emperor is always early when he goes abroad, and if you should miss seeing him to-day, it may be many more before you get the opportunity you desire."

A few minutes after this, Jeannette and her hostess set out on their errand, and in the first instance proceeded to the head-quarters of the emperor, where they watched for some time in the expectation of seeing him come out. In this, however, they were disappointed, for at length, when their patience was nearly exhausted, they inquired of a soldier who was on duty as a sentry, and learned from him that the great man they were looking for, had gone out some time previously to inspect some of the troops who were to form part of the immense army, at the head of which he was so soon to place himself. The two females immediately followed to the place which had been appointed for the review, but on reaching the spot, they had again the mortification of learning that Napoleon had dismissed his troops for the day, and gone to the barracks of the conscripts, where other important business required his attendance. Thither they also proceeded, but with no better success, and at length, wearied by the many disappointments they had met with, they returned home no better off than when they had set out in the morning. Three other days did Jeannette continue to pursue her errand, but still with the same result that had attended her first attempt. Now, however, she had no longer occasion for Madame Germaine as a guide, but proceeded unaccompanied to seek for him, from whom she hoped to obtain the pardon of her lover. Twice, it is true, he had been pointed out to her, but on both occasions he was mounted on horseback, and surrounded by so many of his staff, that it was impossible for her to have approached without imminent danger of being trampled on. But there was one advantage which had been obtained, she now knew the person of the emperor, so that if chance should throw her afterwards in his way, she would at once be able to recognise him, and make the application that to her was of such vital importance. On the fourth day after her arrival, in spite of the threatening clouds that were gathering above, Jeannette set out again, still hoping, yet scarcely daring to anticipate a more successful termination of her labours than she had hitherto met with. As usual, she took her way towards the emperor's head-quarters, but ere she could reach the end of her destination, a heavy storm of thunder and lightning, accompanied by torrents of rain burst forth, and compelled her to seek shelter beneath the porch of a church. Here she had been but a few minutes when the sound of voices met her ears, which seemed to proceed from a sort of side chapel connected with the sacred edifice. Attracted by a sort of curiosity which she could not account for, Jeannette stealthily approached the place, and, clustered by one of the massive columns that supported the roof, she perceived a number of persons, who, by their dress, she knew to be military officers. A single glance at the principal personage of this group revealed to her gaze the well-remembered features of Napoleon Buonaparte—the subject of her anxious search from the moment of her arrival in Toulon. She would have advanced, but her feet seemed to be firmly fixed to the spot, and casting an anxious, supplicating look towards the party, she stood incapable of moving one way or the other. At length the emperor perceived her, and passing through the throng by whom he was surrounded, approached the spot with a look of benignancy, that at once served to rouse and assure her that now was the moment when she might venture to make her appeal to him. In an instant she threw herself upon her knees before the emperor, and in accents scarcely articulate implored pardon for having thus intruded herself into his presence. Napoleon desired her to rise, and then in a voice full of kindness, inquired if she had any request to make to him.

"I have, sire," she replied, diffidently, "but I fear this is no time to trouble you with business that is of no importance to yourself."

"If you have any grievance to complain of," answered the emperor, "I am ready to hear you at once."

"Forgive me, your majesty," she exclaimed, "but my present object is to implore pardon for an offender."

"Humph!—perhaps the offence he has committed is one that I cannot in common justice pardon."

"It might have been a very serious one," she replied, "but happily—in some respect—the person I appeal for, was arrested before any actual mischief took place. Under those circumstances, I have ventured to ask pardon for the offender."

"Who is the person you are appealing for?"

"His name is Jeannot Lamont?"

"What is he?"

"A conscript, sire."

"And his offence?"

"He has been guilty of two;—one of them was gaming against the regulations of the army,—the other of drawing his sword against the man he had been playing with."

"In that case I can make no promise of pardon," exclaimed the emperor, "for the discipline of the army must be kept perfect, or the glory of our arms will soon be tarnished." He paused, and seemed about to leave her, when, as if a sudden thought had struck him, he turned sharply round, and added:—"Have you come any great distance to prefer, what I am afraid is a very useless request."

"Nearly sixty leagues, sire."

"Of course, you rode?"

"Only a little part of the way," she replied, "for my means were small, and I could not afford the expense of riding."

"I see," he exclaimed, after a brief pause, "it is your lover you are pleading for, or I am much mistaken."

"True, sire," she replied with downcast eyes, "Jeannot and I were betrothed, and we should have been married soon, but for——"

"I know what you were about to say," exclaimed the emperor, as she suddenly paused. "You mean that if he had not been taken away from home to serve as a conscript, the young man would not have been in his present awkward predicament?"

"Such a thought has certainly crossed my mind," answered Jeannette, "but I have never repined at the separation, because I knew that the necessities of your majesty, as well as his country, required him to assist in opposing the enemies of France."

"And was the young man willing to serve in the good cause?"

"He never uttered a complaint in my presence," she replied, "and I believe I may venture to say that a more willing soldier is not to be found in all the ranks of your great army."

"You give me a good character of him," exclaimed the emperor, smiling, "and if he deserves it, I——"

"Your majesty means to say that, in that case, you would grant the pardon I have asked for?" interrupted Jeannette, eagerly catching at the hope thus suggested.

"I will not go quite so far as to promise that," answered Napoleon, "because I have not yet had an opportunity of inquiring into the merits of the case. There may not happen to be any redeeming points in the offence he has been guilty of, and I cannot pledge myself to pardon him till I know what sort of character he has previously borne since he has been in barracks here." Then, beckoning to one of his officers who stood behind, he said—"Do you happen to know, Marshal Davoust, anything of the circumstances connected with the arrest of a young conscript named Jeannot Lamont?"

"I only know, sire," answered the marshal, "that a person of that name has been arrested with another, whom they have accused of having broken, on the same evening, two of our military regulations."

"What has been the conduct of this Jeannot, previously?"

"I have never heard any complaint against him, which is more than I can say for a great number of his comrades."

"So far your report is satisfactory," answered the emperor, "but still I must make further inquiries to ascertain whether he is deserving the consideration which this young female has requested."

"The young lady feels deeply interested in him, I suppose?" observed Marshal Davoust, with peculiar emphasis.

"That she does," answered Napoleon, "is sufficiently proved by the fact that she has walked many weary leagues for the purpose of trying what influence she may possess towards obtaining pardon for the man whom she one day hopes to call her husband. The spirited conduct of the girl pleases me, and I will myself make such inquiries into this affair as shall inform me whether he merits the merciful consideration she is so anxious to obtain for him. You say no complaint against him has yet reached your ear, and if his conduct hereafter appears to me to be generally good, I may perhaps yield to the supplication of a fond, faithful girl, who has thought neither of the distance she had to walk, nor the difficulties that were to be encountered when she had this one great object to be accomplished."

"It is not for me, sire, to raise any obstacles against your sovereign will," answered the marshal; "but examples ought to be made when our discipline is broken, and if one instance is afforded of a person being allowed to escape unpunished, it leads to others, till disorganization threatens to destroy the whole army."

"You are right there in one respect," exclaimed Napoleon, "but I flatter myself that those who are under my command know their duties too well to do anything that they are aware would be displeasing to me. Had my soldiers loved me less, I should never have been the conqueror in so many glorious battles."

"Pardon me, sire," returned the courtier, "but you forget that it is you, their illustrious commander, who may take the chief merit of all this glory upon yourself."

"And what should I have been?" demanded the emperor. "What station, think you, would have been mine at the present moment if I had not been backed by some of the finest soldiers that the world ever saw? I have been told before by flatterers that all has been owing to me as their leader, but, for my own part, I feel that my present elevation has been owing to the devotion of my army and the gallantry they have shown."

"I hope, sire," exclaimed the marshal, "you reckon me among those who flatter without reason?"

"On the contrary," replied Napoleon, "I have always found you amongst the most honest and straightforward of those few that I may reckon amongst my friends. But enough of this, Davoust. I would know something of the character this young man has borne, and if it should prove to be pretty good, I will make this female happy by pardoning her lover the offence he has been guilty of."

Then addressing himself to Jeannette, he added—

"You hear that I have put this affair into a proper train for inquiry, and if anything should prove satisfactory, I will to-morrow, in your presence, restore him to liberty."

"Where may I be permitted to wait upon you, sire?"

"At my own quarters."

"At what time?"

"Nine to-morrow morning."

Having said this, the emperor turned away to avoid the grateful expression which he saw she was about to give utterance to, and Jeannette, perceiving that she would best please by retiring at once, left the place, her heart palpitating with joyous emotion at what she conceived to be the certainty of her lover's speedy release. As soon as she was gone, the marshal ventured to interrupt the meditation into which Napoleon had fallen by enquiring, if he really thought of pardoning a breach of military discipline like the one under consideration.

"Most assuredly I do," answered the emperor, "or I should not have suffered yonder girl to take her departure under the impression that the object of her long journey from home was about to be accomplished."

"Pardon me, sire," exclaimed the other; "but an example was required, and I fear that mercy in this case will only lead to the commission of many similar offences."

"Let those who brave my anger be prepared to suffer the consequences of their indiscretion," answered the monarch in a quick, impetuous tone. "There may, as in the present instance, occur cases in which lenity may be exercised, but it does not, therefore, follow that I am to pardon every reckless fellow that may choose to set the rules and regulations of military life at defiance. Besides, I felt interested in the heroism displayed by this young girl, and surely it is not too great a stretch of my royal prerogative to pardon this young man, after the noble exertion she has made in his behalf."

"Your majesty, then, has quite made up your mind to pardon this Jeannot, in compliance with her request?"

"That will depend upon what sort of character I hear of him in the meantime," answered Napoleon. "If he has been tolerably strict in the performances of his duties on all previous occasions, I shall feel a pleasure in restoring him to his former station; but if, on the contrary, his conduct has been unworthy the character of a soldier belonging to the imperial army, then I shall consider it my duty to make him an example to all others who may not yield that implicit obedience which can alone secure honour and victory to our arms. So now, marshal, you know how far my mind is made up with respect to this affair, and it now only remains for you to make those inquiries which are to guide me in the course that is to be pursued."

At this period the emperor's carriage, which had been sent for when they commenced, arrived at the entrance of the church. A crowd of anxious persons was assembled to see the man whom destiny had raised to so exalted an eminence, and Napoleon drove off amidst the enthusiastic applause of his admiring subjects.

CHAPTER VII.

JEANNETTE CONFIDES TO HER FRIEND THE RESULT OF HER INTERVIEW, AND DERIVES FRESH CONFIDENCE FROM IT.—A VISITOR ARRIVES IN THE PERSON OF HENRI DUPONT, WHO SOMEWHAT DAMPS HER HOPES.—THE SERJEANT'S REPORT, AND THE MISCHIEF-MAKER IS DEFEATED.

WHEN our heroine returned to the house of Madame Germaine, she found that the old lady had gone out some time previously on business of her own, but it appeared that she had not forgotten her young friend's wants, for the table was spread with the best her cupboard afforded, and a note was left desiring her to make free with whatever she liked best, and not to expect her return till evening, as the affair that had called her forth would at least occupy her till that time. Grateful for the good-natured attention which had thus been shown her, Jeannette sat herself down to the table, and having appeased her hunger, applied herself diligently to some needle-work, which she knew her kind hostess was anxious to finish with as much expedition as possible. This employment served to divert her mind from other subjects which were at present involved in doubt and uncertainty, and she was still occupied with her task when Madame Germaine arrived just as the shades of evening were beginning to close in. After the first greeting was over, her next care was to light the lamp, and then, seating herself by the side of her young friend, she made eager inquiries as to what had been the result of her attempt to obtain an interview with the emperor. In as few words as possible, our heroine explained all that had taken place, and, arriving at the fortunate conclusion of the task she had undertaken, Madame Germaine was full of admiration and delight at the condescension and kindness which she had met with from the great man who held the destiny of Jeannot in his hands.

"So far you have succeeded to admiration," exclaimed the old lady, as soon as she had come to a conclusion, "and for my own part, I can see no reason why the remainder of your task should not be brought to a satisfactory conclusion. In short, the emperor has almost made a promise to look over the offence your lover has committed; and as a man of undoubted honour, he will not dismiss you from his presence to-morrow without yielding the pardon you have asked for."

"So far as Napoleon himself is concerned, I have the fullest reliance in the success of my mission," replied Jeannette; "but the inquiry as to poor Jeannot's former character has been left to one of the marshals of France, and if he should report unfavourably, the labour I have so cheerfully undertaken will be rendered useless."

"Do you know the name of the marshal?" asked the old lady.

"I think the emperor called him Davoust."

"Then you are in good hands, for people report him to be humane—and it is said that the soldiers regard him as one of the best friends they have in the army. At all events, he is not severe where mildness can be extended, and I therefore think you may venture to hope that to-morrow will see Jeannot restored to his liberty."

"I would fain believe so, dear madame," sighed our heroine; "but somehow I am afraid to indulge my hopes, even though the conduct of the emperor might encourage me to do so."

"Then you are wrong there," exclaimed Madame Germaine, "for I never could see the use of giving way to despair so long as things are going on favourably. For my own part, I'm always inclined to look on the brightest side, whenever there's a doubt, and, in my opinion, it is the wisest plan too, for there's quite grief and sorrow enough in the world, without people meeting troubles half way."

"But how much greater is the disappointment when our anticipations prove to be ill-founded?"

"There may be some truth in that, my dear girl," answered the old lady, "but it is our duty to bear up against misfortunes, and not to crouch down before them, as those only do who have neither fortitude nor resignation. Besides, Jeannot seems to be a favourite with his comrades as well as his officers, so that you have nothing to fear from any evil reports when inquiries are made concerning him."

"Well, Madame Germaine," exclaimed our heroine, "you have taken so much pains to make me happy, that it would be the worst species of ingratitude were I to treat your kind intentions with indifference. I will, therefore, console myself with the assurance that this affair will terminate favourably, and that I shall be able to return home with good news of the result of my long journey."

"To be sure you will, my dear girl," returned Madame Germaine, "for even though it must be admitted your lover has been guilty of a very serious offence, the emperor never fails to reward good actions, and he will therefore yield to the request of a young female who has undertaken so much fatigue and danger for the sake of obtaining pardon for her erring lover. You see I speak confidently, and, rely on it, you will find that I have not proved a false prophet."

"Again I repeat," exclaimed Jeannette, "that I will cast aside my own fears, and place the fullest reliance in the opinion you have been kind enough to express. To-morrow, however, will decide the question, and I shall then know the fate of my unfortunate betrothed."

"Aye," answered her friend, "and, rely upon it, to-morrow will see you as happy as you can wish to be. Jeannot will be restored to liberty, and you will return home with the proud consciousness that all has been owing to your own noble exertions in his behalf."

"That may be very true, my dear madame," sighed Jeannette, "but my gratification will be alloyed by the reflection that he must soon be engaged in fighting against the enemies of our country."

"Exactly so; but how else is he to gain glory and renown?"

"Glory and renown," replied our heroine, "are but false beacons, that have lured many millions of men to their destruction. In truth, I am one of those who can see nothing but wickedness in army being brought to oppose army, and especially as wars are generally supposed to be the mere playthings of the great ones of the earth. Ambition is the leading principle, and to accomplish their ambitious designs, kings care not how many of their subjects fall in the struggle."

"My dear Jeannette," exclaimed the old lady, "if our emperor knew your feelings upon that subject, he would not be much inclined to listen to the petition you have preferred to him."

"It is not likely I should let him know my opinion," answered our heroine, "and yet it is to be regretted that those who govern nations should not sometimes hear the truth, as well as their subjects. War cannot be defended by any argument, and yet, without any apparent cause that we can discover, France is about to pour her thousands of armed men into Prussia, from whence perhaps not one half of them will ever return alive."

A knock at the room door prevented the reply that Madame Germaine was about to make, and the next minute Henri Duport, the conscript, and the comrade of Jeannot, entered the room.

"Well, Jeannette," he exclaimed, after she had introduced him by name to Madame Germaine, "so I hear you have had the honour of an interview with the emperor, and as I could easily guess the object you had in view, I hastened here without delay to learn how you have succeeded."

"If the truth must be told, she has not succeeded at all!" interposed the old lady.

"Then the affair has ended just as I expected it would," returned Henri, "for one of our regulations has been broken, and we all know how determined Napoleon is to preserve the strictest discipline in his army."

"But Jeannot did not enter the army of his own free will," exclaimed our heroine, "and it, therefore, seems peculiarly hard that he should be bound by its severe regulations. Besides, though he drew his sword in a moment of over-powering excitement, not the slightest injury was sustained by either himself or his opponent."

"Aye," he replied, "but the emperor will not look at that circumstance, because an offence has been committed, and he is determined never to overlook even the slightest breach of discipline among his troops. Indeed, everything depends upon keeping the military under subjection; and were I to offend as Jeannot has done, I should expect nothing else but to put up with the consequences."

"And is that really what you think?"

"It is, indeed, Jeannette."

"Then you know not the good qualities of the emperor so well as I do," returned our heroine, "for I have his own gracious permission to see him to-morrow morning, and I believe he will not dismiss me from his presence till he has pardoned him for whom I have made so great an exertion."

"Did he tell you as much?"

"He did, indeed, Henri."

"And you rely upon his promises?"

"How can I do otherwise," she asked, "when the promise comes from our great Emperor Napoleon?"

"I don't mean to say that he would lightly break his word, when once it has been given," answered the young conscript; "but those who are placed so far above us, do not like to be troubled by those who have petitions to make to them, and it is not to be much wondered at, if they now and then dismiss troublesome people by giving a hasty promise that they have no idea of fulfilling."

"Then you would have me believe, that to-morrow Napoleon will so far lower himself, as to acknowledge that he has held out a promise which, when made, he had no intention of performing?"

"Whatever I may think of it," returned Henri Duport, "it would be too dangerous an experiment for me to make, to assert boldly that he will break his word. Opinions, however, are free, and mine is, that, notwithstanding what may have passed during our interview, you will find to-morrow that your hopes will be disappointed."

"I'll not believe it," exclaimed Madame Germaine, "for an honourable man will not stoop to any paltry deception, and my own opinion of the emperor is that, however much it may go against the grain with him, he will sacrifice his own feelings, rather than punish Jeannot, if the inquiries that are making about him should turn out favourable."

JEANNETTE AND HENRI DUPONT.

"And how can that be the case," demanded Dupont, "when he has already broken another of the regulations by getting intoxicated?"

"Is that true, Jeannette?" asked the old lady.

"I fear it cannot be denied," answered our heroine, "but the emperor himself saw him at the time, and pardoned him."

"On condition though," observed Henri Dupont, "that he promised never to commit himself again."

"And he would not have done so," exclaimed Jeannette, with more severity in her tone than she usually betrayed, "but that he was led on by some crafty villain who sought his destruction for purposes of his own."

"How know you that?" asked Duport, shrinking under the somewhat stern gaze that she directed towards him.

"I am sure of it," she replied, "because Jeannot was never addicted to intemperance, so long as he was free from the temptations of those who exult in whatever mischief they can do."

"And who do you suspect of having played so base a part?"

"You!" exclaimed Jeannette, stretching out her arm, and pointing to him as the monosyllable was uttered.

Taken by surprise, and shrinking under a consciousness of his own guilt, Henri Duport started back with a look full of dread and astonishment. He, however, saw the danger of thus exposing himself to still further suspicion, and recovering himself as quickly as he could, he said in a plausible tone—

"Nay, Jeannette, this suspicion is most unworthy of you, for I never expressed any ill-feeling against your betrothed, nor do I regard him with jealousy, though it must be confessed I did at one time hope to have possessed that place in your affections that it seems he is so fortunate as to occupy. You have, however, rejected me, and, with the best grace I could command, I have endeavoured to appear resigned to the doom your lips had pronounced."

"And can you with a good conscience declare that you have never vowed in your heart to be revenged for the preference that was bestowed on him?"

"I see how it is, Jeannette," he replied, endeavouring to avoid this question that was so difficult to answer, "some enemy has been whispering things to my prejudice, and you have believed every evil report that has been spread abroad against me."

"So far from that being the case," she replied, "I never heard that you had any enemies."

"Did Monsieur Narbonne, the notary, never tell you that it would be well to be always upon your guard against me?"

"Monsieur Narbonne is a peace-maker," answered our heroine, "and would not injure any one by an evil report. Indeed he scarcely ever mentioned your name, and when he did, nothing was said to prejudice me against you."

"I'll tell you what it is, Monsieur Duport," exclaimed the old lady, who now thought it was necessary to interfere; "Jeannette is at the present time under my care and protection, and so long as she is a visitor of mine, I will see that neither you nor anybody else shall either molest or intimidate her."

"Have I endeavoured to do either one or the other?" demanded the conscript, in a tone that seemed to say, that if anybody had reason to complain of injury it was himself.

"Of that you ought to be the better judge," she replied, "but considering the the positions in which you and Jeannette now stand with regard to each other, I certainly am of opinion that your visit here this evening would have been much better omitted.

"That's the way one's good intentions are always mistaken," exclaimed Henri Duport; "for the truth is, I came here because I thought Jeannette might depend too much upon her lover's release, and I fancied it would be a great deal better that she should know the worst at once. I have told her exactly what to expect, and for doing so you have both made up your minds to believe that I came only to serve some unworthy purpose of my own."

"And so I verily believe you have," interposed a voice from behind, and directly afterwards Sergeant Lefevre, a nephew of Madame Germaine's, presented himself before them.

"What do you know about it?" demanded Henri, rather disconcerted by so unexpected an addition to the party.

"To speak the truth," he replied, "I have been some time at the door, which happened to be open, and have overheard nearly all the conversation that has been going on."

"Humph!" ejaculated Duport; "listeners seldom hear any good of themselves, and it should have been so in your case, if I had had the slightest notion that you were mean enough to be playing the part of an eavesdropper."

"And who wouldn't have done the same thing, when they heard you telling a parcel of falsehoods to this poor girl, who had no means of detecting the deception you were practising."

"Then perhaps you'll relate the affair in your own way, and then Jeannette will be sure to hear nothing but the truth," exclaimed Henri Duport with a feeling of rage that he could hardly suppress, and striding from the room, he was presently heard clattering down the stairs at a rate that threatened him with a broken neck.

"Oh, never mind him, my dear child," cried Madame Germaine, on perceiving that Jeannette was alarmed at the impetuosity that had been betrayed; "the poor fellow has suffered a defeat when most certain of doing mischief to his successful rival, and it is much better that he should go and vent his spleen anywhere else than here. And now, my dear Louis," she added, turning towards her nephew, "tell us how it was that we happened to receive a visit from you, just when we wanted some one to abash and confound that spreader of false news?"

"I came," he replied, "to let your young friend here know that she may reckon, almost to a certainty, upon Jeannot's release to-morrow."

"And pray, Louis," inquired his aunt, "how do you happen to be so much concerned in this very important secret?"

"Because I happened to be in the barracks when an orderly officer came, by authority of Marshal Davoust, to inquire particularly into the previous conduct and character of our comrade Jeannot."

"Well, and what did the orderly officer hear?"

"Everything, I can assure you, that was most satisfactory."

"What then, no one had a bad word to say against Jeannot?"

"On the contrary, aunt, everybody spoke of him in the highest terms, and well they might too, for if evil fellows would only let him alone, I believe a more harmless chap would not be in the regiment."

"What do you mean by evil persons?" asked Jeannette.

"Why, you see, ma'amselle," he replied, "where there are large bodies of people, there's sure to be some of all sorts—good and evil mixed up together. Now, the army is no exception to the rule, and Jeannot would have been made a victim by some of his comrades, if it had not been for your coming all this distance to see the emperor."

"Then you think she has succeeded?" asked Madame Germaine.

"I don't think it's very likely she can have failed," answered Sergeant Lefevere, "when it's well known that Napoleon always excuses the faults of those who break through his regulations, when it can be proved to his satisfaction who it was that tempted him to do wrong. And it's not often that his majesty is deceived either, for he never minds what trouble it may occasion, when once he has made up his mind to trace out the guilty parties."

"And do you think he has made up his mind in the present instance?" asked Madame Germaine.

"I don't pretend to give an opinion upon matters that I don't know for a certainty," replied Sergeant Lefevre, "but as inquiries have been made this ery day about Jeannot, by command of the emperor, we know that things are going on in a fair train for the young fellow's discharge from prison, if he should prove worthy of the kindness."

"And he *will* prove worthy of it," exclaimed Jeannette earnestly.

"No doubt of it," returned the old lady; "but we must not make too certain of his getting clear off, for the inquiries must prove perfectly satisfactory, or h   l be set at liberty till a more lengthened investigation has taken place. And I don't know but what it's very right, too," she added, "for France takes a pride in her soldiers, and they would soon cease to be what they are, if once they found there was no punishment for those that break the laws they are sworn to obey."

"But your nephew said just now that many are led away by the evil counsels of others."

"No doubt of it," replied Madame Germaine, "but in my opinion it is hardly an excuse for any man to plead that he has been enticed from his duties by designing persons. In short, everybody knows the difference between right and wrong, and——"

"My dear madam," cried our heroine, interrupting her, "you will presently almost persuade me that no excuse can be found for the errors Jeannot has been guilty of."

"And, strictly speaking, I am not quite certain that he don't deserve what punishment he has already received by being placed in confinement," answered the old lady. "However, that is rather a painful subject for us to get upon just at this moment, so we'll say no more about it, lest I should be supposed to mean a great deal more than I really do."

"Then, by way of changing the subject," interposed Sergeant Lefevre, "I suppose you know that we have received orders to be in readiness for marching at an hour's notice?"

"Is it known when the notice is likely to be given?" asked Jeannette.

"Oh, no," replied the soldier; "these things are never published till the very last moment, for the emperor always chooses to keep his enemies in the dark as long as possible; and experience has proved the wisdom of his doing so, for if once his plans were known, he would have little chance of pouncing suddenly upon the enemy and beating them, has he as so often done before now."

"Would to Heaven," sighed Jeannette, "that he were less fond of being at continual strife with foreign powers."

"Aye, so women and children may think," exclaimed the sergeant, "but he who governs France has a clear head and cool judgment, and he knows well enough that if he had not wars abroad he would have no peace at home. We Frenchmen are never so much at our ease, as when we have foreign conquests to look forward to, and as soon as our peace happens, so surely is there always some mischief plotting against the state. The emperor is aware of that; so, like a prudent general as he is in everything, he finds us plenty of employment in fighting the enemy abroad, so that he may preserve his throne at home. And now it strikes me we are going to have plenty of warm work, for the Prussians are brave fellows, and they'll not suffer us to invade their country, without fighting heart and soul to save it from falling, as so many others have done since our great Napoleon has had the command of the army."

"And Jeannot;—is he to join the army that is to pass over the German frontier?" asked Jeannette with alarm.

"If he receives a pardon he will be sure to go," answered the sergeant, "for he bears the character of being a brave and dauntless lad, and is just one of the sort of chaps that the emperor selects to make up his imperial guard, as soon as they have proved themselves worthy of the honour, which, by the by, is no trifling one."

"Alas!" sighed Jeannette, "then I fear there is no chance of his ever returning from this war."

"Then you are mistaken, my girl," answered the sergeant, "for many thousands do survive every battle that is fought, and I don't see why your lover should not be as lucky as anybody else. However, he ought to think himself a fortunate dog to leave behind him a lass that it seems will never forget him in his absence."

"Fortunate!" exclaimed our heroine, "what good fortune can there be in leaving home by force, and having to neglect the only business upon which his future subsistence depends?"

"What business did he follow?" asked the sergeant.

"That of a vine-dresser."

"And his father is still alive, I believe."

" He is."

" Well, then, what's to hinder affairs going on at home in his absence?" demanded the soldier. " Besides, under any circumstances, it is the first duty of a citizen to serve his country, and to give up all selfish considerations, when the glory and honour of his native land requires his assistance."

" So it may be," exclaimed Madame Germaine, " but for my own part, I perfectly agree with Jeannette, in saying that though wars may have been carried on in former times, there can be no occasion for them, now that people have grown wiser, and see that they only lead to an unnecessary waste of life."

" It's all very well to say that," answered the sergeant, " but France has always held a high place amongst nations, and a very pretty thing it would be if she was now to acknowledge that her people are unwilling to draw a sword as their fathers have done before them. For my own part, I should be ashamed of my countrymen if they were to hang back when the emperor, who has been the hero of so many fights, calls upon them to support the honour of the nation."

" Ah !" cried Jeannette, " how smoothly these words sound, and yet what ruin and misery our wars have brought upon thousands of families, who have lost husbands and brothers in a quarrel that they have nothing to do with."

" You must be careful and not let the emperor hear you say as much when you see him to-morrow," exclaimed Sergeant Lefevre, " or you will not have much chance of making a favourable impression on him. He himself sees the necessity for keeping the enemy in continual fear, for he knows the throne he has so lately gained would soon be lost, if foreign sovereigns could only fancy that his subjects were not willing to fight for him as they have hitherto done."

" That may be very true," answered Jeannette, " but peace has always been found the most advatageous for the happiness of mankind, and I don't see why it should not be so at the present time, as well as in those that have gone by."

" I have told you before," said the sergeant, " that while our people are restless amongst themselves, Napoleon can find safety only in employing them to settle his disputes with foreign nations."

" Well," interrupted Madame Germaine, " we women folks cannot be supposed to understand much of such matters ; but all I have to say about it is, that I shall be glad to see the day when our country will once more be able to enjoy the blessings of peace. That will be a glorious time for us indeed ; for now all the youth and strength of the land are being exhausted by these continual conscriptions ; and by and by, when their services are most required, there will be hardly any one left to defend the country from those that would gladly take advantage of our weakness. It is not often that I give my thoughts to these subjects, but when I do, I can see that our ruin as a nation must closely follow that which seems at present to make our greatness."

" Aye," exclaimed the sergeant, " you women always look at matters that you don't understand, on the wrong side."

" Can you deny what I have said ?"

" I don't know about denying it," he replied, " because this happens to be one of those questions that we soldiers have no right to think about. All I know is, that the emperor has always proved himself to be sharp-sighted enough to raise us to the very highest pinnacle of fame, and I for one am willing to follow him even to death, without questioning whether his plans are right or wrong."

" You are a brave fellow, I know, Louis," exclaimed the old lady, " and so have all proved themselves who have risked their lives to extend the honour and renown of their native land. Indeed, if it had not been for the gallantry of his troops, Napoleon would still have been but a poor lieutenant of artillery, as he was when the siege of this town first brought him into notice. Till then he was thought no more of than you are ; but a few years have served to make him the greatest monarch in the world, and to whom all other sovereigns bow with submission, as if he had been born their superior."

" Ah !" returned Sergeant Lefevre, " he has conquered all but those troublesome islanders, the English people, and even they will be obliged to submit at last, or the preparations that have been so long making will have been so much time and money wasted."

"In my poor opinion," replied the old lady, "we had better leave those people alone; for they have proved themselves to be quite a match for us, and by and by they may be too much."

"Psha! they have not soldiers enough to bring against us."

"But they seem to have plenty of money at their command," answered Madame Germaine; "and that being the case they can always purchase the assistance of other nations, who look with jealousy on the rising power of France, that is threatening all the other kingdoms of Europe. Besides, the English have a navy that we have never yet been able to conquer; and they will therefore never suffer us to land our troops on their shores."

"It might be as you say," replied her nephew, "if our soldiers were to be led by any other general; but the name almost of Napoleon is a tower of strength amongst his followers; and wherever he leads there will still be victory, in spite of the high notions you seem to have of these English. But it is in vain to talk of that now, because as soon as this campaign against Prussia is brought to an end, we shall next sail for the British shores; and Napoleon has promised that London shall be ours."

"It's all very well, my dear Louis, to promise great things," exclaimed Madame Germaine, "but it is not always quite so easy to fulfil them. However, leaving those matters out of the question, we will now return to the subject of Jeannette and her interview with the emperor to-morrow, and congratulate ourselves upon the prospect that her lover will receive the pardon she has come so far to solicit."

"Well, poor fellow," returned Sergeant Lefevre, "all I hope is that we shall not be disappointed, and I think that he is very likely to be set at liberty, because, as I told you before, the inquiries that have been made about him are as satisfactory as could well be."

"And that being the case," exclaimed our heroine, "the emperor cannot depart from the promise he made me this day. Besides, his kindness will not be thrown away upon Jeannot, who will be most anxious to repay it by a courageous performance of the duty he owes to the person from whom the favour has been received."

"All I wish is, mademoiselle, that you may see your hopes fulfilled to the utmost," answered the sergeant; "and what's more, I have no doubt of it; for by all accounts your betrothed is as ardent in the cause of his country as even the oldest among our soldiers, and it is by such young men that Napoleon expects to keep up the renown of our victorious armies."

"But I must now leave you, for the trumpet is sounding that calls us to our quarters; and to deviate, even in that trivial instance, is to run the risk of a very severe punishment."

Sergeant Lefevre then left the room, and Madame Germaine, seeing the melancholy of her young guest, endeavoured, by every argument she could think of, to restore her confidence. Not indeed that Jeannette really despaired; but the uncertainty was the more torturing as the time for seeing the emperor approached; and her anxiety became more intense in proportion as the interest became more and more contracted. The old lady could not fail to observe this, and all her endeavours were therefore directed towards the best means of sustaining her against the sad thoughts which still weighed upon her mind. At length our heroine yielded to these well-intentioned remonstrances, and she said, with a forced smile of satisfaction—

"At your wish, my dear madame, and as a duty that I owe to those who take so warm an interest in my behalf, I will so far control my feelings as to prove that I am not indifferent to the kindness that I have received ever since my arrival in Toulon."

"And do you not also rely upon the promise of the emperor?"

"The emperor has only promised to pardon him on certain conditions."

"That may be very true; yet surely you do not expect that any charge will be brought against your lover?"

"Ah!" sighed Jeannette, "that is just what I am most in doubt of; for though he may have conducted himself well in every respect, we know that he has enemies among his comrades, and after what they have already done, may we not fear that they will endeavour to ruin his character by circulating reports that will injure him with Napoleon. Such, at least, I confess, are the fears that prey upon my mind, and, in spite of myself, they increase as the time approaches that is to decide the fate of my poor Jeannot."

Madame Germaine made no reply to this, for she saw that it would be in vain; and shortly afterwards they retired to bed to dream of the events which were to take place on the following day.

CHAPTER VIII.

THE EMPEROR ARRANGES IMPORTANT PRELIMINARIES.—THE REPORT PROVES FAVOURABLE, AND THE PARDON IS GRANTED.—THE LOVERS ARE ALLOWED AN INTERVIEW, BUT JEANNETTE IS AGAIN DRIVEN TO DESPAIR BY LEARNING THAT THE TROOPS ARE ABOUT TO MARCH IMMEDIATELY FROM TOULON.

ACCORDING to custom, Napoleon was early, and was employed at an early hour on the following morning, in attending to those affairs of state and self-aggrandisement, which now occupied nearly the whole of his time. He was seated at a table, and round him were lying maps, books, and numerous other things that were necessary to give him a thorough knowledge of the country which he was about to overrun with his victorious troops. So occupied, indeed, was he with his studies, that he was not conscious of the entrance of one of his favourite generals, though he had been standing near his chair for some time, waiting for any orders he might have to execute. At length the emperor raised his eyes from the chart upon which they had been intently fixed, and perceiving that he was no longer alone, he slightly pushed the paper from him, and keenly eyeing the officer, exclaimed—

"So, Davoust, you bring me pleasant news, I suppose? My orders, as usual, have been obeyed with alacrity, and all things are prepared for this new expedition that is to make such an important addition to my dominions in Europe."

"I have nothing but what is favourable to relate to your majesty," answered the marshal; "you are indeed fortunate in possessing so many countless thousands of willing hearts, which never beat with so much ardour as when you issue orders for fresh conquests."

"Are you not flattering me, Davoust?"

"You never knew me stoop to flattery, sire."

"Very true," answered the emperor, "and yet I can hardly believe that there is no dissatisfaction expressed by those who are compelled by the laws of conscription to enter upon those bloody scenes which the star of my destiny has so often forced me into. Sometimes I feel that the time must come when people will begin to ask themselves if war and carnage are never to be at an end, and if ever that should be the case, my own downfall will not be far off."

"Your majesty," exclaimed Davoust, "is not often given to indulge in those gloomy reflections."

"You are right there, my dear general," returned Napoleon, " or rather you should have said, I am not often given to express to others the thoughts that sometimes cross my mind. The past and present speak sufficiently for themselves, but the future is full of mystery, though I believe I can see troubles accumulating that others little dream of."

"And yet who has ever led so glorious a career as that which has raised you to the throne of France, and made you the master and ruler of the greater portion of Europe?"

"Aye," exclaimed the emperor, "my progress has indeed been a wonderful one, and my brain becomes dizzy when I look backwards and contemplate all that has occurred since the day when I first distinguished myself in this very city. It seems to me like a dream, and I feel often afraid that I shall wake from it, and regret that I ever rose to the proud eminence in which fortune has placed me."

"Is it no consolation, then, sire, to know that you found France groaning under anarchy and confusion, and that you have since made her one of the most exalted amongst the nations of the earth?"

"Yes, yes," he replied, "I feel that I may deserve some little gratitude on that account, but I also know that all this has not been done without a vast loss amongst the bravest and best of our land. But why should I give way to these gloomy thoughts, when visions of fresh conquests are even now leading me to other scenes of strife and bloodshed that—even though thousands will perish—will conduce to what I have most at heart—the honour and glory of the great nation that has chosen me for her ruler?"

"Aye, sire," replied the marshal, "and never yet has she regretted the choice she made, when it fell upon you."

"But what say people about this new invasion of Prussia?"

"All patriots admire the design," answered Davoust, "for the King of Prussia has so often proved faithless, not only to yourself, but to others that have trusted him, that all see the necessity for either dethroning or humiliating him to the utmost. At all events there is the consolation of knowing that his majesty has fallen so completely into contempt, that foreign nations will not think him an object worthy their interference."

"And my own plans are so well matured," exclaimed the emperor, glancing at the charts before him, "that I believe scarcely a month will pass away, before Frederick William of Prussia will be humbled with the very dust. The lesson too will not be thrown away upon Austria, who, in spite of treaties that exist between us, is, I believe, only waiting for an opportunity to join a coalition against me."

"Is she not subdued yet?" asked the marshal.

"To all appearance she is," answered the Emperor Napoleon, "but I know the heart of her sovereign to be hollow and treacherous, and my eye is ever directed towards him with suspicion, that I believe will one day or another be confirmed. But let him beware of such a discovery taking place, for, notwithstanding his boasted high descent, I may yet bring him to a level with the very lowest, who now acknowledge him for their liege lord and sovereign."

"Have you heard, sire, whether he is likely to assist his brother of Prussia in the approaching campaign?"

"That is just what I am anxious to ascertain," answered the emperor, "but hitherto he keeps his designs so close, that I believe no one besides the cautious Metternich, knows what step he intends to take. I, however, cannot be taken by surprise, because he is watched by those upon whose fidelity I can rely, and who will give me the first intimation of any warlike preparations that may be going on. In the meantime, I shall prosecute my plans against Prussia with ardour, and before many weeks the world will see another of its haughty rulers obliged to yield to the bravery of my faithful Frenchmen. You smile, Davoust, but success has never yet failed me, and I have the presumption to believe that, as the favourite child of fortune, I shall never be forsaken so long as I am able to lead our army into the field."

"Has your majesty yet decided when the troops are to march for the Prussian frontier?"

"I have so far decided," replied Napoleon, "that our movement in that direction will not be retarded beyond a few days; probably a few hours will see us in motion, and then let my foes tremble. The tempest which is about to break forth is one that must end in the ruin and degradation of their devoted country.

You and my other generals will, however, hold yourselves in readiness at a moment's notice, for I am only waiting the arrival of a courier from Paris, to issue those orders which are fraught with such important consequences."

"Have you any orders for me, sire, to convey to the officers who are to be engaged in this new expedition?"

JEANNETTE AND JEANNOT'S VOW OF FIDELITY BEFORE M. NARBONNE.

"No," replied the emperor, and then appearing to recollect himself, he added— "by the bye, I forgot to ask how your inquiries ended concerning that young conscript who has been ordered into confinement for a breach of military discipline.   Has his character been previously a good one?"

"It has, sire, but——"

"Ha!" interrupted Napoleon, "he is not worth, then, the pardon it was my intention to bestow upon him?"

No. 9.

"I will not undertake to say so much as that," answered the marshal, "for his character was highly spoken of by all his comrades that I spoke to upon the subject, and I was just coming away perfectly well satisfied with all I had heard, when a young man stepped forward and volunteered to say what he knew about him."

"Well, Davoust, and what said he?"

"Nothing, your majesty, that was favourable."

"Indeed! Had he any specific charges to make?"

"No, sire, he dealt in generalities only, and the chief accusation he made was that the young man, for whom you felt so graciously interested, was always regarded in his native village as a bad example to others, and he further asserted that great satisfaction was manifested by the inhabitants when it was discovered that he was amongst the conscripts ordered to march immediately for the depôt."

"Was your informant a native of the same village from whence this Jeannot Lamont comes?"

"I believe so."

"Perhaps they were rivals?"

"I own it struck me they were, sire," answered Davoust, "but the young man most positively denied it, and declared that he had no other motive for the course he had pursued, than to put your majesty upon your guard against a worthless fellow, who is not deserving the favour you were about to bestow upon him!"

"Do you happen to have learnt the name of this very conscientious man?" inquired Napoleon.

"He told me his name was Henri Dupont."

"'Tis well," returned the emperor, making a note of it in his tablets. "I shall not forget this young man who has made himself so busy, and perhaps the time may come when his character will be as strictly investigated as Jeannot's has been on the present occasion. But tell me candidly, Davoust, what is your opinion of the account given by this volunteer mischief-maker?"

"I think, sire, there is some motive behind, that he is most anxious should not be discovered. Still, however, I cannot say there is no truth in it, for the charge was openly made, and the accuser seemed to have no wish that what he had done should be concealed."

"Did you confront them together?"

"No, your majesty," replied the officer, "I merely performed the task as you had desired me, and left all future proceedings till I had received your orders upon the subject."

"In that case, I think the affair had better rest where it is," exclaimed Napoleon, "for, at all events, his character appears to have been a good one ever since he has been in the barracks, and we have nothing to do with the faults or follies he may have committed previous to his leaving home. Besides, I am of opinion that he has been basely maligned by an enemy, and if it should turn out as I suspect, the traducer shall not escape the punishment his perfidy justly deserves. Indeed, I am almost inclined, as it is, to order him to be brought before me, that I may ascertain at once the motive that has induced him to act so ungenerous a part towards a comrade."

"Shall I desire him to be brought before your majesty?"

"Upon second thought, I believe some other time will answer the purpose better," replied Napoleon, "for I remember this was the hour when I told the young female to be here, and as it is my intention to pardon her lover, it would be cruel to keep her a moment longer in suspense than need be. It now wants a few minutes to the hour appointed," he added, looking at his watch, "and I dare say one who seems so anxious in behalf of her lover, will be punctual almost to a moment."

"In this supposition the emperor was perfectly correct, for before the marshal could return any reply, an attendant entered the room and announced that a young female was without, and earnestly requested an interview upon an affair of importance."

" Let her come in," exclaimed Napoleon ; and no sooner had the marshal retired to the further part of the room than Jeannette entered, and throwing herself at the emperor's feet, implored him earnestly to grant the pardon which had been almost promised on the day before."

" Rise, young woman," he replied, " for the errand you came upon needs not this humility towards one who is ever best pleased when he can with justice pardon those who have fallen into disgrace. The young man you have interested yourself for, seems to have conducted himself well ever since he has been in the army, and as he appears to be sorry for the folly into which he was driven in a moment of excitement, I am well pleased to gratify you by announcing that the punishment he has already suffered through imprisonment will be deemed sufficient to expiate the breach of military discipline he was guilty of."

" Ah, sire !" cried our heroine, " how can I express my gratitude for this kindness."

" You will best do that by not saying another word about it," exclaimed the emperor. " Tell this Jeannot Lamont from me, that I expect better things from him in future, and, though the outset of his military career has been marked by an act of folly, I hope the lenity he has received will act as an inducement for him to win the honour which rewards all those who fight bravely in defence of their country."

" I will not fail to do as your majesty has desired," answered Jeannette, " but I feel assured that he is deeply grieved for the offence he has committed, and that he will do all he can to obtain the favourable opinion of those who are in command over him. He will at least endeavour to wipe out this stain, though I could have wished it had not been his fate to mix himself in strife and battle."

" Ah !" exclaimed Napoleon, indulging himself with a pinch of snuff—like all females, you have a horror of war, though you must know how impossible it is for nations to live in a constant state of peace whilst there are so many contending interests to be regarded. I, myself, have been called a lover of war and bloodshed, though heaven knows I have tried more than any other military ruler to bring about a more kindly feeling amongst the different states which have been most jealous of my rapidly increasing power. I have even tried it with England, my bitterest foe, but her king has treated my advances with scorn, as if they came from some inferior, and I am now determined to chastise his haughty insolence at the very first opportunity that happens to present itself. That, however, he added, checking himself, is no affair of yours, and therefore you will dismiss it from your mind, and remember only that I have granted the pardon which you came here to ask for."

" May I be permitted to ask, sire, when I may see Jeannot ?"

" You can see him within an hour, if you please."

" Where ?"

" At the house of the friend with whom you are staying."

The emperor wrote a few lines, and then having rung for an attendant, he desired the order for Jeannot's release to be conveyed without loss of time to the person in whose custody he had been placed. The man had no sooner received this command than he hastened to execute his commission, and then the emperor, once more addressing himself to Jeannette, said—

" You see, mademoiselle, that I have suffered no unnecessary delay to take place after having once made up my mind for the release of your lover. A few minutes more will suffice to set him at liberty, and I trust the sufferings of the last few days will act as a warning to him for the remainder of his life."

" Alas !" sighed Jeannette, " his life may be but a brief one, for they tell me this new war is likely to be an obstinate and deadly one."

" Who told you that, pray ?"

" All that I have spoken to on the subject, sire."

" Well," he replied, " perhaps they are right, but my own opinion is that the well tried courage of our French soldiers, will bring the war to a more speedy close than many persons expect. Besides, all Europe has experienced the overpowering strength of our arms, and it will need but two or three sharp engagements to convince Prussia that we have not invaded her dominions without a stern determination to conquer her, as we have so many other nations. So you see what glory is to be gained in a brief period, and it is more than probable that your lover will return at the end of a few months as one of the gallant fellows who have reaped honours and renown by the bravery they have exhibited in behalf of their native land."

" If it is not too presumptous, sire," asked Jeannette, " may I inquire if he is likely to return home at the end of this next campaign."

" That is a very difficult question to answer," returned the emperor, smiling at the simplicity of the girl, " for in the first place, it is by no means certain that he will escape all the thousand dangers that threaten those who are in the field of strife, and secondly, I know not whether some other invasion may not succeed the one in which I am about to engage. Of this, however, you may be assured—that no man, nor woman either, within the limits of this empire, will hail a fair honourable peace with grater rapture than I shall. The honour of France is the one thing nearest my heart, and so long as that can be maintained without war, it shall be shown that I am one of the most anxious to secure the prosperity of my country by that peace which we all look forward for."

" Alas !" she sighed, " people are beginning to grow tired of looking for that which they have expected so long."

" The people should interfere only with such affairs as they perfectly understand," replied the emperor. " I have been entrusted with the rule and government of this great empire, and I will lead it on to the very highest summit of earthly grandeur, even in spite of the most malignant spirits that accuse me of having nothing but my own ambition to serve. But never mind—let them call it ambition, or anything else they please, for I have a destiny to fulfil, and none can prevent, however much they may endeavour to oppose it. But enough," he added, abruptly, " you understand not these matters, so return home happy in the consciousness that you have succeeded in your object, and that Jeannot would in all probability have received a severe punishment, had it not been for the generous exertions you have made in his behalf."

Our heroine again knelt at the feet of Napoleon, and having given utterance to the warmth of her gratitude for the favour she had received, she left the emperor's presence and commenced her return home, where she had every reason to expect Jeannot had arrived before her. Impressed at all times with a feeling of profound veneration for the exalted personage she had just seen, how much more was her admiration increased by the graciousness of the reception she had met with, and the readiness with which he had granted the request she had made to him. The gratitude of our heroine, indeed, knew no bounds, and she was still occupied in looking back to the interview that had just passed, when she arrived at the abode of Madame Germaine, at the door of which she found Jeannot, anxiously awaiting her arrival. The joyous meeting of the two lovers it is not necessary to describe ; our heroine for some few moments was unable to give utterance to the words that seemed almost to choke her, and upon being led into the apartment of Madame Germaine, she threw herself into the arms of the old lady, and gave free vent to those tears which it was no longer in her power to restrain.

" Why, my dear girl," exclaimed the kind hostess, " one would have supposed that your errand had proved unsuccessful, instead of having succeeded in your object to the full extent of your most sanguine hopes. Come, come, dry up these tears, for Jeannot has only a short time to stay with us, and you must not suffer him to take his leave under an impression that you are still a prey to grief."

" Oh, madame," returned Jeannette, " these tears of mine are tears of joy rather than sorrow, and therefore my friends need not feel any uneasiness at my giving way to emotions that I could not suppress, without greater fortitude than I can boast of possessing. Indeed, how could I do otherwise than give way to the feelings of my heart, when I saw Jeannot once more at large."

"And all through your generous exertion too, Jeannette," exclaimed her lover, "for had it not been for you, I should have been sentenced to a severe punishment, and then I should never again have dared to present myself before you. Nay, even as it is, I know not how to excuse the conduct that has produced such disgraceful consequences to myself."

"Don't think at all about that," interposed the old lady, "for if it had not been for that, how would you ever have known to what an extent the devotion and affection of Jeannette would carry her. You have now seen how dearly she loves you, and ungrateful indeed must be your heart if ever you forget the tenderness that prompted her to accomplish a long journey on your behalf."

"Can I be suspected of such ingratitude," cried the young man, "when I owe all, even my honour and liberty, to the noble-minded affection with which she has favoured me? Henceforth it shall be my chief endeavour to prove worthy the zeal she has manifested in my behalf, and should an opportunity be afforded me, I will perform some act of valour that shall secure for me the applause of the Emperor."

"Ah, Jeannot!" exclaimed our heroine, "that you will not again dishonour yourself, I am well convinced; but my fear is that, in your anxiety to wipe away this one stain, you will risk your life even in cases of the greatest desperation and danger."

"And ought I not to do so," he asked, "for the man who pardoned, instead of disgracing me for ever?"

"You do indeed owe him a heavy debt of gratitude," exclaimed Jeannette, "but still there are others that you should think of before you plunge yourself headlong into unnecessary danger."

"And foremost among them," cried Madame Germaine, "you should remember her who has been the cause of this happy change in your future prospects. Let the name of Jeannette be ever in your mind, whether in battle or repose, and for her sake you will endeavour to preserve a life which to her is so invaluable."

"But I cannot, nor would I, avoid the post of danger, if it should be my lot to occupy it."

"That of course," answered the old lady, "nor would eannette be easily reconciled if your name was ever to be coupled with dishonour. You are obliged to take part in the wars that distract our country, but, since such is your fate, perform your duty nobly, and it may be that you will return home by-and bye with those marks of distinction that are the aim of all those who desire to obtain the favourable opinion of their fellow men."

"And on the other hand," sighed Jeannette, "he may fall in the s tr if and his name be forgotten, as though he had never drawn a sword in defence of the country of his birth!"

"Very true, my dear," answered Madame Germaine, "but you are now anticipating the worst, instead of looking forward to better things. Your lover may become an officer in time, for in our army men are raised to posts of rank and honour entirely upon their own merits, and I see no reason why Jeannot should not become a great man, as well as numbers of others that we hear of, whose names were never known to the world till they made them famous by deeds of bravery performed in the service of the Emperor."

"But, as all Frenchmen are brave," exclaimed Jeannot, "I don't see that I have much of a chance of being distinguished above thousands of my fellow countrymen, who may all deserve the reward that is due to the brave. That, however, will make no difference to me, for I owe a heavy debt of gratitude to those who have come to my rescue when shame and disgrace had fallen upon me, and I will yet try to prove to them that I am not unworthy the favours I have received."

"I knew it would be so," cried the old lady, "and Napoleon will never have to regret having listened to an appeal for mercy when it was made in behalf of one who erred through too much rashness, and not through any wilful disregard of the laws that were made to govern the army of which our emperor is the head. He has conferred upon you a lasting obligation, Jeannot, and I trust, for your own sake, as well as for those by whom you are loved, that you will never prove unworthy the favour you have this day received from him who is acknowledged to be the greatest monarch in the world."

"You may take my word for it that the kindness shall never be forgotten," answered Jeannot.

"I am sure of it," exclaimed our heroine; "and Madame Germaine only said what she did from a feeling of anxiety that you should maintain your honour without a stain. But why should we talk of this now; for your time is short, and it is even said that in a few days you will be ordered to march with your regiment from Toulon."

"Within a few hours, I believe," returned Jeannot; "for the emperor is anxious to come unexpectedly upon the King of Prussia; and we all know that the greatest of his battles have been won as much by the activity of his movements as by the bravery—great as it is—of the troops he commands."

"Alas!" sighed our heroine, "is it not dreadful to think that all this renown of the emperor's has been gained by the blood of hundreds of thousands of the best citizens of France? Yet such have been the fearful consequences of the ambition of one man, and our beloved country is still doomed to groan for the loss of her children, who are led like sheep to the slaughter."

"Hush!" exclaimed her lover; "you already forget the heavy debt of gratitude we owe to Napoleon."

"Nay, do not think me ungrateful," answered Jeannette; "for never can I forget the favour he has this day granted at my earnest supplication. He has saved you from the shame that punishment must have brought upon you, and for that I thank him from the very bottom of my heart; but are you not to be torn away from me to fight in a cause that all people say is not a just one? and may not your life be sacrificed in the first encounter with the enemy?"

"It may," he replied; "but duty calls me where my services are required, and what a despicable coward should I prove myself were I to murmur at following the example which has been set us by the emperor himself. Besides I may escape the dangers that alarm you so much; and if my conduct should appear to be deserving of reward, I may return home something more than the humble soldier, who leaves you to win his way to glory and renown. Men no better than myself are now field-marshals; some of them even have been raised to the rank of princes of the empire, and none of them have a title below that of duke."

"Ah!" exclaimed Jeannette; "but that is only a golden bait offered to lure others on, in the hope of being rewarded with equal honours. And so indeed may it be with some few, but the great mass must be content to toil on without notice, whilst thousands will be left behind to whiten with their bones the soil on which they fall."

"There is truth in what you say," answered her lover; "but it is not for me to complain of what cannot be avoided. My services, humble as they are, have been demanded, and I am bound to obey the call made upon me by my country without giving a thought to the dangers and difficulties I may have to encounter. In a very short time I believe we shall be marching towards Prussia, but before we go I shall have permission to see you again, and you must then show all your courage, as the betrothed of one who will leave you with a determination to earn an honourable name, even if he should perish in the cause he fights for."

With this the lovers separated; but Jeannette could not control her tears, for a heaviness was upon her heart, and she could not banish from her mind the prognostication of evil that her tears had conjured up.

CHAPTER IX.

AN EVIL SPIRIT IS AT WORK.—JEANNOT IS STILL THREATENED BY SECRET ENEMIES.—TWO FACES UNDER ONE HOOD.—A PARTING.—OUR HERO RECEIVES A WARNING, BUT IS TOO UNSUSPECTING TO PLACE MUCH CREDIT IN WHAT HE HEARS.—PREPARATIONS FOR THE MARCH.

ON the same evening to which the occurrences of the preceding evening belong, two men, evidently of the conscript class, entered a low wine-house in the suburbs of Toulon, and seated themselves in a part of the common room where they might carry on their conversation without much fear of being overheard by the few other persons who were there assembled. The two we have mentioned were no other than Henri Dupont and his friend Jacques Denon, who has already been introduced to the reader as the evil counsellor of the first named personage. After seating themselves, and calling for such refreshments as they required, they looked around them, as if to judge of the company assembled there, and having satisfied themselves in this respect, Henri Dupont said in a half whisper—

"Are you sure that this news you have been telling me is true?"

"So sure am I of it," answered the other, "that I would not mind betting my next month's pay to a single franc piece that everything is exactly as I have told you."

"Who did you hear it from?"

"From several persons," he replied, "but particularly from Sergeant Lefevre, who you must know is the nephew of Madame Germaine, with whom Jeannette is staying."

"And has he confirmed all that the others have said?"

"Every word of it," replied his comrade: "young Jeannot has received a free pardon from the emperor, and if the whole of the report is to be believed, his Imperial Majesty expressed an opinion that your rival must have a secret enemy in some quarter or another."

"The devil!" cried Henri Dupont; "that's awkward at any rate, but I hope his suspicions were not directed against——"

"They are not directed against us in particular," he replied, interrupting him, "so we have nothing to be afraid of. But mind, old fellow, we must keep our own counsel though, for there's no knowing who to trust with one's secrets, and if it should be traced to us we should be sure to fall under the emperor's displeasure."

"As for that," exclaimed Henri, "I don't see what the emperor or any one else has to do with matters that concern him not. This is an affair between me and Jeannot, as to which shall have the girl that we both love, and I don't see what it can matter to a third party as to which of us is to have the girl."

"You are right enough there," answered Denon, "and have only expressed an opinion that I have many a time before now uttered in your presence. No person has a right to interfere in the matter, and if I were in your place I should continue the same course, which in the end will bring you to the very point which you wish to arrive at."

"But Jeannette is not to be moved either by threats or entreaties, and unfortunately her mother is most decidedly opposed to me, because she thinks I have no right to continue my suit after having received a decided refusal from the person I would pay my addresses to."

"Well, but we are not all of us obliged to be of the same opinion," replied Jacques Denon; "and for my own part, I think every man has a right to try his chance, so long as he sees there's any in his favour. It may be all very true that Jeannot was the first to ask for her hand, and that his suit was not rejected; but he has no right to presume, on that account, that she ought not to change her mind if she should afterwards happen to see some one that she liked far better."

"Aye, aye, that's a very capital argument for a man in my situation," replied Henri; "but for my own part, I see very little probability of my succeeding if I were to try my utmost."

"Then you haven't half the spirit I gave you credit for," exclaimed the other, "for no man ever ought to give up, merely because there happens to be a little difficulty in his way. Besides, the girl herself must suppose you don't care much about her, when she finds that you give her up as soon as her first refusal has been uttered."

"But her refusal was so positive, that there could be no doubt as to its having been meant. Indeed, what other notice could I have than that my suit was hopeless, when she told me never to appear in her presence again till I had entirely conquered a passion that could never be encouraged by her?"

"And would you always take a woman at her word when she refuses the offer of a lover?"

"That would depend upon circumstances," replied Henri Dupont; "but in this instance I know she has been betrothed to Jeannot, and there are numbers of persons about her to give their advice against me, even if she were inclined to receive my addresses. Among others, her mother has taken a rooted aversion to me, and besides her, there is one Monsieur Narbonne, a notary, who has made himself particularly busy in doing all he can to spoil my prospects."

"Then why not try my old plan again?"

"What plan do you mean?"

"Why that of pretending a great deal of friendship for Jeannot, and then getting him into some trouble, that would bring with it a disgraceful punishment?"

"How is that likely to serve me, when Jeannot is aware of what I have already done in that way, and would therefore steer clear of any mischief that I might try to do him?"

"'Faint heart never won fair lady!'" returned Jacques Denon, "and I see plainly enough that you have made up your mind to give up the girl merely because you have met with more difficulty than you expected. For my own part, if the case had been mine, I should have persisted the more for having been repulsed, and I'll be bound you would have found yourself in a very different situation at this moment, if you had acted with more determination in the affair. However, I have given you the best advice it was in my power to offer, and it now only remains for you to say whether you will join with me in endeavouring to get your rival into a scrape that will serve to forfeit the high opinion Jeannette at present entertains for him."

"Do you think it possible we may succeed?"

"At any rate, I have a notion it is."

"Without being discovered?"

"That would depend entirely upon ourselves," replied Jacques Denon; "but I think, with a little caution, we might prevent even the most inquisitive person from guessing that we had anything to do with the affair."

"Ah!" exclaimed Henri, "but you don't know what sort of a customer we have to deal with in Monsieur Narbonne. He has all along had a notion that I should not be very particular as to my measures, so that I could supplant Jeannot in the affections of his mistress."

"Then all I can say is, that you ought to have tried to make friends with the old gentleman."

"I have tried to do so," answered Henri, "but he seemed to be suspicious of my real designs, and always avoided me whenever he could do so, without being absolutely insulting."

"Perhaps other persons have been whispering evil things in his ear against you?" observed the other.

"I have reason to believe you are right there; but as the person I suspected was Jeannette's mother, I was unable to take the matter up us as I should otherwise have done. However, be that as it may, I have no chance of making friends with a man who has an unfavourable opinion of me."

"Well, then, it seems, after all, that we had better depend upon our own schemes, and draw him into a scrape as soon as possible."

"How is it to be done?" asked Henri Dupont.

"As easily as it was before."

JEANNETTE AND MADAME GERMAINE.

"But you have seen how completely we failed in our designs."

"Aye, aye," answered Jacques, "we have made a mess of it for once, it's true, but it don't follow that our next attempt will be equally unsuccessful. Besides, you can leave the whole management of the affair to me if you like; and if I am suffered to have my own way, I think everything will be brought about to your satisfaction."

"That is to say, as far as the getting Jeannot into trouble goes?"

"Yes, what can you want more?"

"Why I can see plainly enough," answered Henri Dupont, "that the getting of Jeannot into disgrace will not advance me a single step in the affair that I am most anxious about. The plot, whatever it may be, would at once be laid to me, and instead of getting into the favour of Jeannette, I should be more in disgrace with her than ever."

"Psha! you never look at the fair side of anything."

"That may be," answered Henri, "and I may account for it by saying that I perhaps look before I leap, which I fancy is not the case with you. In short, I have been disappointed so often in my hopes of getting the best of my rival, that I now begin to suspect he is too firmly established in her good opinion for me to have any chance of setting her against him."

"Then why not make up your mind at once, to surrender her without making any more fuss about it?"

"Why, Jacques, I have tried to do so," he replied, "and have even fancied sometimes that I could give her up as easily as I could throw away anything that was of no value to me. But each time I have found out my mistake, and you now see me as much over head and ears in love with Jeannette as ever I were."

"You are a strange fellow," exclaimed his friend, "and hang me if I can make you out, though I fancied a little time ago that you were a chap that would not mind stretching a point or two, so long as there was a chance of carrying out your plans."

"And you judged me rightly when you thought so."

"In that case you will not refuse to join me in one more plot against this rival of yours.—But hark! here he comes with Camille, and, by Jove, they seem to be as thick with each other as if nothing had ever happened to disturb their friendship."

Henri Duport made no reply, but beckoned to the last comers to seat themselves with them; and this having been complied with, a fresh supply of liquor was ordered to be placed on the table. Glasses were then passed round, and Jacques Denon, who really delighted in the perpetration of mischief, alluded to Jeannot's recent arrest, and expressed a wonder at seeing him at liberty again so soon, when all his *friends* expected that he would be disgraced by a severe punishment.

"And so I should," he replied, "but for the exertions of one who indeed proved to be a friend."

"Who was that?" asked Henri.

"One that you know well."

"Do you mean Monsieur Narbonne?" exclaimed Henri, pretending the most profound ignorance of the whole affair.

"No," he replied; "Monsieur Narbonne, though he loves me well, is too old to have taken a journey all the way from our home to this place. No, it was a female that undertook the task, and I love her for the noble heroism she displayed for my sake."

"Love her!" exclaimed Jacques Denon, with a half-suppressed sneer.

"What would Jeannette say if she were to know that your love is divided between her and another?" asked Henri, derisively.

"Ah!" returned our hero, "you may both laugh at me as much as you please, but you cannot make Jeannette jealous, for it happens to be of herself that I was speaking."

"Jeannette!" exclaimed Duport, pretending ignorance of the fact, "do you mean to tell me that she has come all this distance merely because she heard that you had got into a little bit of trouble?"

"I do," answered Jeannot; "and what is more, she would have walked barefooted twice the distance to save me from the dishonour with which she thought I was threatened."

"Well, it was very kind of her to do so, I must say," exclaimed Henri; "but I suppose she didn't come alone?"

"Yes, but she did though."

"Then I must say she acted rather imprudently."

"In what respect?"

"In not having a companion with her."

"Then you and I differ in that respect," exclaimed Jeannot, "for I think she proved herself to be possessed not only of great courage, but also of extraordinary prudence, in undertaking this long journey by herself."

"Her courage I'll not dispute," returned Henri, "but for the life of me I can't see much prudence in a young girl like her coming all this distance without some one to protect her."

"She was better without a companion," answered her lover, "than with one in whose honour she could not place the utmost reliance. Besides, who would be base enough to offer an insult to a young female who was bound on an errand of mercy and kindness?"

"Very true," answered Henri, shrugging his shoulders; "I forgot how useless it would be for me to convince you that she had done anything imprudent. But you'll pardon me, Jeannot, for throwing out such a hint, for, of course, I could have had no intention to wound your feelings by throwing the slightest blame upon a person to whom you are so strongly attached."

"It matters very little to me whether you did intend it or not," replied the young man; "for in this case no mischief could possibly have been done—because neither you nor anybody else could convince me that Jeannette would commit an act that any generous-minded person would say was unworthy of her."

"Bravo!" exclaimed Jacques Denon, slapping him on the back; "I like to hear people stick up for each other, because there's so many folks in the world that delight in doing all the mischief they can. As for Henri and myself, we, of course, can only have the kindest feeling towards the girl, and admire her spirit in coming all this distance to preserve you from the chance of being shot for disobedience to military regulations."

"By the bye," interposed Henri, "how did she contrive to find interest enough to get you off so easily?"

"Only by going at once to the highest source, instead of trusting to the promises of underlings in office."

"What did she consider to be the highest source?"

"The emperor!"

"You don't mean to say that she had courage enough to thrust herself into the presence of Napoleon?"

"But I do mean to say so," answered Jeannot, "and my gratitude will be for ever due to him for the kindness with which he treated one of the humblest of his subjects. He listened to her artless story with attention, and, as there seemed to be little doubt in his mind that I had been made the tool of artful villains, he immediately pardoned my offence, and ordered me to be discharged out of custody."

"What made him suppose you had fallen into bad hands?" demanded Jacques Denon, eagerly.

"I believe Jeannette hinted as much to him."

"That was a bold assertion of her's, at any rate," exclaimed Jacques, "for I suppose, if the question had been asked, she would not have been able to name any particular individuals?"

"About that I am not quite certain," answered Jeannot, "for I am not aware whether she knows who the parties are, and she is too noble-minded to bring disgrace, and perhaps ruin, upon persons unless she were quite certain of their guilt."

"Ah, I see plainly enough how this is," observed Henri Duport, with as much composure as he could assume. "She was in want of a good excuse to make to the emperor, and so, to win his favour, she, without any real cause for the assertion, told him that you had been made an innocent dupe of by others."

"Jeannette," replied the young conscript, indignantly, "would not have stooped to make such an assertion, unless, in her own mind, she had been perfectly convinced of its truth."

" Has she ever mentioned to you the names of the persons she suspects of being your enemies ?"

" She has."

" And do you believe them guilty of the treachery ?"

" I do not," he replied.

"Then, of course, you took the trouble to convince her of the mistake ?"

" Certainly I did."

" Was she satisfied?"

" Apparently so ; but I have fancied since that her opinion and mine did not exactly agree."

"Well," exclaimed Henri Duport, " it must be confessed that women are very hard of belief when once they have taken a notion into their heads. And yet why need we take any interest in this affair, for you know us to be your well-wishers, and that we would at any time rather help you out of a dilemma than into one."

" I should be sorry to believe otherwise," answered Jeannot, " for we are all comrades, serving in the same cause, and it would be hard indeed if we acted falsely, one with the other."

" That's well said, my boy," exclaimed Jacques, " so let's each fill a bumper of brandy and drink it off to our future good understanding."

Quite unsuspicious of any treachery on the part of his comrades, Jeannot raised the glass, and was about to put it to his lips, when Camille, who sat next to him, pulled him by the sleeve, as a hint to be cautious of what he was about. The thought then flashed upon the mind of the young conscript that he was in danger of again breaking one of the military regulations, by drinking to inebriety, and, contriving to throw the liquor under the table without being observed, he rose from his seat and expressed his intention to depart for his barracks.

" What ?" exclaimed Jacques Denon, "are you thinking of leaving us just when our hearts are warming towards each other ?"

" I must go instantly," replied Jeannot, " or I may forget my promise made to the emperor, that I would not again break any of the laws, that he has caused to be drawn up for the regulating of his army."

" Psha !" exclaimed Henri; " do you think Napoleon has nothing else to do but to make himself acquainted with every drop of liquor that his soldiers drink in the course of a day. No, no, when we are not engaged in active services, we have free permission to do as we like, as far as enjoyment goes—and it's well for him that he does so, for people are getting so tired of these heavy conscriptions, that, by and bye, he would not be able to get an army together if it were not for a little indulgence when our services are not required."

" For my part," interposed Jacques, " I see no reason why a soldier should be deprived of his enjoyments any more than other people. When required, we are obliged to fight at the risk of our lives, and it would be hard indeed if we were not allowed to indulge a little when it can be done without injury to anybody."

" As far as that goes, let every one enjoy his own opinion," exclaimed Jeannot, " but for myself, I have so lately got out of a dilemma, that I am determined not to get into another as long as I can help it. So, comrades, I wish you good night, for I am now going to return to our barracks, and they shall see that I go back as sober as I went out."

Upon this he left the place, followed by Camille, and the two conscripts made their way towards that part of the town where their barracks were situated. For some distance they walked in silence, but at length Jeannot, awakening from a reverie into which he had fallen, exclaimed to his companion—

"I don't know how I could have been so foolish, Camille, as not to have seen through it before, but I now begin to discover that those two men were trying to make me tipsy."

"To be sure they were," answered the other, "for I had my eye upon them all the time, and could see plainly enough what their design was. Aye, and if you had drank off that last glass of brandy, the effect of it would have been to make you an easy victim to any plan they might have formed against you."

"Come, come," laughed Jeannot, "that's going a little too far."

"What do you mean by going too far?"

"Why I mean, that though they might have enjoyed the joke of making me drunk, they could have no other object than a hearty laugh at my expense afterwards."

"It would have been no laughing matter though," returned Camille; "for if you had returned intoxicated to the barracks so soon after the pardon received from the emperor, you would have been locked up, and the case would have been reported to-morrow morning. Of course, Jeannot, I needn't tell you what would have been the consequence of such a breach of duty just when the army is about to march for a campaign, that Napoleon fancies will be one of the most brilliant that he has ever been engaged in."

"And what would my being drunk one night have had to do with that?"

"A very great deal more than you seem to think for," answered Camille, "for orders have been given to make examples of all that disobey our regulations, and the severest punishment is to be inflicted in every instance. This was known to the two men we have just left, and it's my opinion that they were trying to draw you into a snare that would have proved your ruin."

"Don't you think, Camille, you are judging them rather too severely?"

"Not more so than they deserve," he replied, "for I several times observed signs passing between them, and that put me upon my guard, or I was as likely to have fallen into the temptation as yourself. However, I made the discovery just in time, and it was lucky I did, for they would have persuaded you to swallow that last glass of liquor, and then there would have been but little chance of your leaving their company till their plan had succeeded."

"You think, then, they would have attempted to play tricks with me?"

"I'm sure of it."

"Well, hang me if I can believe that," exclaimed Jeannot, "we have always been pretty good friends, and for the life of me I can't see what good they could have got by it if they had made me as drunk as a lord."

"As for that matter," replied Camille, "you ought to know more about it than I do, because you are more interested in it. I know, however, that some men delight in doing all the mischief they can, and for aught I know, it may be the case in this instance."

"But men don't often do mischief unless they have some object in view," observed Jeannot.

"Whether these have any object in view or not, I can't say," replied the other, "but I think there can be no harm in acting cautiously towards those that are too forward in their professions of friendship."

"There you are right enough," answered Jeannot, "but in this instance I don't see any reason for supposing that any harm was intended. We all met together quite by chance, and sitting, as we did, at the same table, it is not much to be wondered at that, as fellow soldiers, we should join in companionship."

"But we may suspect them, though, when they tried to make us drink more than we were inclined for."

"Why, that was a mere act of kindness."

"You may give them credit for kindness if you like," answered Camille, "but for my own part, I shall still hold to the opinion that they had some rascally scheme against you."

"And yet I have never heard anybody speak against Jacques Denon, whilst for Henri Duport, I can put in a good word, because he and I happen to come from the same village."

"So I have heard," replied Camille; "and there is a report too that Henri is in love with the girl you are betrothed to."

"He was," answered the young conscript, "but I rather think he has cured himself of that, since he found there was no longer a chance of gaining her affections."

"Has it never struck you," asked his companion, "that people can sometimes conceal their thoughts and feelings when it is their interest to do so? There are hypocrites in the world that can deceive anybody, and I have a notion that Henri Duport is among the number."

"You seem to have taken a dislike to him for some reason or another, and I think it would hardly be fair for me to form an opinion of his character till I have been able to judge for myself. At any rate, he shall have a fair chance, and if I've reason to believe your notion of him to be a more correct one than my own, I'll confess my error and acknowledge myself to be more short-sighted than you are."

"And in the meantime you will give him an opportunity of carrying out the mischief I fancy he is plotting?"

"There you are wrong, Camille, for I will constantly keep my eye upon him, and shall therefore always be prepared in case there should be any foul play going on."

"Well, mind you don't forget yourself," exclaimed the other; "for if mischief is intended, it will fall upon you the moment he can seize upon an opportunity. And, above all things, keep a careful watch over his companion, for, bad as my opinion of Henry Duport may be, I have a still worse one of the other, who, I believe, is capable of any wickedness towards whoever he may take a dislike"

"That may be," returned Jeannot, "but how can he have taken a dislike to me, when we never saw each other till we were both marched to this town as conscripts?"

"Don't ask me how it can be," returned the other, "because I confess it would puzzle me to give an answer that would satisfy you. I have, however, taken a great deal of notice of him ever since we have been in barracks together, and the more I have seen of Jacques, the more convinced am I that he is thoroughly bad at heart."

"Oh, you are prejudiced against him, I see."

"Indeed I am not," answered Camille, "for much as I dislike the man, I would not set another against him, unless I saw good good reason for believing that mischief is brewing, which can only be prevented by caution. Keep your eye upon him as I have done, and in spite of his pretended civility, you will see he is quite as bad as I have said."

"Come, now," exclaimed Jeannot, "tell me why you have formed this notion of him, for, upon my life, I begin to think that all you have been saying is merely from prejudice against the man."

"We are too near the barracks now to enter into a long story," replied the other, "but the next time you and I meet together I'll explain one or two matters that I think will very much surprise you. One thing, however, I will tell you, Jeannot; I believe it was through him and Henri Duport that you and I got into that disgraceful squabble that had nearly been of such fatal consequence to us, and—— But hush!—not another word at present, for we are now among our comrades, and the rest of what I have to say must be told another time."

They had, in fact, entered the great gate that led into the quadrangle, and, making their way through the crowd of young conscripts, they each proceeded to their allotted quarters.

CHAPTER X.

THE NOTE OF PREPARATION.—JEANNETTE'S ANXIOUS WATCHING FOR HER LOVER.—ARRIVAL OF A FRIEND.—NEWS FROM HOME, AND REASONS FOR RETURNING THITHER WITHOUT DELAY.—PARTING OF THE LOVERS.— JEANNETTE LEAVES TOULON UNDER THE ESCORT OF THE NOTARY.

As soon as it was daylight on the following morning, the streets of Toulon presented more than usual bustle, and it soon became bruited abroad that at a late hour on the preceding evening orders had been issued by the emperor for the immediate marching of the conscripts, in order that they might join the grand army, which was then halting within a few leagues of the Prussian frontier. Of course, but little time was permitted for the parting of the young men from their friends; and, as may be imagined, no one waited with more anxious impatience to see her lover than did Jeannette, whose grief was with great difficulty subdued, so that he might not have any additional reason for cursing the hard fate that forced him from her. Madame Germaine, though she was not to be deceived by the apparent fortitude of her young friend, refrained from saying anything that might serve to disturb her assumed serenity, and throwing as much cheerfulness as possible into her manner, she spoke of the coming war as likely to prove the most glorious in which France had yet been engaged, and even ventured to prognosticate that many who were now about to join the army as raw conscripts, would return at the termination of hostilities with the most gratifying marks of the emperor's approval of their conduct. Jeannette listened to her, but was not to be deceived as to the chances that thousands of those who were about to go away, full of youthful hope and courage, were doomed never again to see the land of their birth.

"Alas! dear madam," she exclaimed, "I can foresee woe and wailing for many who have lost husbands, fathers, lovers, and brothers, in a strife that I have heard people say is uncalled for. For what has so much of the best blood of France been shed, if, at the end of all these years of war and carnage, we are still to see that the end of our misery is as far off as ever?"

"Truly, it is to be regretted that such scenes are of daily occurrence," answered the old lady; "but he whom we have chosen for our leader and ruler is resolved to make all foreign potentates bow before him, and if he continues to go on as he has done already, it will not be long before all Europe has submitted to him."

"And will France be the happier for it?"

"That, my child, is more than I can undertake to say, but Napoleon sees farther than I can pretend to do, and depend on it he would prefer peace to war, if he could only make himself sure of the throne to which he has fought his way. I know not much of these matters, Jeannette, from any consideration that I have been able to give them, but people say that there are nations combined against our emperor, and that their object is to overthrow him, and the wondrous fabric he has built up out of the ruins of the revolution."

"So people may say," answered Jeannette, "but in my own mind, I fancy all nations are so tired of war, that they would gladly hail peace as the greatest of blessings, if France would confine herself within the limits that formed her boundaries under the old monarchy of the Bourbons."

"And who, my child, have a right to dictate to the emperor the bounds that he will choose for his dominion?" asked Madame Germaine. "The empire has grown and flourished on the blood of hundreds of thousands of the bravest of the brave, and, after so many have perished, would it not be a shame and a reproach to Napoleon, that he should acknowledge so many had fallen to no purpose, except that of leading armies against armies, and destroying the lives of those who might have been more profitably employed in the service of their country. But it is not for us to judge of such matters as these, for they are beyond the scope of our understanding, and women have nothing to do with those who govern us, or with the wars which they may consider it necessary to wage with foreign countries."

"But they may complain," answered Jeannette, "when they see those they love torn away from them to satisfy the ambition of one man."

"If it is of the emperor you speak," exclaimed the old lady, "I must remind you that you owe him a debt of gratitude for the kindness with which he listened to your appeal for mercy."

"Very true, madame," she replied, "I do indeed owe him a heavy debt of gratitude, and never shall I forget the favour he granted when Jeannot had fallen into the snare that had been laid for him by his enemies. He saved him from disgrace when no one but himself could have done so, yet I cannot feel the less acutely the cruelty of forcing people from their homes and families, to take part in wars which do not in the least concern them."

"I am quite of your way of thinking there," replied Madame Germaine, "but after all, our opinions will weigh nothing against that of the one great man who rules and decides the destinies of France. You regret the loss of Jeannot, who is about to be marched to a distant country, but have I not deep cause for complaint, seeing that my son has also been called upon to serve his country, though a widowed mother had to deplore his absence?"

"How long has Louis been in the army?"

"Nearly five years."

"And was he forced to go as a conscript?"

"No," answered the old lady, "the laws of conscription were not then thought of, for all men were, before that time, eager to enter the army, which was at once the astonishment and terror of the world. Since then, however, so many thousands have lost their lives in battle, that it was found necesary to force the unwilling to become soldiers, in order that our army might still be able to meet the enemy in the field. Such was the commencement of the conscription; and there are many people who have ventured to prophecy that it will prove the downfall of France, through the discontent it has raised, and the shedding of so much of the blood of our youthful countrymen. Others, however, believe that the Prussian campaign will be the last in which Napoleon will wish to engage, and if so, we may, before long, see the establishment of that peace which all are so eager for."

"Most earnestly do I pray it may be so," exclaimed Jeannette; and then she added in a more sorrowful tone, "but why indulge in such a hope, when it is but too likely that Jeannot will not survive the war which you say may be the last?"

"Do you give up already?"

"It has been my dread ever since the moment it was made known to me that he had been drawn as a conscript," answered Jeannette. "Since then it has been the almost constant subject of my dreams, and no other thought have I than that he will be one of those who are destined to perish in the country they are about to invade."

"And has it never struck you that he may escape the dangers you anticipate, and return home with the justly earned honours of his gallantry? You shake your head, Jeannette, as if such a thing were utterly impossible, and yet I have heard of hundreds of instances in which men, with no greater influence than your lover possesses, having been raised to the command of a battalion."

"I have heard of such instances myself," answered our heroine, "but I had much rather that Jeannot had been suffered to remain in his own humble home, than that he should be honoured with the baton of a field marshal."

"Such may be a woman's notion," exclaimed Madame Germaine, "and it is a very natural one for our sex to indulge in. But men have far different

JEANNOT INADVERTENTLY ASSOCIATES WITH HIS ENEMIES.

feelings, and I question whether Jeannot would not prefer the chance of rising to high military rank, to that of being a mere plodding farmer all his life."

Our heroine would have unhesitatingly denied this, but footsteps were just at that moment heard in the passage—a low tap succeeded, and the door then opening discovered the venerable figure of Monsieur Narbonne, the notary. Jeannette turned deadly pale at this most unexpected apparition of a person who she thought was many leagues distant, for her first thought was of her mother, who she feared was either ill or in some imminent danger. Recovering somewhat, her first impulse was to rush into the arms of the good old man, and to implore him in earnest accents to inform her why he had followed her to so great a distance from home.

"First and foremost," answered Monsieur Narbonne, "let me ease your alarm by assuring you that I came on no errand that will occasion you so much grief as I see you anticipate."

"But my mother——"

"Is well, as far as health goes, though I am sorry to add that your absence has filled her with grief and melancholy. She fancies that all sorts of evils have befallen you; and seeing that even your letters have failed to convince her of your being in good health, I undertook a journey here either to induce you to return home with me, or at least to send her a promise that your absence from home shall not be delayed much longer."

"It shall not be delayed longer than this evening," she replied, "for Jeannot is to depart with the troops at mid-day, and when he has gone, I have no other motive for remaining at Toulon."

"Poor lad!" exclaimed Monsieur Narbonne; "he has been in trouble lately, has he not ?"

"He has," replied Jeannette; "but how did you hear of it ?"

"From his father, Monsieur Lamont."

"Indeed! I knew not that he had been informed of it."

"Nor can I tell you the source from whence he received the information," replied the notary. "Certain, however, it is, that the letter which brought the news was not from Jeannot himself, for it was anonymous, and evidently written in a feigned hand."

"Then I can judge how it is," exclaimed Jeannette; "the letter was no doubt maliciously written by the same person who was the cause of getting him into trouble."

"Can you guess who that was ?"

"No one can do that at present," she replied; "even Jeannot himself is at a loss to imagine who the enemy is that has endeavoured to bring all this mischief upon him, for he was not aware of having given cause for the enmity of any one."

"Is there no person that his own suspicion glances at ?"

"None that he would like to accuse.".

"But this," exclaimed Monsieur Narbonne, "is no case in which a man can stand very particular, since the attempt which has been once made may be repeated with more effect another time. It is, therefore, the duty of Jeannot to discover who this disguised enemy is, and I, for one, am ready to assist him with my counsel and advice, if he should deem them useful to him."

"Then you suspect some one in particular ?"

"I do."

"May I ask who ?"

"You may," replied the notary, "though I should not feel inclined to open my mouth quite so freely to anybody else. Henri Duport is the person I suspect, and it shall go hard but I will endeavour to discover whether my notion is well founded or not."

"Monsieur Narbonne," exclaimed our heroine, "I have myself directed my suspicions that way; but, upon more mature deliberation, I cannot bring myself to believe that Henri Duport would be guilty of an act of such cruel treachery as that of betraying the man he has always called his friend."

"You forget, my dear girl," replied the old gentleman, "that he has since garded him as a rival."

"True," she replied; "but can you imagine that through a mere disappointment in love, he would be guilty of an act that, if discovered, must cover him with shame and dishonour ?"

" My dear Jeannette," exclaimed Monsieur Narbonne, " you are too young and inexperienced to know all the intricacies of the human heart, and the good or bad passions to which men are subject. I, however, happen to know that Henri feels your rejection of him as a sort of insult, and, believing as he unfortunately does, that Jeannot is the whole and sole cause of his disappointment, he is very likely to seek some mode by which to revenge himself for the disappointment he has encountered. Far be it, however, from me to accuse him of having been the person who instigated your betrothed to commit an act that might have proved of the most serious consequences ; but I think there is at least probability on my side, and I will not suffer this matter to rest till I have ascertained whether my notions are well founded."

" I know you have undertaken this from pure kindness towards Jeannot and myself," replied our heroine, " but indeed, Monsieur Narbonne, I can see no good that is likely to result from it."

" Why not ?"

" Because Henri Duport is to leave this country immediately, and no discovery that you might make would be of any avail so long as he remains absent."

" But it will be of this use, my dear," replied the notary, " if I should discover that Henri Duport was the author of the mischief that has been done, I can let your lover know of it, and thus put him upon his guard against the evil practices of a supposed friend."

" Jeannot does not look upon him as a friend."

" Very likely, but he does not yet know him for an enemy, and therein lies all the mischief that may occur. You see, therefore, how necessary it is to put him upon his guard, and I can see no harm in doing that, even if there should be no reason for my suspicion."

Scarcely had he finished uttering these words when Jeannot entered the room in search of his betrothed. His countenance betrayed no particular emotion, yet Jeannette felt that this was to be their parting interview, and as she clung round the neck of her lover, she gave way to the tears that no efforts of hers could suppress. The young conscript saw that all his fortitude was now necessary, and with forced composure, he said—

" Dearest Jeannette, this is what I dreaded more than anything, for I knew your affectionate heart would not be able to bear up against our separation, though heaven knows how unwilling I am to witness the sorrow of one who is more precious to me than aught else that the world contains."

" You have come, Jeannot, to tell me that this is to be our last meeting ?"

" Our last for the present only," he replied, " but console yourself with the reflection that we shall meet again at no distant period."

" In heaven," she sighed, " and not till then."

" Come, come, my love," exclaimed Jeannot, " these are not the thoughts you should indulge in, when I am going to leave you full of hopes, and dreaming only of earning a name that you shall afterwards be proud of. Perhaps you think only of the danger that I must run when engaged in the field of battle, but at the same time you must not forget that thousands and thousands escape unhurt, and why should I not have as good a chance as anybody else ?"

" Ah, Jeannot !" she replied, with forced cheerfulness, " you would fain convince me that there is no great danger, and I will not see you part from me full of grief for my too readily giving way to your own melancholy anticipations. I will endeavour to look forward for the best in all things, and should you indeed return in safety, you shall have no cause to reproach me with being unworthy the love you have bestowed upon me."

" My good children," interposed Monsieur Narbonne, " I am much gratified with the resignation you have exhibited in a situation that I must needs confess is a very trying one. Jeannot is imperatively called upon to lend his aid towards maintaining the glory of his native land ; to exhibit any unwillingness to obey that call would be looked upon as cowardice, and all, therefore, who regard his honour ought to submit with resignation to a fate which there is no possibility of avoiding.

" Besides," added Madame Germaine, " it is the duty of every Frenchman to obey the call of his country, whenever she may need his services. Jeannot has proved his willingness to perform his duty without a murmur, and I am glad to find that my young friend here has resolved to take leave of him with the firmness that becomes her."

" Did you ever imagine, then," asked Jeannot, " that she would yield to despair, whilst there was hope yet before her?"

How could I tell what to think of it," exclaimed the old lady, " when I knew her devotion to you, and the grief that has taken possession of her heart, ever since the moment when first she heard that your name was among the conscripts whose services would be required for the next campaign ?"

" Aye, aye, madame," returned Monsieur Narbonne, " she was terribly cut up about it at first, to be sure ; she looked the very picture of grief and wretchedness, and I dare say would have continued the same to the present time, but that she had the good sense to listen to the advice of myself and our good curè, and from that period she has been altogether a different girl. At any rate she has learnt the virtue of fortitude under affliction, and Jeannot will have the consolation, during his absence, of knowing that she is not a prey to grief, however much she may wish for his safe return."

" I will indeed conceal my grief," answered Jeannette, " but I should only deceive both myself and my friends if I said that I shall not be in a state of constant dread lest he should have met with the fate that has befallen so many of his gallant countrymen."

" To die in battle is too often the fortune of war," exclaimed the good notary, " but those who survive them, instead of giving way to their unavailing grief, should console themselves with the gratifying reflection, that those they mourn have sacrificed their lives for the honour and maintenance of their country and its laws."

" That, methinks, monsieur," sighed Jeannette, " is but poor consolation for those who have been deprived of those they love and venerate."

" I admit, the heart cannot be so governed that we can entirely control our feelings," replied Monsieur Narbonne, " but we may so far keep a guard over ourselves, that grief may be deprived of a great portion of its sting. With respect to Jeannot, as I said before, he has a bright career of glory spread out before him, and if he makes use of the opportunity, I have no doubt he will return home a much greater man than he left it. That, in my opinion, is the proper light to view the matter in, for it is time enough to give way: to melancholy feelings when it is quite certain that there is sufficient ground for it."

"Depend upon it, monsieur," exclaimed Jeannot, "my betrothed will not fail to profit by your wise exhortations, and I shall have the consolation during my absence of knowing that she is left under the care of such excellent protection."

" By the bye," cried the notary, as if suddenly recollecting himself, " do you happen to know to whom you were indebted for the trouble you lately got into, and which you escaped with so much difficulty ?"

" I have endeavoured to ascertain," replied our hero, " but as there was little chance of discovering the right persons, I have given up the task as hopeless, fearing that, in my anxiety to get at the truth, I might suspect an innocent person."

" Have you ever inquired amongst your comrades ?"

" I did at first," he replied, " but as the matter has ended in a manner so satisfactory, I have since ceased to take any further trouble about it."

" Yet I think the villain, whoever he may be, deserves some sort of punishment for his baseness."

" Let conscience be his punishment then," exclaimed the conscript, " for if he has any feelings of shame and remorse, he will, to the end of his days, regret the conduct he has thought proper to pursue against me."

"That," observed Monsieur Narbonne, "is all very well as far as the past goes, but do you not think some more successful attempt may be made by the same person some other time?"

"Probably so, monsieur," answered Jeannot, "and yet I should think, after so signal a failure, the attempt is scarcely likely to be repeated. But hark!" he added, "the trumpet is sounding the signal for all the absent to assemble at the barracks, and those who do not obey it will be treated as deserters."

He then drew Jeannette aside, and besought her to act with firmness under the affliction which had befallen them, and uttered promises that appeared to be needless, never to prove unfaithful to the vows which he had so often pledged to her. Jeannette for a moment or two faltered in her resolution, but quickly recovering herself, she at once assumed an attitude of firmness and resolution greater than might have been expected. Still her lover continued to pour into her ears those words of hope and promise that he thought would best serve to sustain her spirits, till at length the trumpet sound was again heard, and then, pressing his lips to hers, he consigned her to the arms of Madame Germaine, and left the room without venturing another look at his betrothed. For a few moments afterwards Jeannette stood as if suddenly bereft of life, but being at length recalled to recollection by her friends, she burst into a flood of tears, which soon had the effect of relieving her overcharged heart.

"I feel better—much better now," she replied, in answer to the earnest entreaties of Madame Germaine, "and since the worst is past, I will endeavour to prove myself worthy of the love of him whom I may never see again in this world."

"You have acted nobly, my dear child, in conquering your feelings at such a trying moment as this," exclaimed Monsieur Narbonne. "Your situation was, I must admit, a most painful one, and it was your duty to endure it, and I am delighted to have it in my power to commend you for your heroism. We will now, if agreeable to yourself, leave this town, which must often bring to your mind circumstances that will be better forgotten, and return without delay to the home where you are so anxiously expected."

"I am ready to accompany you whenever you please, monsieur," she replied, "for in truth, notwithstanding the kindness of Madame Germaine, I shall be glad to depart from a scene that must ever remind me of the greatest sorrow that has yet occurred to me in my brief career of life."

"We will go then immediately," exclaimed Monsieur Narbonne, on looking at his watch, "for I happen to know that the diligence from this place, which passes through our village, will start from an hotel in the next street in the course of an hour."

"Nay, monsieur," she replied, "I walked nearly the whole distance from home to Toulon, and it is my intention to return in the same way, for in truth my means are but slender, and I would not encroach upon those of my mother, when the journey has been undertaken merely for the gratification of my own whim."

"And for the gratification of my whim," exclaimed the worthy notary, "you shall return home at my expense. Nay, it would be in vain to remonstrate, for my mind is quite made up to have my own way in this particular instance, and I am sure you will not refuse to comply with this one favour."

"Aye, my dear child," interposed Madame Germaine, "Heaven has raised up a friend for you in the hour when one was most needed, and it would be wrong to reject an offer that has been made in all kindness. Besides, the journey is a long one, and it would be imprudent to go alone, when you may have a protector whose age and character place his motives beyond all suspicion."

"Monsieur Narbonne is indeed a friend whom I have every reason to regard," answered our heroine, "and I will not therefore refuse the offer of his company back to the house of my mother."

"And when we arrive there," exclaimed the notary, "I will find means to satisfy Madame Corville that it is no less my duty than my inclination to repay the expenses of your journey out of my own pocket; at any rate, you must give me the credit of possessing a heart, my dear Jeannette, and it would be but an indifferent one if I could suffer you to return home with the same difficulties that you had to encounter in coming here."

"The purpose that brought me to Toulon," answered Jeannette, "was alone sufficient to have supported me through far greater hardships than those it was my lot to endure. I thought only of my betrothed lover, and to rescue him from peril I would have willingly sacrificed my life."

"You are a brave, good girl," exclaimed the old gentleman, "and deserve not the sorrow and disappointment that have so unexpectedly come in our way. However, we will hope that peace may soon allow of the return of your lover, and then, at least, you may may look forward to the reward you so richly merit."

"Ah! Monsieur Narbonne," she replied, "it is kind of you to show me the brighter side of the picture, but I am afraid even you will not easily succeed in convincing me that there are not many dangers to be encountered before we can have the peace you speak of."

"Do you then make up your mind that Jeannot will lose his life before the war terminates ?"

"I am afraid he will," she replied, "for he is brave almost to rashness, and the chances are therefore fearfully against him, whatever my friends may say to convince me to the contrary."

"Then you refuse all consolation ?"

"Nay," she exclaimed, "do not think me ungrateful, for Heaven knows how deeply I feel the kindness of those who have generously come forward to rescue me from the despair into which I am thrown, by being torn from him who possesses my love. It is impossible, however, to shut my eyes against the perils he will have to encounter; and, knowing as I do, how many hundreds —nay, thousands—fall in every battle that is fought, I feel a melancholy foreboding that Jeannot will be added to the number of those who are doomed to sacrifice their lives in the fierce war that is now about to take place."

"Cannot you, on the other hand, anticipate the chance of his returning home loaded with honour and renown ?" asked Madame Germaine.

"Honour and renown are scarcely worth contending for when they are to be obtained only by running into danger," answered Jeannette.

"Yet how many are there who think otherwise."

"Such persons are deluded by shadows," answered our heroine, "and there are very few of them, I believe, who do not in the end confess that war is an evil which ought to be abolished, now that the world has grown wiser by experience. It is the plaything of ambitious monarchs, which is dearly paid for, by those who are obliged to leave home, country, and friends, to fight in a cause in which they can feel no interest."

"There is some truth in what you say, my dear," answered Monsieur Narbonne, "but the wars in which we have been so many years engaged were forced upon us by the sternest necessity, for other nations rose up against us, and France must have sunk for ever had she not boldly asserted her right to be ruled by whatever government she pleased. For my own part, I am as much opposed to war as you are, and yet, in this instance, I see so many reasons for drawing the sword, that I am content to abide the result, whatever it may be."

"But when will this fearful contention be over ?"

"That is more than anybody can just now foresee," replied Monsieur Narbonne; "but, notwithstanding the marvellous success which has crowned the efforts of our emperor, I believe he would be glad to seize the first opportunity that offers to procure for his people the blessings of peace."

"Could he not have done so before now?"

"I think not," answered the notary, "for all Europe regards him as being an intruder on the throne of France, and there is a determination abroad to hurl him from the high station he has earned for himself, let the sacrifice of blood and treasure be as great as it may. This is well known to our emperor, and he has resolved to humble those who have vainly combined together for his destruction. And with such mighty armies as he has at his disposal, we may venture to hope that the ensuing campaign will procure for us, at no very distant period, the blessings of peace we are all so anxious for."

"Aye, Monsieur Narbonne," sighed our heroine, "but how many thousands of lives must be sacrificed before that end can be obtained."

"That is indeed a melancholy reflection, my dear child," exclaimed the old gentleman; "but as there is no help for it, we can only resign ourselves to the sad alternative of war. Those who fall will do so in a good cause, and their names will be handed down to posterity as patriots and worthy sons of the country they fight for."

"And those they leave behind them ——"

"Will lament the fall of those they loved, though at the same time there will be some little consolation of knowing that those they weep for were sacrificed in the performance of a sacred duty."

"A poor consolation, Monsieur Narbonne," she sighed, "for losing those whom we most fondly loved!"

"I grant you the blow is a severe one," answered the notary, "but those who are so bereft, must remember that those they grieve for have nobly assisted in saving France from the horrors of foreign invasion. Napoleon has seen the necessity of putting himself upon the offensive, for had he exhibited any want of firmness and determination, we should long ere now have bowed our necks before those who have dared to raise up their armies against us. Under these circumstances, Jeannette, I think we must do the emperor the justice to say that he has acted with becoming vigour for the advantage of the mighty nation which he has been called upon to govern."

"Was there no way, then," she asked, "to settle these differences except by having recourse to the sword?"

"That is a matter which I do not profess to understand much about," answered Monsieur Narbonne, "but from all that I have been able to gather from other people, it seems that we were driven to extremes by the intrigues of foreign powers to restore the old Bourbon family to the throne of France. That, as we had an undoubted right to do, we have resisted, and if we would have a permanent peace, we must not scruple to show our enemies that there is stern resolution in this country to govern ourselves after our own fashion. Submit then, my dear girl, to the necessity which has separated you from your lover, and perhaps, much sooner than you expect, he will be able to return home and fulfil the vow he made previous to his departure. So now prepare yourself for our immediate departure, for the diligence we are to travel by sets out on its journey within half an hour, and if we miss this one it will be three days before another leaves Toulon."

"Ah, monsieur!" exclaimed Madame Germaine, "must you then take her from me at so short a notice?"

"I have no choice left," answered the old gentleman, "for business of a very pressing nature requires my presence at home without delay. Indeed nothing would have induced me to come this journey, but the desire I felt to assuage the alarm felt my Madame Corville at the lengthened absence of her daughter. And now that Jeannot has taken leave of his betrothed, it will be better, for every reason, that we should quit a place which must call up so many painful remembrances."

"Monsieur Narbonne is right," exclaimed our heroine, as she attired herself for the long journey she was about to undergo. "I will leave this town without delay, for my mother yearns to fold me once more to her heart, and it would be cruel to keep her in suspense longer than may be needed. But though we are about to be severed from each other by a great distance, Madame Germaine, you may rely upon it that I shall never forget the kindness I have received from you during my short sojourn in Toulon."

"Then, to prove your gratitude, write to me frequently," answered Madame Germaine, "and in return I will send you word about your lover as often as news reaches this place of the progress of the armies in this new campaign. Here we shall always receive the earliest intelligence from the seat of war, and I hope before long it will be in my power to send you the cheering information of Jeannot's speedy return to those he loves. So now endeavour to forget your grief as soon as possible, for be assured nothing will prove so afflicting to your mother as to see you languishing in despair."

Jeannette promised to remember the advice of her friend, and having by this time got herself in readiness for the journey, she took leave of Madame Germaine with a thousand expressions of gratitude for the hospitality with which she had been received. At length, tearing herself away from the embraces of the kind-hearted old lady, she left the house, accompanied by Monsieur Narbonne, and proceeded direct to the hotel from whence the diligence was to start. Having taken their places, the vehicle shortly afterwards quitted the town, and it was not without a sigh of regret that our heroine looked back upon the city which contained him for whose sake she had undertaken so long a journey. The good notary, however, guessed the cause of her melancholy, and engaging her in conversation upon a variety of cheerful subjects, he succeeded, at length, in banishing from her mind all painful reflections, and even in restoring her in some degree to her usual elasticity of spirit.

CHAPTER XI.

JEANNETTE'S ARRIVAL AT HOME.—THE TWO COUSINS AND THEIR GOSSIPS.—
PIERRE LANGRAIS SEEMS RATHER INCLINED TO MAKE PEOPLE UNCOMFORT-
ABLE.—MADAME CORVILLE INTERPOSES, AND THE INTRUDER IS DISMISSED
AT A SHORT NOTICE.—THE SCHEMES PROVE TO BE TOO TRANSPARENT NOT
TO BE SEEN THROUGH.

IN due time, but after a long and wearisome journey, our travellers arrived at the place of destination, when Jeannette, taking leave of the notary, proceeded without delay to the cottage of her mother, who she found engaged with her cousin Suzette. It is unnecessary to describe a meeting which may be so easily imagined, further than to say that her welcome home was cordial in the extreme. After the first greetings and enquiries were concluded, Madame Corville left the room to make some necessary preparations, and Suzette, whose curiosity was not yet half satisfied, asked a variety of questions respecting the occurrences of her journey, and the result of the extraordinary efforts that had been made to save Jeannot from the consequences that had threatened to follow the imprudence he had been guilty of. Having been satisfied upon these points, she next directed her enquiries to numerous other matters connected with Jeannot, and the dangers to which he was about to be exposed.

"At present," answered Jeannette, "I know very little more than you are already acquainted with. In a few days, however, I expect to receive a letter, and we shall then learn whether there is any prospect of this war being brought to a speedy termination."

"Ah, my dear cousin," exclaimed Suzette, "if once they begin fighting, I'm afraid there will be very little chance of the war being brought to an end till we have heard of more dreadful scenes than even those which have already deprived France of so many of her bravest sons. The emperor, indeed, seems to have an appetite for war that nothing will ever satiate till he has either conquered all his foes, or himself fallen before the mighty powers that are combining to procure his overthrow and ruin."

THE FAREWELL INTERVIEW OF JEANNOT AND JEANNETTE.

"**And do you think,**" asked our heroine, "that Napoleon will ever be obliged to yield to an enemy?"

"I am not able to give an opinion of my own upon such a subject as that," answered her cousin, "but from what I hear from people who may be supposed to understand the matter, it seems there is a firm determination among foreign powers to put a stop to the conquests that we have been making in all directions."

"That such an attempt may be made I think is very likely," exclaimed Jeannette, "but it must be remembered that our emperor is not to be so easily disposed of as his enemies may imagine. He is secure in the love of his brave soldiers, and so long as that is the case there will be little chance of his losing an inch of the ground he has gained."

"I love my country too well to hope he ever will," answered Suzette, "but at the same time I cannot but believe that he is going the very way of all others to make his people heartily tired of his continual sacrifice of human life. Why should we not have peace after these long years of bloodshed and destruction?"

"If the people are tired of such scenes, why have they not remonstrated before now?" asked our heroine.

"But these wars cannot last for ever," exclaimed Madame Corville, "and instead of thinking of the past and present, we ought to look forward to the time when peace will bring back all the blessings that we so much desire. Depend upon it, France will yet be happy, for Napoleon loves the land of his adoption, and if he has so far carried his aggression against other nations, it is that he desires to raise this one far above all the other nations of the earth."

"That may be all very true, aunt," replied Suzette, "but great as has been his good fortune hitherto, mind, change may take place some day or other, and then he will lose his battles as fast as he has hitherto won them. You must observe, however, that this is not my opinion, but what I have heard other people say, who know much better than I can be supposed to do."

"They are no friends of the emperor who say so."

"I don't know how that may be," answered Suzette, "but at all events they are friends of their country, and wish to see her enjoy the blessings of peace, instead of seeing the best blood of her sons shed to satisfy the ambition of one man."

"Hush!" exclaimed Madame Corville, "know you not how dangerous it is to give expression to such thoughts?"

"Oh, yes, I am quite aware of that," replied her niece; "but surely one may give expression to one's own thoughts, when there's nobody by that we need be afraid of."

"Don't be too sure of that, ma'amselle," exclaimed a voice close by, and on looking round they perceived, to their dismay, that Pierre Langrais, the veteran soldier, was standing close behind them. He perceived their alarm, and exclaimed laughingly—

"Pray don't be afraid of me, ladies, for, though I did happen to overhear a few words that it would not be well to repeat, I, as an old soldier, have too much honour to betray things that were uttered in confidence, and without any harm being intended."

"I should like to know what business you have to be creeping and crawling into people's houses, as if you were acting the dishonest part of a spy?" cried Suzette, pettishly.

"Hear reason, young lady," returned Pierre, "and you'll not accuse me of acting dishonourably, when it can be proved that I had no such intention. Your aunt's door happened to be standing open, and I came in without the ceremony of knocking."

"Perhaps you have something to say that you don't want to mention before other people?"

"Oh dear, no," he replied; "I happened to hear just now that Ma'amselle Jeannette had returned home, and was anxious to learn how she had succeeded in that unfortunate affair of her lover's."

"To the utmost of my hopes," answered our heroine.

"Humph!—then he has had the good fortune to escape without the punishment that was expected."

"The truth is," interposed Madame Corville, "he never would have got into the dilemma but for the villany that was practised against him by evil-minded men, and it would have been hard indeed to have let all the consequences fall upon his shoulders."

"Is it possible he can have enemies?" exclaimed Pierre.

"There can be no doubt of it," returned Suzette, "and I should have thought you, of all other people, ought to have known that attempts have been made to get him into disgrace."

"How should I have known it?"

"Because you left Toulon since Jeannette reached there, and you even brought the news of the first disgrace he fell into, when he was seen by the emperor in a state of intoxication. Everybody knew then that the young man had been led away by persons that had a spite against him, and you must have heard it as well as the rest."

"Upon my word," exclaimed Pierre Langrais, with pretended surprise, "one would think, by the way you talk, that I have had a hand in the conspiracy you are speaking of. Instead of that, the young man and I were upon very good terms with each other, and for that matter I believe he had not an enemy in the whole place."

"Then, of course," returned Jeannette, "you must suppose that the fault was entirely Jeannot's."

"Why, the fact is," replied the other, "he is a very young man, and it is not very much to be wondered at, if he has fallen into some of the errors that even older persons are liable to. But he has now had sufficient warning, and he must take heed of his future conduct, for if he should be caught tripping again, it's not you or anybody else that could save him from punishment."

"Oh, I am sure he will not," exclaimed Jeannette, earnestly.

"Say, rather, that you hope he will not," exclaimed the other, "for the army is a bad school for young men, and your lover seems, from what has passed, to have no more fortitude than other people."

"I'll be bound to say," exclaimed Suzette, "that he will be steady enough, if evil-minded people will only let him alone. Besides, I don't know how it is, Monsieur Langrais, but you always seem to take a malicious pleasure in making people believe all sorts of strange things about poor Jeannot."

"Do you think I bear any animosity towards him?"

"It seems very like it," returned the girl, "for it is not very long since you tried to make us believe that he was not faithful to his first love, and yet, as Jeannette knows, there was not the slightest foundation for such a charge."

"I merely said as I had heard."

"Perhaps so; but what you heard turns out not to be true."

"So much the better; I'm very glad of it."

"Upon my word, Monsieur Langrais," exclaimed the elder lady, "I can hardly believe you are glad to hear it, because you seemed to relate the mischievous reports with so much satisfaction. I myself doubted them at the time, and further enquiries have proved that Jeannot was quite innocent of the charge."

"He may be," answered the soldier, "but I couldn't help hearing what people had to say, and, as a matter of course, I mentioned it here, thinking that it ought not to be concealed from folks who were as deeply interested in the matter as you and Jeannette. However, it seems I have acted very foolishly, and all the thanks I receive for my pains is to be told that I have only mentioned the affair for the sake of making mischief."

"And I believe Madame Corville is in the right," exclaimed Suzette, "for you seem to owe the young man a grudge, and are determined to have your revenge."

"Psha! what grudge can I owe to a person that never gave me an offence in his life?"

"I believe he never injured anybody," answered Jeannette, "but for all that we have seen that he has enemies somewhere, who are bent upon his destruction."

"If that's the case," said Pierre Langrais, "how is it that you have not tried to discover who they are?"

"Do not imagine that I have failed in my duty so far as to neglect making inquiries upon that subject," answered our heroine; "but how could I hope to succeed, when those who have been acting this treacherous part have taken good care that their villany should not be traced to its proper source?"

"Yet you fancy I have had something to do with it, and I am to be looked upon as one of his enemies!"

"The truth is," exclaimed Madame Corville, "we have sufficient ground for saying that Jeannot has been made the victim of designing men, and it is only right that we should exert ourselves to prevent any further mischief that may be intended. You have professed friendship towards him, Monsieur Langrais, and if you are really sincere in that declaration you will not be offended at our suspicions, because it is in your own power to prove that they are false."

"I shall leave that for time to show," he replied, "so you had better watch me closely, and judge for yourselves by my conduct whether I have deserved these vile suspicions. As for Jeannot, I have had nothing to do with any follies he may have committed, but I can repeat what I have said before: that he is rather fickle in love matters, and by and by you may hear news to confirm what I have said."

"Can you relate a single instance of his fickleness?" demanded our heroine, anxiously.

"Perhaps I might if I chose to do so."

"Then why do you not?"

"Because I have just had proof enough that my word is not to be taken, and I am not going to subject myself again to the chance of being called a liar and a mischief-maker."

"I see well enough how it is, Pierre," exclaimed the old lady, "you are one of those busy-bodies who deal in hints and inuendoes, but who never dare speak out boldly what they mean. Nothing is more easy than to say that Jeannot will prove false to his love—nor is such an assertion easy to be contradicted—but people are not to be deceived by mere words when proof is absolutely necessary, before you can venture to condemn the person accused."

"The truth is," he replied, "Jeannot is so great a favourite here, that no one can say a word against him without giving offence."

"But he would not have been a favourite if his conduct had not made him so," exclaimed Suzette. "His character has always stood high with every one, and if that's not a proof of his character being a good one, I don't know what is."

"He may have acted the hypocrite to serve his own purposes."

"Then he must have been a hypocrite all his life," exclaimed our heroine, warmly, "for he was born in this neighbourhood, and would have continued to remain in it all the rest of his days, if it had not been for this cruel conscription that has forced him to leave his farm, merely that he may be another victim to the mad ambition that has destroyed so large a portion of our population."

"Remember," said Pierre Langrais, "you are speaking of Napoleon, the man who has twice befriended your lover, but who may not be quite so merciful the next time an offence has been committed."

"Are we to understand," demanded Madame Corville, "that you would be mean enough to cause these words of my daughter to be conveyed to the ears of those who might make use of them against her lover?"

"Not I," he replied; "what is it to me, that I should make myself busy with matters that don't concern me?"

"Would it be the first time you have ever done such a thing?" demanded Suzette, ironically.

"What do you mean by that question, ma'amselle?"

" Is it necessary to explain myself upon a matter that must be so self-evident ?" she asked. " Or, if your comprehension is really so dull, I will plainly ask whether you never in your life interfered in matters that concerned you not, further than that you might perhaps enjoy a little mischief ?"

" Why do you ask me that question ?"

" Only that I might hear whether you could conscientiously deny having been guilty of having done so."

" Well, then, I do deny it."

" How came it then," asked Madame Corville, " that you were the first to come here to tell us of the trouble poor Jeannot had got into."

" Upon my life, there are so many of you to answer at once, that I scarcely know what I'm saying," exclaimed Pierre Langrais. " However, if you wish for a reply to the last one, I must tell you that I thought it only an act of duty to inform you of what had taken place, knowing that Jeannot required the assistance of his friends, and feeling very certain that he would be ashamed to send them word of the disgrace into which he had fallen."

" He had nothing to be ashamed of," exclaimed Jeannette, " and, but for your interference, we should have heard from him by the next post. But luckily matters have taken a favourable turn, and those who were looking anxiously for his ruin, are doomed to see their schemes utterly overthrown."

" So much the better," returned Pierre, with all the composure he could maintain, " I, for one, am heartily gl d for the poor fellow's escape, for there's nobody that respects him more than I do, except for that one fault of his of falling in love with so many girls at a time."

" How many times," exclaimed Jeannette, " are you going to utter that assertion, which you know to be false ?"

" I have uttered it," he replied, " with the same unblushing countenance, " because I know it to be true. Nay, had you asked the question while at Toulon, you would have heard it confirmed."

" I would have asked it had I been so inclined," she replied, " but knowing the utter falsehood of the charge, I should have been ashamed to expose my own want of confidence in one whom I know has never proved false to the vow he uttered ere we parted."

" That's saying a great deal for him," exclaimed Pierre Langrais ; " but even admitting that he has so far been faithful to his pledge, does it follow that time will work no changes in him ? Will he not be thrown into the society of pretty women during the course of this campaign, and can it surprise anybody if he should——"

" I'll tell you what it is, Pierre," interrupted Madame Corville, " this paltry conduct of yours is not to be borne, nor will I suffer my daughter to be annoyed by any more of these inuendoes, that I know are only thrown out for purposes of your own."

" Purposes of my own," retorted the other, " and pray what good can I possibly derive from putting her upon her guard, when I see how cruelly she is likely to be deceived. But it's always the case when a person tries to do a good natured action—his motives are suspected, let them be as good as they may, and he loses the favourable opinion of the very people that he is most trying to serve."

" Between ourselves, Monsieur Langrais," exclaimed Suzette, " I rather think the less you say about this matter the better it will be for yourself. The truth is, we happen to know pretty well that you are doing all this only to make mischief, and if you talk to us for a month to come, you will not be a bit more forward than you are at this moment."

" In short," added Madame Corville, " we are sc thoroughly tired of hearing you speak upon the subject, that you will oblige us by not wasting any more time over it. In short, glad as I am to see all persons who favour me with a call, I trust we shall not receive another visit from you, till this unfortunate gossiping propensity of yours is forgotten."

" Oh, very well, madame," he replied sharply, " if my company is unpleasant to you, it will be very easy to remove the annoyance. When I came here I thought my intentions would be treated with gratitude, but since it seems to be quite the reverse, I shall leave you to form your own conclusions from what I have said."

The mischief-maker then bustled away in high dudgeon, and not a little mortified at the reception he had met with from those whom he thought were so easily to be deceived by any artful tale that he might think proper to relate to them.

" Did anybody ever hear or see such a monster of mischief," exclaimed Suzette, as soon as he was gone. " Why, he would set the whole world by the ears if people would only be foolish enough to heed his idle tales, and I fancy nothing would please him so much as to carry misery and dismay wherever he goes."

" I have always heard that sort of character given of him," said Madame Corville, " but never till now did I believe that he took half so much pleasure in trying to make people miserable. There is one good, however, that we must expect from this last visit of his, he has made the discovery that we are not likely to be imposed upon, and it is therefore to be hoped that he will not make another attempt."

" And better than all," added Jeannette, " is the mortification and chagrin that he must have felt when he saw that all his trouble and ingenuity had been thrown away upon us. So far the triumph has been on our side; but on the other hand, we have reason to believe that he is vindictive and revengeful, and I am afraid whether he may not enter with others into some deeply-laid plot against poor Jeannot."

" Then all you have to do," observed her cousin, " is to send word to Jeannot, in your next letter, that he must guard himself against all temptations that may be thrown in his way. You can, at the same time, inform him of what has taken place to-day, and it will set him to look about him a bit, which in the end may prove useful, as I dare say he will soon find out who the persons are that have been trying to do him a mischief, and what can be their motive for injuring one who never tried to do harm to another."

" It will be well for him to try what he can do in that way," observed her mother; " but for my own part, I don't think he will be very likely to succeed, because those who have been engaged in the plot will, no doubt, take care to prevent any disclosures from taking place. That Pierre Langrais has no little share in it, I think there is every reason to believe; but he, of course will, take care not to let out any part of the secret so long as he can help it; and therefore, I think, under all the circumstances, we had better not quite fall out with him till we can discover whether there is any chance of prevailing upon him to confess why poor Jeannot should have been made the victim of conspiracy."

" Can you have patience to see him again ?" asked Suzette.

" Where there is a purpose in view, I can," answered the old lady, " but it must be confessed I shall scarcely be able to endure the sight of him now that we are aware of the villany he is capable of practising towards a person who has never injured him."

It was therefore agreed that no further notice should be taken of what had passed when next Pierre Langrais visited them, and the conversation was changed to Jeannette's recent visit to Toulon.

CHAPTER XII.

NEWS FROM THE SEAT OF WAR.—CONTINUED TRIUMPH OF THE FRENCH
ARMS, AND A FURTHER LEVY OF CONSCRIPTS DEMANDED.—GROWING DIS-
CONTENT OF THE POPULACE.—A MEETING TO DISCUSS THEIR GRIEVANCES.—
ARRIVAL OF THE MILITARY.—AN AFFRAY WHICH TERMINATES IN FAVOUR
OF THE PEOPLE.

A MONTH elapsed, and the most favourable reports began to arrive of the
success which had already attended the grand army, whenever the Prussians
ventured to throw impediments in the way of the progress of their enemies. No
very important battle had been fought, it is true, but many smart skirmishes
had taken place, which, though not of any very great importance of themselves,
served to show that the French were yet invincible, and that, unless foreign aid
was speedily granted, the kingdom of Prussia was doomed within a very short
time to become a mere province of the French empire. At first this intelligence
was received with enthusiastic joy by the whole population of France, but when,
soon afterwards, rumours began to be spread abroad that many thousands more
conscripts would be immediately required to make up the losses that were continually taking place, the people began to murmur, and many were even bold
enough to declare that they would refuse to serve in any case except in that of
an absolute invasion of their country. Every one, in short, began to see that the
nation must soon become enervated, if the lives of its bravest defenders were to
be sacrificed at the present rate; and much as the genius and military skill of
Napoleon had been lauded, even his staunchest admirers began to foresee that the
time was not far distant when he would find himself nearly deserted by those
upon whom his reliance was placed. So far Jeannot had escaped without even
the slightest wound, though he had been engaged in several skirmishes, and
reports added that he had acted with so much bravery as to bring upon
himself the well deserved commendatonis of his superior officers. This intelligence was most grateful to Jeannette, who, in spite of her fears for the safety of
her lover, could not but feel a pride in the realization of her hopes, that he would
prove worthy of the confidence she had ever reposed in him. Monsieur Narbonne
was always the first to convey to her any intelligence that he knew would prove
agreeable, for he made a point of possessing himself of every fact that he knew
would be most interesting, and was consequently a welcome visitor whenever he
made his appearance at the cottage of Madame Corville. Still, however, Jeannette
never ceased to regret the forced absence of her lover; for in her dreams, as well
as in her waking moments, she saw him surrounded with danger, and, gratifying
as it was to her that he had performed his duty gallantly, she still felt that the
next intelligence she received might be that his life had been sacrificed in a war
which most people declared to be an aggression against a foreign power, which
had not by any act provoked these hostilities. On the other hand, however,
Monsieur Narbonne endeavoured to impress upon her mind the duty of submission; and it was chiefly through his friendly counsel that she supported
herself under a trial which was almost too great for endurance. At
length came a peremptory order from Napoleon, that a fresh conscription
should be made, and this was accompanied by a command, that all those who
had been drilled to the use of arms, should be sent to him without delay, in
order that his army might be so strengthened as to crush the enemy in the
first important battle that was to be fought. A bulletin accompanied this,
assuring the nation that success had attended him in every step that he had
advanced towards the Prussian capital, and the brave conduct of his soldiers was
painted in such glowing colours, that many were led to believe a speedy termination of the war would arrive. But all were not to be so easily deceived by
the highsounding words which conveyed this news, for those who were liable
to fall under the act of conscription, were loud in their denunciations of the

ambition which led to such serious results, and it was openly declared by a great number, that not even the threat of death itself should force them to leave their business and their homes, unless there were more necessity for it than at present appeared to be the case. Meetings were then held among the work-people to form themselves into associations, and a general opposition to the will of the emperor began to manifest itself in almost every town and village in France. Not far from the cottage of Madame Corville was a low, obscure public house, called the Red Hand, in which frequent meetings of this kind were held. These gatherings, though intended to be secret, were well known to the authorities, who, however, contented themselves with keeping a watch upon the discontented, believing that they would soon be able to crush the rebellious movement at any time when it might appear to be necessary. Spies were constantly in attendance, and, as a matter of course, everything that passed was duly reported to those who had employed them. One Stephen Crapean was the host of the Red Hand, and it was chiefly from a desire to increase the custom of his almost deserted house, that he had made it a place of meeting for Bertrand, a young blacksmith, Potier, a carpenter, Vincent, a miller, and about a score of other persons, who had determined to resist a law which they thought pressed too hard against them. Here they assembled three or four times a week to discuss their grievances, and each time that they did so seemed to add to their resolution not to be compelled against their will to enter the army.

"It's all very well," said Bertrand, on one of these occasions, "for those who are idle, or have nothing to do, to leave their families and business for this shadow that they call military glory, but, for my own part, though no coward, I hope, and am determined not to leave my business, when I have a wife and young family to support. The *honour* of the thing may be all very well, but who will take care of those that are dear to me, if I lose my life in a war that's not called for?"

"That's just the opinion of every one of us," exclaimed Potier, "and if we only determine to make a bold stand, Napoleon will be forced to see that Frenchmen are tired of sending all their youngest and bravest men to meet what may be looked upon as almost certain death."

"Aye, aye, let every man stick to his home as he ought to do," cried Stephen Crapean, "and the labour of his hands will be of more benefit to France, than shedding his blood in useless quarrels that none of us feel any interest in. Let the emperor once see that he has worn out our patience, and we shall soon have peace, which, I take it, will prove much better for us than war."

"True," replied Bertrand, "the thing may be as easily done as possible if we only set the right way about it. But there must be no slinking or skulking now that we have once begun, for Napoleon will be in a desperate rage when he sees that people have boldness enough to oppose him, and if we are divided among ourselves he'll gain an advantage over us that will end in our destruction."

"You are right enough there," exclaimed Vincent, "for we shall all be liable to be shot just the same as if we had deserted. Such is the blessed effect of military law, and yet the people have been tame enough to go away as conscripts, when a little spirit would have shown our emperor long ago that Frenchmen are not to be sent like beasts to the shambles."

"Hush!" interposed Potier, "we must mind what we're saying, for I've heard there are spies abroad, and——"

"Let me only know that one is present amongst us," exclaimed the black-smith, looking fiercely round him, "and I'll send my knife through his heart with as little remorse as if he were a mad dog."

"And what good would that do to any of us?" asked the host. "All we want is to keep ourselves out of danger, and not to be doing a parcel of foolish things that would get us into trouble. Let us form our plans to resist the law when they want to force any of us away, and I'll be bound we shall succeed in it the first time they attempt what they have so often done before, without the people having the courage to show that they don't like this system of turning men into soldiers whether they are willing or not to face death in battle."

"As for facing death," exclaimed Bertrand, "I've no great fear of doing that, if I could only see that it was necessary for protecting our country

SERGEANT CLAIRFAIT AND HIS MEN VISIT THE 'RED HAND' MEETING.

against an invading foe. But it's no such thing, for foreign countries would be quiet enough if our emperor would only let 'em alone. Then, look at the misery this system brings upon families who are obliged to part with their main support, and that too with a chance of never seeing them return home alive."

"Or if they do return alive," observed Potier, "the chances are that they have lost a leg or an arm, or have suffered in some other way that makes 'em mere wrecks for the remainder of their days. How many widows and orphans have reason to curse this tyranical system—not to speak of maidens who have lost their lovers, when, but for an unnecessary war, they might have passed a long life of happiness."

" Aye," exclaimed Vincent, " for that matter we have only to turn to the hard case of poor Jeannette, who was the pride of our village till her betrothed was forced away from her, as if he had no right to have a will of his own. And what is she now?—a heart-broken girl, though she has strength of mind enough to appear tolerably cheerful even in the midst of all her misfortunes."

" And for that she is indebted to Monsieur Narbonne," observed Bertrand, " for I often see the old gentleman going to visit her at her mother's cottage, and I'll be bound the kind-hearted old gentleman never goes there but for the purpose of talking good news about Jeannot, who they say, poor fellow ! is likely to turn out a brave fellow in spite of the compulsion that took him away from home."

" So much the worse if he's brave," exclaimed the host, " for it's then more likely that they will put him in the post of danger whenever there's any very difficult task to perform. However, if it's in his blood he can't help showing his gallantry, even if in the end it should be sure to cost him his life."

" If it does that," cried Vincent, " we must not expect Jeannette to survive him long, for she lives only in the hope that he may return safe from the wars, and marry her as he has so long promised to do."

" Why didn't he join us ?" asked Bertrand. " If he and all the rest of the conscripts had done that, the Emperor would have seen that—so long as it's not requisite—Frenchmen have no appetite for war. The whole country is going to rack and ruin for the want of peace, and if we don't have it before long, there will not be grown up people enough left to cultivate the land. These are the thoughts that have at length opened our eyes, so that I don't think it's likely Napoleon will ever be able to keep up his army as he has hitherto done."

" Psha !" exclaimed Stephen Crapean, " he is too reckless to remain at peace for any long time together, so it's of no use for us to expect that brighter times are coming, unless we first show him that there is sufficient spirit left in the country to rise up against him. We Frenchmen made him what he is, and we can unmake him any hour we please."

" Come, come, this is going a little too far," cried Vincent, " for though we may not like his system of keeping up the army, it don't follow that we are to talk treason against the man that has raised our country to the highest pitch of grandeur. Besides, these words might happen to be reported against us, and then you know what would be the consequence."

" And what sort of a fellow must you be to fear the consequences of speaking your mind with boldness and freedom ?" asked Bertrand.

" Why, answered the other," it so happens that boldness and freedom of speech are just the things that Napoleon dislikes more than anything else. Not but what I admire him as much as anybody can do, but this constant drain upon the people has grown to such a pitch that we must either try to put a stop to it, or see ourselves sink into so many slaves of his will."

" That's just my own opinion of the matter," exclaimed Bertrand, " for the more he increases this empire of ours, the more anxiously he looks forward to add other countries to this, and he can only do so by keeping together such an army as will keep those of all his enemies in check. By doing that he is obliged to increase the number of conscripts, so that at last there is hardly a family in the whole country that has not to regret the absence of some member of it whose assistance at home is needed."

"True," said the host, "but is there any one here present that has any remedy to propose?"

"I know of nothing else that can be done, but stoutly to refuse to serve when we are called upon."

"What will be the use of that," demanded Stephen Crapean, "unless we are backed by nearly the whole population? A few showing a little spirit would only end in failure and certain punishment, but if the resistance is general, it will be seen that the people expect to have a voice as well as the person they have raised to be their ruler."

"Especially when their lives are in question," observed Bertrand.

"It's all very well to talk about what we expect," exclaimed Vincent, "but it so happens that Napoleon has got all the power in his own hands, and he'll not part with the smallest portion of it, because he knows that the whole army is in his favour. No one can be more against the conscription than I am, and yet I may venture to say that it would be better to submit for a little while longer, in order that we may take the first favourable opportunity that offers to show that we have power to offer effectual resistance."

"And in the meantime you think we ought to submit to what we feel to be intolerable oppression?"

"As for putting up with oppression," answered Vincent, "I'm as much against it as any one can be, but there's a proper time for doing all things, and when people are in too great a hurry to bring about changes they almost always defeat their own purposes. If I had not wished to see an end put to those oppressions that fall so heavily upon us, I should not have joined with others to get rid of 'em, but it don't follow that we are to throw ourselves headlong into ruin, when by caution we may avoid it."

Bertrand was about to reply, but before he could do so the door was abruptly thrown open, and Sergeant Clairfait, at the head of half a dozen National Guards, entered the room. A general consternation was instantly visible amongst those who had assembled, and some few were making towards the door for the purpose of escape. This, however, was prevented by two of the men who were stationed to guard the entrance, and in the meantime the sergeant advanced towards those who still retained their seats, and exclaimed—

"Messieurs, I suppose you can guess the business that has brought me here, for the news must be known to you that orders have been received from government that a new conscription is to be raised for strengthening the army that has already done so much towards raising the honour of our country."

"Aye, aye," replied Bertrand, who took upon himself the office of spokesman on the occasion, "we don't pretend to be ignorant of the news you speak of, but if the truth must be told, we are none of us inclined to be torn away from our families to increase the honour of a country that is always at the head of nations."

"Do you mean to say that you and your companions here will dare resist the commands of our emperor?"

"Why, when we think he expects too much from us——"

"And who shall dare dictate to Napoleon when he calls upon his people to assist him?" exclaimed the sergeant. "Is there any man here who refuses to serve his country in a time of need?"

"In a time of need we shall all of us be ready to perform our duty," answered Bertrand, "but just now we see no reason why men should be taken away from their families who depend upon their labour for their daily support. In short, the present war is one that few people look upon with favour, and I rather think it will be found that there are thousands besides ourselves that will refuse to obey the call that is made upon them."

"What madness s this!" exclaimed Sergeant Clairfait; "have you never bestowed a thought upon the consequences that will fall upon all those who disobey the commands of the emperor?"

"Oh yes, we know all about that," answered Bertrand; "but when people are driven to desperation they do things that they would not otherwise have thought of. If we must submit to be ruined, it may as well be by one means as another; so, once for all, we are none of us inclined to be included in the conscription, unless better reason can be shown than we see at present."

"In that case," returned the sergeant, "I shall be under the necessity of ordering you all under arrest."

"That's no more than I expected," returned the other, with a sneer, "but it remains to be seen whether we are inclined to love our liberty whilst we have the means in our own hands to resist."

"How dare you go such a length as that?"

"Desperate men dare do anything when they are driven to it."

'Then we must try who is to get the best of this," exclaimed Sergeant Clairfait, and making a sign to his men, they all advanced with the evident design of carrying the last threat into execution. The others, however, in an instant, threw themselves upon their guard; knives were drawn, and both parties were ready to attack each other, when Stephen Crapean threw himself between them, and entreated that no violence should be committed in his house. But the appeal was altogether unheeded by both the contending parties, and a sudden rush being made by Bertrand and those who had enlisted under his banner, the National Guards were, by the suddenness of the attack, overpowered, and in the hands of their adversaries. Instead, however, of committing any further violence against the conquered foe, Bertrand desired that they should be led outside the door, with a caution not to return again upon the same errand, unless they made up their minds to experience rougher treatment than they had hitherto met with. Upon reaching the open air the guards were at once released, and Bertrand, addressing himself to the sergeant, said, in a voice of determination—

"You see, monsieur, that you have men to deal with who are not inclined to be trampled upon whilst they have their own arms to depend on. We expect that this will not pass over without exciting the anger of the authorities, but you may tell them from me that it will be the wiser course not to take any notice of it, for if they do, the news will spread like wild fire from one end of the country to the other, and then France may, perhaps, imitate the example we have this day set."

"I can't answer for what may be the consequence of what you have done," answered Sergeant Clairfait, "but I certainly shall give the message you would send by me, and, as far as I am myself concerned, this defeat shall be remembered in a way you little expect."

"Then you don't deserve the civil treatment you have met with," exclaimed Bertrand, "and hang me if I don't set my comrades upon you again, if you are not off directly."

No reply was made to this, but in a moment, as if by a preconcerted signal, the sergeant and his men turned round and made a rush towards the house. They, however, were not quick enough for those who had so unceremoniously marched them out, for they were immediately turned back, and then Bertrand and his companions once more entering the house, so securely barricaded the doors and windows, that they could bid defiance to any attempt that might be made to break in upon them. This done, they sat themselves down over a fresh supply of liquor, to wait the result of the hazardous exploit they had been engaged in. Most of them laughed over the affair as an excellent joke, but it was not so with Stephen Crapean, who saw that it was likely to get him into a serious dilemma through having allowed his house to be used by men who joined together for the purpose of setting the government at defiance.

"And what more have you to be afraid of than any of ourselves?" demanded Bertrand, after listening to the lamentations of the host of the Red Hand; "ain't we all in the same scrape if anything should happen to come of it, and is it for us to sit down and repeat what has been done, when we ought rather to be thinking how we may best get over it if any notice should be taken of the little rumpus we have been engaged in."

"You may treat it as lightly as you please," answered Crapean, "but for my own part I see nothing but mischief to come of it, and as a matter of course I shall be the first that they order to be arrested for resisting the law."

"Then you must get over it by declaring that the law is so bad a one that it ought to be resisted," observed Potier.

"What good will that do for me?" demanded the host. "Laws, whether good or bad, are to be equally obeyed—at least so say our rulers—and those that oppose them are sure to get punished for their pains."

"Well, then, you have not much to fear," laughed Bertrand, "for you interposed first when the row was about to begin, and if we didn't choose to heed your words it was no fault of yours. So you will soon get over the difficulty, and I would advise you to make yourself comfortable with us over a glass or two of *eau de vie*."

"I'll tell you what it is," exclaimed Stephen Crapean, "this light way of treating a very serious affair don't at all suit me, for I see there's a great deal of danger about to fall upon us, and I, who have less to do with the recent violence than any one among you, shall be made to endure as much punishment as if I had taken an active share in it."

"Why shouldn't you?" demanded Bertrand, with the same levity as before, "when the occurrence took place under your own roof?"

"Then see that neither you nor any of your companions come here any more unless you can do so as peaceable subjects," exclaimed the host; "at first I thought you meant a quiet resistance to what everybody considers to be a bad law, but now I find you are all likely to get into trouble through setting the authorities at defiance, I care not if you never darken my doors again."

"Master Crapean, if you would only listen to reason——"

"Reason!" interrupted the host; "is there any reason in assaulting the military, and turning them neck and crop out of my house when they only came to do their duty."

"Oh, I see clearly enough how it is," exclaimed Potier, "our friend here thinks he has gone far enough with us, and would now come to a dead standstill at the first appearance of danger."

"Or perhaps he hopes to make something by informing the government of what has taken place at our meetings," said Vincent.

"If I thought he'd prove such a traitor as that," observed Bertrand, "he should not live another five minutes. But hang it!—coward as he has proved himself to be, I don't believe he would act the part of a spy upon his old friends and customers."

"You only do me justice there, Bertrand," exclaimed the host, glad to find any loophole to get out of his present scrape. "I have no thought of acting such a villanous part as Vincent has spoken of, but it must be confessed that I care not how soon I get rid of such troublesome customers as you have been to-night."

"You want us to leave your house then, Master Crapean?" said Bertrand.

"The sooner the better."

"Well, that's candid enough it must be confessed, but why should we go out when the chances are that the guards may return in greater force to take us prisoners?"

"The greater reason why you should not be found here."

"Psha! the doors and windows have been well barricaded, and if an attack should be made, there's enough of us here to beat off our assailants, if they should follow us."

"And that they will do, Bertrand," answered the host, "so be satisfied with the triumph you have gained, and every one of you disperse before worse comes of this night's affray."

"Its all very fine to talk about dispersing," exclaimed Potier, " but we are known to the fellows that were here just now, and I suppose they'll make up a rare story in order to excuse themselves for the defeat they have suffered."

" I think it's much more likely that they'll not say a word about what has taken place," observed Crapean, "for if they choose to keep the affair to themselves, they will avoid the laughter and derision that they'll have to endure if this cowardice of their's should be whispered abroad."

" Aye, but you must not flatter yourselves with anything of the kind," answered Vincent, "for this night's rumpus is not likely to pass off very quietly, and by and by we shall find that the mayor will take up this business more seriously than you fancy."

" What!" muttered Bertrand, " are you going to show the white feather already ?"

" As for that," answered the person addressed, " I believe there's as little cowardice to be found in me as in any one that is here present. I thought from the first that we were a great deal too fast in resisting the military when they were sent against us, but as we have got ourselves into a dilemma, I think the wisest thing we can now do, will be to make the best we can of a bad bargain."

" Then," exclaimed Stephen Crapean, " oblige me by making this bargain of yours in any place rather than in my house. I want no police here to make their report afterwards that they found seditious people under my roof, for I received notice a very short time ago that a watch was kept upon my premises, and to be careful lest any further complaints should be made against me."

" Hang 'em, they are always interfering with us poor people," returned Bertrand. "They seem to think we have no right to have an opinion of our own, but if matters don't mend before long, we may perhaps show those who call themselves our superiors, that we are not to be trodden upon any longer."

" Mind what you are saying," exclaimed Vincent, "for if these words should be carried to the mayor or any of his underlings, we may be expected to give an account of ourselves, which would not be very agreeable, considering how severely they punish all people who venture to utter an opinion of their own."

" What a fright you are in about nothing," returned the other. " We have done no great harm that I know of, for we had a right to meet here or anywhere else, and though we certainly turned the intruders away from the place without much ceremony, there's no great harm can happen from that, because they heard nothing that can be reported to our prejudice."

" Aye, aye," exclaimed the host, " it's all very well to take matters so easily as you do, but I can foresee the ruin of my business for one thing, and it's not at all unlikely that we may hear more of this than you expect. The laws are now enforced with more strictness than ever they were, and men are thrown into prison before they are conscious of having done anything wrong."

" Then it's high time that people should begin to show a little spirit," interposed Potier. " We may lie down and be trampled on if things are suffered to go on in this way much longer, so the sooner we make a display of our resolution the better chance there will be of getting back the rights and privileges we have lost. War is the only thing that our rulers think of, and so long as the people will quietly submit to have their bravest men forced away from them, we shall never again know the blessings of peace."

" You are right enough there, my good fellow," exclaimed Vincent, " but how are we to help ourselves, so long as Napoleon's ambition urges him on to conquer and add other dominions to his own ?"

" As for that," returned Bertrand, " our rulers may be taught a useful lesson as well as their subjects, and we have only to express a resolution to submit no longer to an exaction that the country is no farther able to bear. All we now want is peace, and then the trade and commerce of the nation will soon restore happiness and prosperity, which for years past have been lost to us. However, it's no use to talk of these things now, for not a step can be taken till thousands of other Frenchmen join in the same opinion, and resolve to convince our leaders that we are no longer to be led like beasts to slaughter."

"All I can say about it is, that I hope you will not again make this house your place of meeting," exclaimed Stephen Crapean. "I have no wish to get into trouble through your means, and rather than not get rid of such dangerous customers, I would shut up this place and find a new home in some other part of the country."

"Well," exclaimed Vincent, "at any rate, there's no occasion to annoy you with our company any longer now, for I have just been looking from the window, and as far as I can judge, there's not a soul looking out for us near the house. So, if we are all of one opinion, we shall take our leave of Master Crapean, and think this matter over at our leisure."

It is true that all were not quite of one opinion, yet, as the coast was announced to be clear for them, it was agreed that they should quickly take their departure from the house whilst there was nothing to impede or oppose them. Even Bertrand, who was perhaps the most turbulent and dissatisfied among them, made no objection to this latter proposal. He, however, failed not reminding Stephen Crapean that he should continue to frequent his house as much as formerly, and suggested the prudence of taking part with his friends, rather than with those who would crush him whenever an opportunity presented itself. The host returned a half surly answer to this, and having seen his company depart, locked and bolted the door after them, well pleased at having cleared his house so easily.

CHAPTER XIII.

JEANNOT IS WOUNDED.—RECEIVES KINDNESS AND HOSPITALITY FROM STRANGERS.—INTRODUCTION TO JACQULINE.—SYMPTOMS OF WAVERING AFFECTION.—ARRIVAL OF HENRY DUPORT, WHO, SEEING A CHANCE TO DO MISCHIEF, SETS HIMSELF TO WORK FOR THAT PURPOSE.

It would not interest the reader of a work of fiction, to follow the Emperor Napoleon through the succession of brilliant victories that marked his progress whilst engaged in pursuing the conquest of Prussia. It will be sufficient to say that Jeannot exhibited proofs of extraordinary gallantry in every battle in which he had been engaged, and that his conduct had been rewarded by promotion to a sergeant, with promises of a still higher reward, if he should prove himself worthy of distinction, by the time the campaign was brought to a close. Fortunately, though often exposed to the greatest danger, he escaped without even the slightest wound, and it was not till the ever-memorable battle of Austerlitz was fought, that he received a bayonet thrust in the side, which stretched him upon the earth with many of his brave companions in arms, who, like himself had resolved to perish rather than yield to the enemy the honour of that day's victory. After his fall he became utterly insensible through loss of blood, and though the battle raged with fearful impetuosity for more than two hours from the moment that he fell, yet was Jeannot quite unconscious of the terrible scene of strife and slaughter that was going on around him. At length victory declared in favour of the imperial army of France ; the Austrians fled in dismay before their unconquerable foes, and the dead and the dying were left stretched upon the field, whilst the victors retired to the tent to rest themselves, after the unparalleled fatigue they had gone through. Many of the wounded perished on that night with the slain amongst whom they had fallen, and such no doubt would have been the fate of Jeannot, had it not been for the care and humanity of a neighbouring farmer and his son, who, after the battle was over, had left their home for the purpose of affording their assistance to any unfortunate fellow creature, who might not be beyond all human aid. Lantern in hand, these two excellent men traversed the scene of battle, stopping occasionally when they thought they heard a moan, and then passing onwards when they found—as was the case many times—that they had been deceived by the hollow blast that howled over the field of strife, as if mourning for the countless dead who strewed the ground. At length they came to the spot where Jeannot had fallen, and from thence neither of them would proceed a step further, for this time they felt assured their ears had not deceived them, and lowering the light so that it might fall upon the pale countenances of those who had fallen in the day's bloody struggle, they in a short time came to the spot to which the sounds of mortal agony had conducted them. There they found our young soldier, still insensible, and yet showing sufficient signs of life to inspire them with a hope that the holy task in which they had engaged would not have been undertaken in vain. Quickly releasing him from the bodies which had fallen upon and around him, they applied some water with which they had provided themselves to the parched lips of the wounded man. This experiment though it did not restore him to his senses, was sufficient to convince them that there was good ground to hope for his ultimate recovery, and caring nothing for the fact of his being one of the enemy who had come to bring war and destruction into their native land, they resolved to carry him home, and afford him all that care and attention which humanity like their's can bestow. No sooner had they determined to do this than, between them, they carefully raised the wounded man, and supporting him in their arms, made their way, amidst heaps of slain, towards the place where their farmhouse was situated. Madame Gratz, the wife of the elder of the two men, was waiting at the door to receive them, for she had observed the light approaching, and knowing that her husband and her son would not return home without bringing some one with them to whom her assistance might prove serviceable, she had made all those preparations which were most likely to be of use. She eagerly advanced to meet them, but no sooner had the light from the lantern revealed to her sight the uniform of an enemy, than she started back, and returned to the house, as if determined to afford no aid to one who had come armed against the lives of her own country people. Without taking any notice of this, however, the father and son carried their still unconscious burden into the kitchen, where a huge fire was blazing in the chimney, and before which a sort of couch had been hastily prepared for any unfortunate who might be brought in. Upon this Jeannot was immediately placed, and his coat having been removed a deep wound was discovered near the shoulder, from which the blood was still flowing. To stop this was of course the first object of their care, and having bestowed all their skill upon their suffering patient, they administered to him a small portion of brandy mixed with water, as a stimulant. Having thus far attended to the wants of the sufferer as far as his slight knowledge of surgery went, Herman Gratz, the elder of the two men, turned round, and perceiving his wife at the farther part of the room, demanded why she stood inactive when her assistance was so much required.

" Need you ask me that question, Herman ?" she asked; " or is it possible that you can wish me to afford assistance to a foreigner and a foe, when there are thousands of our own countrymen lying on the field of battle, upon whom our care ought to be bestowed in preference to those who enslave and desolate our land ?"

" He is a foe," answered Herman Gratz, " but is that any reason why we should leave him to perish amongst those who have fallen in this dreadful day of strife and bloodshed ? Had he been a countryman of our own, I confess the task I have undertaken would have been all the more agreeable, but as fate has thrown this man into our care—stranger and alien though he be—he shall be treated as a christian and a fellow being."

" Dear Herman," exclaimed the mistress of the house, " you are half angry with me, I fear, and yet I said nothing that might not have been uttered by yourself at any other time. If, however, it is your desire that this young man should receive my attention, I will, as it has ever been my chief pleasure to do, exert myself to the utmost to restore him to health."

"Excellent!" cried Herman, snatching her to his arms; "that is indeed spoken like yourself, and I shall love you for it—if that be possible—more than ever I have. Bestow all your care upon him, and if he should recover, he will owe you a debt of gratitude that nothing can ever efface from his memory."

"Ah, husband!" she replied, "I will not fail to do all in my power to gratify

[JACQUELINE.]

this wish of yours. I will tend upon and watch over him as if he were my own son, though a superstition of our country says 'That they who succour a foe will live to repent the kindness bestowed upon an ingrate.'"

"What have we to do with an idle superstition," he asked, "when a fellow creature would perish but for the assistance we have it in our power to bestow? Besides, though he happens to have fought against us in this battle that has proved so disastrous to him, we must not blame the youth for it so much as the Emperor Napoleon, who expects and insists upon every male subject—from a youth upwards—to devote himself to a military life. They fight against us it is true, but ask any of them if they do it from choice, and I would wager my existence the reply would be that they prefer peace, with the blessed privilege of earning their bread by the sweat of the brow. So think no more of your superstitions, wife, but let me see how soon you can restore this poor fellow to health and strength."

"I think," observed Madame Gratz, "I heard you tell our son Edward just now that the wound is not likely to prove mortal?"

"As far as I can judge," he replied, "I believe it is one that your skill in such matters will soon be able to heal."

"Yet even now he seems almost dead."

"Aye, mother," replied Edward Gratz, "but that is only through exhaustion brought on by loss of blood. The wound, however, is now bound up, and all the poor fellow needs is the care and attention that you and my sister can bestow."

"Your sister!" exclaimed Madame Gratz; "have you forgotten already that she was sent away from home as soon as it was known that a great battle was expected to be fought in our own neighbourhood?"

"But she will soon return again, I suppose, now that it is all over?" observed the young man.

"Aye, aye," answered his mother, "she will not be long away from us, for as the French army will march immediately on its way towards Berlin, she will again be glad to shift her quarters, because they happen to be on the road which will soon be overrun by the foreign soldiers. In a few days at farthest, she will return, though I would almost have wished that it had not been so."

"And why," asked her husband with surprise, "do you wish our daughter to be away from home now that the strife and bloodshed we so much dreaded is over?"

"Because," she replied, "young girls like her ought not to be in the way whilst a stranger of the other sex is present."

"Nay," exclaimed Herman Gratz, "this is no time to stand upon trifles, for the young man that I have brought here requires every attention that can be bestowed upon him, and please Heaven he shall have it, be the consequences what they may."

"You feel interested in him, it seems?"

"Well, to confess the truth, I am," replied Herman, "for if ever I saw honour and honesty expressed in the countenance of any one, it is plainly enough stamped in that of the poor young fellow that we picked out from among so many thousands of others whose fate was even worse than his own. Let us then try what can be done to restore him, and I'll answer for it we shall meet with our reward for it afterwards."

"But won't the government claim him as a prisoner, if it should happen to be known that he is here?"

"Why, there's no doubt he would be claimed," answered Herman, "but as I'm afraid our unfortunate country is likely to fall, as so many others have done, under the overwhelming power of Napoleon, the young man will not be in so much danger as you apprehend. But time will show what is to be the result of this invasion, and, if we should happily be able to resist it, we will then find means to get this youth away before his presence here has been made known."

"Were there no others that you would have rescued from death as well as this one?"

"Doubtless there were many," he replied, "but I brought home the first one that I chanced to meet with alive, and, though he happens to have belonged to the ranks of the enemy, I am not the less anxious that he should, to the utmost, receive our hospitality and attention."

"As you please, Herman," answered the dame; "for, when you are resolved to do a good action, I am always anxious to assist it as far as my humble means will allow me."

"Then you will act towards him the part of a kind and gentle nurse?"

"Of a surety I will."

"I know it," exclaimed the honest farmer with all the warmth of genuine kindness. "I knew well what I had to expect from my ever kind and affectionate Gertrude; or I would not have risked the bringing home of one who has come against our country as an enemy. But, poor lad! the choice was none of his own, for I dare say he has been forced to leave behind him those whom his heart most tenderly loves."

"Aye," sighed the dame, "perhaps a mother who would be heart broken, could she but look upon her son as we now see him."

"Or some maiden," suggested Edward Gratz, "to whom she was to have been united on his return home?"

"Ah," cried Madame Gratz, "how many thousands of broken hearts have been caused in all countries through these wars that have been entered into only to increase the power and dominions of one man! I have never heard that our king gave cause of offence to the ruler of France, and yet, when least expected, legions of warlike men burst suddenly into our peaceful land."

"So it is," answered Herman, "but people, who can judge of future events better than myself, say that they can foresee that the downfall of Napoleon will become more rapid than his rise. Be that as it may, nations are now combining together against him, so that the day may not be far distant when the mighty conqueror will be obliged either to descend from the throne he has mounted, or to reduce his dominions to what they were before France began to make her attacks upon neighbouring states. Heaven send that such may prove to be the case, for till then our own beloved country will be deprived of her liberty."

"Has not our monarch still troops enough to drive away the enemy that ha invaded us?" asked the dame.

"I'm afraid not," answered her husband, "but whether or not, our army has been so dispersed and broken up by this battle here at Austerlitz, that I'm afraid the troops cannot be collected together in time to make a successful stand. In that case the French will march upon Berlin, and the ruin of Prussia will be complete. But don't let us look forward to those melancholy prospects, for the wounded man groans as if a fresh paroxysm of pain had come on, and I will therefore leave him to your care, in the hope that it will not be bestowed in vain."

Intending to rise early in the morning to take another survey of the battle-field, Herman Gratz and his son retired to their beds, leaving the good dame to attend upon her still unconscious patient. After again dressing his wound, she sat herself down to watch beside him, and there remained for hours, with that patience which only a woman can display under similar circumstances. It was not, however, till after daybreak on the following morning that Jeannot began to exhibit symptoms of returning animation, and then, by means of such simple restoratives as she had at hand, she at length succeeded in rendering him conscious of the kindness and attention which had been bestowed upon him. At first he seemed to be bewildered at finding himself in a strange place, but the pain he felt from the wound in his shoulder soon brought to mind the dreadful strife in which he had been engaged, and addressing himself to Madame Gratz, who stood by his side, he eagerly inquired how the French had fared in the recent fight.

"Alas!" sighed the dame, "they were as usual—victorious."

"And you," exclaimed Jeannot, "belong, I suppose, to the country we come to invade?"

"I do."

"Then I am indebted to a foe for my preservation from death?"

"We are no foes," answered Madame Gratz, "nor would this war have been entered into but for the pride and ambition of the man that has led his enemies to our peaceful country. I do not, however, utter this in the way of reproach, for here you shall find yourself among friends, though we could have wished that you had not worn the uniform of a foe."

"How can I thank you for this kindness?" exclaimed the young soldier, wondering at the generosity which was then extended to him by those from whom he might have expected the animosity of enraged enemies.

"By keeping yourself quiet," answered Madame Gratz, "and thus aiding in the cure I have undertaken to attempt. Your wound, though likely to keep you confined to the house for some time, is not a mortal one, and with even such skill as I can boast of, I believe you will have little more to regret from what has happened, except the being detained from your regiment when, it may be, your heart beats ardently for scenes similar to the one that had so nearly proved fatal to you."

"How came I here?" asked Jeannot, "for I remember nothing from the moment when, wounded in a charge upon the enemy, I fell amidst heaps of others who had already perished."

"You were brought here last night by my husband and my son, who went out after the battle to see if they could save any person from amongst those who were wounded and unable to crawl from the place where they had fallen. You were the first they met with, and being brought home, we have endeavoured, as far as our poor skill in such things went, to restore you to animation. Thank Heaven we have succeeded; and therefore is our reward as great as could have been hoped for."

"And I have been cared for, though doubtless many of your own countrymen equally required assistance?"

"They shall receive it as far as our limited means will permit," replied the good dame, for my husband and Edward are again going to search over the battle field for any persons to whom our assistance may be of service."

Herman Gratz and his son now made their appearance in the room, and great was their gratification when they perceived that the wounded guest had so far recovered as to be able to converse. At his request they related to him the result of the battle in which he had been engaged, and having done so, they conveyed him to an adjoining chamber, which was to be devoted to his use so long as it was necessary for him to remain there. Having thus far performed the offices of humanity towards the wounded guest, they again left the farm-house to examine every part of the battle field in order to convince themselves whether there were any others to whom their services might prove useful. A short examination of the spot, however, was sufficient to convince them that the task had already been performed by the armies of both Austria and France, for though they carefully traversed the whole scene, there was not one living person to be found, though doubtless hundreds had been left there on the previous night. Rather gratified than otherwise at the result of their benevolent mission, the father and son returned home with the news that the wounded had been already taken care of by the respective parties to whom they belonged. In a week after the commencement of his sojourn with the worthy farmer and his family, Jeannot was able to leave his bed and take gentle exercise in the immediate neighbourhood of the house which had become his temporary home. He would have written to Jeannette, but for the circumstance of his right arm having been disabled for the present, and perhaps he regretted this circumstance the less from the reflection that it would be the better for her to remain in ignorance of his having been wounded till the information could reach her at the same time that he had completely recovered from the accident. In the meanwhile he heard casual mention of a daughter, who had been sent away on a visit to some friends, when the expectation gained ground that the recent battle was likely to take place in the neighbourhood of her father's farm. This circumstance, however, was not much heeded by Jeannot, and scarcely did he recollect that such a person had ever been spoken of, when, to his surprise, on entering the usual sitting room one morning, he found a strange, though exceedingly beautiful girl, presiding at the breakfast table. She was introduced to him as Jacqueline, the daughter of Herman and Madame Gratz, and from her liveliness and agreeable conversation, Jeannot perceived that she would form an important and pleasant addition to the family circle of which he now seemed to form almost a part. From this period the young people became almost inseparable—in his walks she was always the companion of Jeannot ; at home he read to her, while she busily plied her needle ; and, at length, when his wound was almost healed, the young soldier no longer spoke anxiously of the time when he should once more join the army, which was now in full march towards the capital of Prussia. In short, though he durst not admit such a fact even to himself, Jeannot's heart was almost equally divided between the fair Jacqueline and the still faithful, loving maiden to whom he had been betrothed. It is, however, due to Jacqueline to observe, that no hints had dropped from the lips of her father's guest, either that he felt more than the affection of a brother for her, or that his heart was already engaged to another. At length, one day, when Jeannot happened to be walking alone, he was somewhat startled by meeting an old comrade in the person of Henri Duport, who was then on the road leading to the farmhouse. Their greeting was warm and friendly, for Henri pretended that he had come there full of apprehension and alarm, in consequence of a rumour having reached him that he would find his former associate either dead or at any rate dying from the effect of a wound that he had received in the battle of Austerlitz. In reply to further questions, he affirmed that he had been sent to make inquiries after him; as some had been bold enough to assert that he had clandestinely left his post a short time previous to the strife of battle commencing. Jeannot heard this latter piece of intelligence with no little indignation.

"They who have accused me of this act of cowardice lie in their teeth !" he exclaimed, " for I was in the midst of a charge against the enemy's centre, when a bayonet wound brought me to the earth, and I should have perished there, but for the humanity and kindness of the people who found me after the battle, and who since have restored me to the state you now see."

" And do you feel well, and strong enough to return with me to head-quarters ?" asked Henri Duport.

" So much so," replied the other, " that I intended to have made my way there within two or three days. Indeed, though you may scarcely believe it, my anxiety has been chiefly to rejoin my regiment without delay, though unfortunately my wound rendered it impossible for me to leave this place earlier."

" Well," exclaimed Henri, " at all events, my dear fellow, I have no orders to insist upon your immediate return, if there should be reasonable ground for believing that your absence was occasioned by anything that was not within your own control. Your word is quite a sufficient excuse, so, as I, like yourself, am not limited to time, I should like to stay a day or two with the worthy people who have acted towards you with so much kindness."

" It is not for me to give an invitation for them," answered Jeannot, " but I believe you may reckon upon receiving there as much hospitality as myself."

" Of what does the family consist ?"

" Why, in the the first place, there is Monsieur and Madame Gratz."

" Oh ! they are the old folks," interrupted Henri; " now let me hear if there are any young ones."

" Yes, there is a son."

" And, I presume, a daughter."

" There is," answered Jeannot, with hesitation, " but why do you say you presume so ?"

" Because you have remained at the farm so long, that I fancied it must contain some such attraction."

" Psha !" exclaimed the young soldier; " do you think there could be any attraction for me here, whilst Jeannette is constantly held in my fondest remembrance ?"

"That depends upon circumstances. Is this young lady you speak of pretty ?"

"Do you mean Jacqueline ?"

"Aye, Jacqueline, I suppose, is her name. Is she, I ask, as prettty as Jeannette ?"

"I think she is," stammered Jeannot, "though their beauty is of a widely different kind. The fact——"

"I want no confession from you, my dear fellow," interrupted Henri Duport, secretly exulting in the discovery that he supposed he had made. "I am only pleased to find that you have been able to pass your time so agreeably here, for Jeannette need know nothing at all about what has taken place, and even if she did, I suppose her heart is not so far gone, but that she could still bestow it upon another ; that is to say, supposing you had any wish to be off the bargain."

"You seem to be jesting with me," exclaimed Jeannot, gravely, "and yet I can swear that I never thought of Jacqueline otherwise than as a sister."

"Humph !—when did you last write to Jeannette ?"

"Not since a short time before I received my wound."

"That she must think very unkind of you."

"Perhaps she does," answered Jeannot, thoughtfully, "but she will cease to do so when she hears, as she will by my next letter, that I was prevented by the wound, which had rendered my right arm utterly useless to me."

"But this sister of your's, that I have just heard about, cou d not she have written a line for you ?"

"I never asked her the question."

"Perhaps you had no particular wish that Jacqueline should be aware of the fact that your heart is already engaged ?"

"You are still jesting with me, I find," exclaimed the young man, "and yet there is no more ground for saying that I have fallen in love with this girl than that you have, who are a perfect stranger to her."

"So far I am a stranger," replied the other, "but I hope soon to have the honour of an introduction to the female who has acted with so much kindness to my friend. In short, Jeannot, I expect to find her a very angel of perfection, for already I see clearly enough that your heart has been lost to her."

"Why should you think so," asked Jeannot, half angrily, "when I have assured you that my affection for Jeannette is as strong and as perfect as ever it was ?"

"If you want to know my reason, it is soon given," answered Henri. "Love is very apt to fade during absence, and the fact of your not having written to Jeannette is a proof that she is not so often in your mind as she were. And between ourselves, I don't know that it matters very much, for if you don't choose to marry the girl, there's plenty who would be glad to place themselves in your shoes, and perhaps Jeannette herself might not be altogether displeased at the change."

"Henri Duport !" exclaimed the other, "till this moment I have been foolish enough to believe that you were my friend, but words such as you have uttered prove how grossly I have been mistaken."

"Nay," returned the other, in a tone of remonstrance, "now you are offended with me, though I spoke only in jest."

"Is this a subject to jest upon ?"

"Perhaps I have gone a little too far," exclaimed Henri, who in reality saw that he had done so. "I forgot how sensitive you lovers are, and thought I might speak freely upon even this subject without calling forth so much anger. If, however, I have provoked your wrath, I am heartily sorry for it, and that I hope will be a sufficient apology to obtain my pardon."

"I want no quarrel with you," answered Jeannot, "nor is there any occasion for one, because, as you are going with me to the house of Monsieur and Madame Gratz, you will see and convince yourself that I only pay to their daughter the respectful homage that she has earned for herself, by that kindness and attention which she has paid me ever since her return home."

"That is to say, she has behaved as a sister, and you have returned her kindness with true paternal affection?"

"You are still satirical."

"Nay, on the contrary, I would avoid uttering a word that is likely to give you the slightest offence."

"Remember," exclaimed Jeannot, "that though I may be able to bear these jests, as you call them, when we are alone together, they must not be ventured on in the presence of Jacqueline."

"What! you are afraid, then, that she might by chance let out the secret if it were supposed that I already knew it?"

"You know my meaning better than that," returned Jeannot, "and it is therefore the more provoking that you annoy me with expressions that there can be no foundation for."

"And what of it," still persevered the other, "if there was a foundation for it? You are betrothed, it is true, but that wouldn't be binding unless both the contracting parties are determined to hold by the bargain they have made. Long absence, for instance, may easily excuse forgetfulness, and if you happen to have met with another that you can love better that Jeannette, is it not just as likely that she may have transferred her love to another, under the natural supposition that she is no longer the object most esteemed by the man who has not written to her for many weeks past?"

"It is, indeed, true that she may feel offended with me for that neglect," answered Jeannot; "but as I shall send her a letter in the course of a few days, she will be satisfied when I explain the reason for my seeming want of attention."

"Shall you mention the name of Jacqueline in your letter?" asked Henri Duport, with a sneer that he could not quite conceal.

"Undoubtedly I shall."

"But it will be useless to say that you regard the young lady only as a sister."

"To Jeannette's good sense I will leave the construction she may put upon anything I relate to her," answered the young man. "We have been acquainted together as children—have loved each other with a strength of affection that few feel towards each other—and were mutually betrothed ere I came away from my native village. She therefore knows my heart too well to believe that it can ever be given to another whilst I have the certainty that her's is still faithful to me."

"And yet," observed Henri Duport, "I have heard it said that one of her chief regrets at parting from you was a suspicion that you might meet with some other female whose attractions would be superior to her own. Have you no recollection of her having hinted that you would take some other bride than herself?"

"She certainly said something of the kind," answered Jeannot, "but the words were uttered in the agony of parting, and when she scarcely knew what she said."

"Don't you think it possible that she might have meant what she uttered?"

"At the moment she might," he replied, "but since then she has had plenty of time and opportunity to be convinced that there was no foundation for such a thought."

"Women, my dear fellow," exclaimed Henri Duport, "do not get rid of these notions quite so easily as you seem to imagine. They are, in fact, rather apt to fancy that we of the opposite sex are not remarkable for our constancy in love, and as Jeannette has once pronounced her opinion, I should not be at all surprised if she still clings fast to it."

"Do you want to arouse my suspicions?" demanded Jeannot.

"Not at all," replied the other, with cool indifference. "It can make no odds to me what you think of the affair, but I would rather see you prepared for what may yet happen, in spite of your confidence in your betrothed."

"My confidence," answered the young man, "is not likely to be shaken by anything you may say."

"You still think then," observed Henri, "that I have a mischievous object in what I have uttered?"

"I have always regarded you as a friend," answered Jeannot, "but it will be impossible for me to do so any longer if you persist in following up this subject. Jacqueline is, as I said before, regarded by me in the light of a sister, and in no other way is she ever likely to interfere with the vows that have passed between me and Jeannette."

"So hundreds have thought besides yourself, my dear fellow," exclaimed the other, "but how often do we hear of lovers' vows that are broken and forgotten? Absence from each other frequently begets indifference—then succeeds coldness, and at length neither cares for the other any more than if they had never met."

"Such may be the case in some few instances," answered Jeannot; "but with me, I feel that neither time nor absence can ever make me love Jeannette less than I have always done. And, as far as she is concerned, I feel quite certain that nothing will ever change a heart that I may proudly call my own!"

"Do not suppose that I speak lightly of one for whom I have always felt the highest respect," exclaimed the other. "I was merely endeavouring to show, that even if you should give the preference to this farmer's pretty daughter, the news of your change of opinion would not be of such serious consequence as you imagine."

"You think Jeannette would not scorn me for breaking the vow I have so solemnly sworn to keep?"

"I fancy it quite possible that, so far from feeling angry, she might not be altogether displeased at being released from a promise that was given, perhaps, without due consideration."

"Then, in truth, you would have me believe that Jeannette was never sincere in her professions of affection?"

"Nay, I would not go so far as to say that," answered Henri Duport, "because many people are perfectly sincere when they utter a vow, but it does not follow that they will adhere to it. There are a thousand things that occur in the course of our lives which are not expected when the promise is made, and any one of them may serve to change an opinion, however sincerely it may have been formed."

"This language seems strange to me," exclaimed Jeannot, "and I could almost fancy you have heard news from home, or you surely would not venture to utter what you have."

"Indeed I have heard nothing certain," answered the deceiver, "except a very slight hint that Jeannette does not appear to grieve so much at your absence as was expected."

"Who told you that?"

"No one in particular," he replied. "In fact, I have received many letters from my friends since we came away, and all of them speak of Jeannette as being far more lively and cheerful than when you were almost her constant companion."

"Aye," exclaimed the young man, "these things are reported by those who were jealous of my better fortune when Jeannette preferred me before all her other lovers. They bitterly feel their disappointment, and have written these falsehoods to you because they know it's the most likely channel through which they will come to my ears.   But, though I listen to their slanders, I heed them not, any more than I do the howling of the wind.   So, let me hear no more of this, for we are now at the farm-house, where, as my friend, you will be received with a hospitable welcome."

This was hardly said when they passed through the neatly latticed doorway

PIERRE LANGRAIS SUDDENLY APPEARS TO JEANNETTE IN HER WALK.

and entered the room where Herman Gratz and his family were assembled previous to dinner.   Henri having been introduced to them, was cordially received by the worthy farmer, who, upon discovering that he was a comrade of his former guest, could scarcely heap upon him sufficient marks of esteem and good will.   Henri Duport, who wanted no better chance than to remain where he was for a few days, felt quite delighted with the genuine good feeling manifested by the old man and those by whom he was surrounded. Madame Gratz and her son were equally warm in the welcome with which they received him, and even Jacqueline, overcoming the timidity of her disposition, expressed her happiness at receiving another guest in addition to their former one. With what a scrutinizing eye Henri Duport watched her, may be easily imagined by those who perceive his real character, and the mischievous purpose he had in view. To him it now seemed that the schemes which had filled his mind were on the point of arriving at maturity, for it mattered not to him whether there was any truth in the supposed attachment between Jeannot and Jacqueline, since it was equally easily for him to raise a report that, at such a distance off, was not likely to meet with a contradiction till all the mischief was done. And yet, with feelings like these rankling at his heart, Henri could smile and joke, and exhibit all the exterior qualities of sincerity and friendship. Farmer Gratz, indeed, was so delighted with him, that he would not hear of his departure for at least a week to come.

"You shall not leave us yet," he exclaimed "for it seems our young friend Jeannot is to accompany you back to Berlin, and as we have acted as doctors throughout his illness, we now pronounce it as our opinion that he ought not on any account to be removed till his wound is quite healed."

"If that is my only plea for prolonging my visit here," replied Jeannot, smiling, "I'm afraid it will not be thought sufficient, for I am now sufficiently well able to undertake any moderate duty that may be required of me."

"Do you mean that you wish to leave us?" asked Jacqueline, in a tone of reproach.

"Nay," exclaimed Henri Duport, eagerly interposing, "I can answer for it that my friend is not anxious to leave a place where he has been received with so much kindness."

"Oh, as for that," answered the farmer, "we must have been hard-hearted wretches indeed. to have turned our backs upon a poor wounded fellow-creature, who I believe must have died on the night after the battle, but for the assistance it was fortunately in our power to bestow. Luckily we succeeded in our object, and I shall always think that day most worthily employed on which I saved this young man from a miserable death."

"It was very kind of you, Master Gratz," exclaimed Henri, "and the more particularly so, as the person you assisted was a stranger as well as an enemy."

"Psha!" returned the farmer, "what right have we to ask who or what a man is, when there is a certain duty to perform?—If my son Edward and I had stood wavering about what we should do, your friend must have perished from loss of blood, and I should have deprived myself of the consoling reflection, that I shrunk not from the performance of my duty."

"And Jeannot," said the other, glancing towards him to observe the effect of his words, "would have missed the greatest happiness it has ever been his good fortune to enjoy."

"What happiness do you allude to?" asked Gratz, breaking through the silence that had followed.

"That of being nursed and waited upon by your fair daughter."

"As for that," answered the old man, "I believe the happiness was chiefly upon the side of Jacqueline, for she has a good heart, poor girl, and is never so truly happy as when she is assisting those who are in need of help. Besides, in this instance, she knew that she was pleasing me and her mother, who had both expressed ourselves deeply interested in the recovery of the young man who had been so singularly thrown under our care."

"By the bye," exclaimed Henri Duport, anxious to change a conversation that, if carried much further, might serve to expose the malevolence of his purpose, "I was directed to make inquiries in this neighbourhood, whether any other wounded soldiers belonging to the French army are to be found similarly situated to my friend Jeannot. If there are any such, the orders from head quarters are that they shall, as soon as able, join their regiments, which are now about to join the other forces near Berlin."

"There were a few others a short time ago in different farm-houses about here," replied Gratz, " but I believe all of them have been cured of their wounds, and have gone off to head quarters as soon as they were able."

"And Jeannot, then, is the only one who still remains away from his duty?"

"Come, come, young man," exclaimed Herman Gratz, "I must not have him blamed, when there's not the slightest fault to be attached to him. Perhaps his wound required a longer time to heal, or it may be that we were over impor-tunate for him to remain longer with us, but whichever way it was, Jeannot is not at all to blame in the matter. He would, indeed, have left us long ago if he had been suffered to have his own way about it."

"Perhaps," observed Henri Duport, with a sneer that he managed to conceal, "it may have been the influence of a woman's tongue that prevailed upon him to extend his visit here?"

"Well," exclaimed the farmer, who saw not the drift of this latter observa-tion, "it must be confessed my wife urged him very hard to stay with us a week or two longer, for, as she said, all her care and attention would be thrown away if he were to leave us before being thoroughly recovered."

"Think you a younger female had not even greater influence over my friend than the worthy lady you have mentioned?"

"I don't know but what there may be something in that," exclaimed Her-man Gratz, "for I remember well, that when I was a young fellow I always heeded whatever was said by a young female more than I did the advice of an old one. And it's very natural after all; so I don't see, monsieur, that there was any necessity for that sly allusion of yours."

"You must understand that I meant it only as a suggestion," returned Henri, with a forced smile.

"Ah," replied the former, " of course I couldn't suppose anything else when the words came from the lips of a friend. Nay, even if it had been otherwise, I don't know that it would have mattered, for Jeannot has a right, I suppose, to be persuaded for his own good, let the advice come from whom it may ?"

"Most assuredly—I should be the very last to dispute that point," exclaimed Henri Duport, who saw it was now high time to shift the ground he had taken. "He has every right, as you say, to follow the counsel of his friends, and I should imagine he can have none more sincere than those who have brought him through the danger he was in. However, be that as it may, I would recom-mend him to join his regiment as soon as possible, because there are always people in the world who will attribute unworthy motives for the conduct of those whom they would crush for mere spite or revenge."

"You think, I suppose, that they would dare call me a coward that would shrink from my duty under the excuse that my wounds were not yet healed?" exclaimed Jeannot.

"If any persons did so," answered Henri Duport, "they cannot know your bravery in action quite so well as I do. Still, such things might be said, and it would not be very pleasant for you to hear that your gallantry had been sus-pected."

"Well, never mind that now," exclaimed Herman Gratz, as some of his domestics entered the room bearing various savoury dishes, which were ranged in due order along the table which reached nearly from one end of the kitchen to the other. The good farmer seated himself at the top, and after his family and guests had taken their places, all the servants, male and female, ranged themselves along the forms that were placed on each side the festive board. This was done in accordance with the excellent patriarchal custom of the period, for *there* the master and mistress were not ashamed to sit down to table with their dependents, and thus a feeling of reciprocity and kindness was kept up, which in the present day is rarely to be found.   At the conclusion of the m al the male labourers went away to attend to their several occupations, and the females then set to work to clear away the table which had just been groaning under the weight of good things which had been provided for the meal.   Herman Gratz remained chatting with his guests for about an hour afterwards, and then left to look after the business of his farm, having first recommended them to take a stroll through the neighbourhood till the hour when the family usually assembled to pass the evening in conversation or other rational amusements.

———

CHAPTER XIV.

ALARM BEGINS TO MANIFEST ITSELF AT THE NON-ARRIVAL OF NEWS FROM JEANNOT.—AN EVIL SPIRIT IS AT WORK. — PIERRE LANGRAIS' INTERVIEW WITH JEANNETTE.—THE LETTER, AND THE EFFECT IT PRODUCES.—MONSIEUR NARBONNE INTERPOSES AND ENDEAVOURS TO COUNTERACT THE INTENDED MISCHIEF.

UP to a certain period Jeannette had received letters from her lover as frequently as the peculiar situation in which he was placed would admit, but though she heard from the voice of general rumour that the battle of Austerlitz had been fought, she received no intelligence of the fact from Jeannot.   This, added to many mysterious hints that were thrown out by some inconsiderate persons, began to give rise to a fear that he was among the thousands who had fallen in that dreadful day of strife and bloodshed, and our heroine had to endure the constant torture of hearing the mournful prognostications of those who could only look on the darkest side of the picture.   As for her mother, though she could not but admit within herself that there was but too much reason to fear the worst, she constantly endeavoured to inspire her heart with hope, that, though they had not yet heard from Jeannot, there was still good ground to hope that a short time would bring the glad tidings they were so anxiously waiting for.   In addition to this, Monsieur Narbonne would frequently call at the widow's to inquire whether anything had yet been heard of the young man, and on each occasion, when he received a reply in the negative. he endeavoured, by reasoning ot various probabilities, to convince them that before long they would receive the intelligence for which they had been looking with such intense anxiety.   But, though Jeannette always appeared to be consoled by these assurances of the kind-hearted notary, she felt the same uneasiness as ever, and in the privacy of her own chamber would often give way to the tears which were suppressed only when in the company of those whom she knew would be deeply grieved to witness her sorrow.   One day, however, Madame Corville, on entering the room suddenly, found her daughter in tears.   Her approach had not been heard by Jeannette, whose back was towards her at the moment; but no sooner was her voice heard than the sorrowing maiden hastily wiped away the tears that bedewed her cheeks, and, assuming a tone of cheerfulness that was foreign to her heart, she greeted the old lady with as much apparent cheerfulness as if there was not a care or a thought upon her mind.   But Madame Corville was not to be so easily deceived, and, embracing her daughter, she gently chided her for still indulging in thoughts for which there might possibly be no foundation.

" You must remember, my dear," she added, " that Jeannot is now so fully occupied that it ought not to create any surprise if he is not so regular in his correspondence as you may wish him to be.   It is said, however, that the troops to which he belongs are likely very soon to occupy Berlin, and as then there will be more leisure, I dare say he will make up for lost time by writing to you more frequently than he has ever done before."

"Ah! my dear mother," answered Jeannette, "'tis kind of you, I know, to try and make the best of this affair, but what construction can I put upon the fact of not hearing from him, when all our neighbours who have relations in the army have heard from them since the last great battle that was fought? Nay, even those who have lost their friends by death, have received intelligence of their bereavement by some channel or another."

"Very true," replied her mother, "and the fact of your not having received any such disastrous news ought to console you, for there must at least be a prospect of his having escaped the fate which has befallen so many others."

"How is it then, if he still lives, that we have received no tidings of him for so long?'

"Ah! my dear child," answered the old lady, "if I could satisfy you upon that point, it would set your mind at rest. I, however, hope for the best, even though appearances may be rather against it, and I can almost venture to promise that, if your patience can but hold out a little longer, we shall soon hear that your lover has escaped the perils you are so apprehensive of."

"But what think you of the other rumours that the people have been so industriously circulating?'

"You mean those foolish reports about his having forgotten the solemn vow he made before going away?"

"I do."

"Well, then," replied Madame Corville, "I believe they have been spread abroad by evil-minded people for no other purpose than to do all the mischief they can. There are some who delight in creating misery, and you may depend upon it, that the time is not far distant when you will have reason to confess that my view of this matter is the correct one."

"I hope it may be so, mother dear," exclaimed Jeannette, "and yet I am at a loss to guess what motive any one can have had for raising such reports as those that are in circulation. No person could have expected to derive any benefit from it, and therefore I am the more inclined to think there must be some truth in the alarming rumours that have reached us."

"As for that, Jeannette," answered her mother, "there are a thousand bad motives to be assigned for it, though we know your lover has never done anything to cause the enmity of any living creature. That there is some cause for raising these suspicions is, however, pretty certain, and we may therefore conclude that time will serve to expose the whole fabrication that has led to all this doubt and misery that you have been made to suffer."

"Aye," exclaimed Suzette, who had entered the room while Madame Corville was speaking, "you are right enough there, I am certain, for I can see through the mystery of all these evil doings, and as sure as fate you will find out by and by that Jeannot has never deserved the base things that have been said against him."

"Are your suspicions directed against any person in particular?" asked Madame Corville.

"Why, I am not able to point out any one by name," answered Suzette; "but I have no doubt you'll find that it's the same person that has all along been trying to do him a mischief. Who it may be I am not able to say, but, at any rate, I don't envy them their feelings, whoever they may be."

"Nor I," returned the elder female, "and what is more, it shall be no fault of mine if the author of these infamous reports is not very soon exposed to the scorn and execration of the world."

"Alas!" sighed Jeannette, "of what use will that be if my poor Jeannot should have lost his life in battle?"

"Ah!" exclaimed Suzette, "there has been a report of that kind to be sure, but, for my own part, I believe he is still alive, and that the only reason for not having heard from him is, that no resting time has been allowed to the troops since the day when the great victory of Austerlitz was won. Poor fellow! I dare say, if the truth could be revealed, to us, we should find he is in as much tribulation about those who are at home, as we are on his account."

"You think, then, there is no doubt of the falsehood of the rumours which have reached us of his death?" asked Jeannette.

"In my own mind," answered her cousin, "I feel quite certain that he is alive, for, had he been killed, as many persons suspect, we should have received official imformation of it before now from the war department. 'No news is good news,' as the old adage has it, and I therefore think you may make up your mind that so far nothing serious has befallen him."

"At all events," exclaimed Jeannette, "there is reason to fear that he may have been seriously wounded."

"It is just possible," answered Suzette; "but even if that should be the case, you have the consolation of knowing that he has received every attention, for Napoleon knows so well the value of a soldier's life, that he has given strict orders for every care to be bestowed upon those who are unfortunate enough to be wounded. It must be confessed, however, that I have a very different opinion as to the cause of his long silence."

"You believe he has forgotten me during his absence?" exclaimed Jeannette with a deep drawn sigh.

"Indeed, my dear coz," answered Suzette, "such a wild notion has never once entered my mind. His is not a heart that could be capable of such deception, and great would be my surprise if it should ever be proved that he forgot, even for an hour, the solemn vow he pledged to you before leaving."

"One would think, to hear you speak," exclaimed Madame Corville, "that it is quite impossible for him to prove inconstant?"

"I may be deceived in my opinion of him," returned Suzette, "but, at all events, I have a notion that Jeannot would rather perish than prove faithless to the oath he has taken. When he was amongst us he always had the character of being strictly honourable, and I can see no reason why we should believe it possible that he should have changed so much as to forget her whom he has professed to love beyond all other persons. I therefore still hold to my opinion that he has been captured by the enemy, and that he has consequently been deprived of the privilege of writing to let his friends know what has become of him."

"In that case," sighed Jeannette, "he may linger on for years in hopeless captivity."

"There I believe you are wrong," interposed Madame Corville, "for it is said the war will soon be brought to a close, and when that is the case it happens, as a matter of course, that all the prisoners on both sides are set at liberty."

"But at present the war is being carried on as fiercely as ever it was," exclaimed her daughter.

"So it may be," replied Madame Corville, "but the foe has been beaten in every battle that has been fought, and there will soon be—as people say—a proposal made for peace. So you see, my dear child, there is still a fair prospect before you, and I hope you will not suffer your spirits to sink, just when there is a probability that you will be gratified by receiving cheering news of your lover."

"To be sure you will," exclaimed Suzette, "and as for the reports that have been flying about respecting his having transferred his affection to some other female, I believe it will turn out that it is nothing more than a malicious invention of some enemy."

"I never knew any person that had an ill feeling against him," answered Jeannette.

"Ah!" exclaimed her cousin, "he had none whilst he was here, it is true, but who knows what foes may have risen up against him since he has been away from us ? To be sure, he was always a good natured, kind-hearted fellow, but unfortunately persons of that description are as liable to have their enemies as those who are always quarrelsome and disagreeable. However, I have a notion that he will not suffer much from the malice of evil-doers, because he has plenty of friends who will never believe a word of the rumours that are spread abroad."

"Aye," returned Madame Corville, "and who will stick up for him back and edge, rather than see him sacrificed through the malice of spiteful people. We have only to wait, therefore, till we see what sort of a turn matters are likely to take, and the character of poor Jeannot shall shine forth in as favourable a light as ever it did."

"That is to say," sighed our heroine, "if he has escaped the many dangers he has had to encounter."

"Why shouldn't he have as good a chance of returning home safe and sound as any of his comrades ?" demanded her mother.

"Because," replied Jeannette, "from the news that we have already heard, it seems that he courts rather than shuns those positions which are most dangerous. The risk he runs is therefore very great, and my mind is almost constantly filled with dread lest he should fall a victim to his own daring gallantry."

"Are you then determined to look only at the most melancholy side of the picture ?"

"I would gladly look on the more favourable side of it if I could do so from any conviction of my own," answered Jeannette. "You smile, and fancy I give way to my fears ; but how can I look forward with any degree of hope when there is an inward dread, that I cannot account for, which warns me that some great danger is impending over him ?"

"Then you are a little simpleton for your pains," exclaimed her mother, "for what have you to do with superstition when we have only reality to deal with ? At present all is doubt and uncertainty, but news of a more favourable description may now reach us, and then you will acknowledge that an old woman's opinion is not always to be despised. No doubt we shall have a very satisfactory reason, explaining the causes, whatever they may be, of his long silence."

"Ah! dear mother," cried Jeannette, "I know your kind motives for trying to persuade me that things are not so bad as I imagined, but I fear your labour is thrown away upon one who can see nothing but misery in the future."

"You are determined, then, to see no brighter prospect before you ?"

"Alas !" she cried, "you know not how much I have tried to find consolation in every circumstance that held out even the slightest prospect that my evil prognostications were ill founded ; but all has been in vain, for each day only serves to convince me more and more that some hidden source of grief is yet to be revealed."

Finding that all her arguments and persuasions were in vain, Madame Corville then left the young folks to conclude a conversation in which she had made so little progress that was satisfactory. As if by common consent, they both ceased to say anything more upon a subject upon which they could form no satisfactory opinion, and it was then agreed that Jeannette should accompany her cousin part of her way home, as there were still some few subjects upon which they desired to confer with each other. Occupied as they were in the matters they had to discuss, our heroine proceeded a greater distance than she had intended, and it was not till the sun was seen setting, that she recollected that a portion of her own way back was through a lonely path which she had always avoided when alone, even in the broad daylight. Seeing that she was rather alarmed, Suzette, who was the most courageous of the two, offered to accompany her a portion of the way back, but this our heroine would on no account agree to, and the two cousins separated, each determined to make the best of her way home.   At length Jeannette reached the place which she held in so much dread, and as it was then nearly dark, she redoubled her speed, looking round every now and then to see if any stranger was near.   Having thus traversed a distance of nearly half a mile, she was approaching the further end of the much dreaded road, when footsteps were distinctly audible, and the dim outline of a form was plainly to be seen coming towards her.   Had it been possible to diverge from the path, she would gladly have done so, but it so happened that a broad ditch was on each side, so that no alternative remained but to face the person whoever it might be.   Poor Jeannette trembled in every limb as if some evil was about to befall her, and she felt ready to sink with apprehension, when a voice that she well remembered to have heard before, saluted her with—

"Well, Mademoiselle Jeannette, I thought I should find you somewhere on this road, for I have been watching you and your cousin for ever so long, and followed at a distance, because I supposed you would return the same way."

"And why have you followed me, Pierre Langrais?" she asked with as much composure as she could assume.

"Because I had something to say to you," he replied.

"Then why not have called at my mother's house, where you are almost sure of finding me?"

"Don't ask me anything about the why and the wherefore," he exclaimed, "since you must know as well as I do that there are times when we want not a third party to be listening to everything that is said.   In short, I have heard something about Jeannot, and wanted to tell you the news without delay."

"If you have anything to tell me of, Jeannot," answered our heroine, "you may spare yourself the trouble, for I believe none of the tales that have been told of him, and am resolved never to do so till I have better proofs than you are likely to produce."

"What makes you fancy that I am going to say anything against him?" asked Pierre Langrais.

"Because I have never yet heard you say anything but that which was intended to do him an injury."

"So your partiality for him may lead you to suppose," returned the other, "but the truth is, I am instigated only by a desire to save you from much pain that I can too plainly foresee.   You believe him to be all perfection, but I would fain convince you that he deserves not the love you have bestowed upon him."

"Monsieur Pierre Langrais," exclaimed our heroine in a tone of command, "if your only object is to utter falsehoods against Jeannot, I desire you will spare yourself all further trouble upon the subject.   You have already been warned never again to mention him in my presence, yet, bent as you are upon doing him an injury, you have now dared to intercept me in my path, though well aware that I would have avoided this interview had there been any possibility of doing so."

"You are cross with me this evening I see, ma'amselle," he replied, "and it seems a notion has been allowed to creep into your mind that I have some prejudice against this lover of yours."

"Whatever my notions may be," answered Jeannette, "this is neither the time nor the place that I choose to argue with you about them.   You will, therefore, please to let me pass, or this insolence of yours may be resented in a way you little expect."

"Do you imagine that I would have taken all this trouble if it had not been in the hope of serving you?"

"I neither know nor wish to enquire into your motives," answered Jeannette, "for it matters little what they may be when I know that you entertain an unfriendly feeling towards one who possesses all my confidence and affection. You have tried before now to fill my mind with false impressions respecting him, and now that I know you to be a dangerous enemy, it is high time to warn you that all further interference in this affair will only be regarded by me as the act a man who has some evil purpose of his own to carry out."

"Psha! I have no ill-feeling against the young man."

"Then you have taken extraordinary pains to injure him, without even having the poor plea to offer that you have formerly received some injury at his hands. Be that as it may, however, you have now heard my determination not to listen to any idle tale that you may have to repeat against him. His character is too

JEANNETTE AND JEANNOT.

precious to me to be blasted by the evil reports of those who dare not utter their slanders to his face, and I therefore once more desire that this interview may be the last."

"At all events I must see you on your way home."

"Not on any account," she replied, "for I would rather walk home alone than accept the protection of one whose actions have proved him to be unworthy of my confidence or respect. I know not which way your way lies, Monsieur Langrais, but mine is forward, and I expect you will not require to be told again that I neither want nor will accept your company."

She moved onwards as these words were uttered, but instead of heeding what she had said, Pierre Langrais persisted in walking close by her side. If she quickened her step, he did the same, and if she relaxed her speed, he accommodated his own pace, so as always to remain near to her.

"It's in vain, ma'amselle, that you want to shake me off," he at length said, "because I am determined to fulfil the purpose that brought me out this evening, and I believe that when I have told all, you will begin to perceive that I have taken no little trouble to save you from a great deal of misery that you were likely to fall into. In short, I am able to prove that the rumours you have heard about Jeannot are but too true."

"There have been some idle reports about him, I believe," replied our heroine, "but fortunately for Jeannot, I am not among those who can be prevailed upon to believe them."

"You may, perhaps," exclaimed Pierre Langrais, "when I inform you that I have received a letter from one of his comrades, in which he informs me that it is now notorious that Jeannot is paying his addresses to another female."

"'Tis false!"

"Nay, ma'amselle," returned the other, "don't be too hasty in forming your opinion about the falsehood of this charge, because I am afraid it can be clearly proved with very little trouble. I can rely upon the person who sent me the letter, and he most positively affirms that Jeannot is no longer faithful."

"And I," answered our heroine, "can as positively affirm that there is not a syllable of truth in the charge."

"May I ask, ma'amselle, upon what ground you can deny the truth of what I have told you?"

"My experience of the honour and integrity of Jeannot are quite sufficient to convince me that he would not be guilty of so base an act as you have ascribed to him."

"How am I to decide, when my informant declares that the fact he speaks of has become quite notorious?"

"Who, pray, is your informant?"

"A stranger to both parties, and therefore he cannot be suspected of any ill-feeling in the matter."

"His name?"

"Jacques Denon."

"I have heard him spoken of," she replied, "and, if I am not much mistaken, by Henri Duport."

"It's not at all unlikely that you may," answered Pierre Langrais, "for I believe they are, or at least have been, friends. However, be that as it may, the fact don't destroy the credit that is due to the statement made by Jacques Denon, and I have therefore thought it my duty to inform you of what I have been told."

"You had better have spared yourself the trouble," exclaimed Jeannette, "for I now see more plainly than before, that this is some scandalous conspiracy to ruin Jeannot in the estimation of all those who regarded him with friendship or affection. As far as I am concerned, however, the plot has entirely failed, for I see through the shallow artifice, and at once pronounce the charge to be utterly without truth for its foundation."

"Nay," answered Pierre Langrais, still persisting in the task he had undertaken, "if necessary I can tell you the name of the female who has robbed you of his affection. Shall I pronounce it, ma'amselle?"

"I have no choice left but to hear whatever you may choose to utter," answered Jeannette.

"Then the name of your rival is Jacqueline Gratz, whose father holds a large farm close to the spot on which was fought the glorious battle of Austerlitz. I have no time to relate all the circumstances connected with the affair, but it appears that Jeannot was seriously wounded in a charge that was made upon the enemy, that he was afterwards found by the farmer, who took him to his house and placed him under the care of his wife and daughter."

"Are you sure he was wounded?" asked Jeannette.

"Quite certain."

"Then he has been in danger?"

"I don't know exactly what the nature of his wound was," replied Pierre Langrais, "but at any rate it was the means of introducing him to the girl I have mentioned, and the end of it has been exactly what I have stated."

"That he may have received injury in the fight, I can but too readily believe," cried Jeannette, "but that he has bestowed his affection upon any one else, I can most positively deny."

"Humph! you think then that it is quite impossible for your lover to prove false to his vows?"

"I should little have deserved his affection if I could have believed him guilty of so vile a deception," answered Jeannette. "Our acquaintance has not been one of a few months merely, but has existed from the time when we were children together, and boy or man, I never yet knew him to be guilty of a dishonourable act."

"That is saying a great deal for your lover," exclaimed Pierre Langrais, "but I may perhaps be excused if, in my turn, I doubt his being so immaculate as you imagine. Why should he be able to resist the attractions of a pretty girl, any more than another person?"

"I do not speak of his being utterly without faults," answered Jeannette, "but I know he would not deceive me, and therefore do I fearlessly pronounce these reports to be groundless."

"What motive can anybody have for raising false rumours against your lover?"

"That," she replied, "is a question that may be answered by and by, though at present his enemies have contrived to conceal the designs which have prompted them to this piece of wanton mischief."

"But how can he have any enemies if he is as free from faults as you would make him appear?"

"It is not for me to enquire how it is," replied Jeannette, "for the fact is only too plain, that there are evil persons who seek to injure him for purposes of their own."

"So you fancy," exclaimed Pierre Langrais, "but why should anybody take so much trouble to injure him, if he has never done anything to injure other persons? For my own part, I have nothing whatever to say against the young man, but at the same time I must say, that he is as likely as anybody else to prove inconstant in love, notwithstanding any vows he may have made to remain true and faithful to the object of his first passion."

"And I," replied Jeannette, "will fearlessly assert that he will be able to prove that there has never been any foundation for the scandalous reports that have been published against him."

"Perhaps, then, you can explain how it is that you have not received a letter from him for so long a time?"

"There is no occasion for me to offer any explanation," replied our heroine. "I have myself the fullest confidence in his honour and integrity, and nothing but the most positive proof will convince me that he is no longer deserving of the esteem and confidence I have ever placed in him. Jeannot is well aware that my affection for him is enduring, and he would not sacrifice it merely because this female you have spoken of has treated him with kindness when he so much needed her care."

"Yet, for all that," exclaimed Pierre Langrais, "it appears to be very strange that he should remain at the farm-house so long after he has recovered from his wound."

"It may appear strange to those who trouble themselves with affairs that they have nothing to do with," answered our heroine. "In my opinion, however, there is good reason for believing that he is not yet quite cured, and that easily accounts for his not having sent word to me of the danger he has been in."

"That's certainly putting the most favourable construction upon his omission," exclaimed Langrais, "but I rather think, when you hear more about this matter, you will find that his having failed to write was occasioned by his wish to keep you in ignorance of where he is, and what he has been doing ever since he has been passing his time so agreeably at the farm-house."

"Agreeably!" cried our heroine;—"can he have passed his time agreeably when he has been suffering tortures from the wound of which you have spoken?"

"Even the pain of a wound may be forgotten in the kind attention he has received from your rival."

"Every word you utter," exclaimed Jeannot, "serves to convince me more and more that you are endeavouring to foment a feeling of jealousy in my heart."

"And pray what reasons can I have for doing so?"

"That is a question," she replied, "that I am not at present able to answer. It may be to serve some private feeling of your own, or you may have been employed by others to do that which they fear to do themselves."

"Upon my life you seem to have a very strange opinion of my motives," he exclaimed.

"If I have," she replied, "you may thank yourself for it, since you have been constantly endeavouring to impress upon my mind these cruel slanders that are intended to cause a rupture between Jeannot and myself. Had I lent a ready ear to the libels you have uttered, there would not have been anything to wonder at in your having persisted in the course you have adopted, but when I have plainly told you that I would believe nothing that was stated upon mere rumour, it was surely time to have ceased the annoyance I have been constantly subjected to."

"You give me no credit, then, for having an anxious desire to save you from the affliction I can foresee."

"I desire to receive no favours from Monsieur Langrais!"

"Indeed!—so you would rather have my enmity than my friendship."

"Your enmity I care nothing for," she replied, "because, with a little caution, I can guard myself against it; and as for your friendship, I would shun it as a mere plea to obtain my confidence, when you are most trying to abuse it."

"Upon my word, ma'amselle," he exclaimed, "you seem to have a very strange opinion of me."

"My opinion, whatever it may be, has been caused by the very extraordinary conduct you have pursued ever since you have been in this neighbourhood."

"You are prejudiced against me, I see."

"Call it prejudice, or whatever you please," exclaimed Jeannette, "but at all events I am not to be deceived by the plausible stories you would abuse my ears with. What your notions may be, you are, of course, better acquainted with than I am, and I leave it to your own conscience to say whether it is not time that you should abandon so useless a design."

"I have no design, ma'amselle, but that of endeavouring to open your eyes to the truth, before it's too late!"

"For which I do not thank you, since I know the real motive that has urged you to adopt this cowardly course."

"Cowardly!—In what way have I deserved to have my actions regarded in that light?"

"Really, Monsieur Langrais," she replied, "I wish you would have the kindness to speak to me no farther upon this painful subject. If I am misled by my over confidence in the honour of Jeannot, the punishment will fall upon

myself alone ; but, since I am still content in the good faith of him who ha
pledged his vows, I am quite confident to remain as I am till my betrothed
lover is able to answer these charges for himself."

" And when he does," persisted Pierre Langrais, " he will not be able to deny
the fact of his having paid such attention to this Jacqueline Gratz as you would
not like to witness."

" Do you imagine, then, that I could feel jealous of his returning the kindness
that—according to your own showing—has been bestowed upon him when he
needed the care and attention of those amongst whom he was thrown ? I
can answer for it, he has done nothing more than I should have approved of, even
if I had been present as a witness."

" Would you like, then, to have seen him and Jacqueline strolling about
together like a couple of lovers ?"

" How could I have objected to their walking out together when I have no
reason for believing that they felt for each other any stronger regard than such
as may be supposed to have arisen from the peculiar circumstances in which they
have been placed ?"

" Well !" exclaimed Pierre Langrais, " it's all right enough, I dare say, for
people to take things easy, but I never saw any one so determined as you are to
disregard the warnings of those who are your truest friends. However, you
know best about it, I suppose, though I must say I think you would have acted
wisely to have waited till you had made enquiries as to the truth of the charges
that have been made against Jeannot."

" Why should I wait for a confirmation of these reports, when I utterly dis-
believe them ?"

" Aye," exclaimed Pierre Langrais, " it may be all very well to say so now,
but by and by you will be convinced that I have spoken nothing but the truth,
and then grievous will be your regret that you would not attend to my oft
repeated warnings."

" If so," she replied, " I alone shall be the sufferer, and therefore you need
feel no concern about it."

" How can I help doing so," asked the other, " when my heart is so strongly
enlisted in this cause, that I have continued to repeat my warnings, though certain
at the time that I was only making myself more and more odious to you. But
never mind, I have done my duty, Jeannette, and that will always be a consolation to me, if nothing else is."

" I know nothing about the consolation you may find in it," answered Pierre
Langrais, " but when Jeannot hears of what has taken place during his absence,
you may expect that he will take immediate steps for the punishment of all those
who have been in any way concerned in defaming his character."

" Ah, ma'amselle !" exclaimed the other, shaking his head, " there is very little
fear of Jeannot being seen in this neighbourhood again."

" Why not ?"

" Because it seems pretty certain that he will marry this Jacqueline Gratz,
and then, as a matter of course, he will settle near her father and mother."

" Who, besides yourself, has ever dared to assert that he will marry any other
than myself?"

" Oh, if you ask me that question," returned the other, " I can reply to it by
saying that the story is repeated by many other persons besides myself,
and is believed too, though you are inclined to put so little faith in it."

" If I disregard your report," answered Jeannette, " it is because it can be
traced only to a person who may have some private pique of his own to
gratify."

" What pique can Jacques Denon have against your lover ?" demanded Langrais.
" They have both been comrades together ever since they met at Toulon, and
I can answer for it that Jacques would rather it had been in his power to report
favourably than otherwise of a friend and fellow soldier."

" It may be so," exclaimed Jeannette, " but at any rate I should have supposed that if he had felt any friendship, he would have tried rather to have endeavoured to conceal, than to make public the faults of the man he professes a regard for. However, some people—and perhaps your informant is one of them—have a very extraordinary way of exhibiting what they are pleased to term their friendship."

"Aye, aye, it may be all very well to doubt the sincerity of Jacques Denon, but before long you will acknowledge that you have done him a great wrong, in suspecting that he has intended any wrong, in making known the perfidious conduct of a man who is making love to one woman, whilst he is shamefully neglecting the one he is betrothed to."

At this moment, Monsieur Narbonne was seen to issue from the dark shadows of a tree, beneath which he had concealed himself, on hearing the well known voice of Jeannette. He walked directly towards her, and placing her arm within his, inquired if she wished for the company of Pierre Langrais any longer.

"Mousieur Langrais is already aware that I wished to return home without him," she replied.

"And Jeannette knows," exclaimed the other, "that I should not have sought her out this evening, but that I wished to speak upon an affair in which she is deeply interested. In fact, Monsieur Narbonne, I have heard very disagreeable news of her lover, and I thought it my duty to put her upon her guard, lest, by and by, the disappointment of her hopes should be all the greater."

"And pray, what may you have heard about Jeannot?"

"Nothing much, certainly," replied Pierre Langrais with affected indifference, "but there seems to be a tolerable certainty that he will soon be married to another girl, who he has met with in a foreign country."

"And pray where have you picked up this piece of marvellous information?" exclaimed the notary.

"From very good authority, monsieur, or, you may rely upon it, I would not have reported it to Jeannette. I have received a letter from a young friend of mine who belongs to the same regiment that Jeannot does, and he tells me that he has both seen and heard quite enough to convince him that the report is too well founded."

"Then you may write him word back that his wilful falsehoods have not obtained any credit amongst those he is most anxious to deceive," answered Monsieur Narbonne.

"And pray what reason have you for pronouncing these reports to be founded on falsehood?" demanded the other.

"I have no right to be questioned for having formed a rational opinion," returned the notary; "but as I have no objection to satisfy you upon that point, I must tell you that the story possesses not a single feature that bears the slightest impress of truth. That there is some villany at the bottom of all this, I am quite certain, and those who have had any share in circulating this lie had better look to themselves, for I shall never rest easy till I have exposed the whole plot to the world."

"But suppose there happens to be no plot to expose?"

"That there is one I am certain," answered Monsieur Narbonne, "for falsehoods of the most glaring kind have been circulated against my young friend Jeannot ever since he was forced to leave this place to fight in the cause of his country. I, however, have my suspicions as to one or two of the persons who are engaged in the plot, and am only biding my time to exhibit, in all their hideous deformity, the scoundrels who have been at so much pains to injure my excellent friend Jeannot."

"Jeannot seems to be a mighty favourite of yours, monsieur," exclaimed Pierre Langrais sneeringly.

"He is."

"But your defence will not go far towards convincing people that he is guiltless of deserting the girl he was betrothed to."

"Who will deem him guilty of faithlessness, when I myself give no credit to the story?" demanded our heroine.

"Who will?" exclaimed Perrre Langrais; "why nine people out of ten already pronounce him to be guilty of a gross and cruel act of deception towards you."

"Then those who do so had better mind their own business than attend to that which don't concern them," exclaimed Monsieur Narbonne. "A few may have been deceived by the specious tales that have been spread abroad, but all those whose opinion is worth having, believe him to have been the victim of false reports."

"All I can say about it is, then, that they will by and by find out that they are mistaken, for Jacques Denon can have no motive for telling a lie against Jeannot, yet he says most positively that he is the accepted lover of Jacqueline Gratz."

"Ah!" exclaimed the notary, "these charges are easily made when those who are the subjects of them are at a great distance off. Had Jeannot been near to us, these execrable falsehoods would never have been uttered. However, as Jeannette is not inclined to place the slightest reliance in what has been said, I know not that it will matter if a few choose to give credit to a rumour that bears so palpably the stamp of falsehood upon it."

"Do you suppose, Monsieur Narbonne, that I have anything to do with it?"

"I neither know nor care whether you have," exclaimed the old gentleman, "but at any rate you seem to be most anxious that Jeannette, at least, should believe the charges that have been brought against her lover."

"I have merely informed her of them in order that she may form her own opinions upon the subject."

"For which I do not believe she is at all obliged to you," replied Monsieur Narbonne. "She has no wish, I dare say, to hear all the tittle-tattle that idle people may think proper to indulge in, and you would have acted with much more wisdom and discrimination to have remained silent upon a subject that cannot in the least concern you."

"You give me no credit, then, for having acted from a sincere wish to oblige Jeannette?"

"Oblige Jeannette! What obligation can she be under, when you have done all in your power to make her unhappy?"

"Then you think I ought to have heard all the rumours, without taking any further notice of them?"

"If you had not been actuated by a spirit of infernal mischief, you would rather have endeavoured to conceal a report that could not but fill her with grief, if it had so happened that she was easily accessible to the idle rumours of those who are never so happy as when they are making other people miserable. However, one good may result from what you have this night attempted; you have seen how little likely Jeannette is to be imposed upon by the villanous schemes that have been put into practice, and it may be a lesson for you in future to mind your own business instead of attending to that of other persons."

"Well, hang me, Monsieur Narbonne," exclaimed Pierre, "if you ain't enough to make a man swear that he will never attempt to do another good-natured act as long as he lives."

"I should rather imagine," answered the old gentleman, "that you are not much in the habit of doing good-natured things, or you would not be so very ready in trying to set people by the ears; at all events, you have endeavoured to the utmost to do your worst in this instance, and I should now advise you to take no further trouble in the business."

"Say as you will, monsieur, I have done nothing more than my duty towards Jeannette."

"Over officiousness cannot be called a duty," replied the notary, "nor do I believe that you had any good motive in reporting to her the news you pretend to have received from your friends."

"Pretend!" exclaimed Pierre Langrais; "if you think proper to read it, I can show you the letter I have received from Jacques Denon."

"What use would it be when I am already satisfied that he has written nothing but falsehoods?"

"Ah! Monsieur Narbonne, how easy it is to contradict the statements of another, when it suits our own purpose. You have taken it into your head that there is some plot against Jeannot, and nothing that anybody else can say will ever convince you that there is any truth in the statements. Ma'amselle here chooses to be of the same opinion, and, by and by she will find out, when too late, that she ought to have attended to my warning."

"Once for all, Pierre Langrais, she is convinced that you have either been grossly deceived, or have wilfully been endeavouring to impose upon her. How that may be, will, however, some day appear, and it may therefore be well for you to take your departure from this neighbourhood before Jeannot returns home and hears the part you have been playing in his absence."

"Psha!" exclaimed Pierre Langrais, "it's not very likely that he will return to this place, when he knows that he cannot dare show himself to the woman he has so shamefully deceived."

"Who besides yourself," demanded or heroine, "dare say that Jeannot has proved false to his vow?"

"There are many besides myself that say so, and are ready to repeat the assertion."

"Those who can utter a lie once are seldom ashamed to repeat it," exclaimed Monsieur Narbonne, "and therefore I should not be inclined under any circumstances to give credit to the lies that have been circulated against my young friend."

"Do you think it impossible that Jeannot can be guilty of things that have been done by others?"

"We are all of us liable to fall into errors," answered the notary, "but I think few are less so than the young man who is the subject of our present conversation. In short, I believe him to be free from all blame in the matter, and nothing will ever make me believe the contrary but such positive proof as there would be no possibility of denying."

"Then, of course, there can be no objection to my writing to Jacques Denon for all the evidence that he can send back?"

"Upon my life, Monsieur Langrais, you seem to take a great deal of trouble in this affair, considering that you can have nothing whatever to do with it."

"What do you mean by my having nothing to do with it," asked the other, "when every man must feel an interest for a young female who is in danger of being cruelly deceived by the lover in whom she has placed all her confidence and love?"

"Do you really, then, pretend to be so very sensitive in the affairs of other people that you would excuse yourself for having tried to make all the mischief you can against these young folks?"

"How can you call it mischief," demanded Pierre Langrais, "when my intention is only to prevent the deception that I see is about to be practised?"

"It seems," observed Monsieur Narbonne, "that you must have taken a great interest in this affair, for I have been watching you ever since you took this road, in order to way-lay Jeannette on her return home."

"Ah!" exclaimed Pierre Langrais, "that shows how earnest I was in my desire to save her from the heavy affliction that I know is about to break upon her. I acknowledge coming this way on purpose to meet Jeannette, and surely no one can blame me for that, notwithstanding the doubts you have thought proper to throw upon my motives."

"For my own part," answered Jeannette, "I should have been much more satisfied if you had omitted that which you would persuade us was intended for kindness."

"And yet you seemed to be frightened enough at having to return home alone," he exclaimed.

PIERRE LANGRAIS' IMPORTUNITIES TO JEANNETTE THWARTED BY THE NOTARY.

"I felt rather timid, it must be confessed," she said, "but would much rather have been spared your company than be forced to listen to things that I know to be utterly without foundation."

"How do you know there's no truth in them till you have heard further upon the subject?"

"Because I place the fullest reliance upon the honour of Jeannot, and feel certain that I shall never have cause to regret having bestowed upon him my love and confidence."

"You judge him exactly as I have done myself," exclaimed Monsieur Narbonne; "and for my own part, I apprehend no change that will ever give us cause for regret or reproach. As for you, Pierre Langrais, you seem to be one of those meddling, interfering persons, whose chief delight consists in making other people miserable."

"Upon my life, Monsieur Narbonne," answered Langrais, "I have not much to thank you for, as far as opinion goes. However, that don't matter, for I know the honesty of my purpose, and by and by you will see reason to acknowledge that, whatever mischief may happen, it will not be through any fault of mine."

"Nor is it any fault of yours," returned the old gentleman, "that Jeannette has not before now given up her lover as one who is unworthy a continuance of her regard."

"And perhaps it would have been wise for her to have done so."

"You must have some motive for this enmity that we have not yet been able to discover."

"Indeed, Monsieur Narbonne," exclaimed the other, "I never had any quarrel with Jeannot, nor is there any other reason why I should endeavour to do him an injury. The report ma'amselle has heard from me is exactly as I received it from my friend, and there is no doubt in my own mind that it may be relied on."

"How can you say that," asked the notary, "when the report, no doubt, comes from an enemy?"

"Did you ever hear that he had an enemy?"

"Some persons have said so before now," replied Monsieur Narbonne, "and I think there is pretty good ground for the supposition, when we recollect the attempts that were made at Toulon to get him into all sorts of dilemmas. That a mischievous spirit was then at work there can be no doubt, and it shall be no fault of mine if the whole affair is not sifted to the very bottom."

"Perhaps you suspect that I had something to do with it?"

"Whether you had or not is a matter that your own conscience can answer better than I," exclaimed the notary. "To speak the truth, however, the notion has crossed my mind more than once, and it may even yet be in my power to discover whether there was sufficient ground for the suspicion."

"Well," exclaimed Pierre Langrais, "all I can say is, that the more you inquire into the affair the more you will be convinced that I have had nothing to do with those that you suspect of being concerned in the two or three scrapes that Jeannot has fallen into. All I wish or care for is, that ma'amselle here may learn the truth before it is too late; and for trying to avert what I consider to be a very serious evil, I am now suspected of being one of his enemies."

"The suspicion has arisen from your own extraordinary conduct," answered Monsieur Narbonne, "for all who have ever been acquainted with Jeannot are quite certain that he is not guilty of the hishonourable act he has been accused of."

"Obstinate people will have their own way I know," returned the other, "but for all that, I feel convinced the time is not very far distant when you will hear that the news sent by Jacques Denon is true in every particular. Then you may be sorry that so little heed was paid to my warning; but it will be too late for you to prevent the grief that Jeannette must feel when she hears that her faithless lover is wedded to another."

Determined not to hear any reply to this, Pierre Langrais now turned away, and took a road which led towards the village where he was lodging. Jeannette and Monsieur Narbonne were well pleased at having been thus released from his society, and congratulating themselves upon the circumstance, they made the best of their way towards the cottage of Madame Corville. On their road the worthy notary could perceive that the rumours had not been quite without the effect that had been intended, and referring once more to the subject of their recent conversation, he produced such arguments in support of his own opinion, that, by the time she reached home Jeannette was fully convinced that her lover was entirely blameless.

CHAPTER XV.

HENRI DUPORT TRIES TO WORM OUT A SECRET, BUT MAKES LITTLE PROGRESS IN HIS INQUIRIES.—SURPRISES HIS FRIEND AND JACQUELINE IN AN INTERVIEW.—UNPLEASANT HINTS ARE MET WITH TART REPLIES.—JEANNOT'S SUSPICIONS ARE AWAKENED, AND HE DETERMINES TO LEAVE HIS PRESENT QUARTERS.—THE FARMER AND HIS FAMILY REMONSTRATE, BUT IN VAIN.

CONVINCED by many circumstances that the feeling which existed between Jeannette and Jacqueline was more than that of mere friendship, Henri Duport determined to observe them narrowly. Towards his companion he always exhibited an appearance of the most sincere friendship, never even hinting that he suspected him of having forgotten his vows to Jeannette, but always, on the contrary, speaking of her as his betrothed wife. Jeannot, therefore, had not the slightest notion of the mischief that was in progress against him, and continuing his attentions to the female to whom he was so much indebted, he was thus unconsciously adding to the proofs which were to be brought forward against him. One evening, when Duport was strolling out alone, he met Edward Gratz as he was returning home, and accosting him, it was agreed that they should walk towards a spot in the neighbourhood which was celebrated for the magnificence of its scenery. Though this was the opportunity that Henri had so anxiously looked forward to, he knew not how to commence his inquiries, and it was not till the subject of their conversation was turned towards the circumstance which had led to Jeannot's long visit there, that he ventured to ask Edward if he did not think a feeling of love had grown up between his friend and Jacqueline. The brother appeared somewhat surprised at the question, but after a short pause he replied :—

"The fact is, Monsieur Duport, I have never given a thought towards the subject, but, since my opinion has been seriously asked, I as seriously answer that I believe Jeannot regards her only in the light of a favourite sister."

"At present it may be so," he replied, "but that is just the sort of love that is likely to ripen into a warmer affection, when the parties are almost constantly in each other's society."

"It may be as you say," exclaimed Edward Gratz, "but I have neither seen nor heard anything in confirmation of the notion that you have taken into your head."

"Do you happen to know if her affections have been bestowed upon anybody else?" asked Duport.

"Why do you ask that question?"

"Because if she is already engaged, there is, of course, an end of my suspicions."

"Well then," answered Edward, laughing, "to confess the truth, I have not heard of there being any lover in the way."

"Perhaps you are sure there is none?"

"Not quite certain," replied the other, "for Jacqueline seldom makes me her confidant, so that it is hardly likely she would do so in a love affair."

"At any rate, I suppose you have no reason to believe that her heart is engaged to any one?" asked Henri Duport.

"I have not."

"Then there is no reason why she may not have given her affections to my young friend?"

"I suppose it may be just possible," answered Edward, " but I think the best way to come at the truth would be to put the question to the persons themselves. They might think it rather an impertinent one to be sure, but what of that. if you happen to obtain the information you are so anxious for."

"You think me more inquisitive than I ought to be," said Henri, "but I am interested in the happiness of my friend, and nothing would afford me greater satisfaction than to hear that he was likely to have found favour with your sister."

"So far that is very kind of you," replied the other, "but now, having answered your questions to the best of my power, may I ask if Jeannot has ever been in love?"

"Has he ever been asked?"

"I believe not, for we should have thought ourselves too inquisitive had such an inquiry been made."

"Has he never hinted at any previous engagement?"

"Never."

"Well then," replied Henri Duport, determined not to be too communicative, "I suppose his heart is quite free, or surely he would have spoken if he had formed any former attachment."

"But, as an old friend of his, you surely would have known if he was in love with any one?"

"That's very true," replied the hypocrite, "and there you have discovered why it is that I suspect my friend has never till now seen any female that he could form a sincere attachment to. I have generally been in his confidence, but I believe hitherto he has not given his affection to any one, unless it may be to your sister."

"And even there I believe you have formed a wrong notion," exclaimed Edward Gratz, "for I have taken some little pains to observe them, and from all that I have hitherto seen, it appears to me that it is nothing more than a warm friendship that they feel towards each other."

"But these warm friendships very seldom stop there, when the persons happen to be of opposite sexes. And between ourselves, Edward, a marriage is not an unlikely thing, for Jeannot has a snug little farm of his own at his native place, and as soon as this war is over he will return to it and pass the remainder of his days in peace and contentment. So you see Jacqueline might wait longer for a husband and fare worse."

"Aye, that may be very true," exclaimed the young farmer, "but at present I am far from satisfied that there is any affection between them. Besides, Jeannot is about to leave us very soon, and it is more likely than not that we may never see him again."

"He would be an ungrateful fellow if he was to forget those to whom he owes so much."

"Nay, I can answer for it," exclaimed Edward Gratz, "that he is not ungrateful, for never does a day pass but he acknowledges the services it has luckily been in our power to perform for him. However," he added laughing, "the wish, I have heard, is sometimes father of the thought, and I suppose, if the truth was known, you would be glad to see a prospect of your friend settling in life."

"Depend on it nothing would afford me greater pleasure than to see him the husband of your sister."

"That's kind of you, no doubt; but suppose Jacqueline should have been previously engaged?"

"I hardly think that's likely," replied Henri Duport, "for a secret of that kind is seldom kept long, so that some of your family must have heard of it if there was a lover in the way. Besides, she would not suffer Jeannot to stroll about with her so often, if there was any fear of exciting the jealousy of another."

"Well," laughed Edward, "if it will set your mind at rest, I believe I may venture to say that no offer has yet been made for her hand. She is free, therefore, to make any choice she likes, and, between ourselves, friend Duport, I for one, should not be sorry if our young guest was to be the favoured individual."

"Am I at liberty to tell him as much?"

"Not on my account," exclaimed Edward, "for the proposal, if any is to be made, must come from him in the first instance. But why, in the name of fortune, are you so very anxious to see a marriage between Jeannot and my sister Jacqueline?"

"What other motive can I have than that of witnessing the happiness of the two persons whom I regard?"

"Why are you sure they would be happy?"

"Because their tempers appear to be congenial, and it is quite certain that they do not regard each other with indifference."

"You may have observed them more closely than I have," exclaimed Edward, "but, for my own part, I see no reason for coming to such a conclusion as you have. Jeannot has suffered much pain, even though his wound has been healed, and as his health required exercise, Jacqueline has been kind enough to accompany him in his walks, because no other part of the family could spare time from the business of the farm. This, I believe, is the only foundation for the idea that has got into your head, and depend upon it you will discover before long how much you have been mistaken."

"I don't think it," replied Henri Duport, "and no doubt Madame Gratz would be of my opinion if anybody was to take the trouble of asking what she thinks of it."

"Why do you think that?" asked Edward.

"Because women always detect matters of this kind much more quickly than persons of our sex," answered Duport. "It is more natural for them to do so, I suppose; and there is, besides, the probability that Jacqueline may have confided to her a secret, that she would carefully guard from all other persons."

"That is to say, supposing there is anything of the kind to communicate," observed Edward Gratz. "I, however, am still of opinion that you are rather too hasty in jumping at conclusions, and would venture a wager that the feeling between them is no stronger than such as may exist between excellent friends."

"At all events, I shall try to ascertain the fact."

"How are you to do so?"

"By putting the question boldly to Jeannot. He cannot be offended at my feeling interested in his behalf; and, even if he is, his anger will not last long when he comes to reflect that I have only his own future happiness at heart."

"But if he wished you to know his secret, surely he would have mentioned it to you before now?"

"And in my opinion he has wanted to do so," answered Duport, "but that his diffidence has hitherto restrained him. Several times, indeed, he has seemed determined to make a desperate effort, but something always stopped him before he got to the point, and I was left to guess his meaning as well as I could."

This latter assertion of Henri Duport's was a palpable falsehood, uttered only in the hope of drawing out the secret he was so anxious to discover. The other however, had in truth nothing to reveal, for till now he had never even so much as suspected that an affection had arisen between Jeannot and his sister, and nothing that had now been said would convince him that they regarded each other with more than friendly warmth. Henri Duport saw that he had failed in his attempt, and the mortification he felt was greater than he was willing to show. At length, after walking some little distance in silence, he said—

"You may think it strange, perhaps, that I have spoken to you so plainly upon this subject, but the truth is, it would have rejoiced me so much to hear that my suspicions were well founded, that I was not able to restrain myself any longer from asking the few questions you have heard."

" Then," answered Edward Gratz, " as I have not been able to give a satisfactory reply, you will perhaps next ask Jeannot, who will, no doubt, readily gratify your curiosity."

" So I would," replied Henri Duport, " but I do not wish him to know that I even suspect such a thing."

" Why not? Is it likely that he could suspect you of not feeling rejoiced at the prospect of his happiness ?"

" He knows me too well to suspect anything of that kind," answered Duport ; " but I have another reason, which just at this time I cannot very well explain. All I wished at present was to be certain that he was paying his addresses to your sister, because I know well the *feelings* with which this intelligence would be received at home, if I was to write to his friends, announcing that it is likely he will soon be married."

" Would it afford gratification, do you think ?"

" No doubt it would—to some."

" There would be no objection then, I suppose, to his marrying the daughter of a foe ?"

" How can your father be regarded in the light of a foe, when but for him, and yourself, poor Jeannot must have perished on the field on the night after the battle ? Think you we Frenchmen have no gratitude for so generous an act ?"

" Aye," exclaimed Edward Gratz, " but you seem to think too much of that which we can only regard as a duty. Your friend, no doubt, fought bodily and well before he fell wounded, and it was not for us to stand and deliberate, when a fellow creature must have perished but for the assistance it was in our power to bestow."

By this time they had nearly reached the place which it had been their object to visit, and on suddenly turning an abrupt rock which stood in their road they came to the lofty summit, from which was to be obtained the most magnificent prospect in the country. There, seated upon a ledge that had been cut out of the solid rock for the accommodation of visitors, sat Jeannot and Jacqueline, wrapped in admiration at the enchanting scene that was opened before them. Neither of them seemed to be aware of the approach of intruders till they were close upon them, and then Jacqueline started from the reverie into which she had fallen, sprang from the seat, and threw herself with some confusion into the arms of her brother. Jeannot also appeared to have been taken by surprise, for he also rose hastily, and darted a look of anger towards the two new comers, as if he suspected that their visit was intended purposely to surprise and annoy them. Henri Duport was the only one who seemed to be disconcerted, and addressing himself to our hero, without any appearance of being surpised at the meeting, he said—

" By Jove, old fellow, who would ever have expected to meet *you* here ? Edward and I took a stroll this way to see a remarkably fine view that I had been told of, and neither of us had the slightest notion that we should pounce upon you and the young lady in this sort of fashion."

" Our walk has been rather a longer one than we usually take," answered Jeannot, " and feeling fatigued, we sat ourselves down here to enjoy a prospect that I never saw excelled."

" You have never been here before, then ?"

" Never."

" How strange, then, that we should have come the same walk at the very same time."

" I see nothing very singular about it," interposed Edward Gratz, " for our young friend has said that he would not leave the neighbourhood without seeing the prospect, and I suppose he has taken the opportunity of the first fine day, since his visit here is drawing so near to a close."

" Dear brother, let us return home," exclaimed Jacqueline, in a whisper tha
was intended only for the ear of him to whom it was addressed. Observing
that she still trembled, and remembering the conversation that had recently
passed between him and Henri Duport, he immediately acceded, and leading
her away, the two companions were left to themselves. Jeannot felt so vexed
and confounded at what had taken place, that he would have followed their
e ample immediately afterwards, but that Duport, perceiving his design, inquired
  he felt annoyed at having been interrupted during a *tete-a-tete* with a young
  y."

" That depends upon circumstances," answered the other, " for if you are
schievously inclined, it will be easy to report this affair, so that I shall appear
iculous in the eyes of the world, and guilty in those of Jeannette."

" My dear fellow, do you think I would injure you ?"

" That remains to be proved," answered Jeannot, " for that I have enemies
somewhere is quite certain, by the attempts that have been made more than
once to ruin me in the estimation of those whose regard I most dearly prize."

" I hope you don't suspect me of having anything to do with it ?"

" I know not who to suspect," answered Jeannot, " for my enemies, whoever
they are, take good care to conceal their villanous designs under the mask of
friendship."

" Upon my life, I am almost inclined to fancy that *I* am one of the persons
you suspect."

" Then you may spare yourself all uneasiness in that respect," answered
the other, " for I have not yet been able to decide in my own mind who it
is that I am indebted to for several acts that certainly were not intended for my
advantage."

" You must have made some mistake surely," exclaimed Henri Duport, with
seeming kindness, " for where is the man that would endeavour to injure another,
who, I may say without flattery, is esteemed by all who know him. No, no, my
good fellow, your ear must have been abused by some evil-disposed person for
purposes that we have yet to discover."

" On the contrary, not a soul has ever tried to make me believe that which
my own experience was sufficient to make manifest. However, this is a subject
that I had no intention of speaking to you about, for I am now upon my guard,
and before long I dare say I shall discover who it is that has been trying to do
me all this mischief."

" Surely you must have some notion who it is ?" exclaimed Henri, anxious to
see how far he was safe.

" At present I do not," he replied, " and even if I had my suspicions I should
be very careful not to mention them, lest it should be the means of defeating the
object I have in view."

" What may your object be ?"

" To expose the falsehoods that have been spread abroad, and thus clear
my own character from the charges that these secret enemies have brought
against me."

" Again I say there must be some mistake in this," exclaimed Henri Duport,
" for surely if such reports as you speak of had been circulated, I should have
heard of them ?"

" I don't know that," replied Jeannot, " for it is only in the neighbourhood
of my own native village that these rumours have been set afloat. There
they are known well enough, and I may think myself lucky if they do
not injure me in the estimation of those whose good opinion is most dear
to me."

" And who has been telling you all this nonsense ?"

" One who is not likely to deceive me," answered Jeannot. " I have received
a letter from Monsieur Narbonne, the notary, and he tells me that there have
been charges made against me, which I ought to contradict without loss of
time."

" Why don't you do so then ?"

" I have, as far as a flat denial goes."

" How have you done so ?"

" By means of a letter which I sent back to him by return of post," answered Jeannot.

" That was, no doubt, the proper course to pursue," answered the other, " but if the reports you speak of have made any impression at all, I suspect your denial will not have much effect against the mischief that has been done."

" If that don't do," exclaimed Jeannot, " they'll at least do me the justice to wait till I can return home and destroy the web that has been so skilfully constructed to destroy me. For a time my enemies may enjoy their triumph; but their dismay and confusion shall be all the greater when I can bring forward my proofs to convict them of cowardice and falsehood."

" I suppose," observed Henri Duport, with seeming interest, " they have been trying to injure you with Jeannette ?"

" They have," answered Jeannot; " the good notary tells me in his letter that one Pierre Langrais has been endeavouring to circulate a report that I am at this time paying my addresses to Jacqueline, the daughter of the person who saved my life."

" Well, but my good fellow," exclaimed Henri, " you must not blame people for making a mistake when there may have been apparently good reason for supposing that you may have found favour in the sight of the young lady. On your part it may be nothing but gratitude perhaps ; but those who are mere lookers on may very likely think you have fallen desperately in love with her."

" But surely you don't believe anything of the kind," returned Jeannot.

" Why should I suppose that you are less susceptible to the tender passion than any of the rest ?"

" Because you know I am engaged to Jeannette by a solemn vow, and it would be base indeed were I to deceive one who has ever placed the fullest confidence in me."

" Aye, that might be all very well to say if you had not been parted from her so long," answered Henri Duport ; " but lovers, like other people, may prove forgetful sometimes, and the fact of your not having written for a long period to Jeannette must have convinced her before now that the engagement between you is at an end."

" I'll be bound such a thought has never crossed her mind," exclaimed Jeannot, " and if we could only know for a certainty what she really does think, we should discover that my neglect has been excused on account of the wound I have received. Besides, she knows well enough that nothing will ever tempt me to be faithless to my vow; and though, perhaps, rather surprised at my silence, I am satisfied she will not attribute it to a wrong cause."

" Then you would fain make me believe that you have not fallen in love with Jacqueline ?"

" I certainly should not try to convince you, if so foolish a notion has entered your head," answered Jeannot ; " but I should think my own denial ought to be sufficient, whatever cause you may fancy you have for thinking me unfaithful."

" Why, the truth is," replied Henri Duport, " people may be excused for forming a wrong notion, if circumstances appear to warrant it. In short, you and this young female have become so much attached to each other, that you are never so happy as when together."

" You think so, because we happened just now to be found in each other's company."

" Why, that certainly looked rather suspicious," exclaimed Henri, laughing ; " but there have been reasons before to-day why I have fancied that you think more of Jacqueline now than you do of your first love."

"Surely," returned Jeannot, as a sudden thought crossed his mind, "surely it was not you who spread this report which has reached the ears of Jeannette?"

"Why you must know it was not," returned Henri, "for our old friendship must convince you that I would rather serve a friend than do anything to injure

JEANNOT MAKES A CONFESSION, OF A DELICATE NATURE, TO HERMAN GRATZ.

him. Besides, I have not written home for a long time past, and therefore no communication can have been made by me."

"I only mentioned it," answered Jeannot, "because I know this Pierre Langrais was an acquaintance of yours, and it seemed but too likely that he has acted the part of mischief-maker for the sake of pleasing you."

" Pleasing me ?"

" Yes, you have always loved Jeannette, and how could your cause be so well
served as by making her believe that you are faithless to the vow you have made
her ?"

" Ah! then I begin to see that you really believe me capable of playing the
part of a traitor ?"

" I won't go so far as to say that," answered Jeannot, " but some people
fancy that all is fair in love matters, and you may imagine that it is
worth some pains to secure the affection which has been bestowed upon myself."

" On the contrary," replied Henri Duport, " I considered all hope of gaining
her at an end, and therefore could have no such intentions as you have
imagined."

" Well," exclaimed the other, " it would be in vain for you and I to argue
that point now, for whatever I may say in support of my own suspicions, I have
no proof whatever to bring forward."

" But what the deuce, my good fellow, could have put it into your head that
I had anything to do with the evil reports that have been circulated by Pierre
Langrais ?"

" The thought merely crossed my mind, and I always think it better to speak
out one's mind at once than to remain in doubt and uncertainty, when they may
be so easily put an end to."

" Perhaps it is as well that you did so," exclaimed Henri, " for now you have
given me an opportunity of contradicting whatever false notions may have been
put into your head. Nay, as you have gone so far, I shall take the earliest
opportunity to ask Jeannette whether I have, either by myself or through anybody else, hinted that I still entertain a hope that she may yet be mine.
At all events, I feel certain that you will be satisfied with the answer you
receive."

" Why should you do that," asked Jeannot, " when it will only cause her
uneasiness to learn that a difference has arisen between us with respect to her ?
Let her then remain in ignorance of what has this day passed between us, and I
will, for my own part, think no more of a suspicion that you declare to be utterly
groundless."

" And am I to understand, then," asked Henri, " that you have not fallen in
love with Jacqueline ?"

" Certainly you are," he replied.   " I regard her only in the light of a sister,
and surely she deserves all my gratitude and esteem, after having so largely con-
tributed towards restoring me from the effects of a dangerous wound.   At all
events I cannot help esteeming her for the generous devotions she has exhibited,
and cannot envy those who mistake my gratitude for love."

" Psha ! one would imagine there was some great crime in loving her."

" The crime," answered Jeannot, " would not consist so much in the loving
her as in deceiving one who has placed all her confidence in my honour.   Jeannette, of her own accord, would never have believed that I could prove false to
my vows ; but where others busy themselves in matters that concern them not,
it is scarcely to be wondered at if she believes that I have yielded to the fascina-
tion of a rival."

" Are you sure she has reason to believe there is a rival ?"

" There can be no doubt of it, for Pierre Langrais would not suffer such an
opportunity to pass when there was mischief to be done."

" Surely you must be mistaken about this Pierre Langrais ?"

" How can I be mistaken," asked Jeannot, " when I have received all the
particulars of the strange rumours that have reached home ?"

" But surely Jeannette would not believe the tales that may be circulated
against you ?"

" Who can blame her if she does ?" demanded the young man.

" Why, I should think she ought to have more confidence in you than all that comes to."

" Confidence ! Is there any one that can turn a deaf ear to reports like these, when they are being constantly repeated ? Besides, there is much blame to myself for having neglected to write, when I knew the anxiety and alarm she must feel when news reached her that I had been wounded in battle. Indeed, take it altogether, I can make no excuse for myself for having suffered her to remain in ignorance of my fate, when she ought to have been the first to whom it was communicated."

" Aye, aye, it may have been very thoughtless, I dare say ; but you are not the first person that has been guilty of similar omissions, and I'll be bound Jeannette will be ready enough to pardon you when she finds that there is no rival to be afraid of."

" But Pierre Langrais will take care to keep up this falsehood about Jacqueline."

" I don't pretend to know how that may be," exclaimed Henri Duport, " but I should suppose Jeannette is accustomed to judge for herself sometimes, and if she does, as in the present instance, she will surely make up her mind to wait till she learns from yourself whether or not there is any truth in the report."

" That's very true," answered Jeannot, " but she has no doubt been told that I continued a visitor in the house of Herman Gratz till long fter my wound was sufficiently healed to permit my departure."

" There, between ourselves, is some ground for surprise."

" And yet so it is," exclaimed Jeannot. " There seems to be a spell that leads me to this neighbourhood, and though I have many times made up my mind to take leave of my kind friends, I still remain, as if unable to leave it."

" Then, depend upon it," laughed Henri, " you love this girl more than you would acknowledge even to yourself."

" Nay, if I thought so, I would have taken my leave of her long ere this time."

" My dear fellow," exclaimed Henri Duport, " why should you have done so when it would have been depriving yourself of a great pleasure ? Besides, you owe a very heavy debt of gratitude to these worthy people, and it would have been most unhandsome had you left their house when they were looking forward to your remaining here a short time longer as their visitor."

" But what will be said by my commanding officer when I return to my regiment ?"

" Why what should he say," demanded Henri Duport, " except that you were a lucky fellow to have found yourself in such comfortable quarters at a time when everybody else fancied you were left dead on the field of battle ? For my part, if the case had been my own, I should hardly have regretted the wound, in consideration of its having led to a very agreeable introduction into a very agreeable family."

" That may be all very well," exclaimed Jeannot, " but the gratification is materially damped when I recollect the mischief that an ill-natured report may do me with those whom I most love, and whose esteem is dearer to me than anything else in the world."

" But an explanation will very soon bring everything to rights again," answered Duport.

" It's easy enough to say so," returned the young man, " but there is more difficulty than you imagine in removing an impression that has been seriously formed. In short, the same tongue that has been uttering all these falsehods against me would still be employed in the same task, and who would wonder if Jeannette was to believe the rumour in preference to any contradiction with which I might meet it ?"

" I don't know how that may be," replied Henri Duport, " but I should think she would rather believe your denial of it than the charge itself, which, like everything else of the kind, is all very well till the other side has been heard. By the bye," he added, finding that his friend made no reply, "I have been speaking to Edward Gratz upon the subject, but he either knows nothing, or pretends that he has no idea of your being in love with his sister."

"How could you speak to him upon that subject?"

"Because I found you were not likely to open your mind to me about it, and I thought there was a chance of getting something out of him."

"Wasn't he angry at your presuming to hint at such a thing?"

"I don't know whether he was or not," answered Henri, "but at any rate he was wise enough to conceal his anger even if he felt any. To be sure he seemed to be a little bit surprised, but that was hardly to be wondered at if it was done to deceive me as to the real state of the case."

"Edward Gratz can never have had any suspicion of that which never had any foundation," answered Jeannot. "That I have been much in the society of his sister is very true, but is there anything remarkable in that, when I must ever esteem myself so deeply indebted to her kindness?"

"You'll think me a very inquisitive fellow, I dare say," exclaimed the other, "but as a friend, I would ask, if—supposing your word had not been given to Jeannette—you would not have been over ears in love with the daughter of the people who have made their house your home?"

"I don't know how that might have been," he replied, "but this I can say, I have never regretted the vow I made to Jeannette; and unless she has been led away by the tales related against me, she, and none else, will be my wife."

By this time they had reached the farm-house, which the two young men entered and proceeded to the room which was usually occupied by the farmer and his family. Here they found Herman Gratz and his wife, both of whom welcomed their return with the hearty hospitality for which they were so pre-eminent. Neither Edward nor his sister, however, were there, and Henri Duport, glad of an excuse to leave, hurried away again immediately to seek after the young folks. It soon became evident that Jeannot was anxious to relieve his mind upon some subject that was not very agreeable to him, and no sooner had the farmer made the discovery, than he at once asked what it was that had made him so dull all on a sudden. Thus appealed to, Jeannot advanced towards the farmer, and taking his hand, exclaimed:—

"You have seen by my altered countenance that something weighs heavily upon my mind, and it is now time that I confess to you a secret which I ought to have told before now."

"There may be a secret," answered the farmer, shaking the hand which he still clasped within his own, "but, short as our acquaintance has been, I'll dare be sworn that it is not one which you need I be astounded to utter nor I to hear."

"A thousand thanks for your good opinion of me, my dear sir," exclaimed Jeannot, "and I believe when you have heard me to an end you will still acknowledge that I have done nothing to deserve your displeasure. However, from the time I have been here, and the kindness I have received, it was my duty to have told you before now that——"

"Well, why are you afraid to speak out?" asked the farmer, seeing him hesitating,—"I suppose, if the truth was known, you have fallen desperately in love?"

"You have guessed, monsieur."

"I thought so,—and the object of your affections is——"

"Not her whose name you were about to mention," interrupted Jeannot.

"Who, then, was I thinking of?"

"I may be wrong," exclaimed the young man, "but I fancy you have thought that I was going to propose for your daughter."

"I did so," he replied, "so there's the honest truth of it; but if you don't care about the girl, why there's an end of it, and I can see no reason why you and I should be the worse friends for it."

"Indeed, Monsieur Gratz," exclaimed Jeannot, "I will take care that you shall never have reason to reproach me with ingratitude after the favours and services I have received from you. I have indeed everything to be thankful for, and I can hardly account for it that I have not before now been able to find courage enough to inform you that I was betrothed to the mistress of my first affections ere I left my native village."

"My dear fellow." he replied, "I see no reason why you should have made *me* your confidant."

"Under other circumstances it might not have been necessary," answered Jeannot, "but in this case I see that I ought to have done so, since it would have avoided the painful situation in which we are all placed."

"You mean, I suppose, that we began to look upon you as a suitor for my daughter's hand?"

"I am afraid my attention to her may have led to a supposition of that kind."

"Well, my dear Jeannot," exclaimed the old man, "to tell you the truth, there was a time—and that not very long either—when my good dame and I had a notion that you were looking forward to become our son-in-law."

"And no doubt you were both angry at my supposed presumption?"

"Indeed we were not," answered Monsieur Gratz, "for the truth is, there's a young chap has been paying his addresses to Jacqueline for some time past, and as we had no very great fancy for him, we were rather in hopes that you would be able to cut him out."

"This is the first time that I have heard of your daughter having been sought in marriage."

"It is nevertheless true, for all that," answered Herman Gratz.

"And does your daughter return his love?"

"I believe so," answered the old farmer, "but at all events she knows that, however inclined we may be to humour and indulge her in all other cases, in this one we have a decided objection to the man she has named with favour."

"How is it that I have never seen him?" asked Jeannot.

"Because, like yourself, he is engaged in war far away from this place," answered the farmer.

"But is it not singular that Jacqueline has never once spoken or hinted of such a person?"

"Why, the truth is," he replied, "these are subjects that young girls are not very apt to speak about, and as you have never said anything to lead her to suppose that you were going to make a proposal, she saw no necessity for making you her confidant. It is, however, quite true that the young man I speak of has gained her affections; and the probability is, that if he should happen to return safe and sound, we shall, in the long run, give our consent to the match, rather than do aught that may embitter her future days."

"Is the match a disproportionate one?" asked Jeannot.

"No," replied the farmer, "his family is sufficiently respectable; but the truth is, he has always been of rather a gay turn, and I am afraid to trust him with the dearest treasure I possess."

"Ah," replied Jeannot, "if that is the only thing against him, he may amend before marriage!"

"He has already reformed very considerably," exclaimed Herman Gratz, "but the truth is, I cannot altogether get over the prejudice I have taken against him. However, if Jacqueline is determined not to alter her choice, neither myself nor her mother will oppose the union."

"Is she aware of that determination?"

"I don't know that she is," answered the farmer, "but at any rate she may pretty well guess as much, for she knows we never unnecessarily oppose her wishes, and in this respect I would rather sacrifice my own feelings than her's. However, I had a notion up to the present time that you felt a strong regard for my daughter, and, to confess the truth, I should have made no objection had such a proposition been made to me."

"And for my own part," exclaimed Jeannot, "nothing could have afforded me more gratification than such an alliance, had it not been for the previous engagement that I have spoken of."

"Does the young lady you speak of know the circumstances which have led to your being our guest?"

"She does."

"And is she not rather jealous of the attention you have received from another female?"

"I know not how that may be," answered Jeannot, "for that will depend upon how the affair has been mentioned to her. If she has heard of it through a friend, the impression will not be against me, but if the news has been conveyed to her by an enemy then I may conclude, that she will fancy that I have forgotten the vow I made to her."

"Have you, then, any enemies to be afraid of?"

"I have."

"Do you know who they are?"

"No," replied Jeannot, "they are too cautious for that; but I believe it will not be very difficult to make the discovery as soon as I return home. At all events I will lose no opportunity for the want of trying, and, should I succeed, I will not rest till the whole of their villanous plot has been revealed."

"Take my advice, my young friend," exclaimed the farmer, "and take no heed of the past, unless you should find that any very serious mischief has been done. The young female you speak of has, I should imagine, sufficient judgment of her own to decide upon the probable truth or falsehood of the accusation, and the chances are that she will decide in your favour."

"That she would do so of her own accord I am quite satisfied," replied Jeannot, "but if my enemy has decided upon doing me an injury he will not give up till he has accomplished the devilish mischief he has plotted."

"Well," interposed Madame Gratz, "at all events I should suppose you would soon be able to contradict any falsehoods that may be told against you?"

"Very true, my dear madame," answered Jeannot, "but my contradiction may come too late, since 'tis hard to undo the mischief that has been done by another."

"Have you never been able to discover who these enemies are that you complain of?" asked Herman Gratz.

"I fancy I know the name of one of them," answered Jeannot, "but it may appear strange when I tell you that I have never had any acquaintance with the person, and consequently am at a loss to know in what I have ever offended him."

"Then I should suppose the young female you speak of will not easily give credit to the calumnies of a stranger."

"That will depend upon circumstances," exclaimed the young soldier, "for Jeannette cannot know upon what ground the accusation may be made. She will not, however, very readily yield her belief to any stories related to my prejudice, and in that thought is my chief hope of escaping from the intended mischief of my foe."

"No doubt you will," said the farmer, "and I need hardly say that if any testimony of mine should be required it will be at all times at your service. At all events I can speak as to your conduct ever since you have been here, and my testimony cannot fail to be of some service, when I state that your conduct has never once met with my disapproval."

"There's only one thing that appears rather singular," exclaimed Madame Gratz, "and that is, your silence till the present moment as to your previous engagement."

"Had I suspected what was to take place," answered the young man "I should most assuredly have revealed that which has just now come out. However, the truth is, I thought the affair altogether uninteresting to any one here, and thence arose the apparent wilful concealment of which I have been guilty."

" As for that, my dear fellow," exclaimed Herman Gratz, " it was no affair of mine, and I think you did perfectly right in not saying anything about it. In short, if there was blame any where, we must take it upon ourselves, because it was our duty to have put the necessary questions, when we supposed you had formed an attachment to our daughter."

" My good friend," returned Jeannot, " I see no reason why you should take any blame upon yourself, when there could be no ground for supposing that my promise had been already given to another. My silence, it is true, has turned out unfortunate, but luckily there is yet time for me to amend the error. I will therefore take leave of my hospitable friends, and surely, then, those who have made themselves so busy in my affairs will no longer have an excuse for poisoning the ear of Jeannette with these tales, many of which are inventions intended to answer certain purposes of their own."

" You are not serious, I hope, in this intention to leave us?"

" Indeed, my dear sir, I can see no other way of getting out of this dilemma," answered Jeannot. " I am now sufficiently recovered to return to my duty, and without loss of time I shall repair to the head quarters of our army."

" Then you do intend to go back to Berlin?"

" I do," answered the young man, " for if the news which has reached us is true, Napoleon has been so far favoured by victory that he has taken possession of that city with very little difficulty. There it will be my duty to join my regiment, and as peace is likely to be signed very soon between the contending parties, I am not without hope that a few weeks will enable me to return home to my native village."

" And then, I suppose," said Madame Gratz, " you will soon marry your Jeannette?"

" There will be nothing to oppose our union," answered the young soldier, " unless she has given credit to the foul slanders that have been related against me."

" Surely she will not believe the reports, without first of all hearing what answers you have to make to them?"

" I hardly think she will," exclaimed Jeannot, " but it seems that my foes are determined not to be defeated in their purposes, and that being the case, it is impossible to say how far she may be imposed upon by their artfully conceived plans. And yet, from what my friend, Monsieur Narbonne, tells me in his letter, she seemed determined to believe me guiltless, though almost everybody else thought there must be truth in the circumstances related by the fellow who has made himself so officious throughout the affair."

" Well," exclaimed the farmer, " if she refuses to give any credit to the stories that he has told, you have very little reason to care what anybody else may think of them."

" And especially," said Jeannot, " as I am led to believe Madame Cor-ville is still determined to defend me against all the attempts that have been made."

" Madame Corville is, I suppose, the mother of the female you are betrothed to?"

" She is," replied Jeannot ; " and in her I have always found a friend, ready to take part with me against all slanders that evil-minded persons have heaped upon me. Then there is Monsieur Narbonne, who remains my firm friend under all circumstances, and with two such advocates as they are, I can even now hope that Jeannette will not listen to evil reports until she has heard more evidence than has yet been brought against me."

Just as this young man had arrived at this rather satisfactory conclusion, he was prevented saying any more by the entrance of Jacqueline, who, still pale and agitated, leaned for support upon the arm of her brother. The two last named personages seated themselves by the old folks, and the conversation then turned upon the subject of Jeannot's departure, which it was announced was to take place on the following morning.

———

CHAPTER XVI.

THE DEPARTURE.—JEANNOT ARRIVES AT HEAD-QUARTERS OF THE ARMY.— HAS AN INTERVIEW WITH HIS COMMANDING OFFICER, AND THE SATISFAC- TORY EXPLANATION HE GIVES.—HENRI DUPORT STILL CARRIES ON HIS DE- SIGNS.—OUR HERO BEGINS TO SUSPECT THAT HE HAS AN ENEMY NEARER AT HAND THAN HE HAD HITHERTO THOUGHT FOR.—A FRIENDLY CAUTION.

IN spite of the pressing solicitation of his friends, Jeannot was resolute in his determination to take his leave of them, and accordingly on the following morn- ing, he and Henri Duport left the farm-house and commenced what appeared to be a long and fatiguing journey towards Berlin, where they knew their regiment was then in quarters. It is not our intention, nor indeed is it necessary to follow them on their march, for no particular adventure befell them on the way, and it will therefore suffice to say, that towards the middle of the fifth day after their departure from the farm, they entered Berlin, which they found in full posses- sion of the French army. Their first care was to march to the barracks in which their regiment was quartered, and where Jeannot was welcomed by is companions in arms, like one who had risen from the grave. After this the next thing that was to be done, was to report his return to the commanding officer, who sent back word that he was to repair immediately to the lodgings of Colonel Laroche, to whom he was to explain the reason of his long absence. To Jeannot there seemed to be something ominous in this message, but after a little consideration he reflected that the account he had to give of himself must prove completely satisfactory, and that therefore he had no reason for avoiding the interview. In the full consciousness, then, of having a good cause to plead, he left his comrades and proceeded at once to the colonel's lodgings, upon arriv- ing at which he was conducted into the presence of the officer, a man of most severe aspect, though generally said to be kind and humane to those who were placed under his command. He was seated at a table reading some military documents when Jeannot entered the room, but raising his eyes he surveyed him for a few moments with a scrutinising glance, and then throwing down the papers, inquired the name of the person who stood before him.

"Jeannot Lamont," was the brief, but respectful reply.

"Humph! you have been reported for some time past as having neglected your duty. What reason have you to give for not joining your regiment before now?"

"I fell wounded in the battle of Austerlitz," answered the young soldier, "and it was only by a miracle that I escaped death."

"Was your wound a very serious one?"

"It was, monsieur," he replied, "but I believe was never at any time consi- dered dangerous."

"That is candid, at any rate," exclaimed the querist, "and you will find, young man, that it will be to your own advantage to conceal nothing which it is my duty to inquire into. Where, pray, was the wound you spoke of?"

"In the shoulder, monsieur."

"And was it of sufficient magnitude to render necessary so long an absence from duty?"

"I fancied I might have joined my regiment sooner," answered Jeannot, "but the persons who found me after the battle was over, and to whose care and at- tention I perhaps owe my life, would not hear of my leaving them till all danger was over."

"Then, I suppose, you wish me to infer that your absence was not ⸻ by cowardice."

"Cowardice, monsieur!" exclaimed Jeannot. "Did I prove myself a coward up to the time when, fainting from loss of blood, I fell among a heap of comrades, who had already lost their lives in the hottest part of the battle."

JEANNOT EXONERATED FROM COWARDICE BY HIS COLONEL.

"You are right, my good fellow," returned the colonel, "and the question, it must be admitted, was one that I was not justified in asking. In truth, I have been told that you acted with a great deal of bravery, when death seemed to be the almost certain fate of every one engaged in that part of the field of battle. Indeed, you would not have been subjected to these questions, but that our military laws require that the conduct of every soldier shall be investigated after his sonages, in order that the officers in command may be satisfied that no soldier of the French army has shrunk from his duty. Your conduct appears to have been praiseworthy in every respect, except that there is a probability that you might have left the house of your friends some few days earlier."

"And I should have done so, your honour, but that I heard that the war was not likely to be renewed for some time to come."

"Added to which, the persons who so hospitably received you into their house, were not willing to part with you."

"They were, indeed, most kind," answered Jeannot, "and no act of mine can repay them for it."

"Was there anything particular about the place?" asked Colonel Laroche, smiling.

"I don't understand you, monsieur."

"Then I must speak a little more plainly, I find. In a word, your benefactors, I believe, have a pretty daughter?"

"They have."

"And you were unwilling to leave her society?"

"I was certainly not anxious to leave one who had paid me so much attention during my illness," answered Jeannot. "If, however, any one has said that she had any influence in causing me to remain longer than was necessary, I must at once assure you that Jacqueline Gratz had no such power over me as has been stated."

"Did you not fall in love with her?"

"My regard for her was merely that of a brother for his sister," answered Jeannot, "and from what I heard just before leaving the house, I have reasons to believe that her's for me was of a similar description. At least her father and mother informed me that she is already engaged to another."

"Then it appears," exclaimed the colonel, "that in this repect, at least, I have been deceived."

"Has any one, then, informed you that I was paying my addresses to the girl?" asked Jeannot.

"That, young man," replied the colonel, "is a question that I am not disposed to answer. The circumstance certainly has been reported to me; but as it may be a mere supposition, I am very willing to believe your denial of it—and, therefore, nothing more need be said upon that part of the subject."

"May be, sir, it would be thought too great a liberty if I was to ask who has been making so free with my name?"

"I promised never to mention it," replied Colonel Laroche, "and you will therefore see how impossible it is for me to break my word. The hint, however, has not done you any harm, so that there is the less need for you to know who it was that has been at the trouble of relating that which it is very probable he knew was without foundation. Had there been any truth in the report that you were induced to remain away from duty by the allurements of a woman, I must have laid the facts before the general in command, and it is likely you would have received a severe punishment."

"And who knows but the same concealed foe may spread the same rumour elsewhere?"

"Even if he does so," replied the officer, "it will do you no mischief, for the facts that have come out during this interview will be made public, so that every one may learn that you have exonerated yourself to my entire satisfaction."

"Still, sir, I shall always be liable to the same misrepresentations."

"Supposing you were, the same means as the present would be afforded for clearing yourself."

"Am I then to consider, monsieur," asked Jeannot, "that this enquiry has proved satisfactory?"

"Quite so."

"And my absence has been sufficiently explained to clear me from all blame?"

"I see nothing to blame you for now, Jeannot," replied the officer, "for, in the first place, your absence was occasioned by a wound received whilst engaged in the discharge of your duty, and afterwards you were detained by the attention and care which your wound required. On the other hand, however, I may say that this enquiry would not have been entered into if it had not been for the evil report that was raised by a person, who, I suppose, had some revengeful purpose of his own to serve."

"And yet, monsieur, though I have disproved the charge, I am not to know who it was that attempted to stab me in the dark?"

"Be satisfied with the favourable turn affairs have taken," exclaimed Colonel Laroche, "and leave your enemy to the heavy disappointment that his failure has occasioned. You will now return to your regiment with a character uninjured, and I believe there are very few of your comrades who will not rejoice at the result of this investigation. For my own part, I am perfectly satisfied that no blame is to be attached to you, and, should your future conduct deserve it, I shall feel great pleasure in doing all I can to assist in getting you promoted according to your merit."

Colonel Laroche now took up the papers which he had thrown down at the commencement of the interview, and this being a hint to Jeannot that no further questions were to be asked or replied to, he respectfully took leave of his officer, and quitting the room proceeded with all haste to return to his own quarters in the barracks. Occupied with his own thoughts whilst crossing the spacious quadrangle round which the buildings were ranged, he was startled by hearing his name pronounced, and, turning his head in the direction from whence the sound came, Henri Duport was seen approaching. On a cursory glance any one would have supposed that he felt nothing but friendship for the person he was about to encounter, but a second and more careful examination of his features would have been sufficient to convince a person that there was malice lurking in his heart, whilst, to all outward appearance, he was actuated by no other feelings than those of friendship and kindness.

"Well, Jeannot," he exclaimed, as soon as he had come up, "so I hear you have been sent for by the colonel, and, fearing that some mischief was in the wind, I have been looking out for you to hear how you have come off."

"With flying colours," answered Jeannot, "which I suppose is of as much gratification to me as it is of disappointment and chagrin to the scurvy knave that has been at so much trouble to bring me into disgrace."

"Psha!" returned the other, "why should you fancy that any one would attempt to injure you?"

"Because Colonel Laroche told me as much scarcely half an hour ago," he replied.

"Did he name the person?" asked Henri Duport, with an expression of alarm that he could scarcely conceal.

"I wish he had," answered Jeannot, "but for some reason or another he refused to tell me who the scoundrel was, though I pressed him two or three times to name him."

"He did right," exclaimed Duport, evidently relieved by the answer he had received; "for you are rather hot-headed, my dear friend, and I suppose he knew pretty well what would be the consequence if he were to open his mind any further."

"Do you think it right, then, that a man should be allowed to slander another, and yet the injured person is not to be told who it was that wanted to ruin him?"

"I don't pretend to know how this affair of yours stands," answered Henri Duport, "but you seem to have got off so well, that you have everything to be thankful for, instead of grumbling at not being allowed to know the name of a person in order that you may revenge yourself upon him."

"Well," exclaimed Jeannot, "for all that, I'll never rest till I have found out who it is that has been trying to injure me. It is some one in this place I know, for Colonel Laroche acknowledged that he had seen him not very long before, and I think a little careful inquiry will soon put me upon the right clue. By Jove! after this mischief he has been trying to do me, I should be a fool indeed if I didn't endeavour to find him out."

"Take my word for it, you had better leave well alone," answered Henri Duport, "for it seems you have come off all right enough, and as the colonel refused to tell you the name of your calumniator, you may depend upon it he will be highly offended if you make any more stir in the business."

"So you would persuade me to sit down quietly under an injury like this?"

"All things of this kind ought to be governed by circumstances," answered the other, "and you may depend upon it, I speak only for your own good when I recommend you to bear no malice against a man that has not been able to do you any harm."

"As for malice, I have no wish to bear it against any one," exclaimed Jeannot, "but there's something so sneaking and cowardly in going behind a person's back to injure him, that I don't think it will be very easy to persuade me that this affair ought to drop where it is."

"You know your own feelings best," returned Henri Duport, "but, for my own part, I see no good that can come of it. The person, whoever he may be, that has tried to injure you, knows, I'll be bound to say, before now, that you are determined to find him out. He has heard that before now you may depend upon it, Jeannot; and what will be the consequence? Why, he'll take care to keep you in the dark, and he must be a simpleton indeed, if he can't manage to do that."

"Or rather I should be the simpleton if I couldn't manage such an easy affair as that."

"Well," exclaimed Henri Duport, "and suppose you did manage it, what would be the good of it?"

"Why, at any rate, it would put an end to further annoyance from the same quarter."

"Psha! there's some mistake here, I'm sure."

"What mistake can there be, when Colonel Laroche has just told me that some one has been raising reports that—if believed—would make me out a rank coward."

"Let them make you out what they will, my boy," exclaimed Duport, flatteringly, "for we all know you to be as brave a fellow as Napoleon has got in his army, and that's as good a character as you or any one else can desire to have."

"But how long will the character last, if you persuade me to take no steps to preserve it?"

"Ah, Jeannot," exclaimed his companion, "I see how it is. You are just now warm and irritated at what you have heard from the colonel, but only wait till you get cool, and I'll answer for it you will think very differently of this foolish affair."

"Is it a foolish affair," demanded Jeannot, "when a man sees another trying to rob him of his good name?"

"I dare say you feel it very hard just at first," exclaimed the other, "but you should take these things as coolly as I do, and never suffer trifles to ruffle your temper as this one has done. At all events you may take my advice in one thing; wait patiently till to-morrow morning, and then, if you feel in the same sort of humour that you are in now, I will not say another word to put you off your own notion."

"Wait till to-morrow!" exclaimed Jeannot; "why, if I was to do that, I should deserve to be considered by everybody the coward that I have been represented. No, no, I am determined to find out who this concealed enemy is, and if you, Henri Duport, have half the friendship for me that you have so often professed, you will not shrink back when I ask for your assistance."

"My boy," he replied, with forced composure, "it shall be at your assistance whenever it may be required."

"Then help me at once," exclaimed Jeannot, "to discover the scoundrel that has been telling Colonel Laroche all these infernal lies about me."

"Ah, I'll do that with pleasure," answered Henri Duport, "but remember, I tell you again, this affair had better be left alone, for, as no mischief is likely to come of it, the best thing you can do will be to suffer the affair to die away into forgetfulness."

"It may be all very well for *you* to talk about forgetfulness," exclaimed Jeannot, "but how can I feel myself safe when the same mischief-loving scoundrel will be always plotting to do me an injury?"

"Nonsense, man!" returned the other, "do you suppose the person—whoever he is—will risk the chance of exposure, when the design—if he really has one—has been already exposed? Besides, it seems you are a bit of a favourite of the colonel's, and depend on it he will be offended if you take any further notice of a thing that is scarcely worth a second thought."

"But then reports not only accuse me of having broken my vow to Jeannette, but fix upon me the disgrace of cowardice, which is a stigma that I am determined not to be under while there is a hope left of exposing the falsehoods of my calumniator."

"Psha! who do you think will give credit to such charges as these against Jeannot Lamont?"

"Perhaps no one will do that," answered the young man; "but there would be good reason to believe me guilty if I take no steps to prove that I have been the victim of falsehood. The accusation seems to have been industriously spread abroad during my absence, and it is now high time that I take the necessary measures to convince my friends and comrades that I have never deserved the name of coward."

"Well, all I can say about it is, that I don't think there is any one that would believe such a charge, let it be made by who it might. It would be looked upon only as the ill-natured act of some one that owes you a grudge, and there would be an end of it."

"And have you no idea who it is that has been trying to do all this mischief?" asked Jeannot.

"Not the slightest."

"But you will endeavour to discover who it is?"

"Certainly I will, my dear fellow, for you have always found in me a true and trusty friend."

"I shall know you to be one," answered Jeannot, "if you show an anxiety to assist me in this affair. I feel that a doubt has been thrown upon my honour, and a soldier should not suffer a charge of this kind to remain uncontradicted a moment after he has been informed of the charges laid against him."

"Upon my life, I think you take this a great deal too much to heart," exclaimed Henri Duport, "for as the commanding officer is convinced that there is no ground for such an accusation, you need care very little about what other people may think."

"But what would poor Jeannette say to it, if the news should reach her ears that I have been accused of cowardice?"

"I should say her opinion would be worth very little if it could be so easily forfeited as all that. Besides, she is hundreds of miles away, and nothing can be more unlikely than that she should hear a report that will be discredited everywhere as soon as it is known that Colonel Laroche is satisfied with your conduct."

"True, the colonel is satified, but it does not follow that other persons will be equally as generous. Not that I care for the opinion of ill-natured people, for they might say or think of me just as they please, if it was not for the chance that their evil reports might at last find their way to those whose good opinion I am most anxious to preserve."

"You are still thinking of Jeannette, I find."

"I am," replied the young man, "but not only of her, but of Madame Corville and Monsieur Narbonne, the notary, from both of whom I have always received as much kindness as if I had been their own son. These are persons whose love and esteem I should grieve to forfeit, and, rather than do so, I will leave no stone unturned until I have discovered and exposed the villain who has sought to ruin me with my best friends."

"You have reason to believe that there is only one person engaged in the transaction ?"

"I don't know how many there may be," answered Jeannot, "but that there is only one prime mover in the affair, I am pretty well satisfied, though there may be several who are base enough to lend their assistance for the mere love of mischief."

"Do you think Pierre Langrais has taken the principal part in the transaction you complain of ?"

"I do not, indeed."

"For what reason ?"

"Because I have never had any acquaintance with him," replied Jeannot, "and consequently he can have no injury to complain of."

"Then you think he is merely employed by another ?"

"I am quite certain of it," answered the young man, "and it will be strange indeed if I do not before long expose the whole treachery to the world."

By this time they had reached the room in which the soldiers usually assembled when not on duty, and here they soon separated, for Henri Duport made way through the crowd to join one of his comrades, who he saw at the further end of the place, and Jeannot directed his way towards a spot that was nearly deserted. Here he sat himself down, his mind still intent upon the all-engrossing subject of his recent conversation, and anxious only to form some plan which might probably lead to the discovery of the enemy he had to contend against. The more he turned the matter over in his mind, the more convinced did he become, that the person who had been plotting all this mischief was well acquainted with him, and that the proceedings had been adopted to gratify some feelings of revenge for an injury, real or supposed. But then came the difficulty to discover who could suspect him of having committed a wilful wrong; and being unconscious of ever having done aught to bring upon himself the vengeance of any human being, he began to despair of making the discovery, till chance might assist to bring the whole truth to light. Gloomy and melancholy, he was still lost in his own ruminations, when some one touched his arm, and looking round, he saw that his old comrade Camille had taken a seat beside him. This was the first time they had seen each other since Jeannot's arrival in Berlin, and after a cordial greeting had taken place between them, Camille's first anxious enquiry was to learn the cause of his friend's uneasy looks, when almost everybody else was rejoicing in the successful termination of their emperor's most recent campaign. Desirous of avoiding any further explanation upon the subject, Jeannot quickly assumed an air of greater cheerfulness, and replied that he was merely regretting the circumstance which had prevented his taking a more important part in the victories which had followed the glorious battle in which he had the misfortune to be wounded.

"And is that really the only reason why I find you so full of gloom and thoughtfulness ?" asked Camille.

"What can be more galling," demanded our hero, "than to know that I have done but little for my country, when all my comrades can boast that they lent their best assistance towards extending the glory of France into all nations. How can I do otherwise than reflect that, whilst others were bravely fighting in the cause of their beloved country, I was remaining idle ?"

"Idle !" exclaimed Camille, " do you think, then, there was any blame when you were rendered incapable of serving your emperor any further, by a severe wound that you had received, whilst bravely charging the enemy at the point of the bayonet. No, no, you may take my word for it, that all persons speak loudly in your favour, and there is no one that does not rejoice at your returning amongst us safe and sound."

"You say there is not one that does not rejoice at my safety, but are you quite sure that such is the fact ?"

"I believe so."

"You think, then, I have no enemies ?"

"Well, to tell the truth, I think you have as few as anybody," answered Camille. "There's none of us that can say we have never made a foe in our lives, but at all events, I don't suppose you have an enemy that would attempt to do you a very serious mischief."

"There I must differ from you," exclaimed Jeannot, "for, unfortunately, I happen to have made a discovery very recently, that there are persons busily employed in secretly undermining my character."

"Do you know who they are ?"

"I do not."

"Can you make no guess ?"

"I have tried to do so, but all has been in vain."

"In what way has this supposed enemy been seeking to do you a mischief ?"

"In two ways," answered our hero. "First, he has spread reports abroad that I might have rejoined my regiment sooner, and that I absented myself only to avoid risking my life in the battles that must follow the one in which I fell."

"And are there any that believe such a falsehood ?"

"There's sure to be plenty of persons to believe anything that is said to injure another one," answered Jeannot, "and it's quite certain that even our colonel thought something of it, for he desired me to appear before him immediately after I arrived here, and he then told me that certain injurious reports had been raised against me, which it would be necessary to contradict with as little delay as could be."

"Of course you were soon able to convince him that there was no foundation for what he had heard ?"

"Yes," answered our hero, "luckily he seems to have formed rather a favourable opinion of me, and the slander was therefore in vain, so far as he was concerned."

"Does he know the person who set it afloat ?"

"He does."

"And you, I suppose, were afraid to take the liberty of asking him the name of your enemy ?"

"No, I was not," answered Jeannot, "I did ask him, but for some reason that he didn't explain, he refused to inform me who it was that had been telling him these tales about me."

"Then, if I was you, I should think no more about the matter," exclaimed Camille, " for if those who have the command over us don't give any credit to the ill-natured rumour you speak of, I see no reason why you should care about anybody else."

"You forget the injury it may do me with Jeannette."

"Jeannette would surely be the very last to believe you capable of a cowardly act."

"Left to herself, I have every reason to believe she would put the most favourable construction upon the matter, but I have good reason to know that there is one enemy of mine always near her, and he will take care that the poison shall not fail to operate upon her."

"Aye," answered Camille, "it may be all very well to report those things to her, but the question is, how far will she give credit to assertions that have the stamp of falsehood upon them. But who, pray, is the person that you suspect of making himself so busy with your affairs?"

"His name is Pierre Langrais."

"Oh, I remember the man well enough," exclaimed Camille. "He was for some time ill in the military hospital, and was allowed to return home as being no longer of any use as a soldier. He had the character of being a designing knave, and therefore I should suppose there's not much chance of any one paying attention to what he may say."

"That will depend upon whether he makes out a plausible story or not," answered the young man, "for I have been informed that he has told Jeannette of there being a pretty female in the family that took care of me after I was left wounded on the field of battle, and he has even gone so far as to assert that, forgetful of the solemn vow I made to Jeannette, I have bestowed my love upon a rival."

"Let him tell her that, if he pleases," exclaimed Camille, "for I am sure a story of that kind would not be believed."

"Then I'm of a different opinion," answered the lover, "for in a case of this description jealousy is soon roused, and Jeannette, like anybody else, may easily be deceived by the crafty insinuations of a designing knave."

"But her mother would surely caution her against giving credit to every idle story she hears."

"That she would do so as long as there was any chance of doing me a service I am quite certain," answered Jeannot, "but all of us know how hard it is to remove an impression that has been made upon her mind, and, willing as I am to hope for the best, I cannot help fearing that the old lady's trouble would be all thrown away."

"Then why not write to Jeannette, and caution her against giving credit to any thing she may hear to your prejudice?"

"I have been thinking of doing so, but it has since struck me that such a step might expose me to more suspicion than if I leave matters to take their own course. Indeed there seems to be so much chance of our speedy return to France, that I begin to think it will be better to let matters remain as they are till I see Jeannette, and explain away whatever falsehoods may have been stated against me."

"But in the meanwhile she may think your continued silence a certain sign of guilt."

"She may," answered Jeannot, but even if it should be so, I have the consolation of knowing that I can bring forward the most unquestionable proofs that I never for a moment thought of transferring my affections from Jeannette to another."

"Who are your witnesses?"

"The persons from whom I received such generous hospitality after being found in the battle-field."

"Aye," exclaimed Camille, "they, indeed, can answer for you, and Jeannette must be hard of belief indeed if she thinks you guilty of faithlessness after having heard evidence in your favour from those who ought to be able to judge of your conduct better than anybody else. So, if I was in your place I should make up my mind that this affair will end entirely to the satisfaction of all parties."

"Well, I will venture to hope as much," answered the young soldier, "and now I would ask what advice you have to give as to the best means to adopt for discovering who the person is that has been the chief plotter in all this mischief."

"That's more than I can do as matters are at present," returned his friend, "but I should caution you to keep the affair entirely to yourself at present, because whatever may be said will be sure to reach the ears of your enemy, whoever he may be. That, of course, will put him upon his guard, and defeat any plans that you may form to trace him out."

JEANNOT AND CAMILLE CONVERSING IN THE GUARD-ROOM.

"Can you devise no method by which you may discover who he is?" asked Jeannot.

"Indeed I cannot, my dear fellow," he replied "but I should not be at all surprised if it should turn out to be almost the last person you would have suspected. Some one, for instance, whom you have always trusted as a friend, and have perhaps made a confidant of, even in your most secret thoughts."

"That is exactly what I have fancied myself, and to tell you the truth, my suspicions have lately been directed towards a person who at one period I would have trusted even with my life."

"Who is he ?"

"Henri Duport."

"Ha! Has he any cause for regarding you with dislike ?"

"I have never given him any that I am aware of ;—except, indeed, that I happen to have been long engaged to the female who he has since professed to love."

"One would have thought *you* had most cause for complaint there," observed Camille.

"Any person would have imagined so," answered Jeannot, "but the contrary has been the fact, and I have been told by several persons that he has expressed himself in very angry terms against me."

"And yet you have still continued to regard him as a friend ?"

"I certainly have done so," replied Jeannot, "but that has been because I have never observed anything in his conduct to confirm that which I have only received from the statements made by other persons. He has always been, to all appearance, kind and friendly, and many times have I reproached myself for having suspected one, who, for aught I know to the contrary, may be very much disposed to do me a service."

"At all events, if I was to give an opinion," exclaimed Camille, "I should think that the more guarded you are in your dealings with him, the better it will be. There can be no great harm in acting with caution, and even if he should observe any difference in your conduct, I don't know that that will matter much, since it may be quite as well that he should be aware of the doubts that have arisen in your mind."

"And what if he should ask me the reason of my altered behaviour towards him ?"

"Why, in that case I don't see that you are bound to give him any explanation upon the subject," answered Corville. "You can return any answer that may seem most convenient at the time, and by and by, when you return home to your native village, the whole facts may come out in the presence of those who have been deceived by the falsehoods raised against you."

"But, in the meantime, how am I to guard against a continuance of the schemes of my enemies?"

"I don't know that I should take any great trouble about the matter." replied Camille, "for though some mischief may be done at the time, you may depend on it everything will turn round favourably enough by and by. Jeannette cannot be long imposed upon by these artfully contrived reports of a vindictive rival, and immediately upon your return home it will be very easy to convince her that you have never had a thought of proving unfaithful to the solemn vow you made her. But hush! here comes Henri Duport, so let the subject drop, and, for the present at least, receive him as you have always done before."

The person thus spoken of approached, and, seating himself between the two friends, entered into conversation with them upon the subject of their expected return to France.

CHAPTER XVII.

MONSIEUR NARBONNE IS THE BEARER OF WELCOME INTELLIGENCE.—DISCOVERY OF AN EAVESDROPPER.—PIERRE LANGRAIS FALLS INTO DIFFICULTIES, MAKES AN INDIFFERENT EXCUSE, AND IS CARRIED OFF TO DURANCE VILE.

WE may now pass over a period of three months, during which time letters were received from Jeannot, but in no instance did he allude to the report which had been spread abroad to his prejudice. At first Jeannette regarded this as a sort of tacit acknowledgment that there was truth in what she had heard, and it was not without some difficulty that Madame Corville was able to prevail upon her to suspend her judgment till her lover was present to answer the various charges that had been made against him. By degrees, however, Jeannette yielded to the arguments of her mother, and having promised to look upon the affair with a favourable eye, she desired Pierre Langrais never to come any more with his mischievous tales, but to allow the affair to remain as it was till a thorough explanation could be given in the presence of all the parties concerned. This was a source of no little vexation to the agent of mischief, but remonstrance under such circumstances would have been vain, and he was obliged to yield, though not without a determination in his own mind to watch for an opportunity when he might revenge himself for the impediments that had been thrown in the way of his plans. As for Monsieur Narbonne, his thoughts were very differently occupied, for all his desire was to discover the author of the mischievous reports, and after proving how little they were deserving cf credit, to show Jeannette how utterly mistaken she was in the character of her lover. True enough it is that she listened with attention to the various reasons he gave for the supposition that all which she had heard would prove to be the mere outpouring of a malignant spirit;—she even expressed her own hope that Jeannot would be able to disprove the stories, and expressed it as being her determination to offer no further opinion against him till the whole matter had undergone the thorough investigation that had been promised. Pierre Langrais, therefore, saw all chance of carrying out his designs at an end, but this only served to increase his malignancy, and from that time he was constantly creeping about, and endeavouring to worm out the secret of what was going on, by every paltry means he could devise. As we observed before, three months passed away, and news occasionally reached the village, that as peace had been signed between France and Prussia, the troops of the former nation might be expected to return home very soon. Amongst others who doubted this was Jeannette, for she felt almost afraid that the intelligence was too good to be true, and even the opinion of her mother failed to convince her that the long-wished-for event was near at hand. One evening, however, whilst Madame Corville and her daughter were sitting alone the notary unexpectedly paid them a visit, and it was easy to see by his cheerful countenance that he was the bearer of news which he knew would be agreeable to them. Seating himself, therefore, in the chair which had been placed for him by Jeannette, he rubbed his hands as people are wont to do when they have something to communicate, and then with a laugh indicative of the highest gratification, he enquired if they had heard the news which had been brought to the village. To this question he received a reply in the negative.

" Ha !" he exclaimed, " that's just as I expected it would be. Everybody in the place has been told but you, so I stepped down from home to let you know that our young friend and favourite, Jeannot, may be looked for every day."

" Are you serious, Monsieur Narbonne ?" asked the elder female.

" Indeed, I was never more so in my life," he replied, " for this is not a matter for jesting about, when I know how anxiously poor Jeannette has been looking for his return. To be sure she has been a little bit jealous or so, about some foolish rumours that have got abroad, but when the young fellow comes back he'll soon be able to drive all that nonsense out of her head."

" So I have tried to persuade myself," answered Jeannette, " but Pierre Langrais still persists in his story, and, much as I wish he may be able to give a satisfactory explanation, I am almost afraid it will be impossible for him to do so.'

" Then, between ourselves, ma'amselle," exclaimed the old gentleman, " your confidence in his honour and probity is not so great as I could have wished it to be. Nay, I will venture to say more. This Pierre Langrais is not a man that any one can place reliance in, and I think you will afterwards see reason to blame yourself for having paid attention to his idle tales."

" And don't you think Jeannot is also to blame for not having written to me ?" she asked.

"I'll not give my opinion about that at present," answered the old gentleman, "because I always think it fair to give the accused party a hearing before he is condemned. This lover of yours is not the only person who has had to contend against the malignancy of secret foes, but I have generally found, if fair play is given, the falsehood is sure to be discovered in the end."

"There's no doubt of that, Monsieur Narbonne," exclaimed the old lady, "and I have been trying to convince Jeannette of it, but somehow the foolish girl is more difficult to be persuaded upon this subject than I ever saw her before."

"I suppose that is because she thinks her lover—like Cæsar's wife—ought to be above suspicion," returned the notary, smiling.

"I don't know how that may be, monsieur," answered Madame Corville, "but at any rate I know Jeannot will not return home a moment sooner than he ought to do, if peace is to be made between him and Jeannette. Not that I can altogether wonder at her either, for it's natural that she should feel uneasy as long as these rumours against her betrothed are uncontradicted."

"Perhaps that may be all very true," exclaimed the old gentleman, "but some allowances may be made for exaggerations, even supposing there may have been some blame to the young man."

"You think, then, there may be some ground for the rumours we have heard?" exclaimed Jeannette with evident symptoms of alarm.

"ay, I have not said anything of the kind, he replied, "for I would not mind laying a good wager that he has never so far forgotten either himself or you, as to disregard the vow he made in my presence, shortly before he left home. I can readily believe, however, that he may have walked out this female—who you regard as a rival—but who, at any rate, seems to have watched over him with all the tender care of a sister, when he was left wounded among the people whom he had gone to fight against as an enemy."

"But Pierre Langrais asserts most positively that he made her an offer of his love."

"Pierre Langrais is a fool, as well as a knave, or he would not have made a statement, that we shall easily be able to contradict."

"How is it to be contradicted?" asked our heroine.

"By persons who will be ready enough, I dare say, to speak the truth, when the honour and respectability of the young man are at stake," answered the notary. In short, I have been at the trouble to make enquiries about this M———— G———— and his family, and from all I can hear, they have a most excellent character."

"It may be so," answered Jeannette, "but is not that of itself an argument, rather against than for what you have been advancing?"

"How can it be against me?"

"Because, if the family is as honourable and respectable as you say, there is then the more reason to suppose that he may have sought an alliance with the daughter of Monsieur Gratz. However, I do not wish to prejudge the case, and will therefore, since you wish it, wait till Jeannot returns to offer an explanation, of that which at present appears very black against him."

"You may rely upon it, my dear," exclaimed her mother, "that the report has only been raised from sheer malice, and a short time will serve to prove that I am right."

"Let me hope you are, dear mother," she replied, "but who is it that can be an enemy of Jeannot's, when, up to the time of leaving us, he was supposed not to have one in the world?"

"Aye, aye, that may be," exclaimed Monsieur Narbonne, "but there are thousands of causes for people taking a dislike for one another, and a little time and patience will serve to prove what has been the origin of all this cruel animosity."

"Don't you think," asked Madame Corville, "that Pierre Langrais could be prevailed on to tell all he knows about the matter, if something in the shape of a tempting bribe was offered him?"

" I fancied at one time that such a thing was quite possible," answered the old gentleman ; "but, having sounded him upon the subject, I am bound to admit that the fellow's resolution to keep the secret exceeds anything I ever saw before. When I spoke of making him a present of a large sum of money, he only laughed in my face, and asked if I supposed he had been employed to do the dirty work for anybody else."

" Then he still persists in saying that he has related the report only out of pity for Jeannette ?"

" So he would make us believe, madame," answered the notary, " but for all that, I feel convinced that he is the mere tool of another person. Who his employer is remains to be found out, but it shall not be any fault of mine if the discovery is not made before Jeannot's return home."

" When did you say he was expected ?" asked our heroine, eagerly.

" We may look for him every hour," replied Monsieur Narbonne. " Indeed, all the villagers are full of the news, and are prepared to give him a glorious welcome."

" Then they, at least, do not believe him guilty of having transferred his affections to another ?" observed Madame Corville.

" So far from believing the mischievous story," he replied, " there is not a man, woman, or child in the place but is convinced of his innocence. Indeed, they express their surprise that the falsehood should have been received with credit anywhere, and it is to show their own kindly feelings towards him that they intend to receive him on his return home with manifestations of their respect."

" In that case," exclaimed Jeannette, " I will not be the only one to receive him with coldness and suspicion."

" That's well said," exclaimed the notary, " and I will undertake to say that you will soon see reason to be glad that you have formed so rational a determination. Jeannot, too, will be gratified to find that your confidence remains unshaken, and, as far as I am myself concerned, I will omit nothing that may tend to destroy the unfavourable impression that has been raised against him."

" Oh !" returned Madame Corville, " you are very kind, sir, to take so much trouble ; but I'm afraid very little good will be done unless you can discover who has been the author of the scandalous tales that have been circulated against him."

" Which you may depend upon it, shall be done," answered the old gentleman, " or I shall have less success in this affair than I have anticipated. In fact, I cannot believe this Pierre Langrais will much longer persist in concealing the name of the promulgator of the mischief."

" And what if you discover him, monsieur ?"

" Why, it is impossible to say what will follow," he replied, " but I should suppose it will not be difficult to induce him to confess his motive for pursuing so shameful a course, and then, at least, Jeannot will have passed the ordeal with honour to himself."

" True," exclaimed Madame Corville, " but his wickedness will not be punished as it deserves."

" It will, at any rate, be some satisfaction to know that he will be looked upon with abhorrence and disgust," answered the notary. Such conduct as h has been guilty of must in the end meet with its just punishment, and it wile be gratifying to all of us to see that the traducer will sink into contempt, whilslt the person he has endeavoured to destroy will be restored to the good opinion of the world."

" Aye," replied Madame Corville, " and what will please him more than anything else, will be the clearing of his character in the eyes of his betrothed. The poor fellow, I dare say, has been miserable enough ever since you wrote to tell him of what was said about him here, and now it's high time that he should be made happy by knowing that the schemes of his enemies have not prevailed."

"And if it will be any satisfaction to him," exclaimed the notary, "he will soon have the pleasure of knowing that punishment will follow on the man who has been so busily engaged in carrying on his base designs. By the bye, Madame Corvlle, I have often puzzled myself to find out what can have induced any one to take so much trouble, when he must have known perfectly well that it could not succeed for any long time."

"I suppose there must be revenge at the bottom of it?"

"No doubt of that," answered Monsieur Narbonne, "but I should have thought that Jeannot, with all his good temper, could never have made an enemy, or given offence to anybody."

At this moment, some loud talking was heard in the adjoining room, and presently afterwards, on the door being thrown open, Claude, the man-servant of Monsieur Narbonne, came struggling towards them, with Pierre Langrais held firmly in his grasp. This unexpected occurrence occasioned the greatest surprise, and, addressing himself to his attendant, the notary inquired the reason of the violence which he had committed.

"I don't know what you may think about it," replied the man, "but when a fellow like this is skulking about other people's premises, it seems to me high time that he should be made to give some account of himself."

"Explain yourself, Claude," exclaimed his master; "where did you find this man, that you accuse him of skulking?"

"He was outside the window, listening to every word that was being said by you and these two females."

"You hear what he says?" observed the notary, addressing himself to Pierre Langrais, "and I should now be glad to know what reason you can give for being found near this house?"

"I mean to say that this fellow had no right to lay hands on me."

"That may be," answered Monsieur Narbonne, "but, on the other hand, you had no right to play the part of an eavesdropper."

"I am no eavesdropper."

"Then how was it that you were listening at the window?"

'He tells a lie when he says that I was listening," answered Pierre Langrais. "I was only coming here to tell Madame Corville that her intended ... is likely to return soon—and this is all the reward I get for my good nature."

"You might have spared yourself all this trouble and inconvenience," exclaimed Monsieur Narbonne, "for it so happens that I came here to bring the news, and Madame Corville is already informed that Jeannot may be expected every hour."

"I beg your pardon, monsieur, for interfering," said Claude, "but if he was not here for the purpose of listening, he must have come for something worse, for it's well known that he is Jeannot's enemy, so, of course, he can care very little for the news that he is about to return."

"Then what do you suppose I came for?"

"Why," exclaimed Claude, "if the truth must be told, I have a notion you came here to rob the place, or I should not have handled you quite so roughly as I did."

This hint was eagerly caught at by Monsieur Narbonne, who was really glad of an opportunity of detaining the man, and, addressing him sternly, he said—

"What your motive for coming here may be I don't know, but there is so much suspicion about the affair, that I shall certainly not allow you to go at large again till you have given some reasonable account of yourself."

"Are you going to make a prisoner of me then?" demanded Pierre Langrais, sullenly.

"Of a certainty I am," answered the old gentleman, "unless you can sasfy me that you came here for no felonious purpose."

"A felonious purpose!" exclaimed the other. "Is it likely that an old soldier, who has served his country, would attempt a robbery?"

"That's more than I can tell," answered Monsieur Narbonne, "so, if you expect to be restored to liberty, you must give such an account of yourself as will satisfy me of your innocence."

"And pray what business have you to question me?"

"Your conduct has given me the right," he replied, "and your refusal to answer my questions seems like a confirmation of the suspicions I have formed. However, it is not my intention to proceed any further in the affair, because justice is more likely to be obtained if I cause you to be conveyed before a magistrate."

"Beware of what you are about, Monsieur Narbonne," exclaimed the other, "for I am not going to suffer my character to be taken away, merely because you choose to suspect me of being here with a bad intention. I never intended to commit a robbery; and as for my being found near the house of Madame Corville, I have already explained that, by stating that I came to inform her of Jeannot's expected arrival."

"Which none of us believe."

"I can't help that," he replied, "but it's the truth, and I can defy anybody to say that I was ever guilty of a dishonest action."

"At all events," exclaimed Monsieur Narbonne, "you have been guilty of very base ones, for nothing can palliate your conduct in endeavouring to ruin the character of a young man in the estimation of her who has been solemnly betrothed to him."

"I only told her what I have myself heard," answered Pierre Langrais, "and the question is whether people would not have blamed me if I had not warned Jeannette of the fickleness of her lover."

"You might have spared yourself the trouble of doing that," interposed Madame Corville, "for I don't believe a word you have said against the young man; and as for Jeannette, I believe she is equally resolved not to listen to any reports till she has heard them confirmed by other persons, and that, I rather think, is not likely to be the case."

"Well, we shall see how that will be when Jeannot returns," exclaimed the mischief-maker. "At any rate, he'll not be able to deny that he was for a long time at the house of one Farmer Gratz, and that all the while he was there he was paying very marked attention to the daughter."

"Psha!" ejaculated the notary; "what can you make of it, even supposing he did show her the attention that so much fuss has been made about? Gratitude he may have shown for the favours that were conferred upon him, when he must have perished but for the care that he received from those kind-hearted strangers, but as for any avowal of love, I believe it to be nothing but an infamous calumny, intended to injure him."

"Ah!" exclaimed Pierre Langrais, with a sneer, "Jeannot happens to be a great favourite here, so, of course, anything that may be said to his prejudice must be set down as being untrue."

"That would depend upon circumstances," answered Monsieur Narbonne, "for I should be quite ready to believe any one who had no bad feelings of their own to gratify."

"What bad feelings can I have to gratify, when I know nothing at all about the young man?" demanded Pierre.

"You may have been bribed by others to do this dirty work for them."

"In that case, you must be aware that Jeannot has enemies?"

"I never heard of his having any," replied the old gentleman, "nor do I understand how he should, for he has always been regarded with esteem by those who were acquainted with him."

"You mean to say, then, that it is quite impossible he can have forgotten his vows to Jeannette?"

"At least I will not give credit to the assertion till it is confirmed by the testimony of others, and that I believe will never happen. You, however, will, no doubt, continue in-the same opinion, which will matter very little, seeing that people will pay no attention to the ill-natured reports of a foe."

"If you mean me, Monsieur Narbonne, I was never a foe of the young man's."

"That I leave to your own conscience," answered the notary, "but at any rate you have been untiring in your efforts to injure him in the estimation of those whose good opinion he most values. And now, at length you have overreached yourself, and having given us an advantage, we will not suffer you to be at liberty again until you can prove that your presence here was not for a bad purpose."

"I tell you again, Monsieur Narbonne, that I came here only to tell Madame Corville and her daughter the news that I thought would be most agreeable to them."

"How did you know they had not already heard it ?"

"I only fancied it was very likely they had not," he replied, "and it seemed to me only a good natured act to bring them the news as soon as possible. However, the best of intentions are often turned against ourselves, and such appears to be the case in the present instance."

"How is it," asked Jeannette, "that you have now taken it into your head to feel so much interest for Jeannot, when all along you have been trying to make us believe he was not worth a thought ?"

"Aye," cried Madame Corville, " explain that if you can ?"

"It's not worth my while explaining anything," he replied, "because I can see well enough that I have been set down as a worthless, good-for-nothing fellow, and all I can say or do will never make any of you think otherwise of me. But never mind, every dog has his day, and by and by Monsieur Narbonne will be sorry that he has proceeded in this harsh way against me."

"You have brought it all upon yourself," answered the notary, "for had you remained at home instead of coming here, all the inconvenience that you complain of would have been avoided. As for your excuse about wishing to inform Madame Corville and her daughter, I don't believe a word of it, and you must therefore put up with the consequences."

"Humph! you mean to say that I am to be locked up on suspicion of being here with the intention of committing a robbery ?"

"If you can satisfy a magistrate that you had no such intention, the inconvenience will not be very great, but if you fail to do that, you will be committed for trial, and it will then be for the judge to decide upon the merits of your case."

"It may be all very well for you, Monsieur Narbonne, to treat it in this easy way," he exclaimed, "but for my own part I can see no reason why I should be sent to prison on a paltry charge of this kind. I never was guilty of a robbery in my life, and if this servant of yours had not been quite so officious, Madame Corville would have been convinced that I came to her house for no other purpose than the one I have spoken of."

"So you would like to make us believe," answered the old gentleman, "but when people go on such an errand as you speak of, they enter the house by the door and not by the window, as appears to have been your intention."

"I was near the window when that man saw me, but without any intention of committing a felony."

"Be that as it may, you must submit to be shut up in the cage to-night, and if your statement appears to be a reasonable one you will be set at liberty to-morrow."

"Yes, and I shall come out with a character ruined through the course you are taking," exclaimed Pierre Langrais. "But I warn you to take care of what you are about, for if justice is to be had in the country you shall suffer for this as well as I."

"Your threats will not deter me from doing my duty," answered the old gentleman, "so you need not expect that any fear of the consequences will prevent your being locked up till this affair can be properly inquired into. And as for Jeannot, you will have the mortification of knowing that all the evil reports you have spread against him will not have done him the slightest injury."

"I never wanted to do him any mischief," exclaimed Pierre Langrais, "and

PIERRE LANGRAIS DETECTED AS EAVESDROPPER.

all this ill-feeling against me has been caused by my anxiety to caution Jeannette against what I still believe to be the perfidious conduct of her lover."

"And yet you come—according to what you told us just now—to bring her the news that he is about to return home."

"Well, you can believe me or not, just as you please," exclaimed Pierre, "but there's one thing—your evil thoughts will not do me all the harm you wished.

Let Herman Gratz be questioned upon this subject, and I'll be bound he'll tell you that Jeannot Lamont has been paying his addresses to his daughter."

"How do you know he suspected anything of the kind?" asked Madame Corville sharply.

"Because I have heard as much from other people, and these reports have not been spread without foundation."

"It seems that you, at least, have been very willing to believe them," exclaimed the notary.

"I have done so because there seemed to be no doubt of the fact," answered Pierre, "and it seemed to me nothing more than right that I should tell the story, as I heard it, to those who were most deeply interested in it."

"Do you mean to declare that you have not been employed by some other person to do this mischief?"

"Who do you suppose would do such a thing?"

"That," replied Monsieur Narbonne, "is exactly what I want to know."

"Then, even if there was any truth in your suspicion, I would not confirm it after the treatment I have received here."

"But the treatment you complain of has been occasioned by your own conduct," answered the notary. "Your presence was not wanted here, for you must have been aware that Madame Corville and her daughter would hear the news of Jeannot's expected return before now."

"I wish I had known it," exclaimed Pierre Langrais, "for you may depend upon it I would not have come here if I could have guessed the dilemma it would get me into."

"It's easy enough for you to get out of the dilemma, if you think proper to adopt the right course."

"What do you call the right course, Monsieur Narbonne?"

"Inform us who the person is that has employed you to spread these falsehoods abroad, and you shall not only be immediately set at liberty, but I will reward you liberally for the service."

"I dare say you would," answered Pierre Lagrais, "but I should like to know what right you have to assert that I have been employed to do mischief? I never had any ill-feeling against Jeannot, and as for what I may have said about him, it was only done for the sake of exposing what I consider to be his heartless conduct. So now you see, Monsieur Narbonne, I have no information to give, and therefore your offer is of no use."

"Then you prefer going to prison to obtaining your liberty upon the tempting offer you have just heard?"

"As for that," exclaimed the fellow, "I have no explanation to give, and even if I had, I should not accept your offer, because I know this charge can never be substantiated. Who, I should like to know, will believe that Pierre Langrais ever intended to commit a robbery, when it is well known that, as a soldier of the imperial army, he has always borne a good character?"

"But your character will suffer when it comes to be known that you have acted the part of a mischief-maker. So now, for the last time, I ask if you will obtain your liberty upon the terms I have proposed?"

"And for the last time," exclaimed Pierre Langrais, "I tell you that I will make no sort of bargain with you. I now consider myself your prisoner, and your servant needn't be afraid of my making any resistance, for I'll walk quietly with him to the place where I am to be confined, and in the morning you will find me quite ready to undergo an examination before his worship, the mayor."

And as a proof that he was in earnest, he made a sign to Claude that he was ready to go with him. The latter, however, did not seem altogether to like the duty he had to perform, and it was not till Pierre had again assured him that he had nothing to fear, that he at length left the house, accompanied, without any apparent reluctance, by his prisoner.

"That's a most extraordinary fellow," exclaimed Monsieur Narbonne, as soon as he was out of hearing, "and between ourselves, I am almost sorry that so serious a charge has been made against him."

"You think as I do, I suppose," returned Madame Corville, "that he had no design of robbing my house."

"Whether he had or not," answered the notary, "we have no proof to bring against him, except the fact of his having been found lurking about your premises."

"That was rather suspicious certainly," exclaimed Madame Corville, "but I rather think, if the truth could be known, he was at the window merely for the purpose of listening to what we were saying."

"What could he expect to hear?" asked Jeannette.

"Something of importance, no doubt," answered her mother. "I dare say he expected that our conversation would be about Jeannot, and that he might gather something that would assist him in the plot that was going on against your lover."

"Then he must have been disappointed," returned our heroine, "for there was not a word uttered that could have been of the least use to him."

"I only wish that we could have had a notion that he was there," observed Madame Corville, for I would have made good the old adage, that listeners never hear any good of themselves. But never mind, let his motive for coming here have been what it might, he has got very little good for the trouble he has put himself to."

"He'll find out before long," exclaimed Monsieur Narbonne, "that the principal part of his trouble has to come. Only wait till Jeannot comes back amongst us, and then we shall have the pleasure of seeing how completely he will be confounded by the plain, honest answer of the man he has been endeavouring to traduce."

"Aye," said the old lady, "but what greater annoyance can he feel than in finding that Jeannette, of all other persons, is determined not to be misled by the falsehoods he has been spreading abroad against her lover. He will see all his pains thrown away for nothing, and as for the villain that has employed him, I can exult in the thought of what his mortification will be when he makes the discovery that Jeannot comes out of this affair with flying colours."

"I'd give a hundred francs to know who the fellow is," exclaimed Monsieur Narbonne, "for if we could only get at that fact, we should have the satisfaction of witnessing the chagrin that must follow the frustration of his hopes. But Pierre Langrais seems determined not to reveal any part of his secret, so I suppose we must be content to wait till time and circumstances point him out to us."

"Do you think there is any difficulty in finding out who he is?" asked Madame Corville.

"At present the mystery appears to be as thick as ever it was," replied the notary, "but I am in hopes that the truth will come out before long. Nay, I should think Jeannot will be able to assist in the discovery, for surely he must know if he has any enemy likely to proceed to such extremities."

"Do you imagine it is a comrade?" asked Madame Corville.

"I have no doubt of it."

"Then the next thing is, to discover the motive that could have led to such cruel persecutions."

"Which I should suppose may be easily done," exclaimed our heroine, "for surely Jeannot must be able to remember if he has ever given cause of offence to any of his comrades."

"As for that, my dear girl," answered Monsieur Narbonne, "he would be extremely fortunate if he has been able to avoid giving offence to more than one out of the great number of persons that he is constantly thrown among. Besides, where there are so many, there must be all sorts of tempers and dispositions, so that it would be almost impossible to fix upon the individual who has set all the mischief afloat."

"And why might it not have been Pierre Langrais himself?" demanded Madame Corville.

"I have thought so myself sometimes," answered the notary, "but upon further reflection, I fancy we must look elsewhere for the author of these lies, for I think it hardly likely that he would himself be the person to give utterance to the reports, when he knows the odium it must bring upon him."

"Besides," said Jeannette "he seems to be a stranger to the person he is trying to injure, and therefore I fancy it the more likely that he is employed by somebody else."

"Whoever it may be, deserves to be well ducked in a horsepond for his pains," exclaimed Monsieur Narbonne. "Aye, and it's very likely to be his fate too, if we can only find him out, for Jeannot has luckily plenty of friends, and the grudge they owe his cowardly enemy will carry them to great lengths, the moment they have an opportunity of paying off old scores. So there's some consolation for us you see, Madame Corville, and all I desire is that the pleasure I anticipate may not be long delayed."

"I don't want any violence to be committed," answered the old lady, "but I should like to see him hunted with scorn out of the village, if ever he should be bold enough to show his face here. That would be satisfaction for poor Jeannot at any rate, and I can venture to say that he desires nothing more than to see his enemy treated with the scorn he so justly deserves."

"That may be all very true," exclaimed the notary, "but he must be content to let his friends and neighbours have their own way, when once they find out the man to whom he is indebted for all this mischief. For my own part, I desire to see no violence, and yet, if any should take place, I know not that I should make any attempt to prevent it."

"Well, it must be confessed he don't deserve much pity," observed Madame Corville, "but for all that, I think even Jeannot himself would be the first to go to his rescue, if there was any chance of his being roughly used."

"Then the greater fool he for his pains," exclaimed the old gentleman, "for the fellow deserves almost anything that may befall him after the villanous part he has been playing. It's not for me to advocate violence, and yet there are circumstances that excuse even a rough sort of retaliation."

"But suppose the man was to die under the punishment?"

"That is taking an extreme view of the case," answered Monsieur Narbonne, "for of course our people here know the consequences that would follow such an act, and no doubt they would control their feelings sufficiently to prevent things reaching quite such a pitch as that. At all events, the fellow can avoid the danger, if there is any, and he will act with prudence and foresight if he directs his footsteps to any other place rather than this."

"Well," exclaimed the old lady, "let us hope that, for his own sake as well as that of others, that he will not venture to show his face here. All the harm I wish him is, that he may feel the force of conscience, and that he surely must do if he has any heart at all."

"Which we may be excused for doubting," observed the notary, "for I think if he had had such a thing belonging to him, he would never have been guilty of such evil practices against a fellow-creature. But for my own part, I begin to see that matters are about to take a turn, and Jeannot will yet be happy, in spite of the pains that have been taken to make him otherwise."

"Have you never thought," asked our heroine, "that his enemy may find out some other way to be revenged, when he sees himself likely to be defeated in his first plans?"

"There's no saying what a fellow of that kind is capable of being guilty of," answered Monsieur Narbonne, "but at any rate we have the consolation of knowing that we are in some degree prepared for any mischief he may next think of."

"But sometimes I have feared lest he may even go so far as to make an attempt upon the life of Jeannot."

"Then, by all means, get rid of such a notion as that Jeannette," exclaimed the notary, "for as far as his life is concerned, I believe the life of your lover is perfectly safe. Your mother, too, I dare say, will quite agree with me in that respect; so look forward with hope to the expected return of Jeannot, and by all means delay not your marriage, for I believe the moment that sees you united to him will be the last of your uneasiness."

"Depend upon it, monsieur," returned Madame Corville, "I shall not fail to persuade my daughter to follow your advice. Nor, indeed, do I believe she will need much persuasion from me, since there was an understanding before they parted, that the wedding should take place immediately upon his return."

"Aye," answered Jeannette, "but it was on condition that I was quite convinced of his constancy during his absence."

"And are you not convinced of it?" asked the notary.

"I would fain convince myself that I am," she replied, "but I may perhaps be pardoned for requiring some explanation of the reports that have reached me."

"Oh, as for that," answered the old gentleman, "I rather think he will not have much trouble in doing that. Besides, the occurrences of this night have no doubt somewhat alarmed Pierre Langrais, and I am much mistaken if he don't open his mind a little more freely upon the subject than he has yet done."

"Do you expect he will confess who it is that has employed him to make mischief between the lovers?"

"I think it very likely he will," answered Monsieur Narbonne, "but that will depend upon the humour I find him in when I see him in the morning. In the meantime he will have plenty of time to reflect upon the difficulties he has brought upon himself, and I think it by no means unlikely he will be glad to extricate himself upon such terms as I may deem it prudent to offer."

"If you think anything is to be done by offering him a bribe," exclaimed Madame Corville, "I hardly need say that you are at perfect liberty to do so to the utmost extent of my means. That I am not rich you know, but I would part with almost the last thing I possess in the world, rather than these young people should any longer suffer from the vile conspiracy that has been entered into against them."

"Not a sous, my dear madame, shall come out of your pocket," replied the worthy notary, "for now that I have taken this affair in hand, I'll carry it out at my own expense, let it cost what it may. Nor need you apprehend anything on that account, for I believe Pierre Langrais will be glad to come to almost any terms now that his own wickedness and folly have got him into trouble."

"Well, monsieur, I hope you may not be mistaken," answered the old lady. "At any rate, the experiment is well worth trying, for, though none of us believe the vile things that have been said against Jeannot, it will at least afford the highest satisfaction to all of us to hear the falsehoods contradicted by those who have framed them."

"That is the chief motive that has urged me to the step I am about to adopt," returned Monsieur Narbonne, "and to carry my views into effect I shall spare neither trouble nor expense. A few hours will serve to show how far I am likely to succeed, so for the present I will take my leave, and to-morrow, immediately after my interview with Pierre Langrais, I will come here to let you know the result."

Upon this he took leave of the mother and daughter, and quitting the house, made the best of his way home.

CHAPTER XVIII.

MONSIEUR NARBONNE HAS AN INTERVIEW WITH THE COMMISSARY AT THE
GUARD-HOUSE.—IS SUBSEQUENTLY INTRODUCED TO PIERRE LANGRAIS IN
HIS CELL.—THE PROPOSAL.—A DISAPPOINTMENT; AND THE NOTARY FINDS
HIMSELF AS FAR OFF FROM HIS OBJECT AS EVER.

At an earlier hour than usual, Monsieur Narbonne descended to the breakfast parlour, where, in obedience to previous orders, he found everything in readiness for the morning's meal. As he took his seat, Claude entered the room with the coffee, and having made all the necessary arrangements, was about to retire, when the voice of his master arrested his steps.

"Claude," said the old gentleman, "what did you do with your prisoner last night, after taking him from the house of Madame Corville?"

"I took him to the guard-house as you bade me."

"Did he say anything on the way?"

"A great deal, monsieur, but nothing to the purpose."

"Didn't he speak at all about the charge that has been made against him?"

"He stoutly denied being at Madame Corville's for any evil purpose, and swore he'd make you smart severely for depriving him of his liberty without any just cause."

"Ah!" exclaimed Monsieur Narbonne, "that's always the case with men when they find themselves in difficulties. They vapour and threaten in the hope of intimidating those who are to appear against them, but in almost every instance they tell a very different story when they find themselves in the presence of a magistrate."

"That may be, monsieur," answered Claude, "but I don't think that will be the case with this fellow, for, as an old soldier, he has been used to danger for many years back, and I rather think he expects to get off if he still continues to persist in his innocence."

"Did you tell him that he might depend upon being rewarded if he would only confess who it was that has set him on to tell all these falsehoods about Jeannot?"

"You may rely upon it, I did not forget to do that," answered Claude, "but I might just as well have held my tongue, for he stuck out hard and fast that he had said nothing but the truth, and added, with a look of exultation, that Jeannette would find out, when too late, what a fool she had been to place reliance in the honour of her lover."

"Merely an empty boast that," observed the notary, "for I have been acquainted long enough with Jeannot, to feel perfectly satisfied that he will never deceive the woman to whom he has promised marriage."

"I have always had the same opinion of him, monsieur," exclaimed Claude, "but it can't be denied that lovers are sometimes false, and for aught we know there may be some foundation for what has been said about Jeannot and the young female that was so kind to him after he was wounded at the battle of Austerlitz."

"Ah! Claude," returned his master, "you know not the youth you are speaking of so well as I do, or you would not believe it possible that he could be guilty of so dishonourable an action. Besides, he made a vow to Jeannette in my presence; and were he to break that, he would never be able to show himself again in the society of honourable men. So get rid of your notion, Claude, as soon as you can, and rely in all confidence upon my word, when, in his behalf, I declare that he will come clear out of this ordeal."

"Pardon me, monsieur, if I have said anything to offend you," said Claude. "I have only given the opinion that I have heard from other people, and if I have done the young man an injustice, I shall be heartily sorry for it."

"Believe nothing that you may hear reported," exclaimed his master, "for there are already people enough in the world who are glad to propagate mischief for the mere love of inflicting misery upon others. This Pierre Langrais is one of the class I speak of, and we have only to wait with a little patience to make the discovery that he has been urged to this act by others as wicked, if not worse, than himself."

" Then he must have been offered a good bribe to do it."

" Exactly so."

" How is it, then, that he is not likely to accept of a larger one to tell who has set him on ?"

" I know not how that may be," answered the notary, " but time will show that I have lived long enough in this world to form tolerable correct notions of things. I can see that, in short, there is some devilish scheme at work to injure Jeannot by raising false reports that will lower him in the opinion of his betrothed."

" May I ask you, monsieur, if you know of any motive that Pierre Langrais could have had ?"

" I have no notion," answered his master, " but it seems to me most likely that he is merely the instrument of another who is afraid to make the accusation himself, though he hesitates not to stab his victim through the agency of another."

" And that other, I suppose, will not easily be discovered ?"

" I'm not quite sure about that," replied the notary, " for Pierre Langrais will soon begin to grow tired of his present uncomfortable situation, and I have a great notion that he will be very glad to regain his liberty by confessing all he knows upon the subject."

" But he told me last night that your charge was a false one, and that the case would be dismissed before it was half heard through."

" Indeed !" exclaimed Monsieur Narbonne, " then I rather think he will find himself very much mistaken, for, with all his cunning, he cannot deny being found lurking about Madame Corville's house under very suspicious circumstances."

" He could be there for no good purpose, monsieur," exclaimed Claude, " but still he denies having any evil designs in going there."

" But the late hour in the evening is against him."

" So it is, monsieur," answered the man, " and as far as my own opinion goes I have very little doubt that he was there for a bad purpose. He seems to be a sullen sort of fellow though, and I'm afraid nothing will be got out of him unless it should be done of his own accord."

" At all events I shall try the effect of a bribe upon him."

" I don't think he'll accept of it."

" Surely you have not been foolish enough to put him upon his guard by hinting such a thing ?"

" I merely mentioned something of the sort," answered Claude, " as if it came from myself, and I don't think he could have the least idea that you are likely to speak upon the same subject."

" Did he make any remark upon the subject ?"

" He didn't pay the least attention to it, but for all that, he couldn't have failed to hear what I said. Perhaps he wanted to hear what more I had to say upon the subject, but if that was his object, he was very much disappointed, for just at that time we reached the guard-house, and, of course, our conversation was brought to an end."

" You have not yet told me, Claude, whether he offered any resistance as he went along ?"

" Not the slightest, monsieur." On the contrary, he walked as willingly as if nothing was the matter, and I suppose thought by that means to convince the world of his innocence."

" Whatever other people may think of it," replied Monsieur Narbonne, " I at least shall not easily change the opinion I have formed of that man, and the motives that have actuated him. However, I will now walk down to the guard-house and obtain permission to see the prisoner before he is taken for examination before the mayor."

Monsieur Narbonne having by this time finished his breakfast, rose from the table, and making a few business arrangements that were to be looked to during his absence, set out from his house in order to see Pierre Langrais, and sound him upon the subject of making a full disclosure of the motives that had urged him to act with so much rancour against a man who had never injured him. In due course of time he reached the place of destination, and having acquainted one of the gens-d'armes with the purpose of his visit, was immediately conducted to the room in which the commissary usually transacted the business connected with his office. The worthy notary seated himself as he was requested, and in few words related the object that had led to his unexpected visit.

"Do I understand," asked the commissary, "that you wish to speak to the prisoner?"

"Precisely so."

"Humph!" returned the other, "it is unusual to suffer such an interview before an examination has taken place; but you, Monsieur Narbonne, know the law too well to infringe upon it, and I will therefore grant your request, on your bare promise not to make any arrangements by which the ends of justice may be defeated."

"That I readily give," answered the notary, "and you may the more confidently take my word when I tell you that your prisoner has no quarter to expect from me unless he thinks proper to divulge who it was that set him on to spread these rumours against a young man whose absence deprives him of the power to contradict the aspersions that have been thrown upon his character."

"How is this?" exclaimed the commissary. "Is there no other charge against the prisoner than that of spreading false reports? If that is the only accusation, we had no right to detain him here a whole night."

"At any rate there is a strong case of suspicion against him," replied Monsieur Narbonne, "or I, who pretty well understand the law, would not have committed him to your custody. In short, he was found last night lurking close to the cottage of the widow Corville, and as I happened to be there at the time when he was discovered, I thought it proper to give him in charge, in order that his motive for being there at that hour in the evening might be known."

"That alters the case," answered the official, "and I now perceive that there was sufficient ground for the step you have taken. By the bye, though, I have been making enquiries about this man, who, it appears, has served many years in the army, and from all I can learn he bears the character of having been a brave soldier."

"I have no means of disputing that," replied the notary, "but still his bravery affords no certain proof of his honesty. He may not, it is true, be what I suspect, but if he has suffered any inconvenience the fault is his own, since he can offer no colourable excuse for having been found lurking at a place where he had no business."

"Perhaps he may be able to give a satisfactory account of himself when he appears before the mayor."

"If he does," exclaimed Monsieur Narbonne, "he will, of course, regain his liberty, and the slight inconvenience he may have suffered, will have been richly deserved for the mischievous part he has been acting towards two young persons who have never injured him."

"If I understand rightly," observed the commissary, "you have taken up this affair in behalf of other persons?"

"I have."

"Who are they?"

" Jeannette Corville and Jeannot Lamont."

" I have heard something of them. The latter, I believe, was a conscript when he left this neighbourhood, and had long previously been betrothed to the girl you have mentioned."

" Right."

MONSIEUR NARBONNE'S INTERVIEW WITH THE COMMISSARY.

" And this Pierre Langrais has been endeavouring to sow the seeds of discord between them, has he not?"

" With so much craft and determination," replied the notary, " that I verily believe,.if I had not stepped in to expose the fallacy, his story would have obtained more credit than it deserved."

" You have always been a peace-maker I know," exclaimed the commissary, "but I hope you will excuse me when I ask, if you are quite certain that these rumours are founded in pure invention?"

"I have not the slightest doubt of it in my own mind."

"You have good reason for supposing that there is some plot for causing a quarrel between the lovers?"

"Abundant reasons, my dear sir," answered Monsieur Narbonne, "but unfortunately no positive proof. Indeed, Jeannot is at so great a distance off, that there is no getting at all the facts of the case, but my confidence in his honour is so great, that I could almost wager my existence he would not deceive one to whom he has pledged himself by a most solemn vow."

"At all events," laughed the commissary, "he seems to be fortunate in having at least one staunch friend."

"And the poor lad deserves nothing less," exclaimed the notary, "for a more industrious, honest fellow is not to be found in the whole neighbourhood. He worked diligently for his father when the old man became too feeble to toil any longer on his farm, and everything was going on smilingly when the accursed law of conscription obliged him to leave his business to follow the unholy profession of arms."

"Are you aware whether he has seen much service?"

"More than a great many who have been double the time in the army," answered Monsieur Narbonne. "He has been in many of our greatest recent battles, and at length fell wounded at Austerlitz, where he would have perished for want of assistance had it not been that he was found by an honest farmer who conveyed him home and bestowed upon him as much care and attention as if he had been a son of his own."

"Then he was fortunate at any rate."

"Not so fortunate either, monsieur," answered the notary, "for the daughter of the farmer was his principal nurse, and hence arose the report that he had transferred to her those affections which had already been bestowed upon Jeannette."

"For which you think there is no ground?"

"Not the slightest," answered the notary, "or I will confess myself to have been most palpably deceived in the opinion I formed of my young friend. The circumstance I allude to has been taken advantage of by some one who owes him a grudge, and this Pierre Langrais has, I suspect, been made the tool, because the real concoctor of the plot had not courage enough to perform his own dirty work."

"You speak, Monsieur Narbonne, as a man who is confident that his views are correct."

"I am well convinced they are."

"Then all I hope is, that you may be able to bring the mischief-makers to the punishment they deserve," exclaimed the commissary. "Indeed I can no longer doubt that you have come to a right conclusion upon the subject, for I know you are not likely to suffer prejudice to interfere, where cool deliberation is required. So now, Monsieur Narbonne, you are at liberty to see the prisoner as soon as you please."

Saying this, he beckoned to the same man who had brought the notary into his presence, and desired him to conduct the visitor to Pierre Langrais, and to leave them together that they might converse with perfect freedom. Monsieur Narbonne, after thanking the commissary for the courtesy he had received, followed his conductor, and shortly afterwards found himself alone with the prisoner whom he had desired to see. The prisoner's back was towards the door when Monsieur Narbonne entered, but turning quickly round as he heard footsteps approaching, his countenance assumed an expression of anger; and in a sullen tone he inquired the motive of a visit that was so unexpected.

"My motive is not a very bad one, Pierre, as you will find when I explain the purpose of my visit," answered the old gentleman. "In the first place, then—for I wish to come to the point at once—I have taken the trouble to come here to know whether you are inclined to get yourself out of this dilemma, by answering the fair questions I have to put?"

"First, let me know what your questions are, and then I'll tell you whether or not I shall answer them."

"Very well; then, I would know whether you will tell me who it is that has employed you to circulate these falsehoods against Jeannot?"

"What right have you, monsieur, to call them falsehoods?"

"Because I know the young man who has been the subject of them is too honourable to break the vow which he took just before he left this place for Toulon."

"He may not be the same man as he was then," exclaimed Pierre Langrais; "for at that time he was young and inexperienced, and had not seen so many pretty girls as he has since."

"Pretty faces would not change such a heart as Jeannot's," answered the notary, "nor do I indeed believe that he could find one more handsome than the girl to whom he has pledged his word."

"Humph!—for an old man you seem to have as much prejudice as a good many younger ones have."

"At all events, I speak only as I think," answered Monsieur Narbonne, "and no evil reports that can be spread abroad will ever make me believe that my young friend has proved unfaithful."

"I don't see that it matters much whether you do or not," replied the other, "for it is Jeannette whom this affair most concerns, and if she believes what I have said, my end will have been gained."

"What end do you speak of?"

"That of sparing her the misery of learning too suddenly the disappointment that is in store for her."

"Spare yourself all trouble on that account," exclaimed Monsieur Narbonne, "for whatever you may say to prejudice Jeannot, I shall gainsay with as much confidence in his continued good conduct as if he had never for an instant quitted my sight."

"There is no help for it, if you choose to be obstinate," exclaimed Pierre Langrais, but, hard as you are of belief, there are others who will give me the credit of speaking the truth."

"Jeannette, for one, will not believe you."

"Perhaps not, but her mother will; and her advice may yet save the poor young girl from the misery that would have been in store for her but for the interest I have taken in her behalf."

"Madame Corville's opinion of you and your motives is exactly similar to my own," answered the old gentleman. "She is not to be easily deceived by the artful representations of interested persons, and——"

"Interested persons!" interrupted the soldier.

"Yes," answered Monsieur Narbonne, "try to conceal the fact as you will, the veil is so thin and transparent as to be easily seen through."

"Then perhaps, monsieur, you will be kind enough to explain what motives there are in the present instance?"

"One of them is a design to ruin Jeannot—though why or wherefore I am unable to say, till the case has been more rigidly inquired into. In short, Pierre Langrais, the purpose of my visit to you this morning was to ascertain whether you might not be prevailed upon to desist from giving utterance to those hints and insinuations that can never effect the design you have in view."

"What design can I have?"

"That can be better answered by yourself than by me," exclaimed the old gentleman; "and it would be more to your own advantage to abandon these evil practices than to persist in them for the mere purpose of doing a mischief to those who never injured you."

"Upon my life, monsieur, you seem to have made up your mind that I have some bad intention in view."

"I am sure you have."

"But how can that be, when all I have said has been for the sake of sparing the feelings of poor Jeannette?"

"The feelings of poor Jeannette, as you call her, have been tried as far as your ingenuity could assist you. She, however, is not to be so easily prevailed upon to believe in every idle rumour she hears, to the prujudice of her lover, and it shall be my care to prevent the mischief that is intended, by such advice as age and experience in the world's wickedness will enable me to give."

"You seem determined to believe that I have a motive of my own for the caution I have given to Jeannette," exclaimed the soldier; "and having made the assertion, you will now perhaps tell me what reason I can have for saying that Jeannot is faithless to his vow?"

"I know not at present what it may be," answered Monsieur Narbonne, "but, no doubt, a very little inquiry will serve to put me in full possession of all the facts, and then the world, though perhaps deceived for a short time, will perceive that I was right when I said there was no truth in these rumours that have been spread abroad to prejudice the character of my young friend."

"But suppose, on the contrary, people should learn that nothing but the truth has been said about him?"

"I cannot believe it possible," answered Monsieur Narbonne, "but, were such to be the fact, I should then, indeed, say that reliance is not to be placed in any man. I have known Jeannot from childhood, and during the whole time of our acquaintance, I am proud to say, have never seen him guilty of an unworthy or dishonourable action. How then, let me ask you, can I give credit to the falsehoods that are now spread abroad against him by persons who are interested in injuring him among his friends?"

"How can it be said that I am interested?" demanded Pierre Langrais. "Had I been a younger man, it might have been imagined that I was a rival of Jeannot's, but that cannot be said of one who is now advanced in years, and who has passed the greater part of his life in warfare, which affords very little time to think of love."

"Still my conjecture may not be very wide of the mark, when I say that you may have been employed by some one else who has an eye towards the pretty Jeannette."

"Psha! what can have put that notion into your head?"

"When there is mystery, it is not to be wondered at, if all sorts of notions strike us," answered Monsieur Narbonne. "That there is a reason for spreading these vile calumnies is very certain, and whether my present conjectures are right or wrong, I will never rest satisfied till I have sifted the matter to the very bottom."

"I'm glad to hear you say so, monsieur," exclaimed the other, "for the more you make inquiries into this subject, the less reason will you see for blaming me as you have done."

"At any rate," answered the notary, "it cannot be denied that you have made yourself very busy in propagating these rumours, which, in your own mind, you must know are false."

"Indeed I don't know anything of the sort," exclaimed Pierre Langrais, "for I happen to know it as a fact that Jeannot was for a long time under the roof of a certain Herman Gratz, whose pretty daughter was his nurse during the period that he remained there."

"Very likely it may have been so," replied the notary, "but surely nothing can be argued from it to prove that Jeannot transferred to her the affections which he had already bestowed upon another."

"So you may think," returned Pierre, "but to me it appears very strange that he should have remained at the house of his new friends long after he had recovered from his wound."

"That is one of the ill-natured reports that I place not the slightest reliance in," answered Monsieur Langrais. "From all that has reached us at present respecting the conduct of Jeannot, he has earned for himself the character of a brave soldier, and it is therefore unlikely that he would have failed to rejoin the army immediately after he found himself sufficiently recovered to do so."

"You are determined, then, not to believe anything that is said against your young friend?"

"I will believe anything that reaches me upon good authority," replied the notary, "but not one word will I give credit to that comes from those whom I perceive are bent upon his destruction."

"Upon my life, Monsieur Narbonne, I can't conceive why you should imagine that he has more enemies than anybody else. For my own part, I owe the young man no grudge, and if I had not believed him to be guilty of playing false with the woman that he has proposed to love, I should have been the last in the world to say anything that was likely to do him an injury."

"Of course, it is not to be expected that you would acknowledge bearing him any ill will."

"How can I bear him any ill will," asked Pierre Langrais, "when I have scarcely seen him in my life? But it's always the way when one tries to do a good turn to another;—one's motives are sure to be misrepresented, and the man who steps forward to set matters right is looked upon as a fellow that is trying to set other people by the ears. However, I suppose you have nothing further to say to me upon this subject?"

"Nothing," answered Monsieur Narbonne, "but I would now ask if you will obtain your release from this dilemma, by confessing who it is that has set you to do all this mischief?"

"I have told you before that I have not been set on to do it by any one," answered Pierre Langrais. "One answer ought to be as good as a thousand, and if I am to be kept here all my life, you'll never be able to get anything out of me."

"Then you are an obstinate fellow for your pains," exclaimed the old gentleman warmly, "for I am certain you could give me the information I want, and the giving of it would procure your immediate liberation from this place."

"If you come to that, Monsieur Narbonne," replied the captive, "I should like to know why I am here at all? Suppose I do know anything about this affair that you are talking about—is that any reason why I should be deprived of my liberty?"

"You are here for a very different crime," answered the notary, "and it will cause no little trouble and annoyance to yourself if you persist in not giving the required information."

"Which I certainly shall not do," he replied, "let the consequences to myself be what they may."

"You are paid then for keeping the secret, or you would not hold out, after being so repeatedly urged upon the subject."

"There you are wrong again, monsieur," answered Pierre Langrais with the greatest *sang froid*, "for the truth is, I am no more likely to take a bribe than you are yourself. I, however, don't choose to open my mind to you any further upon this subject, and neither threats nor persuasion will ever make me alter my determination. So keep me here as long as you please, and perhaps by and by I may turn round and demand an explanation of the reason why I am detained here."

"Which explanation will be very easily given," returned the old gentleman, "for you were taken into custody by my orders for being found lurking about the house of Madame Corville without having any business there."

"How do you know I had no business there?"

"Because you have not given any reason."

"I wasn't going to give one to you," answered Pierre Langrais, "but perhaps I may do so to some one else if he can show any right for asking the question."

"You forget what trouble and annoyance you occasion yourself by all this obstinacy."

"I can't very well forget that, Monsieur Narbonne," he replied, "for you have told me so often of it, that I must have been a dunce indeed, not to have learnt my lesson by this time. However, I am too old a soldier to be frightened by trifles, and if I am shut up here for a month, you'll find yourself at the end of that time no nearer to your object than you are at this moment. In short, as I have said often enough before, I have not been employed by anybody to poison the mind of Mademoiselle Jeannette against her lover, who I respect as a brave fellow."

"Your actions belie your words," exclaimed the notary, "for you have repeatedly uttered things of him which—had they been believed—would have lost him the regard of his betrothed."

"I told her only what I believed to be the truth," answered the other, "and surely a man is not to be blamed for putting a woman upon her guard against the faithlessness of her lover. As for Jeannette and her mother, I respect them both, and it would have been wrong of me if I had not mentioned the reports that are in circulation against this young man."

"Do you believe these reports yourself?"

"I should be glad to say 'No,' to that question," answered the other; "but when things are mentioned by so many persons, it's very hard to convince one's self that they are uttered only for mischief."

"Have you ever seen anything to warrant you in coming to the conclusion that Jeannot is faithless to his vow?"

"That's a question that I shall not answer just at present," replied Pierre Langrais. "What I have said, however, I mean to stand by, and before very long Madame Corville and her daughter will be convinced that I had no other than a good purpose in telling them that too much reliance is not to be placed in the good faith of Jeannot."

"Then you must beware of the vengeance of the young man when he returns and hears what you have said of him."

"I am quite prepared for anything that may happen," exclaimed Pierre Langrais in a tone of indifference. "Besides, look at the difference between his years and mine, and then say whether I ought to expect violence from him."

"It's not for me to advocate violence," returned the notary, "but if any should be offered in this instance it must be admitted that you have brought it all upon yourself. A calumniator deserves little pity, and I believe you would find none, were matters to arrive at such a pitch as we are speaking of."

"Well," exclaimed the other abruptly, "it seems to me, Monsieur Narbonne, that you are wasting your time whilst trying to bring me to your own way of thinking. I have made up my mind to remain here quietly as long as they choose to deprive me of my liberty, but by and by it will be my turn, and then we shall see which of us has most reason to exult."

"You have made up your mind, then, not to afford me the information I require?"

"Quite."

"Have you no consideration for those whom you are endeavouring to render miserable?"

"I am only doing my duty," answered Pierre Langrais, "and nobody but yourself would ever say that I ought to conceal the faults of a man when I know the unhappiness that would follow. However, you have heard my determination, and therefore to remain here any longer would be utterly useless."

And so Monsienr Narbonne seemed to think, for, taking the hint, he called the turnkey and left the place no better off than when he entered it.

CHAPTER XIX.

JEANNETTE IS STILL CONFIDENT IN THE GOOD FAITH OF HER ABSENT
LOVER.— APPEARANCE OF MONSIEUR LAMONT WITH GRATIFYING IN-
TELLIGENCE.—THE YOUNG HERO'S RETURN HOME IS HOURLY EXPECTED.

IT was about a week after the interview of the notary with Pierre Langrais that the news was spread like wild-fire of a peace having been hastily concluded between France and her enemies, the consequence of which would be the immediate return of the greater part of the army. As may be easily imagined this intelligence was most gratifying to our heroine, who, with all the ardour of youth, believed it to be almost certain that Jeannot would be one among the first to arrive from the scene in which he had assisted to obtain so much glory for his country. Her cousin Suzette was also of a similar opinion, but her mother, whom age had rendered less sanguine, endeavoured to prevail upon her to wait with patience for the fondly anticipated moment, and not to indulge in hopes which might not be fulfilled for some days, or even weeks to come.

"Remember, my dear child," she said, "that though a peace may have been concluded, it must be some time before an army, so large as that which our Emperor commands, can be withdrawn from the country he has invaded, and its motions must be slow, lest the enemy should imagine that Napoleon is glad to take the first opportunity of leaving the country."

"Aye, mother," answered Jeannette, "that may be all very true, but it is said that one half of the army is already on its march back to France, and in that case why should not I indulge the hope that my dear Jeannot will be among those who first arrive?"

"To be sure you may," exclaimed Suzette, who had just before alled in to see them, "and for my own part I feel pretty well certain that we shall see him in the course of a very short time."

"What ground have you for thinking so, my love?" asked Madame Corville.

"Perhaps you may call it a very simple one," answered the young girl, "but I dreamed last night that he was within a league of this place, and I can assure you that my dreams very often come true."

"So you may fancy," replied the old lady, "but I hope Jeannette will not be induced to place any faith in this one, lest she should find herself grievously disappointed in the end. Let her wait with patience till the anxiously looked-for time arrives, and then she may fairly presume that there is an end of the grief which has so long troubled her."

"It's all very well to say so, dear aunt," replied Suzette, "but you must recollect that youth and age take these matters very differently, and for my own part I can see no harm in Jeannette fancying that her betrothed is on the eve of returning."

"That will depend upon whether she can bear a disappointment."

"Oh yes, mother," exclaimed Jeannette, "I can endure anything now that there seems to be every chance of his return within a very short period. It was only when his life was constantly endangered that I gave way to my despondency, but now hope sustains me, and I can wait with patience and composure till he returns."

"You are still satisfied with his fidelity, then?"

"Perfectly so."

"There I quite agree with you," answered her mother, "and for my own part I have never felt inclined to place any confidence in the vile reports that have been circulated to his prejudice. There are few persons in the world, I believe, who are without enemies, and as for Jeannot, I feel certain he will be able to prove himself as honourable and faithful as he has always professed to be."

"So says Monsieur Narbonne," returned Jeannette, "and he is not likely to give an opinion that has not a good foundation for it. Besides, his enemies will not dare to repeat their accusations in his presence, and depend upon it we shall hear no more of these unfounded charges after his return home."

"No, no," exclaimed Suzette, "the cowards—whoever they are—will shrink back with alarm when they see the certainty of having all their villany exposed to public view. And yet I should like to know who it is that has taken so much pains to injure your intended son-in-law."

"So should I," answered the old lady, "but I am afraid there is little chance of it, now that Pierre Langrais has refused to give up the name of the person that employed him to come here and circulate these falsehoods against the honour of Jeannot."

"Is there nothing," asked Suzette, "that might lead to a clue for the unravelling of the mystery?"

"Not that I am aware of."

"Well then," replied the girl, "I have a notion that I could name him, if it might be done without offence."

"Offence!" exclaimed Madame Corville, "I should be thankful to any one that would assist in the discovery."

"You would? Then I tell you, my dear aunt, that I believe Henri Duport to be the man."

"Henri Duport! Why should you suspect him?"

"Because he was—and perhaps still is—the rival of Jeannot for the hand of my cousin."

"There may be something in that, to be sure," exclaimed Madame Corville, "but it would be cruel to suspect him unjustly of so base an act as the one we have to complain of."

"Nay, if he is innocent, it will be easy enough for him to convince the world of it."

"But he would never forgive those who raised such a report against him."

"That would not trouble me much," answered Suzette, laughing, "for I never liked the man, and the anger he may feel will never serve to convince me of his innocence, unless he can bring forward good substantial evidence in his own favour. That he is at the bottom of all this mischief I am almost certain, and it will be no fault of my own if I do not prove the truth of my charge, if any further reports are raised against Jeannot."

"You are a good, warm-hearted girl, my dear," exclaimed Madame Corville, "but I must caution you against giving way too much to your feelings, lest mischief should come of it. Monsieur Narbonne has already taken this matter in his hands, and we cannot do better than leave him to unravel the mystery."

"Monsieur Narbonne has proved himself to be a good friend in this affair," answered Suzette, "and I am sure he will do his best towards exposing the base-hearted fellow who has taken so much pains to vilify and destroy the character of poor Jeannot."

"Luckily for himself," observed the old lady, "Jeannot's character is too good to be easily destroyed by the breath of slander."

"All that I grant you," answered Suzette, "but the intentions of his enemies are just the same; and, for my own part, I see no reason why the treachery should not be exposed and punished as it deserves."

"Very true," exclaimed Madame Corville, "and yet I believe it would be better to let the matter rest where t is—that is to say, if no further reports are raised to injure the betrothed lover of my daughter."

At this juncture Monsieur Lamont, the father of Jeannot, entered the cottage, and it was easy to see by his countenance that he was the bearer of pleasant intelligence. Jeannette placed a chair for him, when seating himself near Madame Corville, he said—

"I have come, madame, to bring you the earliest news of an event that I believe will surprise as well as delight all who are here present. In a word, my son's arrival may be immediately expected."

"Is Jeannot so near us?" asked our heroine, with an exclamation of sudden joy.

"He was within half a league of our village when he was last seen by the person who gave me the information."

JEANNOT'S CASTIGATION OF HENRY DUPORT FOR HIS VILLANY.

"May I ask, pray, who it was that brought you the news?" inquired Madame Corville.

"A comrade of his, whom we all know," answered the old gentleman. "In fact, it was no other than Henri Duport, who was sent forward to announce the immediate arrival of all those who left this place as conscripts just previous to the last campaign."

"And are you sure Jeannot is coming ?" asked the old lady.

"So Henri Duport told me."

"What did he say of your son ?" asked Madame Corville.

"Nothing more than that he had quite recovered from the wound he received in the battle of Austerlitz."

"He said nothing, then, about the rumours which have reached us of late ?"

"Not a word," answered the old gentleman. "Indeed, he appeared to be in a great hurry, and left me almost directly to go and convey the news to other persons who are as interested in it as myself."

"Do you know, Monsieur Lamont," said the old lady, "that we were speaking of him just before you came in, and my niece expressed it as her opinion that he is the author of all the falsehoods which have occasioned us so much uneasiness."

"To tell you the truth, madame," he replied, "I have thought something of the same kind myself, for I know he used to have a sneaking kindness for your daughter, and it seemed to me more likely that such reports should have come from him than anybody else. Let that be as it may, however, the mischief is not so great as was intended, and we can therefore afford to be generous and forgiving to whoever it was that tried to make the mischief. Besides, Jeannot will soon be once more amongst us, and that will amply repay us for all the anxiety we have felt during his absence."

"Ah !" cried Jeannette, "it will indeed, Monsieur Lamont, and if anything more than another will serve as a punishment to the infamous libeller, it will be in witnessing the fact that the falsehoods have not injured him against whom they were directed. Jeannot will be welcomed back to his home by all those whose regard he most covets, and from his own lips we shall hear the denial of the accusation which it is evident was published only to compass his ruin."

"Do you think then," asked Suzette, "that it is necessary for him to deny that which nobody ever believed of him ?"

"The denial is not necessary," answered her cousin, "but it will be some satisfaction to learn what ground there was for reporting that he was paying his addresses to another."

"Ah !" laughed Suzette, "I see well enough how it is ;—You have not yet succeeded in quite driving that girl, Jacqueline Gratz, out of your head, and would like to know what sort of a rival you might have chanced to find in her."

"I own that I feel interested in the family," answered Jeannette, "but not for the reason you have mentioned."

"What other reason have you, then ?"

"I should like to hear from Jeannot a description of the people who were so kind to him, when he fell wounded in the field of battle."

"Suppose he should launch out in praise of this Jacqueline ?" observed Suzette.

"If he does," replied our heroine, "I can listen to him without the slightest feeling of jealousy. I know his heart has never wavered for a moment from his betrothed, and instead of feeling annoyed at hearing him speak in favour of the young girl you talk of, I shall only think that he is repaying a heavy debt of gratitude which she and her family have laid him under."

"In my son's name I thank you," exclaimed Monsieur Lamont, "and will venture to say that your confidence in his honour will be amply repaid when you have heard all the circumstances connected with his sojourn at the house of Herman Gratz. It must be remembered, too, that his visit there was compulsory, for his wound was of a very serious nature, and he must have perished but for the attention and hospitality of those who found him exhausted on the field of battle."

"Aye," added Madame Corville, "and those, too, to whom he was so much indebted were natives of the country which our troops had invaded and overrun."

"We shall hear more of them from Jeannot," proceeded Monsieur Lamont ; "and now that the war is happily over, I would not mind walking barefoot to their house to thank them for the kindness they bestowed upon my son at a time when he was in need of their care and attention. As for the daughter, the affection of a brother and sister may have sprung up between her and Jeannot, but I feel assured that nothing can have warranted the assertion that they were pledged to each other."

"Do not imagine, Monsieur Lamont," exclaimed our heroine, "that I have ever for a moment believed in the ill-natured reports which interested persons have raised against him. I know the fervour and steadfastness of his affection for myself; and undeserving indeed should I be of his regard, if I could for a moment have listened to the idle tales which have been whispered in my ear."

"Well said, my dear," exclaimed the old gentleman;—"your faith in him deserves to be rewarded, and I can undertake to say that you see no reason to regret your kindness to him. He has always been to me a good son, and from the steadiness of his previous conduct, I believe there is every certainty of his becoming an ornament and an example to those who belong to his own sphere of life."

"Then you," observed Suzette, "like all of us here, never placed any belief in the rumours that have reached us?"

"I was sure there was no foundation for them," replied Monsieur Lamont, "for I was never deceived by him in my life, and it would have been strange, indeed, if he had now begun to practice the art of dissimulation. However, it is not for me to praise or flatter him, for I believe all who knew him will bear testimony to the worth and excellence of his conduct."

"How happy you must feel, Monsieur Lamont," exclaimed Suzette, "at knowing that he is soon to return to your arms."

"I am indeed happy," he replied, "yet it must be confessed there is still one source of uneasiness remaining."

"What is that, may I ask?"

"The probability that he may again be called upon to take part in these unhappy wars."

"You think, then," exclaimed our heroine, "that Jeannot will not be suffered to remain long at home?"

"Such is my fear," he replied.

"But having been so recently wounded," exclaimed Madame Corville, "I should suppose he would have sufficient plea for asking to be spared from the next campaign."

"He would not tarnish his laurels by doing anything that might bring upon him the charge of fear or cowardice," replied Monsieur Lamont.

"Then you think he would prefer fighting to staying at home?"

"Nay, I do not assert that," answered the old man, "but as a soldier, he would rather lose his life than do aught to destroy the honour he has achieved. He may not, however, be put to the test, for our emperor has carried his conquests into so many countries, that there are few now remaining to tempt him again to draw his sword for the extension of his empire."

During the latter part of this conversation Jeannette had prepared herself for walking, and was just about leaving the house when she was observed by Madame Corville, to whose question she replied that she was going to meet Jeannot, whose immediate return had just been announced. Of course no objection was raised to this, nor did any one propose to accompany her, for none wished to be present at an interview which was to take place after so long an absence from each other. Even Monsieur Lamont, anxious as he was to see his son, remained behind at the cottage, and Suzette, though dying with curiosity, so far mastered her resolution as to seat herself down by the side of Madame Corville to wait with patience and resignation the return of those whose appearance was so anxiously looked for.

CHAPTER XX.

CONCLUSION.

JEANNETTE proceeded with hurried steps in the direction that she knew her lover would come, and had gone perhaps a quarter of a league when she saw a figure before her attired in the military garb.   At this sight her heart throbbed quickly, for she thought only of Jeannot, and it seemed to her that the long anticipated meeting was now on the eve of taking place.   Deceived by the darkness of the copse through which she was then passing, she was, however, doomed to be cruelly disappointed, for when the person she had seen approaching was within a few paces, she perceived, to her no small alarm, that it was Henri Duport, whom she had mistaken for her lover.   She instantly paused, and would have retreated, but the young man guessing her design, stepped forward with a quickened pace, and taking her by the arm, asked in a tone of evident vexation, why she was so anxious to flee from his presence.

"Because you are not the person I came here to meet," she replied, trembling with apprehension.

"I see," he replied bitterly, "time and absence have not yet cooled your love for my rival."

"Why should I have changed my feelings towards him to whom I have been solemnly betrothed?"

"Perhaps I might be able to mention many reasons," answered Henri Duport.

"You allude to the foul reports that have been circulated to his injury," she exclaimed.

"It must be confessed I do."

"Know you by whom those falsehoods were invented?"

"How should I?"

"Very easily," she replied, "for there are many persons who do not hesitate boldly to assert that you are the traducer of Jeannot!"

"Then I would tell them to their teeth that they lie!" exclaimed Henri Duport, angrily.   "It is clear that I have enemies somewhere, and you, I suppose, are among those who believe me capable of an act of treachery against my friend."

"Friend!—you abuse the sacred word!"

"Oh, I see how it is," he exclaimed, bitterly, "advantage has been taken of my absence, and some busy meddling fiend has been uttering falsehoods to prejudice me amongst those whose esteem and regard I most covet.   But surely you, Jeannette, do not believe me capable of so heinous a breach of friendship as to circulate rumours that would prove injurious to my comrade in arms?"

"If you are innocent," she replied, "it will be easy enough to make it manifest.   People there are, however, who assert their belief that the rumour has proceeded from you."

"What rumour do you speak of?"

"The one," she answered, "which accuses Jeannot of having forsaken me for another."

"Ah," exclaimed Henri Duport, "now I begin to perceive what you are speaking of.   Jeannot was staying for some time at the house of an honest farmer near the battle field of Austerlitz, and, like yourself, I have heard say that he was rather particular in his attenitons to the pretty daughter of his host and hostess."

"Did you not deny the falsehood?"

"How could I, when I believe in the truth of the assertion?"

"Now," exclaimed Jeannette, "I am more convinced than ever that you, and you only, invented the calumny."

"What reason could I have for such an act?"

"Did you not offer me your hand when you knew that my heart was already given to Jeannot?"

"I did," he replied; "but love is not to be easily controlled, and after a long struggle to subdue my own feelings in favour of my rival, I could adopt no other course than the one you now condemn. I loved you, Jeannette, and surely there could be no crime in endeavouring to secure you for myself."

"Was it not a breach of the friendship you just now boasted of?"

"In all things but love a man may control himself," answered Henri Duport. "I would have yielded you to my rival had it been possible, but the struggle proved to be a vain one, and in my despair I at length implored you to pity me. You, however, met my appeal with reproaches, and I saw with feelings of bitter agony that cannot be described, that you were resolved to become the wife of Jeannot."

"In revenge for which," she exclaimed, "you have basely endeavoured to injure him by reporting that he had given his love to the daughter of the man who had afforded him the shelter and hospitality of his roof when he was found apparently dead on the field of Austerlitz."

"The report was none of my raising," he replied; "yet, if the question was put to me, I should declare my belief in it."

"On what ground?"

"Some other time I will enter into all the particulars," answered Duport, "but at present you must be satisfied with a few of the main facts upon which I found my belief. In short, Jeannot prolonged his visit to the house of Farmer Gratz so long, that his officers began to think that he purposely remained absent from the army in order to avoid the dangers of battle. I was, therefore, sent to warn him that he must immediately rejoin his regiment, and thus it was that I had an opportunity of witnessing his affection for the pretty Jacqueline."

"Was there anything extraordinary," asked Jeannette, "in his becoming attached to the woman who had tended upon him with all a sister's care during the whole time that he was suffering from the effects of his wound?"

"On the contrary, I think it perfectly natural," answered Duport, "and therefore you may the less wonder at the strong hold which she took of his heart. As his recovery advanced they were constantly walking out together, and I have myself seen them strolling about the neighbourhood like a couple of lovers."

"And you would have me believe from that circumstance that Jeannot so far forgot me as to make an offer of his hand and heart to another woman?"

"I don't know what you may choose to think about it," replied the other, "but the affair was the common talk of the whole neighbourhood, and people are expecting, now that the war is brought to a conclusion, that he will return and fulfil the promises he has made her."

"They will be disappointed then," answered our heroine, "for Jeannot has lost no time in coming back to France, and his traducers will soon see that he is faithful to his first pledge."

"I know he is returning to you," exclaimed Henri Duport, "but it is only to deceive you more than you are at present. He will, no doubt, profess for you the same love as ever, and you must beware, or you will have reason bitterly to regret the confidence you have so blindly reposed in him. Besides, he has been raised to the rank of a sous-lieutenant, and would rather marry the daughter of the wealthy Farmer Gratz than wed the humble peasant girl who——"

"Villain and liar!" exclaimed the voice of some one who just at that moment burst from a thicket where he had been concealed, and before Henri Duport could turn himself round to discover from whom the words had proceeded, he was struck to the earth by a terrible blow. In another minute a foot was placed upon his neck, and then it was that he perceived in his assailant no less a personage than the very man against whom he had been uttering so many falsehoods.

"Wretch!" muttered Jeannot, "at length I have discovered the author of all the calumnies I have been suffering under. You it is who have endeavoured to poison the mind of Jeannette against me, in order to accomplish your own base designs ; and 'tis well for you that she is now present, or I could not perhaps have restrained my hand from taking ample revenge for all the injuries you have been trying to heap upon me."

" Would you murder me ?" exclaimed Duport, cowering under the stern glance that was fixed upon him.

" Had I slain you," answered the other, " the penalty would have been richly deserved, for your villany has infuriated me almost beyond my power of control. As it is, however, your worthless life is spared !—but come not again into my presence, or we may not part till one or other of us has lost his life in satisfaction of this, our deadly quarrel."

Then taking the arm of Jeannette within his own, he led her away, leaving Henri Duport to give utterance to his fearful maledictions on the man who had so signally defeated him at the very moment when he was endeavouring to supplant him in the heart of our heroine.   Having exchanged their greetings on the happy occasion that had restored them to each other, Jeannette said, in reference to the reacontre which had just taken place—

" Why do you tremble thus, my love ?` Is it that you are afraid of the vengeance of yonder miscreant, whom I have so recently chastised for the villany he has been carrying on ?"

" Alas!" she sighed, " I am afraid lest his wrath should fall upon you when you are least prepared for it."

" Do not fear anything on my account," replied her lover, " for I know the vindictiveness of his heart, and shall always be ready for him when he is inclined to carry this matter any further.   That, however, is hardly to be expected, for he will find few friends in this neighbourhood, and the probability is, that he will at once seek a home in some other part of the world.   True, his falsehoods will soon be proclaimed, and he will hardly choose to stay in a place where all will look upon him with loathing and abhorrence.   Nay, even should he remain, I believe there would be little fear of violence from his hands after the complete defeat I have just now given him."

" Did you hear much of what he said before you so unexpectedly appeared before us ?" asked Jeannette.

" Quite enough to convince me that he was the propagator of the infamous falsehoods that have been invented against me," replied her lover.   " On approaching towards the place where you were standing, I heard voices, and on listening for a moment or two, easily recognised yours.   I then crept nearer, and from the position which I took, could overhear every word that passed, without being seen.   A short time served to convince me of the object which Duport had in view, and at length being no longer able to control my feelings, I rushed from my hiding-place, and chastised my traducer in the manner you saw. Believe me, dear Jeannette, you have only done me justice in placing your confidence in my continued love.   True it is that I was thrown a great deal in the society of the young female you heard so much talk about, but she knew that my heart was already engaged to another, and during our frequent walks, our principal conversation was about you and the happiness I anticipated whenever the termination of the war would allow me to return home."

By this time they had nearly reached the cottage, and were met by Madame Corville and Monsieur Lamont, both of whom welcomed the return of Jeannot with unbounded expressions of joy.   Suzette, too, soon joined the party, and her satisfaction was marked no less than by those who had already hailed the arrival of our hero on his return home.

*   *   *   *   *   *

Our story is nearly finished.   In a fortnight after the return of Jeannot, the whole village was in a commotion of joy for the celebration of the marriage rites between the affianced couple.   The bells rung merrily from the village steeple, and all being joyously finished, a long life of happiness was the reward for the faithfulness in love of JEANNETTE AND JEANNOT.

www.ingramcontent.com/pod-product-compliance
Lightning Source LLC
Chambersburg PA
CBHW080825250626
47160CB00008B/2858